All in the Family

by

Suzanne Rossi

All In The Family

COPYRIGHT © 2009 by Susan Peek

Cover Art by *Kim Mendoza*

The Wild Rose Press
PO Box 708
Adams Basin, NY 14410-0706
Visit us at www.thewildrosepress.com

Publishing History
First Crimson Rose Edition, 2010
Print ISBN 1-60154-726-9

Published in the United States of America

Dedication

Dedications are tricky. I inevitably omit a name.
Therefore, if I must insult someone, let it be family.
To my son Kevin Peek, his wife, Lisa, and their sons,
Corey and Kyle, thank you for understanding
when I confiscated your dining room table to write
at the crack of dawn.
To my son Brendan Peek, his wife, Danielle, and
their daughters, BriAnnon and Sarah,
thank you for your support and enthusiasm
whenever my spirits flagged.
My biggest thank you goes to my husband,
Bruce Peek, who is always there for me.
When assailed by doubts about my abilities,
he didn't hesitate to take me out to dinner,
ply me with martinis, and tell me I was terrific.
Without all of you, I'd have never made it.
I love you.

Prologue

"Think you can pull it off, Johnny?"

Johnny Scarano stared at his questioner wondering if he should make a crack about stupid questions, and then decided against it. Lou Rizzo had once been a highly respected underboss for the Muzio family.

"Yeah, I can, Lou. Somebody's gotta get outta here and take that bitch down. There are twenty-four of us stuck on this fuckin' island. She's responsible. I'll get her if it's the last thing I do."

Johnny hoped the last portion of his statement wasn't prophetic. He sat back in his beach chair, swigging Evian.

On cue, the other four men seated with him did the same. It was their usual routine. Take a dip in the crystal clear sea—none of them sure which one. One of the guys with experience in gambling had organized an unofficial pool on it. Afterward, they'd sit under the shade of a palm tree, shooting the bull about the old days. Then they had all been important to their various mafia families. Now, they bordered on pathetic.

"Johnny, are you sure you've thought this through?" Carlo asked. "We were drugged, brought here, and drugged again. The Feds ripped information from our guts. If any of us show our faces back in Chicago, our bosses will tear out more than secrets. We'd all buy one in the head after they beat us senseless *and* shoot off our knee caps."

Johnny smothered his irritation. Carlo Marcianni, a consigliere for the boss of bosses, Caesar Casano, and his never-ending logic damn near drove everybody nuts.

"What? You sayin' we should just stay here and see who shows up next? Bullshit!" He allowed the anger and frustration to show in his voice.

Carlo shrugged, brushing sand from his feet. "Why not? This ain't such a bad place. We got an ocean, a pool, there's even a nine-hole golf course. Hell, Lefty Lefkowitz is planning a tournament next month. The tennis courts will be finished in a few weeks. We each have our own little cottage with hot and cold, a kitchen, and cable TV. As retirement, it ain't bad."

"No broads," Joey Bacio complained.

"Like you'd remember what the hell to do with one," Lou replied.

"I wouldn't mind giving it a whirl."

Bobo Rabinsky took a drink. "A tournament? No kidding? Maybe I'll enter. I had a pretty good round the other day."

"Will you assholes listen to yourselves? Are you still on drugs? So, the weather is perfect. So, we have a one-bedroom house, which is probably bugged out the ass. I wouldn't be surprised if this goddamned palm tree didn't have a mike hidden in it," Johnny snapped.

Four pairs of eyes looked up at the swaying fronds rustling in the gentle sea breeze.

"Naw, too much salt air," Carlo said.

"Jesus, I don't know why I bother talking to you guys. Your brains and your ambitions have turned to mush." He jammed his bottle into the sand, rose, and walked a few paces towards the breaking waves.

Turning back, he said, "Sooner or later, the security around here will get lax. A patrol boat will

2

be late, a head count will be forgotten—something. And when it does, I'll be ready. I want Gabriella Vicelli dead."

Johnny swung around, trotted to the water, and dove into the surf.

Chapter One

Three weeks later

Gabriella Vicelli glided up to the front steps of the lakefront mansion in her new Porsche and turned off the key. The sudden silence was almost as deafening as the throaty growl of the powerful engine. Beyond the manicured lawn she caught a glimpse of Lake Michigan through the twilight gloom, its deep blue water stretching to the horizon. Her jaw clenched in anger.

Must be nice to live so high on the hog with my father's blood on his hands.

Gavino Ponzetti had built the two-storied, colonnaded home shortly after Gus Vicelli's murder. Tonight, light poured from every window illuminating the front and side yards. If the same held true for the garden area, she could have a problem. She'd been here a few weeks ago for a cocktail party and had scoped out the garden behind the house. A small service drive ran along the side wall. It would suit her purpose fine.

Twisting the rearview mirror, she inspected her elaborate hairdo using her fingers to adjust a curl and pouf it up a bit more. She smiled at the reflection.

Perfect—absolutely perfect.

A valet opened the car door. She exited and trotted up the steps on her four-inch stilettos to greet the head of the family, the Don, Gavino Ponzetti.

Ponzetti, his slicked back dark hair touched with gray at the temples, smiled. "Gabriella, nice of you to come."

"Thank you for inviting me." She pitched her vocal tone higher, replying in a little girl voice. "I've been so excited and looking forward to this all week. I even got a new dress and spent *hours* at the hair salon."

Perfection again—not too bright and self-absorbed—just what they expected of her. She'd expended a lot of time polishing this act.

"You are a vision." The Don bent and kissed each cheek. He didn't have far to bend. In her heels, she was only an inch or two shorter.

She leaned forward to give him a better view of her breasts in the low cut gown. He looked. They were never too old to look.

"Your father, God rest his soul, would be proud of you," he said, straightening.

"Oh, Mr. Ponzetti, you're too kind."

The lying bastard. He'd had her father killed so he could muscle in on the lucrative South Side numbers game.

"Now, where is that handsome son of yours?" Gabriella asked.

She breathed deeply, her breasts straining against the dress. She'd invested the better part of three months cultivating his son, the empty-headed Frank Ponzetti, with the sole purpose of soliciting this invitation. Most of the Ponzetti family, legitimate and not, would be in attendance.

"Hey, baby, it's about time you showed up."

Frank walked up claiming her like a prize, while his father turned to greet another guest. Two bodyguards stopped the newcomer and patted him down.

"Oh, Frankie, honey, will they search me, too?"

"No, baby, that's my job—later." He ogled her body and drew a finger from her throat to her cleavage before steering her toward a room already filled with people. "How about some champagne?"

"Oh, I just love bubbly." She blew him a kiss as he left to get her a glass.

Gabriella thanked God she hadn't been searched. She'd have a tough time explaining the gun strapped to her right thigh. Tonight would be her twenty-fifth hit. Twenty-five in five years and nobody ever suspected the only child of Gus Vicelli to be behind it all—except those she'd already dispatched, of course. The dim bulb act had proven effective.

Scanning the crowd, she found her prey, Marco Alberti, Gavino Ponzetti's third in command, a capo, and the man in charge of protection rackets. He was slime, and she'd enjoy taking him out. She still worked on the challenge of enticing him into the garden alone with her. Ditching Frankie presented no problem. A small bottle of knockout drops in her purse should do the job.

A waiter stopped by her side offering canapés. She popped one into her mouth. The server bowed and made an almost imperceptible movement with his head. She responded in kind. Good, her backup had arrived. Gabriella hoped the others, one a valet and another masquerading as a cook, had shown up, too. Alberti's love of pasta showed in his hefty frame, and she counted on their help in removing the body. She'd set ten o'clock as zero hour. Dinner would be over and Marco well-oiled with booze and wine.

Frankie returned and handed her a glass.

"Jesus, baby, you look hot." His gaze slithered down her body again, and then back up fixating on her chest. "That dress is very nice." He licked and curved his lips into a sleazy smile.

"Well, I bought it just for you," she said, smoothing her hand over the tiny bodice of the midnight blue, sequined, beaded gown. She deliberately let it hesitate under her breast. Poor old Frankie's eyes bugged out.

"Oh, God, let's get out of here and go someplace a little less crowded."

"But, Frankie, honey, you promised to introduce me to your friends. I've been looking forward to dinner all week." She pouted. "Later, after the entertainment. I just love Jimmy Jett. I've been to every concert and have all his CD's."

"All right, but as soon as he's done you and I go upstairs for a little bump and grind. I've never waited this long for a roll in the hay. I want some snatch."

"Oh, Frankie, don't be vulgar." She leaned forward and slid her hand down the front of his shirt to his crotch where she gently squeezed. "I'm worth waiting for. I promise. Trust me."

Sweat popped out on his brow, and he drained his champagne. He was putty in her hands. Silly putty.

"I need more champagne," he muttered. "How about you?"

"Not yet, honey. I want a clear head for what I'm planning." She sipped from her full glass, winking.

Never had she meant it more. The look on Frankie's face was priceless, like a kid on Christmas morning. She bet his feeble mind had kicked into high fantasy mode. Too bad. He would soon discover Santa Claus didn't exist.

Frankie left for a refill, and Gabriella located her victim. He stood alone on the opposite side of the room near the French doors. She wove her way through knots of people until reaching his side.

"Oh, Mr. Alberti. It's so nice to see you again. Do you remember me? I'm Gabriella Vicelli. We met last month at the All-Italian Club dance."

In her stilettos, she towered over him by at least a head. She allowed the tip of her tongue to trace her upper lip and stepped closer, his nose practically in her cleavage. He couldn't help but to see down her dress.

Short and squat, like a fireplug, the balding Marco smirked with fleshy lips, taking full advantage of the view offered. His gaze slid down to her hips, and then up again.

"Yeah, I remember you. You here with Frankie?"

"Oh, yes. He's off getting some more champagne. I really like Frankie a lot, but sometimes he's such a little boy. He doesn't like it if I talk to other men. Isn't that silly?"

"Miss Vicelli, some women can change men into boys."

"And boys into men. Please, call me Gabriella."

He took a huge gulp of his drink. Quickly scanning the room, he said, "And I'm Marco. So, are you and Frankie an item or something?"

"Sort of. I mean, he's a lot of fun and all, but I prefer the company of older, more mature men. If you know what I mean." She lowered her eyes to sip from her glass, looking at him through her lashes.

Marco's gaze riveted on her chest. "Yeah, I think I understand."

"I just knew you would. The first moment I saw you, I had the feeling we were..." she paused, "...simpatico. I'd love to talk with you some more."

"How about lunch tomorrow?" He looked over her shoulder, and then cupped her breast with his hand, rubbing his thumb over the nipple.

She forced herself to breathe heavily and focused her attention on his bulging fly.

"Oh, Marco. How about later tonight? After dinner? In the garden at, say, ten?"

"Yeah, ten's fine. We can...talk...uninterrupted

for a few minutes."

He leered, then slid his hand into her bodice and leaning down, kissed the swell of her breast.

Gabriella gasped at the audacity of the move. Only now did she realize he had maneuvered her so he faced the crowd. A tall, potted plant partially screened them. For the first time in years, she was flustered. She hadn't expected this.

Miserable, fucking pig. She stepped back, readjusting the bodice.

Gabriella resisted the urge to ball up her fist and deck the son of a bitch. Instead, she wagged her finger and said, "Naughty man! Behave yourself. What if someone saw?"

Marco smiled. "A small sample, baby. Wait'll you see what I can accomplish in ten minutes."

He proceeded to whisper the lewdest, most vile acts she'd ever heard into her ear. She wanted to plant her knee in his crotch. The sleazy bastard. Taking him out would be a pleasure. Gabriella counted to ten and allowed tense muscles to relax, regaining her composure. It wouldn't do for Alberti to notice she hadn't enjoyed his actions or suggestions.

Swallowing, she heaved what she hoped sounded like an excited sigh and replied with perfect truth, "I can hardly wait."

"Trust me, neither can I. Here comes Frankie."

She turned as Frankie approached.

"Where the hell have you been? I was looking all over for you. Hello, Marco, how's it goin'?"

"Hey, Frankie. Things are goin' just fine. I'm havin' a great time. Miss Vicelli has been keeping me company."

"Yeah?" He shot the two of them a suspicious glance.

"I was telling Mr. Alberti how much fun I had at the All-Italian Club last month. Frankie, honey, can

9

we go back again?"

"Yeah, sure, baby. Whatever you want." He slid a possessive arm around her waist. "Marco, if you'll excuse us, there's someone I'd like Gabriella to meet."

"Not at all. Nice chatting with you, Miss Vicelli."

Frankie steered her away. She threw a parting glance at Marco over her shoulder, winking. He smiled back and took a long swig of his drink.

Having made the connection, Gabriella went through the motions of social chitchat for the next forty-five minutes, perfecting her plan of attack and hoping her backup could get Alberti out of the garden before anyone missed him—or her.

Dinner was prime rib so tender she could cut it with a fork, but tonight Gabriella barely noticed the feast.

Calm down. Relax. Don't forget to smile. Keep your mind on the conversation. Everything is planned out to the tiniest detail. It'll go just like clockwork.

She repeated the words in her head. With each passing minute, her nerves stretched, and she kept an eagle eye on Frankie's liquor consumption, pleased to see him slugging down the champagne and Cabernet with abandon.

Dessert was being served when she looked at her watch. Nine fifty-five. She slipped a hand into her purse and uncorked the knockout drops, then palmed the bottle. One drop would make him drowsy. Two would have him nodding off, and three would put him sound asleep in the Cherries Jubilee in ten minutes.

"Frankie, could I have a sip of your wine? You've had a lot of it, so it must be good."

"Of course it's good. The Ponzettis only serve the best." He shoved the glass towards her. "Here, have a taste. Don't gulp it. Let it roll around on your tongue for a moment to enjoy the flavor."

They sat at the end of a long table opposite from his father. She was to Frankie's left. She picked up the glass and raised it as though in a toast. On cue, the crash of falling china and glassware along with oaths filled the air. Her confederate had dropped his tray right on schedule. Frankie's head whipped to the right, along with everybody else's. Leaning forward to obstruct the view of the diner on her left, she squeezed three drops into the wine, and then replaced the glass in front of her date.

The confusion cleared within a few seconds, just enough time to slip the bottle back into her purse. Without missing a beat, Frankie turned back, grabbed the glass and took a generous swig.

So much for savoring the flavor.

"Frankie, would you excuse me for a minute? I have to visit the little girl's room." She kissed her finger and put it on his lips, then glided out of her chair.

Another quick glance at her watch showed she had three minutes. Gabriella sped through the drawing room and the French doors, pausing long enough to remove her gun before hurrying to a dark corner of the garden. A light rustling in the bushes as she rushed by indicated where her backup hid. She stopped along a perimeter wall near a back gate, the gun held under her purse.

Her heart pounded. It always did. This would be the best one yet. Oh, they all got what they deserved, but this one would be special. It would put a sizable dent in the Ponzetti chain of command, and the perverted Marco Alberti would never again defile another woman.

She didn't have long to wait. Within a few minutes, Marco rounded the corner, a cigarette dangling from his lips.

Wasting no words of greeting, he shoved her

back against the wall and dropped to his knees. Flinging the cigarette away, he ran his hands under her dress and along her legs.

"Spread 'em, baby. I want a real dessert." His lecherous grin froze when he found the holster strapped to her thigh. "What the hell?"

Her hand whipped out, and she pulled the trigger. It was almost too easy. The tranquilizer dart disappeared into the folds of his neck. A look of stunned amazement replaced the grin. Marco Alberti's eyes glazed and rolled back into his head. He toppled like a felled ox.

"Nighty-night, asshole."

Instantly, the men appeared from their hiding place to her right.

"Jesus, what did you promise him?" one man whispered.

"Never mind. Just get him the fuck out of here. I have to get back inside. Can you handle him?" She unfastened the holster handing it and the gun to him. He placed it on Alberti's chest.

"Yeah, no problem," the second man said. The two of them lifted the unconscious mobster. "Dave is waiting in one of the catering trucks. We'll have this clown on the plane in less than an hour."

They carried their burden through the gate, and disappeared into the darkness. She ran for the house. As Gabriella entered the drawing room from the terrace, she noticed the whole incident had taken less than ten minutes.

A new world's record. Now, to stage my exit.

She slid back into her seat, kissing the cheek of a sleepy Frankie. "Miss me, baby?"

"Huh?" Frankie blinked as if trying to focus his eyes.

"I said, did you miss me? Is something wrong?"

With an undignified grunt, Frank Ponzetti, heir to the throne of the Ponzetti family business, fell face down into his dessert.

"Frankie!" she yelped, jumping to her feet.

Everyone in the room stopped their conversations to stare. She shook his shoulder and said in a loud voice, "Frankie, are you all right?"

Gavino Ponzetti hurried to her side. "What's going on?"

"I—I don't know, Mr. Ponzetti. I went to the ladies room, and when I came back he just fell over. He's—he's not dead, is he?" She injected just the right amount of fear into her voice while clutching her throat.

Gavino pulled his son's head up from the plate by his hair. Frankie was out cold. The syrupy sauce mixed with the melting ice cream dripping from his chin and eyebrows. A cherry stuck on the end of his nose. He looked like a snoozing clown. Luckily, the flames had been extinguished.

"Dead drunk I'd say," his father said in an angry tone. "He's passed out."

"Well! I've never been so insulted and humiliated in my entire life!" She stamped her foot.

Outraged lady—acting class at Miss Cameron's School for Young Girls. She'd aced the course. All the money her father spent on that snooty private school had not been wasted, although she doubted if this was what he'd had in mind.

"Miss Vicelli, please accept my deepest apologies and allow my driver to take you home."

"No, thank you. I have my own car. Tell your son I never want to see him again as long as I live."

On that clichéd exit line, Gabriella whirled and flounced from the room. Outside she rushed up to the parking attendant, telling him, "Electric blue Porsche."

Two minutes later, she roared down the driveway. Turning onto the street, she laughed out loud.

"Damn, I love this job!"

****

Lane Hamilton stared at his computer screen in disbelief, his frustration level rising, and then re-read the operations report from Medusa for a third time. Everything was in order. The plan had gone off without a hitch—except the target was not Larry "The Lump" Fazio, a recently made mid-level thug for the Rinaldi family. Medusa had taken down yet another Ponzetti family member, Marco Alberti.

"Damn her!"

The whole point of hitting the Rinaldis had been to set up the division's man in place. With Fazio gone, the informant could move up in the organization. He didn't think his boss had anyone ready to make such a leap into Alberti's shoes.

"Doesn't this woman ever obey orders?"

Lane ran a hand over his weary face and glanced at the clock—4:15. Unable to sleep, he'd come into the office early for the sole purpose of reading the report, hoping things had gone down with no problems.

"Yeah, right, no problems. The operation was perfect. The hit was wrong," he muttered to himself. "I may have to kill the bitch."

That was assuming, of course, he ever met her. With any luck *that* would never happen. She'd been a pain in his ass ever since he'd joined Alpha-Omega. He'd had it. He'd request to be removed as her controller. His other operatives did as told, no questions, no complaints. Why the hell couldn't she?

They'd clashed on the first assignment, arguing about who, when, and where the hit would occur. He thought he'd won the battle, but in the end, she'd done it her way—a sign of things to come. Her work, in spite of an inability to follow directions, was damned good. Even he had to admit that. Still, operatives who didn't obey the rules ended up dead.

Besides, the bullheaded Medusa was driving him nuts.

"What makes her so goddamned special? And why does Roger tolerate her?"

His irritated voice bounced off the walls of his office. Lane forwarded the report to his boss. He included an angry postscript detailing his frustration with Medusa, and then took his anger out on the send button, his finger almost jamming it through the keyboard. There, done. Now, she was the head man's problem. Sometime tomorrow, when his temper had cooled, he and Roger would have to talk.

"This can't go on. Something has to be done about Gabriella Vicelli."

****

Johnny gazed at the cloudless sky. The sun shown with the intensity expected of a late spring day in the tropics.

Just another fuckin' day in paradise.

At least when the rainy season began, he wouldn't feel obligated to comment on the perfect weather like he was happy to be here enjoying it.

Teeing up the ball, he took a giant swing and topped it. Jesus, he hated this fucking game.

"Johnny, you're still lifting your head," Bobo said. "Keep it down until after you hit the ball."

"Yeah, yeah." He shoved his driver into the bag and glared at the ball sitting a mere twenty-five yards down the fairway.

"Well, at least it's straight," Lou offered.

Johnny wanted to smack them both over the head with whatever club would do the most damage. Apparently, he was the only one who wanted revenge on that bitch, Gabriella Vicelli. Everyone else seemed content, like a herd of cows. He refused to let their indifference influence his determination. For the past three weeks, he'd observed every bit of security the island had to offer. It looked impregnable. However, looks didn't always translate into reality. If nothing else, Johnny Scarano was patient.

He walked the short distance to the ball. Reaching into his bag, he pulled out a fairway wood.

"Johnny, I think you'd be better off using a three wood. That five has too much loft." Lou sounded almost apologetic.

With exaggerated patience, Johnny took the advice, replacing the five wood.

"Now, don't forget to keep your head down. Swing through the ball, and follow through to the end of your swing. That way..."

"Bobo, shut the fuck up!" He addressed the ball again and swung, slicing it deep into the woods. "Shit!"

Bobo winced. "Aw, hell, Johnny, not another one. You're going to have to go find it. The last shipment that came in was short by several boxes. We gotta conserve until we can get replacements."

"Bobo, do me a favor. Just go on without me. I'll catch up."

He grabbed his clubs and headed for the woods. At least it would be shady.

Dropping the bag, he made a half-hearted effort to look for the lost ball. He really didn't give a shit if he found it or not. Using a club, he poked at the tropical vegetation while slapping at the pesky insects buzzing around his ears.

Goddamn it! He should have stayed in the cottage and watched TV or something. Why the hell had he agreed to play in this half-assed tournament for a game he hated?

Johnny continued walking, no longer trying to look for the ball. Who cared? So they'd be short one more.

The shortage of balls on this island ain't got

nothing to do with golf.

He had no idea how much time had passed since he had left the others. He'd stopped wearing a watch almost two years ago. What good was a watch here? It's not like he had a train to catch.

The whine of a jet engine brought Johnny out of his self-pity. The trees had thinned, and he found himself near the edge of the woods, the airstrip just in front of him.

Instinctively, he ducked behind the cover of some bushes as a plane swooped in low and landed. It taxied to a stop fifty yards from the Quonset hut serving as a flight center. The door opened. Two men drove up in a truck, and after offloading several large boxes, drove away.

To his amazement, the pilots deplaned and walked into the hut. No one guarded the jet. Hope surged. *Finally, a lapse in security.*

Johnny ran across the field separating the tarmac from the woods. He stayed low and tripped over a rock, falling flat on his face. He lay still for a moment before cautiously raising his head. Nobody noticed. He got up, his heart pounding, and continued on, making it to the plane's steps where he halted, sucked in an excited, shaky breath, and listened.

If they had another person on board, he'd be caught like a fish in a net, punished with house arrest, and no privileges for a month. He figured the odds at fifty-fifty. Boots scraping on the concrete spurred him into action. The guards were coming. Scrambling up the steps, he entered the aircraft.

I'll be goddamned. This is my lucky day.

The plane was empty. Johnny hurried aft searching for a place to hide. He made his way to the back of the corporate jet. A gap of about eighteen inches separated the last row of conventional style seats and the bulkhead. Johnny squeezed in, and curled up in the corner wondering if the pilots would check the plane before taking off. He shrugged. If they did, they'd find him. If they didn't, he'd get away. He'd always been a bit of a fatalist.

He also wondered how long it would take until the bulls discovered his escape. The Feds took a head count every night at nine o'clock and again at seven in the morning. Bobo's threesome had teed off at nine-thirty. They'd been on the fifth hole when he left. He estimated the time now to be around eleven. Would the other two golfers raise the alarm when he didn't show up? Hell, knowing Bobo and Lou, they'd just figure he'd been pissed and quit.

More footsteps approached the aircraft. Johnny held his breath. The pilots entered after a short conversation took place outside. One turned for the cockpit, while the other secured the door before joining him. The men spent several minutes going through a pre-flight checklist. He sweated bullets and wished he had a weapon in case they discovered him. He might be able to hijack the damned thing. Then the engines started. A few minutes later, the plane taxied to the end of the runway. The jet rolled, picked up speed, and took off.

He'd done it! He had no idea where the plane was headed, but it had to land somewhere in the States. When it did, he'd find his way to Chicago.

His elation faded, replaced by cold anger and fierce determination. He needed a plan. Once back home, he'd have to dodge both the Feds and the mob, but if he maintained a low profile, he could pull it off.

As for Miss Gabriella Vicelli...she would soon be history. He envisioned a slow, painful death for her. And Johnny intended to administer every painful moment.

Trust me, payback's a bitch. I'm coming for ya, sister. Count on it.

Chapter Two

Johnny grasped the seat and hauled himself up slowly, groaning when his cramped muscles protested every inch of movement. He eased his way out of his tiny hideaway in almost total darkness, and wincing with pain, moved his legs for the first time in several hours. He knew they had landed near D. C. He'd heard snatches of conversation from the pilots on the radio through the open cockpit door calling Washington approach. It hadn't been that long a flight. The island must be in the Caribbean.

He made his way forward. Pausing for a moment in the doorway, he listened for signs of life. Silence greeted him. Off to his right, a small light glowed, throwing the hangar into a mosaic of deep shadows and dim light.

The pain in his legs forced him to cling to the handrails as he exited, stumbling once and almost falling. On the ground, he massaged his calves and tried to walk off the effects.

Fuckin' bitch. This is all her fault.

He examined his surroundings. The large hangar doors were closed and probably locked. Two other planes took up space. The feeble light source came from a small fixture over a doorway.

Limping, Johnny made his way over and discovered an office. Without hesitation, he checked for possible alarm wires, snatched a hammer from a workbench, and smashed the glass, the noise deafening in the silent hangar. He unlocked the door and entered. Offices always kept petty cash around somewhere. He found it in a drawer and stole the entire hundred and fifty dollars. The phone book on the desk told him he was in Bethesda, Maryland.

He stuffed the cash into his pocket and left, not bothering to wipe down the surfaces he'd touched. The Feds would know who'd done it.

Toward the back wall a lighted red "Exit" sign glowed.

A sudden noise snapped his attention to the door under the sign. Someone, a guard most likely, inserted a key into the lock. Johnny grabbed a wrench and hurried to stand behind the door. It had been a long time since he'd killed someone, and he wondered whether his heart pounded in fear or anticipation.

The door opened and the security guard entered. He swung a flashlight around the interior of the hangar, stopping at the sight of the broken office window.

Johnny didn't hesitate. He leaped from behind the door and brought the wrench down on the man's head. The guard cried out and fell. He hit him again. The elderly man didn't move. Now, he had to hide the body. It wouldn't do for someone to come in early and find it lying on the floor. A door on the far wall of the hangar marked "Mechanical Room" caught his eye.

Grabbing the collar of the guard's shirt, he dragged the hundred and fifty pounds of dead weight across the floor. Johnny turned the door knob, relieved when it wasn't locked, and shoved the man inside.

He stared at the guard's prostrated body. The unmistakable fumes of cheap bourbon drifted to his nostrils. Bending over, Johnny searched the man. He found the bottle tucked into a back pocket, pulled it out, and cursed. Only a dribble remained. He drank it anyway, smashing the bottle against the wall. The guard groaned.

Johnny stared down at the man, his heart pumping hard and his breath coming in short bursts. He raised the wrench and struck him again, and then again to make sure. Damn, it felt good. He hadn't lost his touch after all.

A rapidly expanding pool of blood formed little streams on the cement. He dropped the wrench next to the body, not bothering to check if the man still breathed. He didn't care.

He ran back toward the door. Passing the workbench, he rummaged for a weapon—something easy to conceal, yet deadly enough to kill—before settling on an awl. Its sharp, pointed tip would do the necessary damage. He shoved it deep into his pocket, and then poked his head out of the open door. Another taxiway and hangar stood opposite him.

Johnny drew in his breath and ran, his stiff legs hampering the movement. In the shelter of the other building, he slid around the corner to the back. A simple chain link fence separated the airport from a field beyond. He sprinted for the fence, scaled it, and then trotted through the weeds to a road. Unsure of which way to go or where it would take him, he walked.

The road widened into a street. He entered the town of Bardsville passing businesses and warehouses, and stopped in a twenty-four hour gas station where he bought a cup of coffee and a pack of smokes, then asked directions to the bus station.

On the island they'd been allowed to dress in shorts and golf shirts, so he blended in. Even so, he didn't want to linger. The Chicago bus departed in less than an hour. He purchased a ticket.

Johnny tried to sleep on the bus, but a shrieking

baby and people talking permitted only brief catnaps during the trip. He wanted to kill them all.

After arriving in Chicago, he bought some second hand clothes and a bottle of hair dye, then scurried to the nearest cheap hotel. Later, he looked in the cracked mirror and smirked.

Not bad. Unless he ran into a family member, no one would recognize him. He hated losing the mustache. He'd had it since his early twenties, but without it and with the salt and pepper hair gone, Johnny decided he looked younger. Maybe even better looking.

The smirk turned into a grin. He ran his hand over his newly shaved face.

Might even get a piece of ass. The thought cheered him.

A baseball cap, glasses, oversized jeans, and shirt completed his disguise. He was home. He was ready.

****

"Lane, we have a small problem," Roger Warwick, director of Alpha-Omega Division, an ultra-secret branch of the FBI, said.

Lane Hamilton lounged in front of his boss's desk expecting to discuss Gabriella Vicelli.

A small problem to Roger represented a catastrophe to most people. Did it involve his nemesis? Whatever the problem, it had to be more exciting than sitting in front of a computer all day. His natural propensity for sarcasm blossomed. "Did the copier run out of paper again?"

Roger frowned. "Don't be a smart ass. This is serious. Johnny Scarano is missing."

Lane jerked upright, alert, no longer bored. "Missing? As in gone off the island? Are you sure?"

"Yeah. He didn't show up for dinner and missed the head count. Security had to wait until daylight to search properly."

"We *do* have a problem. We just sent Alberti to the island last night. He should be arriving any moment."

"The pilots of a cargo plane delivering supplies left to stretch their legs and grab a cup of coffee. They swore they were gone no more than fifteen minutes."

Lane ran a hand over his face. "Lemme guess. Nobody guarded the plane."

"According to the head of security, there was a small lag time between the pilots deplaning and security arriving."

"The planes are never to be unattended." Anger roughened his voice. "If both pilots leave, security is supposed to be called before they go."

"Obviously, we had a breakdown."

Roger's clipped words told Lane heads would roll somewhere. As former head of the FBI, Roger had garnered a reputation as a ruthless son of a bitch when it came to breakdowns.

"It's always been a possibility. Now, it's happened," Lane said.

"We found Scarano's golf bag on the edge of the woods and a golf club on the other side near the airstrip. Bobo Rabinsky and Lou Rizzo claim Johnny was playing with them in a golf tournament when he went into the woods to retrieve a lost ball."

"A golf tournament?" Lane stared. "They live too well for thugs."

"Probably, but it keeps them busy. The new tennis courts are a big hit, too. A couple of the guys have requested art supplies on the next shipment."

Lane shook his head. The conversation had veered off track. "Didn't any of our hidden mikes or videos give us a clue?"

"Not if he spoke on the golf course or while swimming. Rabinsky said Scarano had been making noises about escaping for the last few weeks. Nobody else seems to be all that interested in leaving."

"Why should they? They're living in paradise."

Roger sighed and twirled a pencil between his fingers. This was about as agitated as his boss got. A calm demeanor had served him well during his official years whenever he had to go before a congressional committee. The public loved him. His mane of white hair and good looks parlayed into *People* magazine's "Sexiest Man Alive" several years ago.

"I assume the plane has been searched," Lane said.

"Of course." Roger paused, his jaw clenched. "Scarano may have been busy. A security guard is missing. According to his supervisor, the guy is some kind of relative of the owner and has been known to relieve his boredom with a pint of bourbon."

"Swell. So, this guy could just be on a bender and not missing at all. When did the plane land?"

"About five o'clock last night."

Lane did some fast calculations. "The pilots would go directly to debriefing, and then home. Once the plane was secured in the hangar it would be unguarded. Scarano would know to get out of there before the nine o'clock bed check on the island."

Lack of security had loused up more missions than he could count.

"That's what we think happened."

"What time did the plane leave the island?"

"A little before noon."

"It's ten now. That's a huge head start. He'd have to travel in disguise. He can't afford to attract the attention of his former bosses."

Roger agreed. "He's a dead man if he does, and he knows we'll be looking for him." Roger paused again, and then said, "And we both know where he's going. Rabinsky said Johnny was one pissed off gangster."

Lane closed his eyes, silently cursing. "Vicelli."

"He wants revenge. If he can take her down, he just might convince his boss to reinstate him."

"And if Johnny Scarano lives long enough to do that, our operation is history along with a lot of good men, including us."

"I have an assignment for you, Lane, out from behind that desk you hate." He raised his hand, forestalling the words about to spill from Lane's lips. "Don't deny it. I know you hate it, but remember it was your decision to break cover from the Witness Protection Program. Well, your wish is granted. You're going back into the field."

Roger had uttered the words in such a smooth voice Lane was instantly suspicious. *Oh, shit. Now what?* He didn't like this one bit.

"Yeah? Where?"

"You'll go to Chicago and keep Gabriella Vicelli safe. I've already sent her a message to expect a visitor and to follow your orders."

Lane stared at Roger. Chicago? Vicelli? Dammit! "You want me to babysit Vicelli? Roger, the woman is a loose cannon. She doesn't follow instructions and has her own agenda. I oughta know. I've been her controller for four long years."

"She's important to Alpha-Omega Division. We can't afford to lose her. She's too valuable."

"Roger, if you hadn't browbeat her into spreading her hits around, all of the Ponzetti family would be on that island. She wants her own slice of revenge."

"I know. Marco Alberti wasn't supposed to be the next detainee." Roger shrugged. "But I gotta admit, she pulled it off. We're getting good information out of him."

"But he wasn't the target. Dammit. She's volatile, unwilling to take orders, and a major league bitch. Send someone else."

"Nope. You're it. Your job is to protect and keep her in line. Get her out of the city if possible until Scarano is back in custody or dead. Spend your time making her see the error of her ways." He handed Lane a manila envelope. "Here are your documents and your cover story along with the pilots' debriefing and statements. Go home and pack. A car will pick you up in an hour. We'll fly you into Detroit where you can catch a commercial airline to Chicago."

Lane had no choice. Sure he wanted back in the field, but not with that hellcat Vicelli anywhere within a hundred miles of him. He rose and headed out the door.

"Lane? Have a nice trip."

"Go to hell, Roger."

His boss's laughter rang in his ears.

****

Gabriella tossed and turned, gripped in the depths of a nightmare, knowing she dreamed, but unable to awaken. She ran for her life, dashing down the gravel pathways of a garden maze. The thick bordering hedges reached skyward into infinity. From behind, her pursuer's footsteps pounded.

The long skirt of her beaded gown hampered movement. Grasping the material in her free hand, she yanked the weighted folds.

The twisting path gleamed, the white pebbles a stark contrast to the black of the hedges and the night.

She paused, glancing at the nine-millimeter clutched in her hand, its cold, heavy weight cramping her fingers. On the other side of the obstructing shrubbery, a party was in progress. If she found the exit, she'd be safe, one of the revelers.

"Gabriella," Alberti taunted. "You bitch! Where are you?" Footsteps crunched on the gravel. "You can't get away. I'll get you and do all the stuff I promised."

She shivered trying to control her ragged breathing and galloping heartbeat, one step ahead of total panic. Her mouth, dry as cotton, had the metallic taste of fear. The incongruous scent of jasmine permeated the air.

A burst of laughter from the other side of the hedge spurred her back into action. She ran down the path to the next intersection. Gabriella bore left and ran into a dead end. She turned to retrace her steps. The dark silhouette of a man barred her way.

"Hello, bitch."

With her heart hammering under her ribs, she backed away until the stiff, sharp leaves of the hedge scraped and pricked her bare shoulders.

Displaying calmness she didn't feel, Gabriella raised her gun hand. She clutched a TV remote control. Desperately, she pushed the buttons waiting for the channel to change. It didn't.

Marco laughed, raising his arm. She stared down the barrel of his semi-automatic. The party, just inches from her back, continued with chatter and the clinking of ice cubes in glasses.

Marco advanced, stood in front of her, and placed the gun between her eyes.

"See you in hell, bitch." His finger tightened on the trigger.

Gabriella awoke, jerking upright, her fist in her mouth to stifle a scream. Bathed in sweat, she choked back a sob, running her hands through tangled hair, the jasmine perfume worn the evening before still strong on her skin.

God, she hated these nightmares. They terrified her. Still shaking, she held her head in her hands until the tremors receded, and her thudding heart and labored breathing slowed.

She glanced at the clock, before flopping back onto the pillows. Four-thirty. Should she get up or try to go back to sleep? She was exhausted. Sleep had not come easily these last few weeks while she'd planned the details of Alberti's departure.

Sliding out of bed, she shuffled into the bathroom, drank two glasses of water, then returned and slipped beneath the covers. She closed her eyes, praying for dreamless sleep.

****

Hours later, Gabriella sat at the dining room table glaring at her computer screen, and re-read Roger's e-mail for the fourth time. She twirled a lock of hair around her finger and sipped from her third cup of coffee. A visitor? Warwick had never sent her a visitor before. What could be so important he wouldn't put it in an encrypted e-mail? Son of a bitch. She hated an interrupted routine. What was going on?

Her cell phone rang, the mellow tones of *The Godfather* theme intruding on her thoughts. She didn't need to look at the caller ID. It was Frankie. He'd called every hour on the hour since ten o'clock this morning. The ringing stopped, and a few seconds later the tone sounded indicating another message had been left. That made six, so far. Let him call and grovel.

I don't need the miserable bastard anymore.

Shoving aside a pile of papers, Gabriella returned to her problem of a visitor. She'd sent her report as soon as she'd gotten in last night. Her controller demanded instant reports. It was the only demand she ever obeyed—not because she enjoyed following orders, but because it kept the asshole off her back. She hated being nagged, and doing it Tinkerbell's way kept things quiet.

Gabriella sniggered. Tinkerbell. What the hell kind of a code name was that? She had often speculated on her code name being Peter Pan. It made sense. She also bet Tinkerbell was a woman. Surely, no guy would have that as a code name. She laughed at the image of a male fairy with a magic wand flitting from operative to operative.

But man or woman, Tinkerbell was a pain in her ass. That's why she was certain she had a female controller. Women in charge loved to nag women under them. Well, nobody nagged or gave orders to Gabriella Vicelli.

She glanced at the clock with a groan. Four-fifteen. She felt like hell. Keyed up after a successful mission, she'd arrived home last night, turned on some music and danced off the excess energy before writing her report and going to bed. After the nightmare, she'd slept until almost one o'clock.

Gabriella polished off the lukewarm contents of her cup. Who would be next? Maybe somebody from the Muzio family. Yeah, Muzio was about due, although the temptation to nail another Ponzetti thug ranked high on her list. *Better wait. Tinkerbell will crawl up my ass otherwise.*

She closed her eyes, twirled a lock of hair, and thought. *The Muzio family is weak right now. Another disappearance might break them.* She made a notation to investigate on her computer to-do list, and then exited the program.

Enough work for today. She'd take a shower, order in, and have an early night. Her visitor could fend for himself.

I'm not a goddamned babysitter.

Gabriella was halfway to the bathroom when someone leaned long and hard on her doorbell. Her guest already? She turned and had only taken a couple of steps when the buzzer sounded again.

Impatient asshole.

"I'm coming, I'm coming. Keep your fuckin' shirt on!"

Looking through the peephole, she stared at a stranger. Her visitor? She slipped the safety chain into place, and then cracked the door open to observe a damned good looking man. Her mind automatically slipped into descriptive mode as if writing a report. Tall—six feet or so—trim build, about two hundred pounds with dark hair, dark eyes to match.

He glared and snapped, "Do I get to come in or are you going to leave me standing in the hall?"

"Who the hell are you, and why should I let you in?"

"My name is Leo Carpetti and you're expecting me. You do read your e-mail, don't you?"

She wanted to tell him what he could do with himself. Instead, she unfastened the chain and opened the door. He said nothing, picking up his duffle bag and laptop case, then brushed past her.

"Hey! Come on in. Who am I to refuse entry to such a charmer? It's just *my* apartment."

"I'm sorry, but I've been traveling. I hate planes and airports. We have a situation and need to talk."

The stranger dropped his bags next to the cluttered coffee table.

"What's your name again?"

"Carpetti...Leo Carpetti."

"Is that your real name?"

"It is as far as you're concerned."

The temptation to smack him one was strong, but she resisted—at least for the moment.

"So, Carpetti, what's this situation?"

"Johnny Scarano. Remember him?"

He sent her a sharp, penetrating look. She had the feeling it wasn't a rhetorical question.

"Yeah, about midway on my list of hits. He was a henchman for Benny Rapido and the Ponzetti family. He had delusions of grandeur. What about him?"

"He escaped from the island last night."

A chill washed over her and her heart hammered in a burst of fear. *Oh, shit! Just what I needed to hear.*

"And how the fuck did he manage that?"

Leo told her.

"Son of a bitch! Don't you assholes do anything right? If you think I'm going to catch him for you again, you're crazy. Go get him yourselves. He's your problem."

A slow flush spread over Leo's cheeks. "No, he's your problem. The report from the island is that Johnny wants your head on a platter so he can present it to his boss."

She flicked a strand of hair over her shoulder. "I'm not afraid of that little weasel." She lied. She knew Scarano well enough to realize he'd track her down like a bloodhound. "Why did Warwick send you? He could have e-mailed me."

"You *should* be afraid of him. The Director of Alpha-Omega sent me to make sure nothing happens to you."

So that was it. *He* was the babysitter.

"Fuck off. I can take care of myself."

"Lady, I personally don't care if your head does end up on that plate. I've been given an assignment and intend to carry it out."

"And what is it you do at Alpha-Omega?"

He stuck his chin out. "I do what I'm told by Director Warwick." His voice took on a dangerous tone.

"Terrific. Go back to Washington, Carpetti. I don't need a smart-ass, anal, flunky protecting me."

He picked up his bags. "Where's your spare room? I need a couple of hours' sleep before we go. Pack enough for a week."

"I'm not going fucking anywhere."

"You'll do as I say. My job is to keep you safe until Scarano is either back on the island or dead. You're going if I have to hog-tie and gag you. That's my favorite option."

The look on his face told her he meant it. Damn those fools on the island. They must have shit for brains.

"The spare room's down the hall on your left," she said abruptly.

Gabriella stifled a laugh as he turned and tripped over her shoes of last night. A denim jacket, a cardigan, a pair of running shoes, and a tote bag full of books littered his path. He wove his way around them like a broken field runner.

She whirled and stomped back to her computer where she fired off a blistering e-mail to Roger Warwick demanding to know this Leo person's real name. It would come in useful for his tombstone because she was gonna kill him.

Walking into the kitchen, she reached for the coffee pot, and then glanced at the clock. Hell, it was almost five. She rummaged in the cabinet for a clean glass. Finding none, Gabriella picked up a dirty one from the counter, rinsed it, pulled a bottle out of the freezer, and poured straight vodka. She wandered back into the living room, shoved a pile of magazines off the sofa, and sat sipping her drink. She preferred it to Xanax. The smooth liquor sent a shot of warmth straight down to her stomach helping bring her temper under control.

She didn't need a babysitter. Let the director deal with Scarano. And under no circumstances would she run. She had a mission, and no third rate wise guy like Scarano was going to divert her from completing it.

****

Lane closed the door of his room. Slinging his duffle and laptop on the bed, he plopped down next to them and closed his eyes. Damn. Vicelli in the flesh was ten times worse than Vicelli on the computer. He was tempted to call Warwick, telling him to forget it. Let Scarano get her. It would serve her right.

He opened his eyes and gazed around the bedroom, the only reasonably clean room he'd seen. Then he spied the thick layer of dust on the nightstand. Taking out a handkerchief, Lane wiped the grime from every horizontal surface he found.

The woman lived like a pig. The living room was strewn with magazines, newspapers, and used glasses. Clothing littered the floor and the furniture. CDs and DVDs formed towers on the tables. The entertainment center looked as if a bomb had exploded. He couldn't see the top of the dining room table, and the glimpse he'd had of the kitchen when he'd passed turned his stomach. The countertop was covered with dirty dishes, and the sink crammed full of the same. He made a mental note to never eat here. Lane suppressed a shudder at the thought of her bathroom.

On that note, he rose and entered the bath in his room. Okay, not as bad as he'd feared. Opening the vanity doors, he found cleaning materials and proceeded to give the place a quick scouring. He hated filth and sloppiness—a holdover from his childhood.

He asked himself how a woman as attractive as Gabriella Vicelli could live like this. He admitted to being surprised when she'd opened the door. He'd come to Alpha-Omega after its inception. The only photos in the files were the mobsters on the island.

Now, he understood her success. She was taller than he expected, maybe five-feet-seven or eight, and possessed a voluptuous figure. Dark brown hair fell in a cloud past her shoulders. Her face had a lean, hungry look, and her targets would succumb in an instant to the soft brown eyes. And those lips! Made for kissing. A little tug of awareness plucked at him.

He took a deep breath. "No, no way. Not this

trip, buddy," he muttered to himself.

No matter how beautiful, there was no way in hell he'd ever contemplate starting anything with bitch central. Lane liked his women polite, quiet and refined. Gabriella Vicelli possessed the personality of a porcupine along with the vocabulary of a longshoreman.

"You're just tired, pal. Tomorrow, she won't look nearly as good," he muttered out loud again.

He looked at his duffle bag. He should have known Gabriella would never leave, even for her own safety. But he was stuck with her until Scarano was recaptured or dead. He had to convince her.

Lane decided to unpack a few things. This might take longer than expected.

****

Gabriella sipped her drink and waited, foot tapping, for the beep of incoming e-mail. The door to the spare room opened and Leo walked out.

"Are you ready to listen to reason?" he asked.

"Only if you are. It's not my fault Scarano escaped."

"In order for this operation to work, you need to remain undiscovered. To be honest, your time is running out. Sooner or later, someone will figure out you were the last one to see the victims."

He bent over, picking up several magazines on the floor, and arranged them in a neat pile on the coffee table.

"How many informants are in place?" She crossed her legs, taking more than a sip from the glass this time.

"That's not your department."

"May I remind you, I am an integral part of Alpha-Omega Division? Roger Warwick and the President *of the United States* think highly of me."

Gabriella stalked into the kitchen where she freshened her drink, and returned to the sofa.

"I know, but keeping a bunch of mobsters on an island in the Caribbean is no easy task. The cost is enormous."

He toted six or seven dirty glasses and coffee mugs to the kitchen, dumping them on the counter.

"I thought we owned the island." She resumed her seat, taking a large gulp of vodka, and propping her feet up on the coffee table.

"We do," Leo said, returning from the kitchen. He pulled out a dust-streaked handkerchief and proceeded to wipe down the end table. "But, with Congress cutting spending, we may have to curtail new admissions. Running a secret organization with hidden funds takes a delicate touch. As far as Congress is concerned, Alpha-Omega is just a little offshoot of the FBI taking care of field operatives. That's why it's so important for you to be protected. If word of what we're doing gets out all of us will be unemployed and probably in jail. In case it's escaped your notice, Alpha-Omega is illegal as hell." He grabbed a stack of CDs and replaced them in the holder. "Tomorrow morning, we leave for a nice little vacation in the Alaskan wilderness. I hope you like camping."

She choked on her drink. Camping? Was he nuts? "Are you outta your fucking mind?"

"Trust me, you'll love it. Lots of wide open spaces."

It dawned on her that Leo had been cleaning during the entire conversation. She'd been so distracted she hadn't noticed.

"You know, if I wanted a maid, I'd pay for one," she said, taking another swallow to stifle the laugh threatening to break through her irritation.

"You need one. This place is a pigsty."

She leaped to her feet, instantly defensive and pissed off. "So what? It's my fuckin' apartment. I'll do what I want. Who the hell are you to come in here and criticize my housekeeping?"

"I don't even want to think about the diseases I could get in the kitchen. You have a dishwasher. Why don't you use it? How many months has it been since you cleaned?"

"Damn you! It's only been a few days. I was busy. Have you forgotten about Alberti? So what if I'm not Mrs. Clean? Why the hell should you care?"

Leo pulled a lacy, black bra out from under a chair and dangled it from his fingertips.

"Gimme that!" she snarled, snatching it from his hand.

"Because I hate sloppiness. And I resent having to clean up other people's messes. God only knows what kind of fungus is growing in your sink. A cluttered house is the sign of a disorganized mind." He tossed a pair of pantyhose at her. "And a disorganized mind can get you killed."

"Disorganized my ass!"

The pantyhose settled over her left shoulder. She snatched them off, throwing the offending article on the floor, and then finished her drink in a single gulp. For an instant, the room spun. She needed food or she'd end up drunk.

"Go pack while I tackle the mess in the kitchen." He rolled up his sleeves. "You do have dishwashing soap, don't you? How about detergent for the dishwasher?" He turned on the faucet, opened the cabinet under the sink, and recoiled at the sight of the almost full garbage pail.

She held her breath at the rancid smell.

"Good God. We'll have to get rid of this right away. I'm surprised you don't have roaches."

"The only roach in this apartment is you. Turn off that water and get outta my kitchen."

She might as well have been talking to a deaf man. He grabbed the Ivory Liquid and the Cascade as though he hadn't heard a word she'd said. She stamped her foot and snatched the vodka bottle. Slopping another shot into her glass, she bolted it down.

"Better go easy on that," he said. "It's hell hiking with a hangover."

Anger overwhelmed her common sense, trying to take control. Who did he think he was? Nobody, but nobody ignored Gabriella Vicelli. This errand boy treated her like a child. And why the hell didn't Warwick answer her damned e-mail?

She wanted to scream and hurl her glass at the calm, composed man at *her* sink loading *her* dishwasher. Breathing deeply, she focused on curbing her temper. Then the doorbell rang.

"Don't answer that," he demanded.

"Go to hell!" She didn't care if Scarano stood on the other side. Leo Carpetti—or whatever his name was—didn't give *her* orders. She jerked the door open.

Oh, shit!

"Hey, baby," Frankie said with a grin.

Chapter Three

Gabriella stared at the biggest bouquet of long-stemmed, red roses she'd ever seen and immediately slipped into her alter-ego.

"Frankie! What are you doing here?"

Frankie shoved the flowers into her arms and laid a five-pound box of Godiva chocolates on top.

"These are for you. Sorry about last night. I swear to God, I don't know what happened. I just couldn't stay awake. Please, forgive me, baby. Can I come in?"

She raised her arm to slam the door in his face when her houseguest strolled out of the kitchen and stood in plain view of the doorway.

"Hey, Gabby, whatta haul."

Whirling, she glared at Leo who calmly wiped his hands on a dishtowel. Gabby? *Gabby*? She hated that name. His accent had also turned less cultured.

"Who the hell is this?" Frankie said.

Her head snapped back to the entryway. Frankie's stance, with outthrust chin and hands on his hips, indicated a jealous tantrum about to erupt. She needed to lower the testosterone level. Now!

"This is my—my cousin, Leo Carpetti. Leo, this is Frankie Ponzetti."

Frankie's face cleared. He walked past her and into the room. "No kiddin'? I didn't know you had a cousin." He and Leo shook hands. "So, where ya from, Leo?"

"Detroit." Leo flashed a cocky grin.

"Like I said, I didn't know Gabriella had any cousins."

"Sure. My grandmother on my mother's side and her grandmother on her father's side were sisters."

Frankie shot a suspicious look at the dishtowel, and then at Gabriella. She held her breath.

"Huh? That's pretty distant."

"Hey, family is family, if you get my drift," Leo replied with a smile.

Understanding crossed Frankie's face. "I get it. How?"

Leo draped the dishtowel over his shoulder and crossed his arms. "Cousin Gus helped set my father up in business."

"Yeah? What kind of business?"

"The banking business."

"So, how's business?"

"Damned good."

Frankie rubbed a hand over his chin. "You know Antonio Morelli? He runs a kind of lottery in Detroit."

"I've seen him around. How about a drink?"

"Yeah, sure. Vodka—rocks. What about Sal Fabrizio? He's in waste management."

Leo jerked two heavy crystal glasses from a china cabinet, filled them with ice, grabbed the bottle, and poured, handing one to Frankie.

"Yeah, I've met him. My father knew him better."

"My father's good buddies with Gino Scala. You know him?" Frankie took a gulp of his drink, his gaze glued on Leo.

"Whew, man! Way outta my league. I ain't that far up the...ah...social ladder."

The suspicion in Frankie's eyes cleared and his stance relaxed. He looked at Gabriella.

"Hey, babe, aren't you gonna put those in

water?"

Gabriella had stood frozen ever since Frankie walked through the door. The conversation held her riveted. She didn't know whether to be terrified or fascinated.

"Oh, yeah," she muttered, making her way into the kitchen. She flung open a cabinet, grabbing the first vase she found, then dumped the flowers into it. She had no idea where to put the damned thing, finally shoving some junk off the coffee table.

Gabriella had to give Leo his due. He'd handled Frankie like a pro, and since Frankie was a birdbrain, he'd bought the whole cousin thing.

Her computer beeped, signaling incoming mail.

Oh, fuck! Not now! Her heart slammed into her chest as Frankie strolled into the dining area.

"Hey, baby, I didn't know you had a top of the line Dell. I'm impressed."

She shoved him out of the way to get to the laptop before he could see what was on the screen. Moving fast, she exited the program.

"Oh, phooey! I got outbid." She pretended to pout.

"Outbid?" Frankie's face bore a puzzled expression.

"Yeah, on eBay." The eBay screen flashed into place. She breathed easier.

"E-Bay? Why the hell you lookin' at that? It's a waste of time."

"Oh, Frankie, you're so funny. I buy all kinds of stuff. I just love it."

"Women and shopping," he said, and then turned back to Leo. "So, tell me, Leo, have you ever done any...uh...manufacturing?"

Gabriella's heart rate shot up again. Oh, shit. Did this pencil-pushing flunky know that "manufacture" was a euphemism for "made", which in Frankie's world meant being accepted into the brotherhood, usually through an act of bloody violence?

Leo shrugged his shoulders. "I've been forced to do manual labor a few times in the past."

She released a pent up breath, but her nerves still hummed.

Any more of this testosterone driven bullshit and I'll have a fucking heart attack. She grabbed a lock of hair and twirled.

"Hey, all right." Frankie turned to her. "Babe, let me make last night up to you. How about dinner at Giuseppe's tonight?"

Dinner was the last thing she wanted, especially with Frankie, but knew if she said no, he'd hound her until she agreed. In the long run, it would be easier to go out with him. And once she unloaded good, old cousin Leo, she'd take a vacation as far away from Chicago as possible.

"Well, I really shouldn't. Everybody was laughing at me. I don't know how I'll ever show my face at the All-Italian Club again. Your father was embarrassed, too."

Frankie ran a finger under his turtleneck and a hand through his longish, dark brown hair, with an uncomfortable look on his face. "Yeah. He wasn't happy. Told me so, this morning. So, how about it? Giuseppe's makes one hell of a Veal Marsala."

"Well, I don't know." She cast a quick glance at Leo who glared like a snake ready to strike.

"Ah, please, baby. I brought you flowers and candy. What else can I do?"

Watching Frankie beg made her day. "All right, but dinner and that's all. As soon as we're done, I come home."

"Hey, that's my girl. I'll pick you up in the limo at nine."

Leo's lips thinned into a stern line. He gripped the dishtowel until his knuckles turned white. She thought he looked ready to explode. Let him. It might make for some interesting entertainment.

Still putting on a reluctant-to-agree act for Frankie's benefit, she finally said, "Okay."

Frankie beamed, and then turned to Leo. "Have a seat. Let's talk. How're things goin' in Detroit?"

Gabriella sat behind the computer pretending to shop, occasionally throwing out sentences like, "Oh, what a pretty necklace" or "I've just gotta have that," but all the while listening to the two men swap mob related stories.

"Here," Frankie said, handing Leo his card. "If you need anything, just give old Frankie a call. I'll take care of you."

"Thanks, I appreciate it. *Frank J. Ponzetti, Vice-President, Ponzetti Construction.* Construction?"

"Yeah. Cement's our specialty!" Frankie laughed.

Leo roared with him. "Hey, man, we have something in common. I've dug a few foundations of my own."

"I'd hate to tell you who makes up some of the cornerstones of Chicago's tallest!"

"I hope the cops never decide to drag the Detroit River. They'd run out of grappling hooks."

"Lemme guess, Jimmy Hoffa, right?" Frankie said with a sputtering laugh.

"And just my size, too," Gabriella squealed, feigning eBay interest, but watching the men slap each other on the back at their brilliant repartee. Leo actually wiped a tear from his eye.

My God, they're bonding.

He couldn't have gotten all this out of books or reports. He spoke as though he'd lived the life. Gabriella almost choked. In fact, she was amazed at the breadth of knowledge a desk jockey like Leo possessed. He knew the right people, the right terminology, and had used it to ease Frankie's jealousy. The two of them glad-handed and laughed like old buddies.

Earlier, when Leo had barged in like Genghis Khan, she'd been too pissed to pay much attention to him, but now she used their banter as an opportunity to further study him physically.

He stood about six-two and looked fit. There didn't appear to be a spare ounce of flesh anywhere on his body, at least none she could see. Straight, dark brown hair, brown eyes, and a killer smile complete with a dimple in his left cheek made him damn good to look at, much as she hated to admit it. He threw back his head to laugh and suddenly it hit her like a punch to the stomach. Leo Carpetti was drop dead gorgeous *and* sexy as hell.

Her eyes settled on his wide, mobile mouth and flashed into a fantasy of it on hers, not to mention other more intimate parts of her anatomy. Hot, pulsating waves of heat surged through her radiating outwards from the pit of her stomach, and then back again.

Oh, shit! A guy she didn't like, who didn't like her, and who knew way too much about the mob, turned her on. This would never do. She narrowed her eyes and stared.

Who the hell is this guy?

****

Lane slapped his knee and laughed at Frankie's latest story. The minute Frankie had questioned his presence the old personality had slipped into place like a long-lost friend. He felt at home. The blood ripped through his veins, and his nerves hummed with the thrill of once again walking on the dangerous, dark side of life. God, he'd missed it! It was as though he'd spent the last five years in purgatory. He was having the time of his life. If Roger knew, he'd have a coronary.

He'd often wondered how Gabriella had

managed to penetrate the cold, cynical shells of the men she'd taken down. The minute she opened the door to Frankie, he had his answer. The self-centered little girl act was perfect. Who on earth could take the narcissistic Gabriella Vicelli seriously? By the time the poor schmucks realized they'd been had, it was too late.

Her reports, short and to the point, had never hinted at her alter ego. And her e-mails—pithy, acerbic, and usually profanity-laced messages—hadn't clued him in either. For the first time, he felt a sense of admiration. He related to acting a part.

He brought his attention back to Frankie. From what he knew about the Ponzetti family, Frankie would someday take over. The heir apparent was a jerk—arrogant, smug, and not nearly as smart as he thought, thereby proving the Peter Principle of everyone will be promoted until they reach their level of incompetence. Since the opportunity presented itself, Lane decided to use it.

He leaned forward and lowered his voice. "So, tell me Frankie, what's cookin' in Chi? I hear you got some new blood into the organization."

"Yeah? Where'd ya hear that?"

Lane shrugged. "Here and there. We've had a few changes ourselves." He was safe saying that. A couple Detroit families had gone through a bloody period two or three years ago. Lane sipped his drink. "Heard you lost some boys."

"Johnny Scarano, Tony Langhetta, and Duke Anceletti. They just vanished. One day they were drinkin' at the All-Italian Club and the next, gone."

"They get whacked?"

"We thought so, but other families swear they had nothin' to do with it. Said they'd been losing people, too, and blamed us. A war damn near broke out."

"No shit? Better keep your eyes open, Frankie."

"I got my ass covered."

Maybe the seed of foreign-based suspicion would grow, diverting possible questions regarding Gabriella and the All-Italian Club. Lane drained his glass.

"You think it could be someone from outside? That's what happened five or six years ago in Miami. The Russians came in and damn near took over the whole city."

As if on cue, the voice from the dining area piped up. "Oh, goody. I've got the high bid, so far."

He leaned in closer, lowering his voice another notch. "Frankie, what's with you and my cousin? I'm not being nosy, you understand, but as her oldest male relative, I feel kinda responsible for her."

Frankie glanced at Gabriella. "For the last two months, I've been tryin' like hell to get her into bed, but last night things changed."

"Yeah? How? And this better be good. Gabby's a good girl." He tried to sound outraged and allowed a threatening hint of displeasure to enter his voice. "I wouldn't take kindly to someone—anyone—trifling with her affections."

"No, Leo, honest. That was before. Last night I made an ass of myself. This morning, I realized she's kinda special. My father hopes something'll come of us seeing each other, because of Gus. I think I'm gonna pop the question soon."

Damn. That's all he needed. A lovesick Frank Ponzetti hanging around. He had to get Gabriella out of Chicago.

"I'm glad to hear that, Frankie. A union between our families will help heal old wounds, don't you think?"

"That's what my father said. We took over most of Gus's organization after his death." Frankie drained his glass and poured another.

"You think Gabby is a commodity, a business

deal? I gotta tell you, I was really hoping she could marry a nice guy with a legitimate job."

Lane pretended to look disappointed at Frankie's motives. He'd counted the drinks poured and watched Ponzetti take a generous gulp. One more and he could lose any subtlety of pumping him.

"Hey, you got it all wrong. I really like her. She's funny and sexy as hell. I know she's a good girl. We've never—I mean, aw, hell, you get my drift."

Frankie looked like a teenager being grilled by his date's father. He took another gulp of his drink before refreshing it again, and wiped a bead of moisture from his temple.

Good, let him sweat a little.

"I'm glad to hear that, Frankie. How long have you been dating?"

"I met her for the first time about a year ago at The All-Italian Club." Frankie paused to take a drink.

Gabriella mentioned the All-Italian Club several times in her reports. She used it to contact her targets, and that alone made it dangerous. Use it too many times and people remember. The first rule of undercover work is don't get set in your ways. Lane made a mental note to caution her about her MO.

"So, a year, huh? Is it serious?"

"We got reacquainted about three months ago. She ran into my car. I was pissed, you know? It was a brand new Mercedes. She was sweet about it. I couldn't resist."

I'll just bet she was, and of course, you couldn't.

Lane wanted to laugh. He could see it now. The high-pitched voice, the breathless dismay, and the pouting lips. She'd probably gone the whole nine yards. Frankie must have fallen like a boulder rolling downhill.

The voice sounded from the dining area. "I won! I think I'll try jewelry now."

Lane wanted to laugh again. She didn't fool him. It was her way of letting him know she still had her ears open. They had been discussing Gabriella in low tones, and he knew she tried like hell to eavesdrop.

Later, Lane would write a report and send it to headquarters. He turned his attention back to Frankie who now guzzled his sixth drink.

The stupid jackass talked about people, places and events that would buy anyone less than the son of a Don a quick bullet in the head. Roger would put the data to good use.

Frankie droned on, interrupted every once in a while with comments from the dining area. Finally, unbelievable, bragging accomplishments replaced useful information.

Lane picked up the vodka bottle. "Whoa, Frankie. We damn near killed this thing. I'd better slow down. How about you? Can I give you a refill?"

Even half-potted Frankie must have gotten the hint. "No, I've had enough." He rose from his seat, wobbling. "Whew! Grey Goose is damn fine."

Lane stood. "Hey, my cousin has expensive tastes." He laughed, slapping Frankie on the back, then leaned over, whispering, "Get used to it."

Frankie roared. "I guess I can handle it. Hey, baby, I gotta go. I'll pick you up at nine."

Gabriella left the computer and followed him to the door. "Okay, Frankie."

He pulled her into his arms. Lane stood ten feet away his arms folded over his chest, rocking back and forth on his feet.

Frankie smiled, kissing Gabriella on each cheek. "Leo, great to meet you."

"We'll talk again."

Frankie left. Gabriella closed the door behind him, sagging back against it as though exhausted. Her face relaxed when she shut her eyes and heaved a sigh.

I have to get her out of here. The sooner the better.

With arms still folded, Lane ordered, "Break the date and get packed."

Chapter Four

Gabriella's eyes snapped open. Straightening, she remembered she had another battle to wage.

"Go to hell. I'm not canceling a damned thing." She thrust out her chin and widened her stance, hands fisted on her hips.

"Frankie thinks he's in love. I don't want him panting after you like a teenager. I can have a plane waiting for us at the airport."

"Look, dumb ass, I can deal with Frankie. Tell him no and he'll hound me to death. This way he'll stay happy for a while. And he's not in love with me or anybody else. He's like all the rest of his kind. They use women, discard them, and move on to the next available female body. He's been trying to get in my pants since we met. He's putting on an act for you."

Leo picked up the dirty glasses and took them into the kitchen, then returned to cap the vodka and replace it in the freezer.

"Don't argue. Hurry up. I want to be gone before he shows up with that limo."

"Goddamn it! What part of this don't you understand? I have no intention of leaving Chicago. Besides, Frankie will have his hands full with family matters as soon as they realize Alberti is missing."

"Sooner or later, someone will remember seeing you with Alberti. Which reminds me, we have to talk about your M.O. You're getting repetitive and that leads to sloppiness."

"What? Sloppy? You stupid asshole! I plan everything down to the tiniest detail. I spend hours perfecting an attack. What the hell would a desk jockey like you know about it anyway? And while we're on the subject, how is it you know so much about the mob and its inner workings? Who the hell are you?"

"That's not important. We'll discuss your methods on the plane when you've had a chance to calm down."

She'd had it with this interfering jerk-off. She reached for the closest object—an ashtray—and cocked her arm, prepared to hurl it at his head.

Panther quick, he leaped in front of her, catching her wrist in his hand, tightening his hold until she relaxed her grip.

He set the ashtray back on the table and hauled her close, his face just inches from hers.

"Quit behaving like the spoiled child you are and do as I say. I'm here to keep you alive."

Gabriella wanted to argue, but his closeness played havoc with her body. This near to him, she noticed his eyes had small flecks of green. He smelled of fresh air like a crisp autumn day—a male scent that suddenly had her thinking of mountains and tumbling streams. She swallowed. What the hell was happening? She didn't want these thoughts or visions, dammit. She had to regain control of herself and the situation. Nobody, but nobody, commanded her.

She stepped back and pulled her wrist free. "I don't like people telling me what to do. That includes you. I see no danger. It'll look suspicious if I suddenly disappear. Then Frankie and the rest *will* start asking questions. Did you, Warwick, or that idiot controller of mine ever think of that?"

Leo also backed up, putting space between

them. "I have a job to do and intend to do it. I want to get as far away from Chicago as I can until Johnny Scarano is either recaptured or dead."

"You're fucking paranoid."

"What is it with you? Why won't you listen? I'm here to help you."

"I don't need your help. Johnny Scarano? He's a moron. It took me all of ten seconds to nail him."

"Johnny Scarano is as dangerous as they come. A security guard in Bethesda is missing and he's probably responsible. All of the men on that island are killers. If they ever return to society, they'll kill again."

"So a security guard is missing. So what? If they look hard they'll find him sleeping one off in a corner somewhere. I still say you're paranoid. I'm going to dinner. Continue with your maid service until I get back. I can handle Frankie. I've been doing it very well for the past three months."

Leo's eyes narrowed and his lips compressed into a thin line. "Trust me. You're not going anywhere without me."

"Yeah, like Frankie will accept a chaperone."

Leo didn't answer. Instead, he whipped his cell phone out and fished Frankie's business card from his pocket, then dialed.

"Hello, Frankie. It's Leo. I have a little problem... Naw, nothing like that, but I got to thinking. Since I'm Gabby's protector and in light of your declaration this afternoon, I think I should look out for her interests... Well, I think I should come along to this dinner tonight... It ain't a matter of trust, Frankie. It's a matter of what's right. Cousin Gus would see it my way. Your father would understand, too...Hey, I don't want to spoil your fun. Scare up a broad for me. We can double date. I'd like to get to know you better... That's great, Frankie. You're a sport... No, we'll meet you there. I need to run an errand first, and Gabby takes forever in the bathroom...Yeah, women. Get used to it, pal. Can't live with 'em, can't live without 'em... No problem, see you at Giuseppe's."

He hung up and smiled. "We go to dinner and when we get back, we leave."

"Are you nuts? What the hell are you thinking?"

She couldn't believe he'd called Frankie and arranged a double date. And Frankie, that knucklehead, had agreed.

"I have Frankie convinced I'm looking out for you. Gavino is from the old school. He'll appreciate that I'm taking care of my cousin, especially if he's hoping for a union between the Ponzetti and Vicelli families."

"A union! I'd rather die than marry into that family. Where did you get something like that?"

"From Frankie. Apparently, his daddy has plans."

"That's crazy!" Her hand strayed to a lock of hair. She twirled it around her finger.

"And while we're on the subject, what is it with you and the Ponzettis? I know Gavino ordered the hit on your father, but you've got to rein in your revenge. Forget them. They aren't that important."

"The hell they aren't."

"Why?"

"None of your business. I hate them all."

"Hate is the one emotion you can't afford. It'll overwhelm and consume you."

She didn't answer. She couldn't. She'd already been consumed.

"I'm going to take a shower and send a report to headquarters," he said. "During our conversation, Frankie let slip several nuggets of information that'll interest Roger."

He headed down the hall to his room and closed the door. Marry Frankie? Was he hallucinating? It was ludicrous. Oh, she had to get rid of this clown. Tonight if possible.

Gabriella marched back into the dining area and pulled up the agency screen. She hadn't dared open her e-mail with Frankie present, but now she needed answers.

Typing in a series of codes and passwords, she opened the message from the Director of Alpha-Omega Division. She read it, and then re-read it in growing disbelief.

"As far as you are concerned, Leo Carpetti is who he says. There's no need for you to know any more. He is there for your protection. Do as ordered."

She sat back, her mouth hanging open as anger bubbled in her chest. Condescending bastard.

"'There's no need for you to know any more,'" she read out loud. Who had been putting whose life on the line for the past five years? If it hadn't been for her, Alpha-Omega wouldn't exist. *And this is the thanks I get?*

"'Do as ordered,'" she muttered. Fat, fucking chance. She wanted to know more and she wanted to know it now.

Not about to take no for an answer, Gabriella fired off another angry e-mail. In it, she reminded Warwick that she had never had any trouble handling problems in the past. She sent the message, then sat back to seethe while waiting for a reply.

It hadn't all been a breeze, of course. Her scariest moment had come with Lorenzo Nestore. He'd seen the gun and had fought like a tiger. She'd laid low for three weeks afterwards to let a black eye heal.

Lefty Lefkowitz had been the first. A small time thug with the Soretto family, she remembered. Nervous, but dedicated, she had almost missed his neck.

She added up all twenty-five hits. The easiest? Marco Alberti. Or maybe she just thought of it as easy because by now she had honed her skills to an art. Did she regret any of them? No.

Gabriella glanced at the clock on the screen, noting it was nearly time to get ready for her big double date. Leo had laid the cousin-protector groundwork, but she resented his interference. His presence only complicated matters with Frankie. She could have ended things with a few choice words and gone on to her next target.

Damn those morons on the island! If they'd done their jobs, Johnny Scarano would still be locked away, vegetating, and I wouldn't be sitting here with an anal-retentive agency babysitter. Her computer beeped. *About time.*

"I order you to do as instructed because you are so important to this agency."

She fired off the blunt, two word, "Fuck you" reply, then turned off the power and shoved the laptop across the dining table.

Stomping into her bedroom, Gabriella slammed the door with a resounding crash. Glaring at the mess of clothing littering the floor and unmade bed, she pounded her fists against her thighs. "Shit!"

****

Lane sat on the bed, his back braced against the headboard and typed out his report. Years of practice had taught him to keep it short and to the point, but this was one report in which he rambled due to sheer frustration. He concluded with, "She resents all attempts at control and refuses to follow procedures. Her M.O. is dangerously repetitive. She may be important to Alpha-Omega Division, but she will also be its downfall if not reined in. She is obstinate and puts her agenda ahead of that of the agency. She is not a team player. Medusa is a security disaster waiting to happen. Anyone in the field or doing covert work, operating in such a manner, would not live.

"My advice is to temporarily terminate the entire operation for the sake of everyone involved, including the twenty-four men on the island. If Congress finds out what we've been doing, we'll all be publicly exposed, not a pleasant thought for someone in my position."

Lane sent the message, then logged off, closed the lid of his laptop, and carefully set it aside. He pinched the bridge of his nose, pondering his next move.

Gabriella had forced him to revise his plans. He had to get her out of Chicago. Even now, Johnny Scarano could be in town. A public dinner with Frankie was the last thing either of them needed, but short of shooting her with her own tranquilizer gun, he was fresh out of ideas. Never had he had this much trouble with an operative. Until now, he'd had no idea how volatile her personality was.

On the other hand, he should have seen it coming. Every time she had deviated from the original plans, he'd sent a message demanding to know why. And every time she told him in less than ladylike language what he could do with himself, the changes had been necessary, and leave her alone she was doing just fine.

Dammit! Her vendetta against the Ponzettis would get them all in trouble. She needed to slow down. Twenty-five hits in five years represented a lot of missing mobsters. If Frankie could be believed, the families had already discussed the disappearances. She lived on borrowed time.

Lane got up and wandered into the bathroom. Turning on the shower, he stopped to inspect his face in the mirror. The plastic surgery five years ago had gone well. Not even his mother would recognize him—if he had a mother. The doctor had aged him a little and although he was only thirty-seven, he looked in his early forties. He worked out religiously. The rarely missed routine had paid off.

Entering the shower, Lane tried to banish Gabriella Vicelli from his mind and failed. Okay, he admitted she was gorgeous, but he had expected immunity to her charms. Her eyes slanted slightly beneath arching brows, and the rather square face ended in a pointed chin. One frequently thrust out in anger, he noted.

Her father's death six years ago must have been the catalyst for her to take the drastic action of contacting the FBI. Lane knew little about her past, and that's the way he wanted it. He didn't need any more information. He also handled three other undercover men and didn't know their stories from birth either.

He turned off the faucets, stepped out of the shower and chuckled. The look on her face when he'd said Alaska had been worth all the hassles. She'd bought it. The image of Gabriella Vicelli hiking through the wilderness in those silly high-heeled shoes with a full backpack was hilarious. In reality, he had reservations under assumed names at a small motel ninety miles away in Rockford, Illinois.

Still, he had to confess she fascinated him. Toweling off, he asked out loud, "So, why is she such a total bitch?"

****

Gabriella pawed through her closet looking for something to wear. A shower had helped cool her temper, but not by much. She formed ways to get rid of Leo, and then discarded them, although shooting a tranquilizer into him had its merits. It wouldn't take care of the problem, but at least it would shut him up, and she wouldn't have to listen to him give her orders she had no intention of obeying.

Holding up two dresses, she finally decided on

the red one. It screamed, "Look at me." Short, low-cut, and clingy, it would drive Frankie crazy and send good, ole Cousin Leo into a rage. Maybe he'd have a stroke or something. The thought cheered her.

Gabriella wiggled into the dress, applied make-up, and then decided to leave her hair down. Several tendrils found their curly way into her cleavage. She wanted Frankie engrossed with her, not speculating on Leo.

She twisted and turned, inspecting herself in the full-length mirror, then stopped and stared at her reflection. Leo's words about Johnny echoed in her mind. Was he right? Was Johnny more of a threat than she thought? Should she leave? *Fucking Alaska?*

"Don't be silly," she muttered to her image. Johnny was just another thug with his brains in his pants. If he hadn't been, he'd have never landed on the island.

She grabbed an evening bag and slipped into a pair of bright red stilettos, coming to the conclusion she looked like a hooker—or at least, an expensive call girl. She hated projecting that image, but the job sometimes called for it. She pulled the neckline a little lower, then opened the door, and strolled into the living room.

She stopped dead and stared. Leo was lounging in a chair. When she entered, he rose and Gabriella noted with satisfaction he took in her appearance as only a man could do. His gaze slid down, and then back up her body. She saw admiration mingled with exasperation. Leering usually set her teeth on edge, but something in Leo's eyes made her want to yank his clothes off and wrestle him onto the sofa.

She gathered her wits and viewed him in the same way, assessing him like a prized bull. Dressed in a pair of navy slacks and a white, open-necked shirt with the sleeves rolled up, he exuded a sense of casual elegance. She tried not to notice how the crisp white contrasted with the darkly tanned skin of his throat and forearms. A hint of chest hair peeked out from the vee of the shirt.

She took a deep breath to steady her nerves. Leo didn't compliment her looks, and she couldn't decide whether to be irritated or relieved.

"Are you ready?" he asked.

"Yeah. It's almost nine and Frankie's always on time. I always arrive late. It's expected."

He placed his hand on the small of her back as she passed him out the door. Gabriella suppressed a shiver of delight, wondering just what the hell was wrong with her.

****

Johnny lay on the thin mattress covering the squeaky bed in his hotel room and checked his watch, hoping his luck continued to hold. He'd love to sleep longer, but knew he couldn't hide in his room forever if he wanted to find Vicelli. Darkness had fallen. It was time to begin the hunt.

He took a chance on the streets, but had to make contact with someone he trusted. He left his hotel making his way to Hooligan's Bar. Seeing no familiar faces, he had a drink and left, fingering the awl in his coat pocket when a patron eyed him as he walked past.

Moving on, he sauntered into The Tavern and recognized a man at the bar. Not his first choice, but what the hell?

Johnny slid onto a stool next to him and said, "Hey, Ralphie. Long time, no see."

Ralph Puccio glanced over and then did a double take. "Johnny? Is that you? Geez, what did you do to your hair? And what happened to your moustache? You don't look like you. Jesus, I haven't seen you in a coupla years. I heard you got whacked."

"Yeah, it's me. I just had to leave town for a while. What's happened since I been gone? Anything interesting?"

He needed to play this carefully. Ralphie wasn't a member of any family, but a wannabe who liked to hang out with mobsters. It made him feel like a big shot. He reminded Johnny of a pair of perky tits on a stripper's chest—all bounce and enthusiasm. He wasn't the brightest bulb in the pack either.

Ralphie gushed information. Most of what he said confirmed his suspicions. The holes Vicelli had created caused trouble, especially in the Ponzetti family. His resolve hardened to put the bitch away permanently. Once he did, he could resume his old position. When the others knew how she'd tricked everyone, they'd forget about retribution and welcome the rest of the guys back, too—assuming those idiots could give up their golf and tennis games.

Ralphie droned on until finally running out of steam, and Johnny asked, "What about Gabriella Vicelli? Is she still around?"

"Boy, I'll say. Now, there is one hot broad. Long legs and tits from heaven. I heard she's been dating Frankie Ponzetti. I think they're engaged."

Son of a bitch! He had to get to Gavino and warn him. She wouldn't have the balls to take out Frank, would she?

"No kiddin'? Any idea how to get a hold of her or where she lives? I'd like to congratulate her."

"Sorry, pal, but I can ask around if you'd like," the stooge said with an eager expression.

That was the last thing he needed—Ralphie Puccio asking questions. The stupid ass might keep his mouth shut for a while, but sooner or later, he'd spill his guts to whoever wanted to know. Ralphie was no longer an asset.

"Naw, that's okay. I'll probably run into her at

the All-Italian Club. No big deal. Look, I gotta run. Do me a favor. Don't mention to anyone you've seen me. I'm doing something for the big man, and he wants it kept real quiet. You get my drift?"

Ralphie's eyes bugged out. "Yeah, yeah, I get it. Mum's the word. I haven't seen you in years." He winked.

Johnny slid off his barstool and crossed off ever walking into The Tavern again.

"Nice talkin' to ya." He started to leave, then came back to clap Ralphie on the shoulder. He needed to take care of business. "Hey, maybe you *can* do something for me. Just a little job."

The man's eyes blazed with excitement. "Yeah? No kidding? Whatcha need? I'm your man. You can count on me."

Johnny's gaze scanned the other people in the bar. "Not here. It's too crowded. Too many ears. It's an important job. Meet me in the alley out back in five minutes. Okay?"

"No problem. I'll look real casual. Five minutes."

Nodding, Johnny slipped out of The Tavern and walked down the street to the narrow passageway behind the bar where he waited next to a dumpster. With his eyes fixed on the alley entrance, he removed the awl from his pocket. Darkness would hide the weapon.

Ralphie didn't wait five minutes, but showed barely a minute after Johnny had taken up his position. He stepped out and waved.

"Over here," he called in a low voice.

Ralphie trotted up like a lamb to the slaughter.

"Yeah, Johnny, what do you want me to do?"

Quick as lightning, he plunged the awl into Ralphie's chest just under the breastbone. The man's eyes went wide, and he uttered a short, gasping sound. Johnny pulled the awl out, stabbing repeatedly until Ralphie's eyes glazed over and he slumped to the ground.

Wiping the blood off on the dead man's shirt, Johnny heaved the body into the dumpster and left. Another problem solved. He turned and made his way through the alley toward the street dodging dumpsters and garbage bags, his mind already on other matters—like how Gabriella Vicelli's mutilated body would be a warning to others.

Weaving his way through the crowded sidewalk, he decided to get a little food, sleep, and then resume his bar hopping tomorrow. Somewhere, someone had to know where to find the bitch.

Get ready, sweetheart. Your time's almost up.

Johnny walked down the street with a spring in his step.

Chapter Five

Lane walked into Giuseppe's with Gabriella, scanned the room, and then cursed silently. Damn! Nearly every table was occupied. And if Frankie dined here he could only assume other mobsters did, too—maybe even some from New York. This had become dangerous for him as well. He searched the crowd again, but saw no one he recognized. Breathing easier, he followed Gabriella and the maitre d' to Frankie's intimate booth in the far back corner.

Frankie rose, his eyes bugging out at Gabriella's dress, or in Lane's opinion, the lack of it. The clinging red fabric sent his temper and his hormones up a level. He wanted to yank a cloth from one of the tables and throw it over her.

"Hey, baby, you're looking fine," Frankie said, kissing her cheek. His gaze slid down and up again before he turned to Lane. "Hi, Leo. Good to see you."

"Sorry I had to foist myself on you like this, but I'm an old-fashioned kind of guy."

"Hey, I understand and respect your wishes. I want to do things right with Gabriella."

The two men shook hands as though making a pact. Then Frankie moved aside, giving him his first look at his date.

Lane stared and for a moment wondered if Frankie had substituted an inflatable doll as a joke. Then the inflatable blinked, smiled, and took a deep breath. He wondered if her upper anatomy would stay in the dress.

"Leo, your date, Bubbles LaRue."

Long blonde hair fell over her shoulders, and blue eyes framed with thick, dark lashes—heavy on the mascara—gazed up at him, loaded with sexy promises. Her face had the perfection only a surgeon's scalpel could achieve. He tried, but failed to keep his eyes off her chest and wondered where a doctor had found implants that big.

Every man's dream—Barbie come to life.

Only able to inspect her from the waist up, he assumed she wore a dress. The pink top tied around her neck and plunged to her navel. He had no idea how she kept those breasts inside. He bet if he slipped his hand under the tablecloth to her leg, he'd feel nothing but skin.

Bubbles simpered, batted her eyelashes, and presented a hand. Lane kissed it. "Miss LaRue, you are a vision of loveliness. It's a pleasure to meet you."

"Mutual, I'm sure," she replied in a breathy voice.

"Gabriella Vicelli, Miss LaRue," Frankie said.

Lane noted the two women barely nodded. In fact, Gabriella had a look on her face clearly indicating she'd like to poke Bubbles' forty-two inch chest with a fork to see if it exploded. The three of them slid into the booth.

A waiter appeared. "Would you like a cocktail before dinner?"

"I'll say," Lane said. "Bourbon and water."

"Grey Goose martini, straight up," Gabriella snapped.

"Bourbon and water for me, too," Frankie said, eyeing Gabriella's cleavage.

"Isn't a Cosmo that pretty pink drink? I just love pink. I'll have one of those," Bubbles cooed. She batted her eyes again and placed her hand on Lane's thigh.

Lane made the mistake of looking at Gabriella. Her eyes narrowed and riveted on him while Frankie whispered in her ear. She shifted her gaze to Bubbles. For an instant, he wondered if the tranquilizer gun would make an appearance.

Lane couldn't explain the little sense of satisfaction running through him. It lifted his spirits, making him want to smile. He had pissed Gabriella off and rather enjoyed doing it. It was fun to yank her chain, like with threats about Alaska.

Turning his attention back to his date, he said, "Bubbles. That's an interesting name."

"Oh, it's not my real name. It's my professional name. I'm in show business." She winked. "My real name is Wilma Hotchkiss."

The waiter brought their drinks and Lane downed half in a hearty gulp.

"Is anything else real?" Gabriella shot from across the table.

Bubbles giggled. Lane decided the name also applied to the contents of her head. Trouble was brewing and he tried to head it off. "Show business, huh? Are you a singer?"

"Naw, Bubbles works at The Topsy-Turvy Club down on Rush Street. It's one of our joints. She's a stripper," Frankie said, his finger playing with a long strand of Gabriella's hair.

"Exotic dancer, Frankie." Bubbles pouted, inching closer to Lane.

"Whatever." Frankie toyed with the strand of hair moving it back and forth against the swell of Gabriella's breasts like an artist's brush, then caught Lane's eye. He ceased the movement and dropped the tendril.

Gabriella flashed a nasty smile. Turning to Frankie, she kissed his cheek while her hand disappeared under the table. Frankie jumped as if he'd been shot and grabbed his drink, draining it in a single swallow before signaling for another.

Lane shifted to face Bubbles and used one of her curls to caress her chin. Two could play this game.

"So, Bubbles, tell me, are you a native of Chicago?"

"Oh, goodness, no. I was born and raised on a dairy farm in Wisconsin. I really hate cows."

"And you came to the big city to find fame, right?" He winked and rubbed the blonde curl under his nose. Her hair smelled of some kind of flower, roses he guessed.

Bubbles giggled. "Yeah. At first I was hired at The Topsy-Turvy as a waitress, but a friend of Frankie's said if I got nose and boob jobs I'd make more money dancing. He's gone now. I really miss him. Johnny was nice."

Almost choking, Lane looked across the table at Gabriella, and then wondered if she'd even heard the comment. How could she when she was practically in Frankie's lap, nibbling on his ear? Frankie kept glancing at Lane and sidling away. In another couple of minutes, *he'd* be in *Bubbles'* lap.

The waiter brought another round of drinks. Taking their dinner order helped defuse the situation, but as soon as he left the games renewed.

Under the table, Bubbles slung her leg over his, breathing heavily in his ear. Lane pulled back and draped his arm over the back of the booth. Out of the corner of his eye, he watched Gabriella up the ante by giving Frankie a wet willy while Frankie tried to avoid Lane's observant glances.

Frankie yelped. "Waiter! Champagne for the ladies."

"O-o-o, Frankie. I love champagne. The bubbles tickle my nose," Gabriella purred, shooting another nasty look across the table.

"Me, too," Bubbles echoed, and then laughed. "Get it? Bubbles loves bubbles. That's funny."

"I love a girl with a sense of humor," Lane said.

"From the looks of it, I'd say you'd love just about anything," Gabriella growled, her eyebrows drawn together in a scowl.

Lane shot her a glance. She'd used her normal speaking voice, but Frankie apparently didn't notice the slip. He was too busy composing himself and smoothing his hair. Lane almost laughed at the man's dilemma. Gabriella exuded a come hither attitude and a frustrated Frankie could do nothing about it.

The champagne arrived and while the waiter poured, Lane used the time to compose himself, too. Bubbles might be a bimbo, but she packed a powerful sexual punch. He needed to cool down.

He lifted his glass. "To love, wherever we may find it."

"To love," Frankie echoed, smiling at Gabriella.

She smiled back and turned her gaze on Lane as she sipped. The tight smile did not show in her eyes.

His date chugged her champagne. "Oh, that's just the most beautiful thing I've ever heard. You're so sensitive, Leo. I love that in a man. I want to see more of you."

Bubbles' hand stroking his thigh told him exactly how much more.

"Yeah, don't lean over, baby, or we'll all see more of you," Frankie cracked, laughing at his joke.

Bubbles giggled and narrowed the gap between them. Lane scooted away. Any further and he'd wind up on the floor.

A hand grasped Lane's upper thigh and squeezed, then slid higher. Bubbles scooched closer.

"Frankie said you're from Detroit. I've never been there. What's it like?"

"Just like Chicago only further east."

He eased away from her. She followed. Her hand found its mark—his crotch. He jerked as though poked with a cattle prod.

"Oh, Leo," she whispered. "I am s-o-o impressed."

Gabriella glared. Suddenly, he was tired of this silly game. He'd had enough of both Bubbles and Gabriella.

The waiter arrived with their food and for the next twenty minutes they all behaved. Already Lane tried to think of a way out of the evening. He had an idea of what was in Frankie's mind—fob Leo off on Bubbles who could probably boff his brains out, and then have Gabriella to himself.

No, can't let that happen.

With the meal almost over, he still had no plan. Then his cell phone vibrated in his pocket. Since it was an agency phone, he knew the caller had to be Roger and the message urgent. He answered.

****

For Gabriella, the evening reminded her of physics class at Miss Cameron's School—for every action there was an equal reaction or something along those lines.

She turned up the heat on Frankie. And Frankie, the idiot, apparently had taken Leo's protective cousin routine to heart. To show she didn't give a damn about Leo and the five-dollar whore, she increased her efforts with Frankie.

"Oh, Frankie, I just love this place," she whispered in his ear.

"Yeah, yeah, baby. It's nice," he replied, sliding a little further away from her.

"Fra-an-kie," she drawled. "I'm sorry I was so mad at you last night."

"That's okay, baby. By the way, my father sends his regards and hopes you'll visit soon. He really likes you."

Oh, shit! Could what Leo had said about Gavino wanting Frankie to marry her be true? Did he really think she was too stupid not to know he had killed her father, his two bodyguards, and an innocent bystander?

"Well, your daddy is a sweetie. Frankie? Why don't you kiss me?"

She almost laughed out loud as Frankie glanced across the table at Leo.

"There's a time and a place for everything."

This from the guy who made lewd comments and grabbed her ass in the middle of Marshall Field's as she'd modeled a new dress for him. The garrulous saleswoman had been shocked into speechlessness. Gabriella suppressed another laugh.

Under other circumstances, she would have loved the Veal Marsala, but tonight she was too wound up to enjoy it. Then Leo got a funny look on his face and pulled out his phone.

Gabriella knew it was an agency phone. She had one just like it tucked into her purse. The by-play of the evening receded in importance as the reason for Leo's being here took priority.

"Uh, sorry, but I'm expecting a call," Leo said. "Yeah, Carpetti here...Hey Rocco, how's it going? What's up?"

Rocco? Who the hell was Rocco? Roger? Oh, shit. Warwick was calling? That meant it was not only urgent, but dire as well. He always communicated through e-mails. Her heart thudded, and her mind shifted into high gear. Something bad had happened. She sensed it.

She listened to the conversation with growing dread and tried to keep her face impassive. Frankie watched with curious eyes. Bubbles kept right on eating and downing champagne.

"Look, Rocco, here's what I suggest. Go ahead and make him the loan. He won't be able to pay it back any more than the last one. When he's late on the payments, we become his partners in the nightclub business. We can use it as an outlet for other things. *Capisce?* Yeah, keep me informed." He hung up.

"Hey, I like the way you handled that," Frankie said in an admiring tone.

"Thanks. I'm sorry to let business interfere in a social situation."

"No problem. Sometimes it can't be helped."

Lane rubbed his stomach and shook his head. "Will you excuse me for a minute? I'll be right back." He slid out of the seat and disappeared toward the restrooms.

Frankie took advantage of his absence to plant a wet one on Gabriella's lips while his hand crept up her thigh. Out of the corner of her eye, she saw Bubbles beam and shovel the last of her food into her mouth before washing it down with champagne. *Stupid bitch.*

She let Frankie cop a feel. Something was up— other than Frankie's dick—and intuition told her the evening would end soon.

Frankie broke off his sloppy attention and stared up at Leo standing next to the table. The look on his face reminded her of a kid caught with his hand in the cookie jar, only this time it was up her skirt. The expression on Leo's face was entirely different. He looked sick.

"Uh, Frankie, I'm really sorry, but Gabby and I have to go." He rubbed his stomach and licked his lips.

"Go? Why?" Frankie stared with a blank expression.

"Yeah, why?" she asked. She'd argue for appearance's sake.

"I'm not feeling well. Guess it must have been something I ate. I had lunch in the airport. Must have gotten a hold of some bad food."

"But, Leo, you were just fine a minute ago." Bubbles pouted and batted those damned lashes again like it would make everything all right. Gabriella glanced at the knife on her plate. *Not sharp enough.*

"Yeah, I know. Came on real sudden like. One minute I was fine and the next... At any rate, I think I'd better head for home. Sorry. You ready, Gabby?"

Gabby again. She wanted to smack him. "Sure, Leo." She gathered her purse and tossed the napkin on the table.

Frankie laid a hand on her arm. "Why don't you go on? I'll bring Gabriella home."

"Aw, that's out of your way. Besides, I'm not sure I should drive. I may have to puke again."

"That's okay, Frankie," she said, giving him a light kiss. "I'll talk to you later."

Frankie looked like a little boy being denied a piece of candy. "I'll call you tomorrow, baby. Take care, Leo."

Bubbles still pouted. "Will I see you again, Leo?"

"Yeah, sure. I'll give you a call. Maybe stop by The Topsy-Turvy in a day or two when I feel better."

Gabriella tugged at his arm. "Come on, Leo. We'd better get home. I don't want you throwing up in my car. It's brand new. See you all later."

They hustled out of Giuseppe's and waited while the car was brought around.

"What's up?" she asked.

"Not so loud and not here," Leo replied in a low voice. "I'll tell you in the car."

Leo handed the parking attendant a five, then holding his stomach and groaning, got into the passenger's seat. He played the scene out to the end. It was a good thing he did. As she drove away, Gabriella spied Frankie watching from the doorway.

"Okay, what's this all about? Was that Warwick

on the phone?"

"Yes. He called to say Johnny Scarano was spotted by one of our informants in a bar called The Tavern on the South Side early this evening."

Her heart thumped harder in her chest. "Well, so what? We knew he'd be heading here." She hadn't expected him to make such good time.

"All the more reason for us to get out. Those were Roger's orders."

Gabriella braked for a stoplight and tapped her fingernails on the steering wheel.

"I don't see any reason to panic. Who was this informant?"

"Just a guy we employ now and then. As soon as we knew Scarano had escaped, Roger contacted several people in Chicago to haunt Johnny's old hangouts. He said he almost missed seeing him. Johnny shaved off his moustache and dyed his hair. If it hadn't been for a guy at the bar calling him by name, our informant might never have noticed."

"Johnny found a friend? He likes to live dangerously. Who was he?"

The light turned green and she roared away, shifting with short, jerky movements. She didn't like the fact he'd made contact so soon. A small dart of pain flashed behind her eyes, signaling the beginnings of a headache.

"A guy named Ralph Puccio. Ever hear of him?"

"Not that I can remember. Whose family?"

"None as far as we can tell. He just likes to hang with gangsters."

"That could work to our advantage. Those clowns can't ever keep their mouths shut. Word will get back to Gavino Ponzetti in a flash."

"And if they capture Scarano, they'll use torture to get answers. He'll tell them all about Gabriella Vicelli and her magic tranquilizer gun."

"Not necessarily. They might just plug him."

71

"Do you want to take that chance?"

No, she didn't, but she had a hard time taking Johnny Scarano seriously. She still saw the stunned expression on his eager face when she'd shot him. He'd looked about as dangerous as an oversexed rabbit.

Arriving at the complex, she punched in her access code, activated the gate, and then pulled into her parking spot, remaining silent until they entered the apartment. They came to a halt standing on either side of the coffee table, Leo near the sofa, and she by the chairs.

"I think you're crediting everybody with more brains than they have."

"Including you?"

"Shut up and listen," she replied. "Things have changed a lot since I put Johnny away. This is a new apartment. I moved in about six months ago. I never renew leases, so I'm hard to find. Besides, I'm sure you noticed the security gate."

"I managed to get in just fine. The cab dropped me off and when a resident activated the gate, I slipped through before it finished closing."

Her heart lurched. Damn. She'd been so pissed when Leo showed up, she'd forgotten all about the gate, never questioning how he'd gotten in.

"How did Frankie gain access? Does he have your code?"

"That's different. Frankie is a tool and as soon as this mess with Scarano is over, I'm going to break it off. I'll change my code, take a nice long vacation, and by the time I return, he'll have latched onto someone new. When it comes to women, his attention span isn't too long. Hell, Bubbles is probably giving him head right now."

"I don't know why I'm standing here arguing with you."

"I don't either." She ignored Leo's glare and

continued, eager to press her point home. "I use a disposable cell phone—no land lines to track. I change numbers every few months. That wonderful little agency phone is hidden in the bottom of my purse disguised as a business card holder. It even has business cards in it. If I wanted, I could disappear tomorrow."

"You're going to," Leo stated in a confident voice.

Gabriella bulldozed on. "And keep in mind Johnny has limited resources. He can't track me through his usual mob channels. He has to rely on chumps like that Ralph person who will, in the end, betray him. By necessity, he'll have to lay low. Do you really think he's going to walk into the All-Italian Club and say 'Hi, how's it going'?"

"He doesn't have to. You do a good job of that to set up your marks. You use it way too much."

His condescending tone and words made her want to slap him silly. "Look, dumb ass, wait a couple of days. If he isn't out of commission by then, I'll say I'm going with you to visit relatives in Detroit."

"Why wait?"

Gabriella rubbed a hand over her forehead, attempting to ease the growing pain. "I've never cut and run in my life. I don't like losing, especially to someone like Scarano. Damn, what do you know about the situation? You're in your nice, safe little cubicle day in, day out. I'm the one on the front lines, risking her life to bring down the mob."

"I know more than you think. Why would a mafia princess want to bring down the mob?"

"They murder innocent people."

"What are you talking about? Your father was one of them. He wasn't innocent."

"Forget it." This guy was driving her crazy.

Leo dropped to the sofa, heaving a sigh and clutching his head. "God, you are a royal pain in the ass. How long do you think it'll be before Frankie mentions your cousin Leo to his father? Frankie may be an imbecile, but Gavino isn't. He'll start checking." He released his head and turned his gaze up to her. "It won't take him long to discover your father's mother had no sister."

"So what? Frankie will think I'm two-timing him and drop me like a bomb. He'll be angry and jealous for a while, and then get over it."

"Did you listen to any of the conversation tonight?"

"What conversation? You and Miss Tits-R-Us spent the entire time sucking face."

Leo leaped to his feet, anger flashing from his eyes. "You were all over Frankie like a rash. I thought you'd climb aboard and hump him right there."

Gabriella fisted her hands on her hips. "Yeah? And what were her hands doing under the table? Giving you a massage?"

"Did you hear anything Bubbles said?"

"How could I? Your heavy breathing drowned out anything she might have said. I thought you were having an asthma attack!"

He thrust his chin toward her. "Bubbles knows Johnny. Now, since her bra size and her IQ are the same, it seems reasonable to assume that with her Ponzetti connections, he could look her up and ask questions. I'm sure your name would pop up—along with mine."

"Bubbles won't even remember I was there. The only thing the woman can do is take off her clothes to a beat."

Gabriella's head throbbed. She closed her eyes and sighed. If she didn't get out of this room now, she'd kill him.

"Look, it's been a helluva long day. I didn't get much sleep last night, and I'm exhausted."

She walked toward the bedroom, dumping her purse and earrings on the coffee table, and kicking off her shoes in the middle of the room. "I'm going to bed. We can discuss this in the morning, unless, of course, you figure Scarano is going to miraculously appear on my doorstep in the next few hours."

"If I got in, so could he. And if he found one Ralph Puccio, he could find another—one with better information." Leo ran a hand through his hair.

She marched into her room and slammed the door, twisting the lock. Within seconds Lane pounded on it, rattling the doorknob.

"Gabriella, open this door."

Gabriella peeled off her dress and underwear, dropping them on the floor, then jammed the back of her vanity chair under the doorknob and crawled into the unmade bed.

"Gabriella, do you hear me? Dammit!"

She hadn't been lying about the exhaustion, but the fight with Leo still had her nerves humming. His probing of her motives hadn't upset her as much as his actions with the stripper.

"Gabriella, I'm warning you."

"Shut up! And stop that racket. If you don't, I'm calling the cops. Go away and leave me alone." Silence ensued. *Thank God.*

She drew in a shaky breath. For the life of her, she couldn't figure out why she cared one way or another if Leo and Bubbles got it on in the center ring at the circus. He was nothing to her, other than a pain in the ass.

Yet, she admitted watching Bubbles fawn and paw him had made her want to snatch the blonde bimbo bald. She recognized the feeling as plain, old-fashioned jealousy.

Okay, he was handsome as hell and emitted a sexy aura, but that was no excuse to get hot and bothered. She'd found Guido Randucci, her tenth—or was he the eleventh—hit attractive, too. She'd certainly never felt jealousy over any of his bimbos.

Gabriella rolled over and punched her pillow into a more comfortable shape. She didn't want to deal with this now. Her head still ached. Ripping back the covers, she stomped into the bathroom, downed two aspirins, and then returned to bed.

Go to sleep. Worry about sexy agents and escaped killers bent on revenge in the morning.

****

Lane sat on the sofa staring into space. He'd lost it. He'd lost his cool and argued with her. He tried to remember the last time that had happened. The jabs he'd thrown out regarding her and Frankie at the restaurant troubled him. Hell, his behavior with Bubbles troubled him.

He had no doubt Gabriella would call the cops, so it looked as if he was stuck here tonight. He spotted a dirty glass on the table and carried it into the kitchen where he washed, dried, and then put it away.

From his earlier report on Frankie's information, Roger knew he was once again in contact with dangerous people. The clipped, cold words over the phone tonight had told him his boss was not happy about it. Couldn't be helped. He'd deal with it later.

As a matter of course, Lane picked up the clutter in the living room and on the dining room table, stacking papers into neat piles. He found a bottle of cleaner and paper towels, then wiped the glass-topped coffee and end tables.

He needed to burn off the pent-up energy still lingering from the evening. It had always been this way once the danger ended. He knew guys who could fall asleep at the drop of a hat, but not him. He remained on alert, staying busy until his mind stopped whirling.

Lane alphabetized her CDs and was halfway through the videos when the churning stopped. Picking up her discarded shoes, he set them next to her closed door, and then stared at them.

His gut clenched as he remembered her with Frankie. A dart of anger shot through him. Dammit, why with Frankie? His mind conjured up visions of himself in the mobster's place. The thought had him grinding his teeth and running a hand through his hair.

"Why do I care? Why *should* I care?" he muttered.

He walked into his bedroom, closed the door, undressed, and slid into bed. Lane stared at the ceiling for a few minutes trying to put his emotions on the back burner. He had a job.

The fact Scarano had made it to Chicago so fast should worry them all. He'd worked up the profile on the mobster years ago. Besides being a cold-blooded killer, Johnny Scarano was a complete sociopath. And he had to make Gabriella see it.

Chapter Six

Gabriella jerked into consciousness, hands pressed against her chest to prevent her pounding heart from exploding. She sucked in gasping breaths to fill her oxygen-starved lungs.

God, another nightmare, starring Johnny Scarano this time. She'd been in a warehouse dodging from crate to crate trying to elude her pursuer. But Johnny kept following until she ran out of places to hide.

She climbed a ladder to a series of catwalks and looked down. The ground below spun, forcing her to grasp a low railing to keep from falling.

Johnny's head poked over the top of the ladder. "Gotcha," he called out.

With her heart lurching, Gabriella ran. The catwalks narrowed and the railing disappeared. She fled, her arms outstretched for balance. Then, her foot slipped. She clutched the beam, her legs dangling over the dark abyss below.

Turning her gaze upward, Johnny appeared. Bubbles stood next to him sipping a lurid, pink Cosmopolitan.

"So long, bitch," he sneered, stomping on her hands.

Screaming, she lost her precious grip and fell. Johnny threw back his head, laughing while Bubbles waved. Their images grew smaller as Gabriella plummeted.

She sat up, pushing sweat-dampened hair off her face. Her breathing and heart rate had slowed, but she continued to shake. The dream seemed so real that for a moment she'd had a problem distinguishing fantasy from reality.

Johnny and Bubbles. Goddammit! This was all Leo's fault. If the son of a bitch hadn't been such an asshole, she'd have never had this nightmare.

She glanced at the clock. Shit. She'd love to sleep some more, but it was time to get up and argue with Cousin Leo again.

Gabriella lay back, staring at the rotating ceiling fan, her thoughts centered on Leo Carpetti.

Yeah, right. Leo Carpetti. She hated the name Leo. One of Ponzetti's sleazier thugs had had that name. He'd tried to cop a feel at the All-Italian Club when she'd been sixteen. She told her father. No one had ever seen that particular Leo again. Her father had shielded her from the gruesome aspects of his occupation, but in this case, she'd known Gus had indeed taken care of business.

Forget about him. You have a bigger problem with this Leo. Who the hell is he really and how do I get rid of him?

The former posed no difficulty. He had to have his real ID on him somewhere, especially if he needed to ditch the Leo character. As soon as the opportunity presented itself, she'd search his room. He hadn't brought much.

She realized getting rid of Leo might not be the smart thing to do. A niggling little voice inside her kept asking, what if Leo was right? What if Scarano was camped outside the gate waiting for a chance to sneak in? Should she leave? It would mean giving up control, and she hated not being in control.

The news of Johnny being spotted in Chicago had sent an icy chill down her spine. If Gavino Ponzetti got to him first, one of two things could happen. He'd be shot on sight or captured. As to the second, she had no doubts Johnny would spill his guts about everything. His escape could mean her mission, her goal in life, would be over, and as much as she hated to admit it, she'd be better off doing as Asshole Leo wanted. If she went to Cold-As-Frozen-Shit-Alaska under an assumed name before Johnny got nailed, Ponzetti and the rest would never find her. If the Feds rounded him up first, she could go back to Alpha-Omega and continue her quest.

She didn't know what to do and she hated indecision. Her father had taught her that.

Weigh the situation and make a decision quickly, sweetheart. Your first instinct's usually right.

Of course, he'd been talking about her personal life.

Gabriella placed her hands under her head and closed her eyes. She often wondered what her father would have thought of her current...what? Profession? Life's mission? She wasn't sure what to call it. Sometimes, she fantasized he approved. At other times, she wasn't so sure.

He'd always had a rather pragmatic view of life and she speculated on whether or not he accepted the possibility of a sudden, violent death. Had he considered it an occupational hazard?

That's how she viewed her circumstances. Death, while she'd certainly like to avoid it, did not frighten her. Torture did, but she crossed it off as unlikely to occur. They'd just shoot her and get it over with. Even if the entire Alpha-Omega operation were blown wide open, the mob would have a hard time deciding who to clean out. At least on that scale she had been successful. She'd confused the hell out of them.

If only Daddy could have foreseen the future. He'd spoiled her rotten and the last words he'd spoken to her had shown she was number one in his thoughts.

I love you, baby. If he makes you happy, then I'm all for it. I'll talk to you more when I get back from dinner.

Only he'd never come back.

Ever since her life had been a quest, a thirst for revenge and eradication of those who had taken his life and the lives of his bodyguards, Guido and Eddie, and a man who happened to be in the wrong place at the wrong time. She'd sacrifice everything and anything to achieve her goal.

Friends? She had none. Her work was too dangerous and she couldn't expose another innocent bystander to danger.

Family? Her father had made sure his younger brother and sisters were not involved in his line of work. They and her cousins lived hundreds of miles from Chicago.

A family of her own? Yes, of course, but once again, how could she expose them to the danger of what she did?

Loneliness? A tear slid down her temple to lose itself in her hair. Sometimes the loneliness was unbearable, but she had accustomed herself to loneliness years ago, and the hard-bitten bitch had emerged to shield her from the hurt. That and a fierce determination to rid the world of mob scumbags were the only things that had kept her sane after the killings.

A loud knocking on her bedroom door ripped her out of her somber thoughts.

"Gabriella, wake up. We need to get out of here."

Gabriella squinted at the clock. It was barely ten o'clock. She ignored the summons and rolled over.

"Gabriella, I know you can hear me. Quit behaving like a child and open this damned door."

She jammed a pillow over her head.

"Gabriella, I'm warning you. Don't make me use force."

The covers followed the pillow. She heard a couple of thumps as though Leo had rammed his shoulder against the door. *Like that will work.* Even though common sense told her she should leave, his steadfast insistence on it got her back up. He'd have to drag her out, and wouldn't that look good for the neighbors?

The sound of a vacuum cleaner brought her upright. Mr. Hopelessly Anal was doing *housework*? How long had he been awake? Too long, she decided. From the sounds and smells drifting under her door from the kitchen, she figured he'd made coffee and probably had emptied the dishwasher as well. All the mugs had been dirty. Now this.

Heaving an exasperated sigh, she swung her legs onto the floor and fished her robe from under the bed. If he didn't like her housekeeping, he could move to a hotel. She dragged the chair away, jerked her door open, and breathed deeply. The coffee aroma kick-started her brain.

It had better be damned good.

Gabriella staggered into the kitchen and poured a cup. The counters gleamed. The sink hadn't looked this good since she'd moved in. Leaning against the doorjamb, she blew into the steaming mug while Leo swept the vacuum back and forth. A pile of discarded clothing graced one of the chairs. The glass topped tables sparkled. Even the damned CD tower looked organized, and for the first time in a long while, the shelves of the entertainment center held things neatly.

She sipped her coffee. Damn. It was perfect. She'd been hoping it would suck. A part of her wondered if she could chain and lock this domesticated animal in a closet. *But then I'd be permanently stuck with him.*

"You know, you really don't have to do this," she said. When he ignored her, she raised her voice. "Hey! This isn't necessary."

Leo shut off the vacuum. "What?"

"I said what are you doing?"

"I'm cleaning, of course. I figured the noise would piss you off enough to come out of your lair. How can you live like this? The garbage under the sink stank to high heaven. I threw it down the trash chute and disinfected the can it was in. And I found all these clothes under the sofa and chairs. You might want to toss them in the laundry hamper."

He made her feel guilty and incompetent. "Look, asshole, I would have gotten around to it sooner or later. I told you...I've been busy."

Wanting to kick him, Gabriella stomped into the dining area and fired up her laptop. He'd even made progress with the chaos on the table. Leo had discarded the newspapers and stacked other papers out of the way. *Sheesh!*

She entered her agency e-mail and read the only message from Roger warning her about following orders. So, what else was new? She deleted it, and then moved on to her personal messages, also few in number and mostly spam.

She poured another cup of coffee. "I wasn't in much of a mood to listen yesterday. Can you give me more details of how Johnny escaped and managed to get to Chicago so fast?"

Leo drained the last of the coffee into his mug and joined her in the living room. Sitting, he replied, "You know as much as we do about the actual escape. As for getting here, he had the devil's own luck. The hangar manager says he closed up shop about seven in the evening. When he arrived in the morning he found the door window had been smashed and the petty cash stolen."

He sipped some coffee. His jaw clenched and his

lips thinned. She read the frustration on his face.

"By that time, we knew Scarano had disappeared. Didn't take a genius to figure out how. We sent our guys out showing his picture to various shopkeepers. We finally hit pay dirt with a convenience store clerk who remembered him asking directions to the bus station. The videotape confirmed it. With the golf shirt and shorts, he blended in well. No one suspected a thing."

"Golf shirt and shorts? Why was he wearing those?"

"It's kind of like a minimum-security type retirement village. Roger thought they'd be more cooperative and content if they didn't feel like they were in prison."

She couldn't believe it. "Retirement village? What? They play eighteen, then sidle up to the nineteenth hole and quaff a cold one?"

"We don't allow liquor, at least I don't think we do," Leo said with an uncomfortable look on his face.

Was he kidding? Of course not. He didn't have a sense of humor. "Let me get this straight. They have a golf course and may or may not observe the cocktail hour? May I assume they also have an Olympic-sized pool and tennis courts? Oh, and don't forget the cable TV in their three bedroom houses, too."

"It's not Olympic-sized, and the tennis courts were just finished a few weeks ago. They live in individual cottages and yes, they have cable."

She choked on her coffee and stared. The look on his face told her he meant every word.

"I should live so fuckin' good! I've busted my ass for the past five years to send these slime balls away, and you clowns are treating them like deposed royalty. Where's the justice in that?"

"Gabriella, this isn't about justice. These men weren't arrested or brought to trial. We've violated their rights out the ass." He drained his cup and set it on the table. "You want to eliminate the mob. We want to control it. We have people who sooner or later will move into positions of authority. Our vision reaches beyond the next few years."

Gabriella didn't know how to answer that. She had been an integral part of Alpha-Omega's birth and now realized she was part of a team. She'd never viewed it that way before, preferring to think of herself as The Lone Ranger.

Uncomfortable with the revelation, she asked, "So, how come your informant in the bar didn't follow Johnny? If he had, you could have picked him up, and we wouldn't be having this discussion."

"He tried, but he's an informant, not an agent. He had no idea how to trail a suspect and lost him. We're combing the area, but if Scarano has an ounce of brains, he won't be seen in that bar or neighborhood again. He'll fish in other waters."

She finished her coffee. Taking a deep breath, she said, "If I agree to leave, what happens if the mob gets Scarano first? What happens to me?"

Leo sighed and shrugged. "I'm not sure. We have to go on the theory they'll believe what he tells them. You'd probably have a name change, a little plastic surgery, and be set up in a different town. If we get him first, its business as usual once the heat has died down."

Gabriella rose. She needed to think about this. "I'm going to get dressed."

By the time she'd showered and changed, she'd come to a reluctant decision. Logically, the Feds had a better shot at finding Johnny before the mob. The Feds were looking for him. The mob hadn't a clue. The odds stood in favor of the good guys. Relinquishing control for even a few days grated on her nerves, but in this case she saw no other choice. She concluded Leo wouldn't leave and visualized living with Mr. Clean for an indeterminate time. At least he wouldn't vacuum in the Alaskan wilderness.

Entering the living room, she looked Leo straight in the eye.

"All right. You win. I'll pack a few things and we can leave in an hour."

Before he could answer, the doorbell rang. Leo looked through the peephole and swore. "It's lover boy."

"Shit. What's he doing here?"

"If we ignore him, maybe he'll go away."

"He knows I'm here. My car's parked out front. Might as well let him in."

Leo inhaled deeply, and then opened the door.

"Hey, Leo," Frankie said, barging in. "Hiya, baby."

"Frankie, what are you doing here so early?" she said, slipping into character.

"I've got a couple of things to talk about, but I wanted to check on Leo here. How're you feelin'? You looked like hell last night."

Leo rubbed his stomach. "Better. It was a rough night. Man, never have the meatball sub at the Detroit airport. Whew! I damned near camped out in the bathroom."

"Poor Leo. I felt so sorry for him. I even went to an all night drugstore to get him some medicine so he wouldn't—"

"Yeah, yeah, I think he gets the picture, Gabby. You don't have to go into nauseating detail. No pun intended," Leo interrupted.

"Yeah, I get it. Bubbles sends her regards. She says come on down to the club and she'll put on a special show just for you." Frankie laughed and winked.

"Uh, yeah. Tell her I can hardly wait. Maybe in the next couple of days."

Leo glanced at her. It took all her self-control

not to throw something at the two of them. She imagined the kind of show Bubbles would put on. She ground her teeth and pretended to look happy.

"Could I come, too, Frankie? I've never been in a strip club before."

"No, no, baby. Strip clubs ain't for ladies," Frankie replied firmly.

"But Bubbles is there."

"Bubbles ain't no lady. Take my word for it."

"How about some coffee?" she asked, knowing Frankie would decline. He hated the stuff, and she wanted him gone.

"Naw, I ain't got time. I only dropped by to see how Leo was doin' and to invite you to the wedding."

"What wedding?" Leo asked.

"Yeah, what wedding?" she echoed. News of upcoming nuptials regarding mobsters usually spread like wildfire, and she'd heard nothing.

"Caesar Casano's granddaughter is getting married on Saturday. You're invited too, Leo, if you're still here."

"I'm not sure. I kind of doubt it, but thanks anyway."

"Too bad. Bubbles would have enjoyed it."

"Which granddaughter?" Gabriella asked. "I didn't know any of them were even engaged."

"It's his oldest, Angelica Martinelli. Apparently, her boyfriend knocked her up. Her mother is furious, demanding an instant wedding. And if Caesar's daughter is unhappy and wants something then, by God, she gets it."

"Sounds like the poor guy's got a gun to his head," Leo said.

Frankie roared with laughter. "Yeah, in more ways than one. That was good, Leo. You're a card."

Gabriella's mind slipped into high gear. Caesar Casano in a crowded social setting? It was the kind of thing she'd dreamed of for years, and Frankie had just presented it to her like the grand prize at a county fair. Holy shit, how long would it take to plan? She needed more information.

"Where's it going to be held, Frankie?"

"St. Jerome's. The reception will be at the All-Italian Club. It's just around the corner."

The All-Italian Club! Oh, this was too good to be true. If Alpha-Omega had to be closed down, then this would be her swan song. She'd go out with a bang. Caesar Casano represented the biggest and strongest of all the Chicago families. He was a modern day Al Capone. The thought of taking him down caused her nerves to hum with excitement. She had to do it!

"Oh, Frankie, that sounds like fun. I'd love to go! I remember Mr. Casano from when I was a little girl. He was nice to me," she gushed. "What should I get them as a wedding gift?"

"I don't know. Anything, I guess."

She tried to avoid looking at Leo, but couldn't resist sneaking a peek. He stared back, his eyes wide with disbelief.

"I'll get them towels. I just love lots of soft, fluffy towels, don't you?"

"Yeah, sure, whatever. Look I gotta get going. I have to meet with my father and some of his associates."

"That sounds important," Leo said.

"It is. Nobody's heard from Marco Alberti since our party the other night. We can't find him in his usual haunts." Frankie looked worried and confused. "My father's not happy. He says Marco had an altercation regarding certain territory with one of Muzio's henchmen last week."

"Think they got him?"

Frankie shrugged. "It's possible. He's valuable. Sure hate to lose him." He glanced at Gabriella. "You remember him, baby. You were talking to him."

Her heartbeat soared. Why would he ask her that? Did he suspect something or was it just Frankie talking?

"I was? I talked to so many people. I don't remember him. Maybe he's gone on vacation," she said, cheerfully.

"I don't think so. I've gotta go. I'll drop by later, Leo. We can go out and have some laughs, if you feel okay."

"Yeah, sure."

Frankie left, but Gabriella barely noticed. Her mind raced to plot the downfall of the boss of bosses.

****

Lane closed the door behind Frankie and turned to face Gabriella. She stood mute, a strange triumphant smile on her lips and the light of battle in her eyes. He didn't like it. She had something up her sleeve.

"I guess agreeing to go helped get him out the door. Give him a call in a while and say you have to break the date. Tell him a family matter has come up in Detroit."

She gazed at him, surprise on her face, as though she'd forgotten he was here.

"Break it? Hell, no! Didn't you hear? Caesar Casano will be there. It's like a gift from the gods."

"You just agreed to leave with me," he reminded her.

"Are you nuts? Leave now? This is a golden opportunity to nail the big man. We only have a few days to plan."

She whirled and picked through the pile of papers on the dining table until unearthing a legal pad. Lane gaped. She wasn't joking. She meant it. She wanted to plan another hit to take place within a week of her last one.

"You're the one who's crazy. Forget it. There's not enough time to plan anything. An operation like that requires weeks of detailed preparations."

"Let's see, I'll need to know how many people are invited. I'll call Angelica." She made a notation on the pad. "I hope the wedding's in the evening. It'll be easier to get him if it's nighttime."

"Gabriella, shut up and listen. We are not going to hit anyone."

"I'll contact Roger. Tell him to have some back up ready. He won't like it, but tough shit."

"Are you deaf?" He shouted. He never lost his temper like this, but she could piss off the Pope.

"Unfortunately, I have perfect hearing. I hear you screaming. Knock it off. I have to think." She paced the living room.

"Then listen. We can't do this."

She stopped and stared at him. "Of course we can. It'll be hard, but we should be able to pull it off."

Now, he stared at her, feeling he was about to lose an argument. The aura of a zealot glowed around her.

"What difference will one more hood make?"

She bit her lip. "Because this will probably be the only chance we'll ever have to nab the big boss. He's surrounded by bodyguards and rarely goes out. He holds court in his mansion on the lake. I'd never make it inside the compound. I faced that long ago. Security is tighter than a virgin's ass. But if my retirement is imminent, I'd like to have this be the ending."

"It'll be an ending all right—ours. There isn't enough time. You heard Frankie. He's going to a meeting about Marco Alberti's disappearance."

He had to make her see things his way.

"I heard Frankie. He's dumber than a brick. He should never have discussed the meeting with you, an outsider, or mentioned anything in front of me. With a little luck and some pumping, he'll tell you all about the meeting, word for word. Why don't you do that? Go out with him tonight while I plan."

"And leave you here alone? No way."

She stepped in front of him and placing her hand on his chest, looked up with soft, chocolate eyes.

"Think about it. If we pull this off, it'll make both our careers. The Chicago mob will be in the worst disarray since the twenties. Our people can move up to be capos or underbosses and feed us information on families in other cities. Leo, it's why Alpha-Omega exists."

Lane wanted to argue, but the pleading eyes and husky persuasive voice won. Her idea was insane, but he saw the possibilities of a talk with Frankie. He couldn't leave her alone, however, which meant he'd have to find a place to stash her. After a couple of hours, he would plead illness again and return. If Frankie spilled his guts, he might be able to convince Gabriella that would be almost as good as grabbing Mr. Big. And if that didn't work, he'd gag her, tie her up, and carry her out under the cover of darkness. But first he had to contact Roger.

He walked towards his bedroom. "I'm going to make a report, ask Roger for advice, and then take a shower. Keep the door locked and don't answer the phone. Give me an hour. Let's see what shakes out of the tree."

"Good idea. I'll do the same."

He closed the door and opened his laptop. Now, he had to tell Roger he needed the location of a safe house and why.

****

Gabriella made sure the door closed before sending a brief summary of the situation to Roger. Finished, she marched into the kitchen, grabbed a Coke out of the fridge, and filled a glass with ice. She carried everything into the living room and poured the fizzy soda over the cubes, swearing when the

91

foam overflowed onto the coffee table.

Kicking off her shoes, she sat cross-legged on the sofa jotting down ideas. Soon several sheets of paper lay scattered on the seat next to her. Those plans made sense. The rejects littered the floor.

Leo and Roger would have to see it her way. For the first time since beginning her mission five years ago, she needed outside help. It killed her to admit it, but she needed Leo and Roger to make this happen.

She weighed her options. Separating Casano from his bodyguards had to be the top priority. Then they'd have to get his body out of the club unseen.

But most importantly, she and Leo would have to get the hell out as soon as possible. The minute his thugs discovered Casano missing, they'd seal the exits and check everybody from head to foot. Leo's credentials might not hold up under such intense scrutiny. His cover had only been intended to last a short day or two. *And* she'd have to deal with Frankie.

She chugged her Coke and returned to the kitchen for another before resuming her seat. A few minutes later, she heard the sound of water running.

Gabriella sat upright. If he was in the shower, then now would be a good time to search his room. She might find out more about him.

Padding down the hallway, she opened the door and cautiously looked in the empty bedroom.

She started with the dresser drawers. Everything lay neatly folded. It took only a second or two for her to determine she'd find nothing. She turned her attention to the closet. Everything hung in perfect, color coordinated order. *Talk about anal retentive.* She riffled through the hangers. The search yielded a big zero.

Spotting his laptop on the bed, Gabriella made a beeline for it. Maybe he'd left the agency screen on.

He hadn't, and she didn't even waste time bringing it up. Leo probably had as many passwords and codes as she did.

Then her eye fell on the duffle bag in the corner. It looked empty, but what the hell? Unzipping every compartment, she was about to give up when a thought struck her. She felt along the bottom of the bag until her fingertip touched a small plastic rivet, then another two all lined up in a row, hidden under a fold of the lining.

Pulling gently, the rivets popped open to reveal a small space in the bottom. She found what she'd sought, a thin wallet and several sheets of even thinner paper, folded into thirds.

She read them. According to the driver's license and credit cards, his name was Lane Hamilton and the papers stated his mission to take her to Rockford.

Rockford? And the bastard told me Alaska. I'll get even with him for this. She found another driver's license, Social Security and credit cards under the name James Kennedy and the same for her, Sarah Kennedy.

We'd better be brother and sister. She could see Roger getting a kick out of making them pretend to be married.

Suddenly, the door to the bathroom swung open. Gabriella had been so intent on her search, she hadn't heard the water stop. Leo—Lane stood in the doorway, a towel wrapped around his waist.

"What the hell do you think you're doing?" His angry words dripped ice.

Chapter Seven

Gabriella *should* have noticed his angry voice. She *should* have noticed his furious expression. And she certainly should have realized she'd been caught snooping. But God help her, all she noticed was that damned loosely tied towel draped around his lean hips.

She forgot about the incriminating evidence in her hand. Instead, her gaze roamed freely up and down his body. She stared in fascination at his broad shoulders and wide chest, the latter liberally covered with curly, dark hair. And how could she *not* avoid seeing the six-pack abs?

Oh, shit! Desk jockey or not, this guy obviously worked out on a regular basis. The abs funneled down to a trim waist. His thighs and calves had ropes of muscles, which indicated he not only worked out, but probably jogged as well. She didn't even want to speculate what the towel hid. During her search, she'd seen his size thirteen shoes. Oh, God!

Gabriella swallowed hard and tried to regain some of her composure. Caught red-handed, she had no defense. Before she could bluster her way out of the situation, the object of her search repeated the question.

"What the hell do you think you're doing?" His eyes narrowed into slits, and he stood with his hands fisted on his hips.

"I had to find out who you were. I hate the name

Leo."

"If Roger thought you needed to know, he'd have told you. It could be dangerous knowing my real name."

"*Is* Lane Hamilton your real name or are you faking that, too?"

"It's my name." He ran a hand through his hair and took several deep breaths.

Gabriella rose from beside the duffle bag and tossed the papers onto the bed. "James and Sarah Kennedy? I do hope we were going to be brother and sister."

"Does it matter?"

"What did Roger have to say about my plan to get Caesar Casano?" she countered.

"I haven't heard back yet, but after I tell him you've blown my cover, he'll give it a thumbs down. Now, leave so I can get dressed." He made a grab for the towel as it slipped a bit further down his hips.

A delicious gush of heat rolled over her. He tightened the navy blue strip of terry cloth and glared. Her fingers itched to rip it away. In her mind's eye, she saw the two of them rolling around on the bed, naked. God Almighty, she could even feel the smooth texture of his skin and the chest hair rubbing against her breasts. Sweat popped out on her brow. Holy shit, if she didn't stop this line of thought right now, she'd tackle and throw him on the bed or the floor, whichever was closest.

"If you've given any kind of a decent, unbiased report, he'll have to agree," she snapped, trying to refocus.

"I told him exactly what was on your mind. I doubt he'll agree to it."

"I'll just bet you did! I'm going to amend my version and we'll see who's right."

Keeping the towel in place with one hand, Lane ran the other through his shower-dampened hair again. Frustration had replaced the angry expression on his face.

"Damn! No wonder your code name is Medusa!"

Medusa? *That* was her code name? It sounded familiar, like something out of mythology. Gabriella racked her brain to place it. Finally, she remembered and a deep sense of hurt crept through her.

How could he? How could Roger have given or allowed her to be given *that* code name? Is that how he viewed her?

Gabriella swallowed the hurt. She thought nothing could penetrate the hard shell she'd grown around her, and hadn't seen this coming. Stiffening her emotional spine, she allowed anger to replace hurt feelings. After all the good work she'd done for Alpha-Omega this was the thanks she got?

"Medusa! Isn't that the chick that screwed around with some God and got changed into a freak with snakes for hair? Why the hell would that be my code name? You tell Roger to fuckin' change it— now!"

"Before she fooled around with Poseidon and angered Athena, she was considered beautiful. Technically, Medusa was a gorgon, a female monster. It's said that anyone who looked upon her turned to stone."

"I don't need a Goddamned mythology lesson, you asshole. I want it changed. Stone, my ass! I don't see you rock hard!"

Oh, shit, did I really say that! She wanted to drop through the floor.

"Maybe it's prophetic. She ended up with her head chopped off." Lane heaved a sigh. "Look, we both need to cool down. Why don't you go make us some lunch and let me get dressed? We can talk more in a few minutes."

"Do I look like the chief cook and bottle washer

around here? Make your own damned lunch. And while we're on the subject, do you ever say 'please'?"

Lane's eyebrows rose. "Do you?"

Gabriella curled her hands into fists, sucked in a couple of deep breaths, and turned on her heel. The last thing she saw as she closed the door behind her was a view of Lane's naked backside when he whipped off the towel.

Oh...my...God!

****

Lane wanted to smack his head against the wall. How could he have done that? How could he have been so careless? He'd seen it—the look of hurt on her face before her temper flared. Her code name had been changed to Medusa shortly after he'd come to work at Alpha-Omega. Her controller at the time requested it and refused to work with her. At first, it had been a joke. The name stuck.

He also kicked himself for not having left his real ID back in Washington, but everything happened so fast, he'd forgotten. He realized his error at the Detroit airport and hid it in the false bottom of his bag. Five years ago, he'd have never made such a mistake.

I've been behind a desk too long.

He should have known Gabriella would search his luggage, yet when he'd come out of the shower to see her crouched beside his duffle, shock damned near robbed him of speech.

He dressed quickly. Rock hard. If only she knew how badly he wanted to toss that towel into the corner and drag her onto the bed, she'd have run like hell. He wondered what he'd do if he did manage to get her out of Chicago and into a motel in Rockford.

He spent a few minutes e-mailing Roger with the latest development. Roger rarely lost his temper, but somehow Lane had the feeling this would be one of those times. Lord, why hadn't Roger sent Loomis instead of him? A simple protection job had turned into a nightmare. He considered drugging Gabriella, heaving her into the trunk of her car, and taking off.

He returned to the living room and found her at her computer. "What are you doing?"

"E-mailing Roger my side of the story. I just gave him the necessities earlier. Now I'm going into more detail," she replied shortly. "Between the three of us, we should be able to come up with a good plan. Don't tell me you've never worked under a deadline."

His mind flew back in time to New York seven years ago and a deadline that had almost gotten him killed. "Yeah, I've had deadlines and time frames. We have to talk."

"When I'm finished. Your sandwich is on the coffee table," she snapped.

He sat on the sofa and picked up the food, and then noticed the mess she'd left behind.

"What is this? I just cleaned in here. Two hours and you have the place looking like a garbage dump again. You've got papers scattered everywhere. Doesn't the mess bother you?"

Gabriella stopped and glared a hole in him. "Not particularly. Why are you this hopelessly anal? I'd clean it eventually. God, chill out." She resumed typing.

Once again his mind did a quick flashback, only this time he saw his mother passed out after a drunken binge with empty bottles, clothes, and garbage scattered all over the tiny apartment. He remembered his disgust and anger, before transferring it to the present.

"What's wrong with wanting to live in a clean house? We all have our little hang-ups and this is mine. I like things neat and clean. A messy house indicates a messy mind."

She stopped again. "Oh, for God's sake! My mind is not messy. It's crystal clear. It stays that way because I don't let unimportant details like a little clutter bother me. I'll bet you wouldn't be so obsessed with Windex and Pine-Sol if Bubbles dropped by."

"Lady, you are a legend of nightmare proportions around Alpha-Omega. Why the hell are you such a bitch?" he asked in a resigned tone.

Gabriella typed a moment longer, then closed the laptop and walked into the kitchen. She returned with her sandwich and a Coke and sat in the uncluttered chair.

"Because it's all I've ever known," she said, taking a bite. She stared at the tabletop, refusing to meet his eyes. Her voice was tinged with a combination of anger and sadness.

"What do you mean?"

She put her sandwich down, rose and strolled over to the window keeping her back toward him.

"I barely remember my mother. She died when I was six. Daddy spoiled me rotten. I went to a private school and it never occurred to me that the other kids didn't have two bodyguards take them and pick them up every day. I can still recall my eighth birthday party. Not one kid from school attended. Their parents wouldn't let them, although I didn't realize it at the time. The only attendees were the kids of Daddy's business associates. It wouldn't be my last taste of being ostracized."

Gabriella crossed the room and stopped before a picture he'd noticed on the shelf of the entertainment center. It was a photo of her and Gus Vicelli. It depicted a younger Gabriella, maybe at age eighteen. She picked it up and ran her finger lightly over her father's face, then smiled. He sensed her vulnerability.

She turned, a hard expression in her eyes. "When I was twelve, my whole world collapsed. Daddy informed me I would be going away to a boarding school. I cried, I pleaded, I threw the loudest temper tantrum of my life, but nothing worked. Daddy said he wanted me to be a lady like my mother."

"Was your mother from one of the families?"

"No. She came from old St. Louis money. Her family disowned her when she married Daddy. Her oldest sister was the only one who stayed in touch."

"Where did you go to school?"

"Before I knew it, I was shipped off to fucking Connecticut where I enrolled in Miss Cameron's fucking School for Young Girls. I would receive a top-notch education and always know which fucking fork to use."

Her voice had a hard, bitter edge. She rubbed her forehead as if in pain.

"I was deep into resentment and didn't notice little things for a couple of weeks. Things like how all the other girls shared a room. I was alone. And while I had companions at the dining table, no one spoke to me. I felt invisible and cried myself to sleep every night."

She replaced the picture on the shelf.

"Then one day, two of the older girls cornered me in the hallway. They told me they didn't want 'my kind' at Miss Cameron's and to go back to the gutter where I belonged. I had no idea what they were talking about. One girl gave me the lowdown.

"Funny, I can still remember her name, Vanessa Chadwick—all WASP with blonde hair and blue eyes. She was from B-a-h-ston."

Gabriella's brown eyes churned with loathing.

"She waved a newspaper in my face and I read the headline. *'Mob Boss Gus Vicelli Trial To Begin Next Week.'* The little bitch sneered and said, 'Your father's a cheap gangster who kills people. I hope he gets the death penalty.'"

Gabriella pounded her fist into an open palm.

"I smacked Vanessa Chadwick right in the mouth—knocked her tooth out, too. And that's how I found out what my father did for a living."

She walked back to the window, her hands clasped behind her back. "Vanessa may have wanted me gone, but the other girls seemed fascinated to have a real, live mobster's daughter in their midst. They'd ask questions like, *Did you ever meet John Gotti? Did your father kill anyone? Have you ever seen someone get killed?* I hated them." She choked back a sob. "I hated them all. I decided to show the world I didn't give a flying fuck what they thought. I developed an attitude. I didn't need a bunch of snooty, rich, East Coast girls for friends anyway. I kept to myself. Miss Cameron wouldn't allow newspapers into the school for a while after the incident, but every time we went to town, I'd manage to buy one and sneak it in. I followed his racketeering trial and gloated when he beat the rap."

Lane didn't interrupt and allowed her to talk. He had the feeling this was the first time she'd ever told anyone. It certainly hadn't been in her file.

He realized her life had been as lonely as his, always being on the outside looking in as a kid, wishing he had a father, and a mother who was not a drunk. She had experienced the same gut-wrenching hurt, maybe even worse. She'd loved and idolized her father only to find he had feet of clay. At age ten, he'd known his mother's feet were anchored in mud.

"I loved my father very much and for his sake pretended I didn't know what he did. I begged to come home after the trial, but he refused. So, I stuck it out to make him proud. I graduated valedictorian." She laughed softly. "My father attended the ceremony along with several business associates. If he invited family—my real family—to the shindig, they didn't show. To this day, I can remember the shock on so many of the other parents' faces. I gave a heartfelt speech on the value of a good education, all the while laughing inside at the irony. One of 'my kind' beating out those high-brow girls and their snobbish society families."

Still laughing, Gabriella returned to the chair and ate the rest of her sandwich in a couple of bites, then downed the Coke.

"How come you didn't go on to college? With those credentials you could have gotten in anywhere," Lane asked.

"I wanted to come home. I missed my father and decided to attend a school closer to Chicago, but before I enrolled, I wanted to get reacquainted. Knowing what he did for a living opened my eyes to a lot of things, most of which disgusted me."

"Like what?"

She leaned back in her chair and closed her eyes.

"I saw how they treated women. These guys have a very simple philosophy. Women are either Madonnas or whores. They marry Madonnas, often the protected daughters of other mobsters, and use them in an effort to solidify their standings within the family. Kind of like nailing down a trophy wife. Then they go out and find a mistress—a whore.

"The Madonna rarely leaves the house. She takes care of the kids, sees to it everything runs smoothly and ignores what her husband does for a living. They are deep into denial."

Lane knew all of this, but let her talk. He wanted to see what made her tick.

"The whore shows up at clubs and night spots on the hubby's arm." She shook her head and made a face. "I vowed I'd be neither. I refused to marry into the mob, and I certainly won't be one of their whores."

"So, you put on an act and a damned good one at

that." Lane couldn't keep the admiration out of his voice. "None of them ever suspected a thing."

"I know."

"How did you get involved with Alpha-Omega?"

"My father's death was the catalyst. The police knocked on the door about midnight with the news that Daddy, his two bodyguards, and a man who shouldn't have been there had been gunned down in front of La Scala Bravo restaurant. His chauffeur was wounded. I later learned Gavino Ponzetti had ordered the hit. He and Daddy had argued over territory. A month later the entire South Side was firmly under the wing of the Ponzetti family."

Lane wanted to offer condolences—after all, she'd lost a father—but couldn't bring himself to do it. Gus Vicelli had killed and ordered hits of his own. He had no sympathy for the man or his demise.

"And so you went after the Ponzetti family."

He didn't phrase it as a question. It was the truth.

"Oh, I want to see Gavino Ponzetti destroyed, but the mob is to blame. I want the mob brought down."

"But how did you know to contact the Alpha-Omega? What did you do? Knock on the FBI's door and offer your services?"

Lane had a hard time visualizing Roger or anybody at the FBI accepting her at face value.

Gabriella rose and, twisting a lock of hair around her finger, resumed pacing. She resembled a tightly coiled spring about to explode.

"I kept a low profile for a while after the murders. During that time I read in the papers about an undercover FBI agent in New York. He spent years infiltrating the mob. He had names, dates, photos, taped conversations—everything. Years! And he was never caught or even suspected. For some reason, the Feds finally pulled him out."

She laughed. "Can you imagine? Those guys must still be wiping the egg off their faces—from prison cells, of course. I followed the trials. He put away over a hundred wiseguys. Day after day he'd testify, knowing he had a contract out on him worth over a half a million dollars. One shot and he'd be dead, but he had guts and did what was right."

She quit pacing and threw her head back to gaze at the ceiling, a smile on her lips and a look of admiration in her eyes.

"I thought maybe I could do the same, so I came up with a plan and took it to the head of the FBI. It took months to finalize everything, but in the end Alpha-Omega was born. It was born out of the actions of a man the New York mob knew as Dante Borelli. He's my hero. I wish I could meet him some day."

Lane sat frozen in his seat, unable to move or think of a thing to say. He had no idea Alpha-Omega had been her idea. No wonder she resented taking orders. She must have viewed it as her personal arm of revenge.

Except Alpha-Omega was illegal as hell. He knew it and so did Roger. The Feds used Gabriella as much as she used them and if the ax fell, she'd go down with everybody else. Gabriella Vicelli had a vision and the guts to carry it out. Her bitchiness had begun as a shield from hurt, but now served to protect her from the Frankie's of the world. She would never allow any man to control her.

Lane realized he'd found a kindred spirit—daring, dedicated, and determined. Even though a polar opposite in personality and temperament, this woman would keep him on his toes and never be boring.

As for Dante Borelli, he wanted to laugh at the irony, but didn't dare.

Chapter Eight

Gabriella picked up her plate and carried it into the kitchen, mentally kicking herself with every step. Why had she spilled her guts like that? She'd just aired a butt load of baggage to a man she'd only known for twenty-four hours and who didn't like her in the bargain. She ground her teeth remembering the funny look on his face.

Probably pity. She didn't want pity from anyone.

Thank God, she hadn't told him the whole truth, like how important Dante Borelli was in her life. She didn't tell him she'd compiled a scrapbook. After each hit, she pulled it out and re-read every article. It gave her a sense of companionship, as though she'd found a friend who understood her passion. Whenever she had doubts, she thought about the man who had the balls to take down some of the worst of the New York mob.

She hadn't needed to infiltrate. All she'd needed was determination. Her hero gave her the inspiration to carry things out. She had the feeling Dante Borelli would approve of Alpha-Omega.

She also didn't reveal that over the last couple of years, she'd fantasized about Dante Borelli and sometimes wondered if she didn't love him a little. She laughed at the absurdity of it. In love with a man whose real name she didn't know and was never likely to meet? Maybe she was just in love with what he'd accomplished.

Gabriella returned to the living room to find Lane still seated with an unreadable expression on his face. He looked up, and then away as though embarrassed.

God, what had possessed her to tell him anything? It must have sounded like the most self-pitying narrative on the face of the earth.

Poor little Gabriella. She had no friends. No one liked her. Her father was a gangster. Well, he may have been a mobster, but she remembered him as Daddy. No one deserved to die that way.

Lane turned to her and opened his mouth when the beeping of her computer distracted both of them. It had to be Roger Warwick answering her e-mail.

They both rushed for the dining room. She got there first and pulled up the agency screen.

"It's from Warwick." She shot him a smug smile. "We'll see what he has to say about things now."

"If he's e-mailed you, he's probably e-mailed me too," Lane replied and headed down the hall to his room.

Gabriella quickly signed in and crossed her fingers. If Roger gave her the go ahead, Lane would either have to do as *she* said or head back to Washington.

She read the first two sentences of the message, "Your plan has been approved for the elimination of Caesar Casano. I want all details within seventy-two hours."

She jabbed her fist in the air shouting, "Yes!" Then she read the rest of it and said, "Shit!"

"Also consider this a reprimand for violating orders and searching Lane's luggage. It will go into your file. To be successful Lane must be in charge of this mission. He has more experience. Obey him. If I have one negative report, I will personally dismiss you from Alpha-Omega."

Obey him? Oh, hell! Fired? He'd fire her? Damn,

he meant it. He wouldn't dare fire her. Without Gabriella Vicelli pulling the trigger, Alpha-Omega would be nothing more than day care for mobsters. And what the hell did more experience mean? *Son of a bitch.*

She was about to protest when Lane came storming out of his room.

"What the hell did you tell Roger?" Lane demanded.

"I told him we could work together and that we already had a plan in mind."

"You're going to get us killed," he said, glaring.

"No, I'm not. Look, we can do this. The wedding is only a few days away. Between the two of us, we can come up with a plan." She lifted her chin and glared right back.

"I'm worried about the security around Casano. Even at the All-Italian Club, they'll cover him like a blanket. Neither one of us will have a prayer of getting to him. I'm an outsider from Detroit. They'll check me out before I get in the front door, and Casano isn't stupid enough to traipse off with you for a tryst in the garden."

"You'll get in. The All-Italian Club is neutral territory. Frankie accepts you, and you'll be with me. I'm Gus Vicelli's daughter."

"I don't like it."

"Tough shit. Roger's okayed it."

The look on his face changed from angry to smug. "That's right. He's okayed it—with *me* in charge."

She wanted to hit him right in the mouth. Then she remembered the wording of the message. *He has more experience.* Experience at what? Gabriella recalled the way he'd slipped into wise guy mode with Frankie.

"Roger says you have more experience. What does that mean? What experience? I thought you were a desk jockey at Alpha-Omega."

Lane shifted his gaze away. "It doesn't matter. If we have to come up with a plan in three days we'd better start thinking."

She knew a dodge when she saw one. "Oh, no you don't. Who are you really? You know way too much about the mob and its inner workings. You couldn't have gotten all of it from reports or research. You've lived the life, haven't you? What are you—a wise guy turned informer? How did you get into Alpha-Omega? Pardon a cliché, but I can't see Roger letting a fox into the henhouse."

He scowled. "That's none of your concern. Let's get down to business."

"No way. Not until you tell me the truth. How do I know I'm not setting myself up? If Alpha-Omega can infiltrate the mob, why couldn't the mob place informants in the FBI? I'm sure it's been done before." She stared, determined to wrench the truth out of him. "You know, all I have to do is get on that computer. You'd be surprised what you can find on Google, and I can probably hack my way into a few files at the division," she said, breaking the stare down.

"And where did you learn how to do that?" His voice sounded smooth, but his eyes looked hard.

She shrugged. "I once had a friend who showed me the ropes. He was brilliant with computers. In fact, he had his own software company. Now, who are you?"

He stared at her for a moment, and then gestured to the sofa. "Sit down. It's a long story, and I'm putting my life in your hands."

Gabriella sat, her heart thumping with anticipation and hoping he wasn't part of the mob—even a reformed part. Lane sat in a chair opposite.

He clenched his fist and rubbed the knuckles over his lips while his other hand massaged the back of his neck. His spine was ramrod straight. A frown grooved deep lines in his face.

"I always wanted to do something exciting. When I graduated from USC, I went straight to the FBI. For a couple of years I worked in the bowels of the building doing analysis and psychological profiles on various mobsters."

"Did that include my father?"

"No. My section dealt with the New York mob, the Tiziano family to be precise. One of their guys came to us with a proposition—give him immunity, set him up in the Witness Protection Program, and he'd help put an FBI informant into the family. At that time, Roger Warwick was the head of the FBI and asked if I wanted the job. I knew more about the Tiziano family than anyone else."

"You were undercover?" she asked with a gasp.

"It was the job I'd always wanted. I had no family, no one to miss me or to endanger, and wanted to make a difference. I knew how the mob operated, and I knew how gangsters thought. They worked up a background for me that said I was this guy's cousin from Miami. The computer whizzes gave me a foolproof identity by hacking into the computers of real businesses in Miami to give me a work record, a rap sheet, a Social Security number, addresses—everything."

"So you pretended to be connected."

"One of my offenses was murder of another gangster in Miami. They even infiltrated the court system to make it look as if I'd beat the rap."

"So, you came to the Tiziano family as a made man. What happened to your so-called cousin?"

She couldn't help herself. The story paralleled that of Dante Borelli. It explained how Lane had known the terminology and so much else. Maybe he had even known Borelli. She'd love to pick his brain about that.

He smiled and ran a hand over his face. "It took six months for them to accept me. As soon as that happened we faked my 'cousin's' death in an automobile accident, and he disappeared somewhere quiet and safe. I was on my own."

"How long?"

Lane rose and paced much the way she had earlier. Tension knotted her stomach and her palms grew damp.

"I decided to go slow. I'd be a buddy, someone they could talk to. I didn't want to push it and get them suspicious. One capo took me under his wing and showed me the New York ropes. I built their confidence in me, and took small steps up in the chain of command. I had a lot to learn. The streets were a whole lot different than an office in the basement of the Hoover Building. These guys lived by jungle law where strength was measured by power. The lying, cheating, and scheming were vicious."

Gabriella picked at an imaginary piece of lint on her slacks and twirled her hair around her finger. From his tone of voice, she concluded he hated the mob, too.

"I never saw that side of it," she confessed.

"Of course not. You're a woman. If you'd been a boy, your father would have initiated you damned fast."

"No, Daddy wouldn't have wanted his kind of life for any of his children, male or female."

"Face reality, Gabriella. Your father had a business and if a son had existed, he would have passed it on."

She wanted to argue, but bit her lip instead. She didn't want to think about her father at the moment.

"Did you get good information?"

"I got excellent information. I sat in on lower echelon meetings, gradually working my way up to lunches with underbosses and dinners where discussions took place about how to take over territory and who got hit. I never kept a schedule for reports, but when I had solid information, I'd let Roger and my controller know. We tried to save lives, even mobsters', whenever possible."

"Were you ever scared?" She swallowed, not wanting to remember the nightmares.

"Yeah, but I liked the dangerous side of life. In the end, I wasn't so much afraid as cautious."

"How long did you last undercover?"

He stood in front of the window and shoved his hands into his pockets, balling his fists.

"Almost six years."

"Six years? That's a helluva long time." Suspicion prickled her scalp. This was so much like...no it couldn't be. "How old are you?"

"Thirty-eight in another month. I could have stayed longer, but the higher I infiltrated, the worse the infighting. One day I was handed the contract on a low level thug. If I carried it out, I'd be one of them."

His voice had taken on a tight, almost toneless quality, deepening her suspicion. Her chest tightened.

"But you couldn't do it, could you? You couldn't actually kill a man."

"No. I couldn't do it in cold blood. My controller and Roger decided I'd outlived my usefulness. They warned the target and pulled me out."

He turned, a strange, questioning look on his face as though waiting for some specific reaction. Goosebumps broke out on her arms. Wetting her lips, Gabriella asked, "What happened to the information you compiled?"

"It was used against them in their subsequent trials. They all went to jail. Most of them are still there."

"How long ago was this?"

"Six years."

The time frame, the place, the trials—they all matched. And he'd infiltrated the Tiziano family. The same as...No! It couldn't be...Gabriella leaped to her feet. Oh, God, it *was* him!

"You're..." She stopped for a moment and drew a steadying breath. "You're Dante Borelli!"

Lane nodded. "I was." His face looked impassive, but his eyes held a wary almost fearful expression.

She wanted to throw something, scream, curse, anything. She'd already confessed Dante Borelli had been her hero and the inspiration for Alpha-Omega Division. Leo—Lane—the hopelessly anal retentive thorn in her side was the man she'd worshipped from afar. Oh, God, he must be getting a good laugh out of this.

"And you let me babble on like a high school cheerleader praising the quarterback?"

He shrugged, and some of the wariness left his eyes.

"I never knew how Alpha-Omega had been formed. Roger only told me you had been a key in the organization." He ran his hand over his chin. "Look, Gabriella, I shouldn't have told you. It's dangerous information for you to know, and compromises me. I can't think of why I did. Maybe it was what you said about Dante Borelli. Maybe he *did* make a difference." Lane dragged in a deep breath. "Maybe it was your childhood story. We have several things in common."

"I thought you were in the Witness Protection Program. The papers said you'd disappeared after the last trial."

"I did for a while. I was bored to tears, so I broke cover and called Roger. He brought me into Alpha-Omega."

She had to get out of the room. If she didn't

she'd either throw something or burst into tears of embarrassment.

"I have to get out of here. I need to be by myself and think." She reached for her purse.

"Gabriella, you can't go out alone. Not with Johnny so close. Besides, we have to plan how to nail Casano."

"I still need to be alone." She turned and headed down the hallway. "I'll be in my room."

Gabriella closed her bedroom door and leaned back against it. Her fists pounded her thighs and tears flowed.

Oh, God, she must have sounded like a fool going on and on about how much she admired Dante Borelli, what an inspiration he'd been, and all the time he'd been sitting on her sofa. Thank goodness she hadn't said anything about her silly fantasy.

Over the years, Dante Borelli had taken on a larger than life, almost fictional, persona. Now she discovered he was very much flesh and blood, and staying in her guest room. She needed time to absorb Lane as Borelli.

Gabriella pushed away from the door and paced the room, stepping on discarded clothing. For want of anything better to do, she picked up the clothes and tossed them into the wash hamper or hung them in the closet. But even that didn't calm the agitation churning inside. She needed something else.

The gym. *I'll go to the gym and work out.*

It had been a couple of weeks since she'd exercised. The final planning for Alberti's take-out had claimed all her attention. Rummaging in the dresser, she finally found her workout clothes, changed, then slipped an elastic band with a card and a key attached around her wrist.

Lane still sat on the sofa where she'd left him. Oddly enough, he looked upset, too. A frown pulled those chiseled lips down at the corners and a furrow wrinkled his brow.

"Where are you going?" he asked when she headed for the door.

"I need to vent because quite frankly, I can't decide whether to kill you or myself. I feel like a fool. I'm going to the gym to work out—alone!"

"Gabriella…"

"Don't worry. I'm not leaving the complex. The spa is in the club house. I have a swipe card to get in, so nobody will follow me."

"I'll come with you." He rose.

"No! I told you, I *have* to be alone. I'll be all right. Do you really expect anyone to find Gabriella Vicelli in a gym?"

"Gabriella, there's something else you should know. If I go out with Frankie, you'll have to go to a safe house until I get back. Those are Roger's orders. You *cannot* be alone tonight."

"A safe house? How am I supposed to plan anything from there? That's crazy. I'll lock the doors and be fine."

"No. From now on you play it my way. I'm in charge. And if I say we pull the plug, that's what we do. How badly *do* you want Casano?"

She stood mute for a few seconds. Was Casano worth giving up control?

"All right, but I don't want you in the gym. Clean something while I'm gone."

"I don't want you alone anywhere. I need to work out, too. We don't have to talk to each other. Give me a minute to find some shorts." Lane disappeared down the hallway. "And you'd better be here when I come back," his voice called.

Gabriella tapped her foot impatiently. When he returned, he opened the door and checked the corridor before allowing her to leave.

"All clear."

She walked out, slamming the door behind her.

****

Lane watched with mixed emotions as she pumped iron. Part of him wanted to reassure her she hadn't been a fool. Her words had filled him with a sense of accomplishment. Dante Borelli *had* made a difference. Oh, yeah, a bunch of mobsters had gone to prison and it would be decades before the families involved could trust one another again, but to be the inspiration for a super-secret government agency made it all worthwhile. He hadn't left his ego at home after all.

Another part of him wanted to kick himself in the ass. He had no business confessing his former identity and didn't know why he had. His re-entry into the real world from the Witness Protection Program had been between him and Roger Warwick. Lane Hamilton was just another name in a long line of aliases. He'd had so many identities since going undercover he barely remembered his birth name. Not even Larry Landau, the deputy chief of Alpha-Omega, knew about his past.

He understood her anger. She felt duped by the very organization she founded.

Let her work it off. He headed for the equipment. The treadmill and Stair-Master would do a lot for his frame of mind, too.

****

Gabriella exhaled violently as she worked her abs on the machine. This was her last set of reps. Sweat dripped from every pore and she knew she'd pay the price for missing all those workouts the last couple of weeks. Tomorrow, she'd probably hurt like hell. Lane had kept his word and worked out nearby in silence.

"Thirty!" she gasped when finished. Lying back on the bench, she fought for breath before sitting up. She caught a glimpse of herself in the mirrors surrounding the room. Her face, red from exertion, shone with perspiration and her tangled hair was a mess.

"God, I really do look like Medusa," she muttered.

Prying herself off of the apparatus, Gabriella staggered to the locker room. Normally, a workout like that left her tired, but today she was exhausted. The last couple of days had been sheer hell. Her mental and emotional states had needed cleansing, too. The anger had abated, but not the embarrassment.

She stripped and left her clothes on the bench by the locker, then walked into the whirlpool room. Turning on the switch, she watched the bubbles build to a writhing froth and slid into the heated water. With a sigh, she leaned back and let the air jets pummel her body.

Okay, so what if Lane knew some things about her childhood and her feelings regarding his past career?

You made an idiot out of yourself. Get over it and move on. Concentrate on Casano.

They needed a plan. For this mission, the backup would have to be substantial. The lower level of the All-Italian Club housed the legitimate business of a restaurant and bar. The back door was only a few feet away down a hallway past the kitchen. The reception would most likely be held upstairs in the banquet room. A back stairwell also emptied into the hall.

Her mind rolled ideas over until the timer on the hot tub dinged. She resisted the temptation to reset it. Instead, she got out, grabbed a towel off the shelf and showered quickly. Dressed, she used the brush in her locker to tame her hair.

Time to deal with snatching Casano.

****

Lane flipped on the TV in Gabriella's living

room thumbing the remote, finally settling on the movie *Casino*. An ironic touch. He'd seen it many times and his attention slipped from Sharon Stone to Gabriella. He'd placed her in a cab thirty minutes ago and the agent at the safe house had just called to confirm she'd arrived. Frankie had also called to say he'd pick Leo up in a few minutes.

A knock on the door told him Frankie was here.

"Hey, Leo. You feelin' better?" Frankie asked, pushing his way in.

He should pay Gabriella rent. "I'm feeling much better. That stuff Gabby got at the drugstore really worked."

Frankie made himself at home on the sofa and looked at the TV. "Hey, *Casino*. One of the best. I love it. All those guys getting whacked. It's based on the truth, you know. The Joe Pesci dude was from Chicago. My dad says he was a real asshole and out of control. Nobody was sorry to see him bite it."

"Yeah, but I like *The Sopranos* better."

"Where's Gabriella?"

"Aw, she's out shopping for a wedding gift or something," Lane answered. He wondered how the meeting with Gavino had gone. He picked up the remote and turned the volume down. "Wanna drink?"

"Yeah, bourbon's fine. How come her car's here?"

"She took a cab. Probably afraid she couldn't fit everything into the Porsche. I've never known a woman yet who can buy just one thing."

Lane poured them each a drink and sat opposite Frankie. "You look upset. Anything wrong?"

Frankie took a huge swallow. "Marco Alberti, one of our capos, is missing. That makes the fourth in the last few years."

"You figure he's been whacked?"

"Don't know. We never find any bodies. If someone's icing them, we sure can't figure out who.

You leave a body to send a message."

"You think the Feds got him?"

"That's what my father thinks. He thinks the Feds are kidnapping them or something. Dad called from Martha's Vineyard. He's pissed about cutting short his vacation to deal with it. He just got there yesterday."

Uh-oh, we got trouble. "Why? I mean, there haven't been any trials and you got enough informants to know if they'd been taken into custody."

"That's what I said. I think this is the work of Caesar Casano. We were going to make a move on the Muzio bunch. They're ripe for picking. Now, business is on hold."

Lane couldn't believe Frankie was telling him this. He hated to think of Gavino's reaction if he knew. Both he and Frankie would be dead men. And would Gavino's presence be a problem for Casano's takedown?

"Casano's big, but maybe he wants to be bigger. Kind of like Capone. I agree with you, Frankie."

"You and I think alike, Leo." Frankie finished his drink. "Hey, enough about business. You ready to go?"

Lane rubbed his stomach. "Maybe, for a little while."

"You look better than last night. Bubbles likes you. She's got a special strip for special friends." Frankie grinned. "Let's head down to The Topsy-Turvy and get an eyeful. Bubbles in action is something to see. Trust me."

God, not Bubbles again.

"Bubbles beats TV any day," Frankie added.

Indeed, who needed TV when Bubbles was available? Frankie could be more useful drunk than sober. Even Bubbles might contribute information.

"Sounds like fun. Let me change clothes and

leave a note for Gabby."

He grabbed a clean shirt and returned to the living room where Frankie sat engrossed in the closing minutes of the movie. He scribbled a note and left it on the coffee table.

"Hey, here's where the bitch buys it," Frankie said. "The Robert DeNiro dude survived everything. I heard he moved to Florida. Died a few months ago."

"Yeah, I heard that, too. You ready?"

Frankie shut off the TV and rose, following Lane to the door where he clapped him on the shoulder and said, "Leo, you are in for one hell of a night!"

Chapter Nine

Gabriella gazed at the dingy living room of the safe house. The slipcover on the sofa was threadbare and through the numerous holes, she caught a glimpse of the original tan upholstery now stained with God only knew what. The old lady keeping her company drove her nuts with reminiscences of the good old days. Her grating voice drowned out the blaring television, not that Gabriella cared about the silly game show.

The remains of a bad pizza littered the coffee table and her babysitter, seated in a sagging faux leather recliner, poured herself another glass of wine. Lane would pay for this. She could have stayed at home and done some real work on the plan.

"Yes, things have sure changed. I can remember when J. Edgar Hoover was in charge. We didn't have all this bullshit about civil rights and privacy. He just did what had to be done," the woman, known to Gabriella as Mama Cass, said. It was an apt description. She resembled the late singer to a "T."

"I haven't had an assignment in over five years. Guess everyone else was occupied tonight. You're lucky I'm available. It's good to get back on the horse again." The woman emptied the glass and slopped more wine into it.

The horse is about to throw you on your ass. She couldn't wait to report the drunken slob to Roger. Apparently, no one had checked on this woman in years. She'd see to it the stupid cow never worked again.

"Have some more pizza, honey. How about another glass of wine?" She slurred the words.

The world's worst pizza accompanied by the world's cheapest wine for dinner turned Gabriella's stomach.

"No, thanks, I think I'll just sit here and watch TV," Gabriella said, picking up a remote and flipping through channels.

"Hey! Stop there. *Cops*. I love that show."

Gabriella sat back and stared at the TV, not paying any attention. Her mind had slipped to Lane.

What was going on at The Topsy-Turvy Club? Was Frankie getting drunk and telling tales out of school? Was Lane? And what about Bubbles? Bubbles The Bimbo was there.

She could see the stripper now, bumping and grinding down a runway, shedding clothes like a maple would leaves in autumn. Was Lane enjoying the show? Was he getting a hard on?

She ground her teeth and in her fantasy, jumped onstage and beat the shit out of the blonde. Then she turned and beat the shit out of Frankie. Her mental fist aimed for Lane when a loud snore interrupted her thoughts.

The old lady had fallen asleep. Passed out was more like it. Her arm hung over the side of the chair, the empty bottle clasped loosely in flaccid fingers. It looked as though Mama Cass was out for the count.

Gabriella gazed at the clock on the mantel. How much longer did she have to wait, for God's sake? Lane had said he'd call when he returned to her place, and then come pick her up. She'd been trapped in this dump for hours.

A large snort from the recliner spurred her into action. She leapt to her feet.

"This is ridiculous," she muttered. "If Johnny

did walk in the door, this stupid bitch would be useless."

Yanking out her cell phone, she dialed a cab company and requested a pick up. Forty-five minutes later, she opened her front door and flipped on the light. The creepy silence sent a chill up her spine. With her heart thumping, she looked out the peephole. The corridor was empty.

Lane's constant harping on how easily Johnny could nab her had taken its toll. She was scared and, goddammit, she didn't like being scared.

Just one more reason to get him out of her life. Although at this point she wasn't sure how badly she wanted *that* either.

"Fuck you, Hamilton or Borelli or whoever the hell you are," she cursed again.

Whirling, she entered the kitchen and jerked food out of the fridge. She was starving. The pizza had been cold and tasteless. She'd eaten only half a slice.

Lettuce, tomatoes, a few scallions, the remains of a red onion, and a carrot would make a decent salad. She rummaged in the pantry until finding a can of tuna.

The act of chopping the vegetables had a soothing effect. She visualized each veggie as one of Lane's body parts with the carrot having a starring role in the scene.

She opened, and then dumped, the can of tuna onto the salad. Uncorking a bottle of good Chardonnay, she settled on the sofa, propped her feet up on the coffee table, and used the remote to turn on the TV.

How boring and pathetic is this?

Gabriella shoveled the uninspired salad into her mouth wondering once again what Lane was doing, and who he was doing it with.

****

Lane sat back in Frankie's limo, trying to relax. He didn't have any worries about Frankie. The don-in-waiting had accepted him, but he worried plenty about Gabriella. The look on her face when she'd left had spoken volumes. She'd been pissed.

"Hey, Frankie, nice wheels. How come a limo?"

His companion snorted. "A cop pulled me over a few months ago. I failed the breathalyzer. My father took care of it, but read me the riot act about DUI and the Ponzetti image. Now, I take the limo. By the way, Leo, I want you to meet our driver, Joey. Joey, this is Gabriella's cousin, Leo Carpetti. He's from Detroit."

Lane didn't like this. The job of chauffeur was the first rung on the ladder of responsibility. The men who held that job were also ambitious as hell. Now, someone in the Ponzetti family other than Frankie had his name and cover.

"Hi, Joey. Pleased."

Joey nodded, his eyes, reflected in the rearview mirror, hard and dark. Lane knew he was being memorized.

"A pleasure, Mr. Carpetti. Detroit, huh? I never been to Detroit. What's it like?"

"Not bad."

Keep it short. Don't give the driver anything to report back to his boss.

"Yeah, I set Leo and Bubbles up last night, but Leo had to leave early. We'll go see Bubbles' act and hoist a few, eh, Leo?" Frankie said.

"Yeah. Was Bubbles pissed off?" Lane asked.

"Naw. Nothing pisses off Bubbles. That broad rolls with the punches. She'll scratch your itch tonight." Frankie roared with laughter and dug an elbow into Lane's ribs.

Swell. Bubbles wanted to screw him blind and all he wanted was to pick up information in as short a time as possible, then get back to Gabriella. Could he make out with Bubbles and get her to talk in the bargain? She might be a Bimbo-of-The-Year candidate, but he suspected she missed little. That was the advantage of being considered stupid. No one paid any attention to what you said or what was uttered around you.

He laughed along with Frankie. "I'll just bet. Bubbles strikes me as a girl who knows her way around the cock—er, I mean block. I'll bet she's damned inventive."

"She should take out a patent. The girl has a tongue and lips that'll drive you wild." Frankie shut up and shot a glance at Lane. "Uh, or so I've heard. Some of the guys told me that."

"Hey, Frankie, don't sweat it. I won't hold what you did before you started dating my cousin against you. I'm sure you wouldn't look at another woman now."

Frankie swallowed and gave him a weak smile. Gabriella had been right. Bubbles and Frankie *had* probably banged like rabbits last night.

They pulled up in front of The Topsy-Turvy Club. A flickering neon sign showed a naked woman shaking her rear end. The posters outside listed Bubbles as the star attraction complete with pictures of the chesty blonde in a G-string and pasties.

Joey opened the car door and they slid out onto the sidewalk. Frankie clapped him on the shoulder and said, "Welcome to The Topsy-Turvy Club—the best damned strip joint in Chicago," then led him inside.

The Topsy-Turvy didn't look much different from any other strip club Lane had seen. Perhaps bigger. A tiny foyer with a couple of bouncers standing guard served as the pat down and ID checking area. Neither dared to frisk Frankie, and because he was with Frankie, they passed straight through a black velvet curtain into the main room.

It took a few seconds for Lane's eyes to adjust to the dark interior. Most of the lighting emanated from onstage where a redhead gyrated to a thumping beat. Two long bars stood opposite each other. Both had patrons and the two dozen or so tables were about two-thirds full. Lane figured the management crammed in more on the weekends.

Frankie led him through a maze of the tiny disc-shaped tables towards the front. Several had been shoved together and were occupied by what he assumed were Ponzetti family members.

Ignoring the redhead's final grind, Frankie introduced Lane. "Hey, everybody. This is Leo, Gabriella's cousin from Detroit. Leo, over there, that's Carlo, and that's Lucca. The mug with the bad haircut is Sal."

"Sez you," Sal shouted, waving a drink in the air.

Frankie laughed and continued, "Next to Sal is Gino and this is Renzo. Have a seat and let's get a drink."

The music changed and a sultry black woman with long legs slithered onstage to the sound of sexy blues.

"Hey," a voice called from several tables back. "Sit your asses down. I can't see the broads. Who the hell do you think you are?"

Frankie turned a cold stare in the man's direction. Lane hoped the guy was drunk, because the look Frankie sent was downright deadly. He looked every inch a killer.

"I'll stand where I want. I own the joint. You got any complaints?"

Even in the dark, Lane saw the man turn pale. His companions urged him to sit, but scared or not, he must have felt it important not to show fear.

"Yeah, you come charging in here, laughing and

talking during the show and show no respect for your customers. The customer is always right."

The man slurred the last few words. Drunk or not, the guy had to have a screw loose. Six pairs of Ponzetti family confederates' eyes glared at the misguided patron.

Frankie shot a furious glance over towards the bar and jerked his head. Within seconds, two beefy men had the guy by the arms dragging him away. His friends followed and Lane figured the drunk would soon be sitting on his ass on the sidewalk—if he was lucky.

"Sorry about that, Leo. I don't tolerate loud-mouthed drunks. We run a respectable joint. Have a seat."

Lane sat down and ordered bourbon and water from a waitress. He pretended to watch the stripper, buying time to plot his next move. He needed to be subtle about pumping the new guys. Subtlety was wasted on Frankie.

The stripper's finale and his drink arrived at the same time. The black woman left the stage to scattered applause. The music changed again and another girl took her place. Her routine involved a boa constrictor.

Lane took a cautious sip of his drink. Watered down, but not enough to keep him sober for the entire night. He'd have to nurse it or find a way to dump half the contents on the floor.

The guy with the bad toupee—Sal?—lifted his glass again. "So, Leo, what's your line of work?"

"I'm a kind of banker. Business loans a specialty."

"Leo here is in the business. He's cool. Gus set his father up in Detroit," Frankie offered.

"Oh, yeah?" an older man—Renzo, he thought—questioned. "I liked Gus. I used to work for him in the old days. I was real sorry to see him go." He made it sound as if Gus Vicelli had moved to another state.

"Yeah, the family misses him a lot." What else could Lane say?

"I don't ever remember Gus saying nothing about having relatives in Detroit." Lane turned his eyes to the suspicious gaze of the man named Lucca.

"My grandmother on my mother's side and Gus's mother were sisters."

At the other end of the table, a mustachioed man, asked, "So, how goes the banking business?"

"Carlo, right? Business is good."

"He's good at his job, too. Last night I heard him maneuver to take over a guy's nightclub in Detroit." Frankie downed his drink and signaled for another round.

"How'd you do that?" bad hair asked.

"This guy's into us for a lot of money and wants more. I told them to go ahead with the loan. When the asshole can't pay it off we become his fuckin' partners."

"Leo says they had a problem similar to ours a couple of years ago."

"Frankie, maybe we shouldn't discuss family business in front of a stranger," Lucca suggested in a cold voice.

Lane agreed. Not only was he a stranger, but they were in a very public place, mob owned or not.

"Ah, shit, Lucca, lighten up," a man with a crooked nose said. "If he's here with Frankie, then he's okay."

"Gino's right. If I say Leo's okay, he's okay. Jesus, you've become a suspicious son of a bitch."

"I have a right to be. Too many of us are disappearing. I don't like it."

"Have a drink, Lucca." Carlo drained his glass as another round arrived.

"Keep 'em coming, Tilly. Put the orders in as

soon as you serve a round," Frankie said. The waitress nodded and turned to her other tables. "Leo thinks I'm right. He thinks someone is whacking us down to size so they can muscle in on our territory."

"But who? Everyone's losing people," broken nose said.

"Leo reminded me the Russian mob damn near took over Miami a few years ago."

Renzo, his eyes glued to the stripper, answered, "I heard those Ruskies are an amoral bunch of bastards."

"They're also mean as snakes," Lane commented.

He didn't like Frankie freely discussing Lane's knowledge of the disappearances. Most of the guys were half in the bag, but Lucca would remember. Coming here with Frankie may have been a serious mistake.

"So, you think the Russians are trying to take over Chicago?" Sal wondered.

Lane shrugged and sipped.

"So, how come they didn't take over Miami?" Lucca quizzed him.

"It seems one of their assassins got careless and shot a city commissioner by mistake. By then, the Feds knew what was going down. They ended up nailing them on simple charges and deported most of the bastards."

Lane had still been undercover in New York when it happened. The FBI worked quietly and few Miamians had known how close they'd come to speaking yet another language.

The expressions on the men's faces at the table ranged from thoughtful to astonished. Even Lucca raised his eyebrows as though digesting new possibilities for the disappearances. Lane breathed easier. He'd deepened his cover.

Tilly arrived with more drinks.

He glanced at the stage. A brunette was shaking her entire body as though possessed. With each twitch another piece of costume drifted away. They all watched until the last piece hit the floor.

"Ain't Ruskies," Carlo maintained. "It's one of us."

"Hey, come on, let's talk about something else," Frankie protested. "I didn't bring Leo here to solve our problems. Drink up, Leo," Frankie urged, signaling the waitress and leering at the new stripper in front of them.

Another redhead, she ripped off her costume to the beat of the *1812 Overture* blaring from the speakers.

Frankie grinned. "How do you like the place?"

"It's real interesting. Great show."

"Only the best." He nodded towards the stage. "Wait for Zenda's finale. Little flags pop out of her tits. Come on, drink up. Can't fly on one wing." He roared at his wit.

Lane downed the rest of his bourbon as Tilly reappeared with doubles for everyone.

Frankie gulped half of his in one swallow. "Hey, Tilly! Tell Mark to put some goddamned booze in these things. I'm the boss, not some half-assed tourist."

The waitress nodded again and scooted to the next table, her tray held high.

Lane caught Lucca's eye. The man didn't appear to be affected by the liquor and watched him. He'd have to drink more and sip less. Quaffing down a large portion, the lightheaded feeling that comes with the beginning of impairment nailed him.

On stage, Zenda stood right in front of them. She must have changed her act since Frankie had last seen it. She palmed a remote control. The next thing he knew, the flags sprang out of the crotch of her G-string and little propellers on her pasties whirled.

Frankie roared, clapped, and whistled along with most of the other club patrons.

"How's that for a fuckin' blow job!" he yelled, slapping Lane on the back.

Lane laughed with him. Even Lucca chuckled. In unison, everyone drained their glasses dry and reached for the second.

"Reminds me of the first hit I ever made," Frankie reminisced. "The sorry son of a bitch was a pilot. Used to smuggle weed and coke in for us. I offed him when we found out he was dealing on his own with our stuff. What about you? What was your first hit?"

Frankie must be damned drunk. Discussing past hits in the front row of a strip club was not a smart idea. Feds could be watching and more important, listening. Lucca glared at them. No doubt about it, Lucca would report this entire evening to Gavino.

"Hey! You gone deaf? I said who was your first hit?" Frankie's tone had taken on a hint of belligerence.

"I don't know that we should be talking about things like that in here."

"I agree," Lucca said in a hard voice.

"Bullshit! It's my club, and I'll talk about what I want." He finished his drink and waved his empty glass in the air as Tilly walked by. "One more time with feeling, honey."

Turning cold eyes on Lane, Frankie demanded, "Now, about that hit."

Lane looked around as if to check out who sat close to them. He wanted to appear as reluctant as possible to answer, especially with Lucca giving him the eye.

"It was some do-gooding preacher—a political wannabe. He was going after some of our more profitable ventures like he was on a crusade. He met regularly with a city councilman he thought was helping him. The councilman was in our pocket, but we couldn't control the fucker. So, one night when they were having dinner, I walked in the front door of the restaurant, shot both of them and walked right on out the back. Witnesses had six different composites."

He'd told a true story—only it had happened decades ago in New York.

"That's pretty impressive for a first time," Renzo said, his words slurring.

"Yeah," Lucca echoed. "How did you draw the assignment?"

"Cousin Gus was in town a few days before and suggested me. He thought I was cool under pressure."

The drinks arrived and Frankie raised his glass. "Tilly, we'll want another round right away. Here's to Leo and one hell of a busted cherry!"

He had no choice but to chug both glasses of bourbon. It exploded like a bomb in his stomach and for a moment, the room spun and his eyes refused to focus. Dammit! He was half shit-faced and if this kept up, he ran the risk of slipping out of character or saying something he shouldn't. During his undercover days, he'd been younger and better able to handle it.

Lane's gaze darted around the table. Carlo stared at the present stripper, his eyes half-closed. Bad-hair Sal sat sagging in the chair, his chin resting on his chest—out cold. Gino with the crooked nose continued to drink and make kissing gestures toward the stage. Renzo's movements had slowed to almost a standstill. Lucca watched everyone, especially him.

Tilly brought yet another round. Frankie was way too drunk to notice what Lane did. When Lucca turned to say something to Carlo, he took the opportunity to dump his drink on the floor.

Dancers came and went in a regular procession as did the drinks. Lane had no idea how much time had passed, but if he poured any more booze on the floor, they'd all be swimming. Most of the tables were occupied and the noise level of conversation rivaled that of the music.

The last stripper gyrated off stage and the lights dimmed. After a short pause, a voice came over the loudspeaker.

"The Topsy-Turvy Club is proud to present our star attraction, the one, the only...Bubbles LaRue!"

The spotlight hit the stage and Lane gaped. He'd actually forgotten about her. She posed in the light wearing the most absurd pink clothing he'd ever seen. The damned thing resembled a harem costume and it took him a few minutes to place the look. Then he remembered. Christ, she looked like a cross between Barbie and *I Dream of Jeannie*. Her blonde hair was pulled up in a ponytail and as a slow heavy beat drummed from the sound system, Bubbles stripped.

The Dance of the Seven Veils had nothing on Bubbles. Diaphanous pieces of clothing drifted onto the floor. She danced her way toward the front of the stage where the gauzy material now cascaded over him. Bubbles may have been an airhead, but she sure knew how to strip. It was the best routine he'd ever seen. More and more of the costume disappeared and when she whipped off the bra a collective gasp arose from the audience.

Frankie dug his elbow into Lane's ribs and slurred, "Tits of iron, man. Tits of iron."

Lane agreed. Implants or not, those breasts didn't jiggle or sag. They defied gravity and all the other elements of physics. Bubbles neared the end of her act. He held his breath when she reached down and tore off the harem pants as the music built to a crescendo.

Striking a finale pose, Bubbles stood before the crowd in the tiniest G-string he'd ever seen. The pasties were adorned with tassels.

Tassels? He hadn't heard of strippers using tassels in decades. God, were the damn things so old they'd become new again? Bubbles as an innovator in the business? Who'd have thought?

Using precise movements, the blonde rotated her shoulders until the tassels twirled in opposite directions. The music ended with a resounding crash. Bubbles bowed to a screaming, cheering clientele.

Lane was on his feet with the others, stomping and whistling like a madman. Bubbles blew him a kiss, and then trotted offstage. Her boobs never moved.

"Hey, what did I tell you, huh? Is she great or what?" Frankie said when they sat down.

"She's terrific," he replied in all honesty.

Tilly slapped another round of drinks in front of them. This time, Lane had no problem drinking half and spilling half. He was getting wasted, but then so was everyone else at the table.

Frankie stood and declared in a shout, "To my beautiful soon-to-be fiancée, Gabriella Vicelli, and her cousin, Leo Carpetti!" They all drank solemnly. "Leo, ole buddy, don't go back to Detroit. Stay here. We can use someone like you in the organization."

Lane gulped his drink and had a hard time focusing on the ensuing conversation. *Slow down, buddy. The booze will trip you up if you're not careful.*

A hand riffled through his hair and a voice cooed in his ear, "L-e-e-e-o. How did you like my act?"

He turned to find Bubbles beside him wearing nothing more than a thin, silk robe. Before he knew what he was doing, Lane slid a hand around her waist and down to squeeze her ass.

"Baby, you were fabulous."

"Yeah, baby," Frankie slurred. "Fab'lus." The rest of the men at the table agreed in varying degrees of drunkenness.

Bubbles pulled up a chair and sat next to Lane. Grasping his head in her hands, she jerked it around and planted a big, wet one on his lips, shoving her tongue halfway down his throat.

"Whoa, baby! Let me breathe," he said when she came up for air.

More drinks arrived. He drank it all. The room whirled and his ears buzzed. He was totaled, but Bubbles didn't seem to mind. She slammed down her tequila shooter in a smooth motion, then nibbled on his ear and unbuttoned his shirt to slide her hand across his chest. Lip locked again, he cast a quick glance around the table. Lucca stared at him. To continue the charade, he kissed her back.

Bubbles suctioned his tongue into her mouth and, wasted or not, his body stirred. Then her hand strayed to his crotch and squeezed.

He almost screamed and sat up straight as though hit with a bolt of lightning. His mind cleared enough for him to know he had to put a stop to this now.

He pulled Bubbles away and heard Frankie laughing like a lunatic. The rest of the guys were too drunk to notice. Even Lucca had given up and sat in a stupor watching one of the strippers shrug out of her clothes.

"What's the matter, Leo? Don't you like it?" Bubbles asked, her eyes wide and innocent.

"Yeah, baby, I like it just fine, but I don't like fucking in public."

She straddled his lap and brushed her breasts against his chest. "Then why don't I show you my dressing room? I don't have to share with anybody 'cause I'm the star."

Frankie fell over and crashed into him. Lane reacted quickly, shoving him upright and dumping Bubbles back into her seat.

"Hey!" she protested.

"You okay, Frankie?"

The heir apparent blinked several times before replying, "Yeah, I think so. Boy, am I ever shit-faced."

"I ain't feeling no pain myself. Why don't we call it a night? Where's Joey?"

"Waiting outside."

"Let's go."

"You're leaving me again?" Bubbles wailed.

"Sorry, baby. I'll call and we'll take up where we left off. Okay?"

She looked petulant for a moment, then smiled brightly and shrugged her shoulders. "Okay."

Dumber than a box of rocks.

He stood and helped Frankie to his feet, praying they'd make it to the car before Frankie passed out.

Outside, Joey assisted them into the backseat, and Lane breathed a sigh of relief the evening had ended. As they drove away, he realized the night had not been a total waste of time.

For starters, he'd finally seen that other, deadlier side of Frankie. The man might be an arrogant ignoramus, but to underestimate him would be a serious mistake. Frankie had shown a cold, mean streak. And he knew there was no way in hell Gabriella had ever seen it. If she had, she would never have treated the don-to-be in such a dismissive manner.

****

Johnny knew he took a chance coming to The Topsy-Turvy Club, but did it anyway. He'd spent most of the day scrounging in bars trying to filch information on Vicelli while remaining invisible. He wished he hadn't been so hasty in offing Ralphie. Over-eager babbler or not, he could have been useful.

He chose a table in a dark corner near the hallway and exit in case he had to make a speedy departure. His disguise held up. No one paid any attention to him. He drank sparingly and watched the show, waiting for Bubbles' act. He hoped to meet later.

The only person Johnny knew dumber than Ralphie was Bubbles LaRue. He could be on his knees with his head between her legs and she'd babble all the latest gossip, and then prattle away more after she returned the favor.

He twitched. How long had it been since he'd had any? Too long, and Bubbles had always obliged a friend in need. She also knew when to keep her mouth shut as well as open.

Johnny's heart lurched and a thrill of fear raced along his spine when several Ponzetti family members strolled in, taking seats in front of the stage. Shit! One of them was Lucca Calesso, a hard ass and Gavino's eyes and ears, the last person he wanted to see. Johnny scooted his chair back further into the shadows.

Then, Frankie entered with a man he'd never seen before and joined the group. All eyes were riveted on the stage. None of them paid much attention to anyone else, except for some drunk who pissed Frankie off.

He touched the gun, bought from a street punk and now nestling in his waistband, with nervous fingers. He'd avoided the goons out front by slipping in a rarely-used side door. It had been unlocked, not an unusual occurrence since some customers preferred to enter and exit unseen. It had proven useful for moving certain guests in and out during high echelon meetings.

He kept a close eye on the Ponzetti family. Who was the new guy? He must be in good because Frankie backslapped and laughed like he'd found a long lost relative.

The men drank for over three hours. Johnny stared at the newcomer. He looked vaguely familiar, but couldn't place him. It wasn't his face so much as his voice and actions. As the booze flowed, their voices rose. He had no trouble hearing when the music stopped between acts.

The man with Frankie threw back his head and laughed. *I've seen this guy before.* Closing his eyes, he concentrated on where. It refused to come. *Never mind, it will in time.*

Then Bubbles oozed onstage. He scribbled a note, ready to hand it to the waitress when Bubbles finished. The waitress, busy with other customers, did not stop by his table.

Bubbles ended with a hell of a finale. Then Frankie rose, shouted a toast to his fiancée Gabriella, and welcomed her cousin, Leo, from Detroit.

Detroit? Johnny had never been in Detroit. He'd spent a few months in New Orleans and New York several years ago as a kind of liaison for his immediate boss, Benny Rapido. So, why did the bastard look familiar? He shrugged. He had other things to worry about.

Bubbles came out and joined the group, then proceeded to crawl all over the cousin. It didn't look like Johnny would be joining her any time soon. He tore up the note.

He'd follow the cousin when they left. Maybe he'd bunked in with Vicelli. It was worth a shot. He paid up, exited by the back door, then found a cab and waited. The limo out front belonged to Ponzetti. He recognized Joey. *So he's a driver now.*

His patience was rewarded when Frankie,

barely able to stand, and Leo stumbled to the car.

"Keep the limo in sight, but not too close," he ordered the cabbie.

He tailed Frankie and Leo until they turned into a gated apartment complex. Johnny paid off the cab and slithered behind the bushes. The limo slid through, the gate closing behind it.

He followed the car's progress until it stopped in front of one of the buildings. The three men emerged and entered. A few minutes later, Joey helped Frankie back into the car.

When the limo left, Johnny slipped through the gate before it closed. In the foyer, he read the mailboxes—G. Vicelli, number two-oh-one.

Johnny pulled the gun out of his waistband. Now he had the bitch. He'd take her to Ponzetti, make her talk, and by tomorrow morning, he'd be back in the good graces of his former employer. As for the cousin...too bad. *Everybody has to die sometime.*

Like a stalking cat, Johnny climbed the stairs.

Chapter Ten

Gabriella glared at the clock on the DVD recorder, and then shifted her attention back to the TV screen. Ten-thirty. Where the hell was Lane? Getting it on with Bubbles?

He'd better not be porking that damned bimbo.

With an angry motion, she hit the off button on the remote pressing so hard her thumb nearly broke the damned thing. She'd sat all evening like a dutiful mob wife, unable to concentrate on any kind of plan, wondering and worrying. Owned and operated by the Ponzetti family, The Topsy-Turvy Club gave her a pretty good indication as to Lane's drinking companions. She visualized it now—the laughter, the booze, the stories, and Bubbles shaking those over-inflated tits in Lane's face.

Gabriella clenched her teeth and curved her fingers into claws, mentally shredding the bitch as Bubbles' chest exploded like a pricked balloon, sending the blonde flying around the room backwards until crashing in a flattened heap. Or maybe the vacuum-headed bimbo would shoot right out a window and into orbit, never to be seen again.

A thumping, fumbling sound from the door brought her out of the daydream and set her heart hammering. Johnny!

Be sensible. It's not Johnny Scarano.

She walked to the door, peeked through the peephole, and ground her teeth, then opened it.

Frankie and Lane staggered into the living room, falling to the floor.

Shit! They were drunk on their asses, although Lane had managed to regain his footing. Gabriella recognized the third man with them as a driver for the Ponzetti's.

Frankie lay on the floor laughing like a loon. "Hey, Joey, you wanna help me up?"

Slipping into character, she said, "Frankie, are you all right? What's wrong?"

"Nothing, baby. Just had a good time," he slurred.

Lane stood, but swayed back and forth like a punch drunk boxer, an idiotic grin on his face. "We've had a little too much to drink."

She wanted to kick him in the ass. "So, I see."

Joey had hauled Frankie to his feet, supporting him before he fell again.

"Hey, I had to introduce my buddy Leo here to all my friends. We're good buddies, right, Leo?"

He tried to pat Lane on the back, but missed. If Joey hadn't had a firm grip, Frankie would have landed on the floor again.

"Ap—ab..." Lane belched. "Absolutely."

Ass-kicking was too good. She'd kill him. But first, she had to get rid of Frankie. Time to draw on Miss Cameron's acting class again, although with her temper about to boil over, the performance wouldn't be a stretch.

"Shame on you, Frankie! You got my cousin drunk, and you can't even walk! This is the second time in two days." She sniffed and let a couple of tears fall. "And you promised it wouldn't happen again."

"Aw, come on, baby. We're guys. It's what men do."

Joey, stoic and protective, grabbed the back of Frankie's shirt to keep him upright.

Gabriella cried harder and grabbed a tissue from a box on an end table. "And what about Bubbles? Is she a guy thing, too?"

"Yeah, definitely," Lane replied.

The laughter in his eyes added fuel to the fire already burning in her gut. The bastard.

"Don't be mad. I never touched Bubbles. I swear it. I wouldn't cheat on you," Frankie defended.

"I don't care. I'm very disappointed. And your daddy wouldn't like it either."

"Aw, Jesus, don't bring my father into this. What I do with the guys is my business."

To her surprise, his tone took on a belligerence and his eyes hardened with anger. She'd never seen or heard either from him before.

"Well, I think you should go home and sleep it off. Don't call me again until you're sober." She stamped her foot for emphasis.

"The lady's right, Frankie. Let's get you home. Can you handle your cousin, Miss Vicelli?" Joey asked.

She shot a glance at the swaying Lane, wanting badly to punch him in the nose.

"Yes. I can manage."

"Night, baby," Frankie mumbled as Joey maneuvered him out the door. She pushed it shut.

Lane stopped rocking back and forth. "Whew! Thank God. I thought this night would never end. What the hell are you doing here? I told you to wait for my call."

Gabriella whirled and snapped, "Because that stupid old sot supposedly watching over me is a fucking drunk. She passed out, and I felt safer in my own home. Besides, the place was a dump."

"You should have stayed put."

"You asshole! You got drunk!"

"I'm only as drunk as I want to be. I picked up plenty of information."

141

"Who the hell cares? You're supposed to be protecting me from Johnny Scarano, not boozing with Frankie and his family of thugs. We've got *work* to do."

She refrained from mentioning Bubbles. It could only lead to more arguing. She swallowed her anger.

Lane stared for a moment, and then looked away. "You're right. We need to plan a kidnapping. *And* we need to get out of here. Frankie drops by too often. We can't plan a damned thing with Frankie apologizing every day. I guarantee he'll show up tomorrow with more flowers and candy. By the way, he drunkenly announced to the entire Topsy-Turvy Club that you were his fiancée-to-be."

"Fuck him and fuck you!" The anger simmered behind her breastbone, slowly radiating outwards.

Lane laughed, infuriating her more.

"I'm going to e-mail Roger." She knew it sounded childish, like 'I'll tell my mother on you,' but he was laughing at her. No one did that. No one! Jealousy clawed straight through her gut and into her pride. The hell with him. She had to know.

"What else did you do at the club? Was Bubbles there?"

"Of course. I didn't think it was anatomically possible to get those tassels twirling in opposite directions. She puts on one hell of a show."

"On stage or off?" The simmering reached a boil. Damn, why couldn't she control it?

Lane raised an eyebrow. "Jealous?"

"In your dreams, Hamilton."

In spite of her snotty answer, the little inner voice she'd been ignoring all evening screamed, Yes.

He walked over and placed his hands on her shoulders. "I think you're lying. You're damned jealous."

"Why you conceited son of a..."

He brought his mouth into crushing contact

with hers, cutting off her pithy reply.

For a moment she froze in shock, and then the scorching heat spread from the pit of her stomach to the tips of her fingers and toes, liquefying her bones and muscles. She clutched his shoulders to keep from falling. Gabriella wondered how hard a person's heart could pound before exploding, and how close she was to the occurrence.

Tangling her hands in his hair, she opened her mouth and kissed him for all she was worth. He tasted of whiskey and smelled of cheap perfume, but she didn't give a damn.

His arms pulled her against his body, and she had no trouble realizing he was as turned on as she. His erection nestled just north of heaven, rapidly changing the heat into a forest fire. Her nerves hummed, and the roaring in her ears blotted out all other sounds.

She wanted more. Grasping his shirt, she pulled it from his slacks and ripped it open, the buttons flying through the air. With a groan, she ran her fingers over his hair-covered chest. The muscles, hard as rocks, sent a shiver down her spine.

Lane took the opportunity to cover her breast with his hand, the thumb massaging the nipple into a hard point. Then his hand slid under her top to unsnap her bra. Pushing it up, he palmed the globe, his fingers pinching the erect center.

Gabriella arched and threw her head back, moaning as the room spun. Oh, sweet Jesus, she throbbed all over, and when his hand pulled her even tighter against him, she ached with desire, something she'd not felt in years.

Bending her backward over his arm, Lane fastened his lips over her nipple, his tongue and teeth licking and nibbling. A sharp, hot flash of lightning stabbed deep in her core.

She squirmed and panted, a climax of

indescribable proportions building. Holy shit! She had to have him. Now! Her fingers fumbled with his belt buckle, then with the waistband of his slacks. Finally, Gabriella yanked the zipper down and shoved her hand inside his boxers to grasp a rod of steel fresh out of the furnace.

With a tortured groan, Lane picked her up and laid her on the sofa, divesting her of her top and bra in the process. Her slacks disappeared down her legs followed by her bikini panties. He shed the rest of his clothing. She shivered and quaked with anticipation.

Oh, God, Lane Hamilton—Dante Borelli—the man of her dreams stood naked in front of her and looked magnificent. All sinewy, hard muscles, the hardest of which jutted out in front, made her shiver again. Gabriella reached, encircled it, and stroked. A look of ecstasy crossed his face. He closed his eyes and growled like a pleased lion.

Then he nestled between her legs, his lips caressing her throat, her collarbone, her breasts, and on down her body. His tongue played havoc with her navel and his fingers drew sensual circles on her thighs. She burned hotter. A drop of carelessly spilled water would boil away in an instant on her superheated skin.

Gabriella jerked and cried out when his circling fingers found, then massaged that pinpoint of sensitivity at the heart of her core.

She lifted her hips and rode the rhythm for a few seconds, then said with a gasp, "No. I want you inside of me—now."

He covered her mouth with his and obliged, plunging in with one swift motion.

Wrapping her legs around his waist, she hung on and lunged to meet his fast and furious thrusts. The forest fire crowned. His lips transferred to the side of her neck where he buried his face. His rasping breath incinerated the pounding pulse point above her collarbone. His musky male scent drove her insane with desire.

Forever. Gabriella waited suspended in that wonderful world of almost there for an eternity. Panting, she begged for release in disjointed, sobbing sentences, pleading with Lane and God to send her over the edge.

With a suddenness and violence she'd never before experienced, her prayers were answered. She climaxed, the throbbing contractions almost ripping her to shreds as she shattered into a thousand pieces like a sheet of glass dropped from The Sears Tower.

Lane came with her, shouting and thrusting, the pulsations of his orgasm prolonging hers.

Drained of all energy, Gabriella unlocked her ankles and let her legs fall back limply to the sofa. Without uttering a word, Lane moved his body down to pillow his head on her breasts, his lips caressing the valley between them. It took several minutes for her breathing to return to normal and for her heart to cease its erratic thumping.

Opening her eyes, she gazed at the ceiling, then the top of Lane's head. Reality returned.

"Oh, shit! What have we done?"

He kissed each breast and moved his hands gently up and down her waist.

"I'd have to say we made love," he murmured.

"But we shouldn't have, dumb ass."

"Why do you swear like that? You sound like a teamster with a balky eighteen-wheeler." His voice had a drowsy, satiated quality.

She should have insisted he move, but damned if she didn't enjoy his body relaxing against hers. God, it had been a long time since she'd experienced anything this wonderful. Her fingers stroked his hair in a rhythmic pattern until Lane emitted a tiny, pre-sleep snore.

Typical male. She pushed at his shoulders.

"Hey, don't you dare fall asleep on me."

Rising up on his elbows, he smiled like a contented tomcat. "You didn't enjoy it?"

"Never mind. Get off of me. This was a serious mistake."

He grinned, his face resembling the Cheshire cat. "You liked it. As a matter of fact, so did I."

"All right, you conceited son of a bitch. I liked it. It was stupendous. I never had it so good. Does that satisfy your ego?" Damned if she wasn't telling the truth, but she'd die before admitting it. "Now, get off me."

Laughing, Lane slid off the sofa and reached for his clothes. "Yes, my ego is satisfied, along with my libido." He dressed then faced her. "Okay, so it shouldn't have happened, but it did. What are we going to do about it?"

"Forget it," she replied, pulling her top over her head. "We have a job to do, and I refuse to let sex get in the way. Trust me."

"Sex won't get in the way. I'm going to e-mail Roger."

Oh, shit. "About what?"

"Don't look so horrified. What kind of a man do you think I am?" He avoided looking at her. "I'm going to tell him about tonight at the club. Maybe we can get someone in there. I won't be long. Then we'll plan."

He dropped a light kiss on the top of her head before exiting the room.

****

Lane had no intention of e-mailing Roger. He'd used it as an excuse to get out of the room before he threw her back onto the sofa for round two. The fact that he *wanted* round two bothered him. She was right. They should never have made love. If Roger knew, he'd fire them both.

He hadn't meant for things to get so out of hand, but when she'd started arguing, something snapped, and he shut her up in the only way he could.

"Dumb, dumb, and even dumber," he muttered.

What had happened to all that vaunted self-control he used to possess? The tension and awareness between them had hung in the air like an invisible curtain waiting to smother them in soft, clinging folds ever since she'd opened the door yesterday. If all he'd wanted were sex, he'd have let Bubbles do her thing. But he hadn't wanted Bubbles. He wanted Gabriella.

"Aw, shit!"

He walked into the bathroom. Turning on the cold tap, he stuck his head under the water to clear it of the bourbon left in his system.

He rubbed his hair dry with a towel and sat on the edge of the tub, his face buried in the soft terrycloth. Now, what was he going to do? The instinct to protect surged through him. In a little over twenty-four hours, the woman—hard as nails and foul mouthed—had gotten under his skin and penetrated his inner core. The word love had never been a part of his vocabulary.

Dammit! What had he done? What had she done?

****

Gabriella's fingers shook as she smoothed her hair. Forget the best sex she'd ever had? Not a chance in hell. She'd just made love with a man she'd admired and been half in love with for years. The mental had become physical.

How could she forget it? She didn't regret one single kiss or touch, and if he did either to her now, she'd peel her clothes off for an encore performance.

Shit! She didn't need this kind of distraction. She had to concentrate on how they would snatch Caesar Casano from a wedding reception. Time was running out.

"And we can plot right here," she muttered aloud. "I'm not going anywhere, so don't think fabulous sex will change my mind."

She rose, surprised her legs still contained a slight wobble. In fact, her whole body continued to throb and she gulped in several deep breaths to steady her shaky nerves.

A faint noise from the front door reclaimed her attention. Before she could react, it burst open.

Gabriella screamed.

****

Johnny hid on the third floor landing of the stairwell holding the gun in a tight fist. His heart pounded with anticipation. In a little while, he'd have the revenge he'd sought for so long. Then maybe those bums on the island would see the light. He, Johnny Scarano, would save them all. They'd owe *him*. Once the operation was blown, the Feds would have to release their prisoners. The fucking courts would see to that. He'd end up being a hero to all the families. Maybe even move up in rank and stature. Hell, with a little luck, one day he could take over for Casano. He'd be a Don. He'd have respect from every goombah in the fucking city.

Breathing deeply, he broke off his fantasy and looked at his watch. He'd decided to let the drunken cousin, Leo, go to bed. With that much booze in him, he'd sleep through a nuclear explosion in the next room. If he did, then Johnny wouldn't have to kill him. He didn't mind killing for killing's sake, but he didn't want to start out his renewed life pissing off the Detroit mob.

Vicelli would probably be in bed also. The thought of shoving the gun in her mouth and doing her made him hard. All those images of Bubbles and her sweet little mouth had given Johnny the itch.

But fucking Vicelli wasn't a smart idea. Grab

148

her and haul her ass to Gavino Ponzetti, then torture the bitch until she talked. He wondered how many Feds had taken family members' places in the last few years. From his barhopping, he'd gleaned enough information to know new faces had appeared on the scene.

Impatiently, he glanced at his watch again. He'd wait another fifteen minutes. That would make it a full hour since Frankie and Joey had left. He froze at the sounds of the elevator doors opening and two people laughing in the hallway above. Then the couple entered an apartment and closed the door. Once again, silence reigned.

Johnny wished he had a silencer for the gun. If he had to shoot, the noise would be heard by anyone still awake. It could make getting Vicelli out harder.

He shrugged. *Fuck it, I'll deal with it later.*

Nervous and too antsy to stand still any longer, Johnny inched his way down the stairs to the second floor. Number two-oh-one faced the front of the building. He placed his ear against the door, but heard nothing through the wood. Good. He tried the doorknob. Locked. It didn't matter. His adrenaline pumped like Old Faithful. Using his foot, he slammed it against the lock as hard as he could. The door splintered and crashed open. Vicelli stood in the middle of the living room, and let loose a scream.

"Shut up, bitch."

"Johnny," she said, gasping.

He liked the panic-stricken look on her face. "Yeah, Johnny. Bet you didn't think you'd ever see me again, did you? Where's the cousin?"

Insolence replaced her look of utter horror as she sneered and said, "In bed."

"He's lucky. I was gonna kill him. Move your ass. You're coming with me. You have some explaining to do to Mr. Ponzetti."

"You third rate thug, I'm not going anywhere

with you. Do you really expect Gavino and Frankie to believe a single word you say? They'll never believe I'm responsible. I'll say you kidnapped and tried to rape me. They'll think you're crazy and blow your fucking head off."

The contempt dripped from her voice. Shit, the bitch could be right. But for now his fantasies and the thirst for revenge overwhelmed possible reality.

He waggled the gun towards the door. "Shut the fuck up. Get going."

"Go ahead and shoot. The whole damned building will hear it."

"Don't bet on it. You'd still be dead. Trust me. Now move, you fucking bitch!"

She sneered, but did as ordered and sidled toward the damaged door. He followed, turning his back to a hallway. Victory and redemption would soon be his.

****

The sounds of wood ripping and Gabriella's scream jerked Lane out of his thoughts. Voices carried through the bedroom door, and he didn't need any second guesses as to who had just paid a visit.

Some protector! While he'd been daydreaming, Johnny Scarano had come through the front door bold as brass. Cursing to himself, he pulled a gun from under the mattress and cracked the bedroom door open.

The voices became clearer and from the conversation, Lane figured Scarano was about to make off with his captive. He prowled down the hallway on silent feet and peeked around the corner. Johnny waved the gun towards the door. Gabriella moved, putting Johnny's back between him and the door.

Good girl. She's acting like a pro.

Lane raised the gun, and then stopped. A shot

150

would be heard. The one thing Alpha-Omega didn't need was a bunch of cops asking questions. The Ponzettis probably had a mole in the police department. News would reach Gavino's ears in record time. He shoved the gun in the back of his waistband. He'd have to tackle Johnny from behind.

Gabriella stared over Scarano's shoulder. He motioned with his head and hoped she understood to hit the floor if Johnny started shooting. She blinked. He took it as acknowledgement.

Taking a deep breath Lane charged, hitting his target square in the middle of the back. Amazingly, the gun did not go off, but neither did Scarano drop it. With one hand locked on Johnny's wrist and the other in his hair, the two men rolled in a clinch, banging into the coffee table. It overturned sending the contents scattering.

Johnny landed a weak punch to the side of Lane's head, and then tried to knee him in the crotch. Lane moved nimbly out of the way, giving Johnny a shot to the jaw. Grunting, Johnny heaved his body and threw Lane off to the side, breaking the wrist grip, but before he could get off a shot, Gabriella nailed him in the head with one of her stilettos.

"You fuckin' bitch!" Johnny roared, blood flowing from a wound near his temple. His fist shot out and connected with her jaw. She dropped like a stone, striking her head on the entertainment center, and lay still.

Lane regained his feet, head-butting Johnny in the gut. The air rushed out of his opponent in a loud whoosh and he fell backward. The gun flew from his hand to skitter under the sofa.

Lane landed a hard one-two on Johnny's jaw, sending him staggering into a bookcase. Grabbing a book, Johnny let fly. He had good aim. The heavy tome hit Lane in the face.

Careening back, Lane grasped a chair to keep his feet. He failed. The momentum carried him and the chair to the floor. His face stung and he tasted blood from where the book had jammed his lip into his teeth.

Johnny charged after him, fists ready to hammer. He rolled to his right and leg-whipped the thug at the knees. They ended up in another clinch, using fists and feet whenever possible. It was a fight worthy of any bar brawl. Lane couldn't believe he hadn't knocked the mobster into oblivion. Trained to fight and fight dirty, his only excuse was the booze had impaired his abilities.

Then Johnny got off a lucky one. Lane's head simply exploded into an ocean of pain. Bright, glittering stars danced across his line of vision. For a moment, everything went dark.

When his senses returned a second later, Johnny had scrambled on his hands and knees toward the door, where he grasped the jamb, hauled himself upright, and ran for it.

Lane heard the frantic retreat down the stairs and out onto the street. Still woozy, he crawled over to shut what was left of the apartment door, and then sat on the floor to regain his breath. Opening his eyes, he spied Gabriella lying in front of the TV.

"Gabby!" he cried, dragging himself toward her, wincing as his knee made contact with the stiletto sandal. As a weapon it had been damned effective.

Lane quickly inspected her head, but found no blood, only a large goose egg just above her right ear from where she'd struck the entertainment center. Her jaw had already turned an interesting shade of blue.

He rose, then lifted and carried her to the sofa. Propping her into the corner, Lane ran to the kitchen, held a dishtowel under the cold water, gathered ice in a bowl, and grabbed a second towel.

He bathed her face, relieved to hear her groan. Her lashes fluttered. Wrapping some ice in one towel, he held it to the lump on the side of her head and placed the wet towel against her jaw.

Gabriella moaned, opened her eyes, and stared at him with a puzzled expression.

He wanted to kiss her senseless, but instead opted to say, "Hey, baby. You throw one hell of a party."

Comprehension replaced puzzlement. She scowled, and then snarled in her customary manner, "Fuck you!"

Doubling up her fist, she aimed for his nose.

Chapter Eleven

Lane dodged, grabbing her wrist in a viselike grip. She was tempted to try again, then decided it wouldn't be worth the effort.

"Is this the thanks I get for saving your ass?" he asked.

"Damn you, let go of me! Where's Johnny?"

He dropped her wrist. Her head and jaw hurt like hell. Tentatively, she moved the latter.

"Gone. After you hit the floor, we fought. Luckily, we're both out of practice, *and* he lost his gun." Lane rooted under the sofa, and then placed the cheap weapon on the end table. "He got in a good one. By the time I recovered, he was out the door. How about you? How do you feel?"

She touched the side of her head and felt a lump. "Okay, I guess. What happened? The last thing I remember is Johnny slugging me."

"You fell and hit your head on the entertainment center. How many fingers do you see?" He held up his hand.

"Two. There's nothing wrong with my vision."

"You could have a concussion. Maybe we should go to the hospital."

"No. If I go in looking like this, they may think *you* hit me. I'm fine. Quit hovering. What are we going to do?"

"We'll say you got mugged in the parking lot. Are you sure there's no double vision?"

"I told you, my vision is fine. How many fingers do *you* see?" she asked, raising her middle finger.

Lane's lips twitched, but she couldn't tell whether in amusement or exasperation.

"Ah, still the same sweet person." He rose from the sofa. "I guess you're all right. Keep the ice on that lump. I've got to call Roger and tell him what's happened."

Gabriella grabbed the towel as he disappeared down the hallway. She closed her eyes and leaned her head back. Her memory was hazy, but she recalled Johnny's fist coming at her in slow motion. Then her head had erupted in painful flashes of brilliant lights before a curtain of darkness descended.

Gabriella swallowed the sour taste rising in her throat. Never had she experienced fear like the kind when Scarano had kicked in her door. It clawed everywhere from the pit of her stomach to the tiniest recess of her mind. To her disgust, she'd reacted the way all those wimpy fiction heroines react when confronted with danger, by screaming. If Lane hadn't been here, she would be either dead or trussed up like a Christmas turkey on her way to the Ponzetti dinner table.

Inside, she quivered as though living through a personal earthquake. Damn! Lane had been right. Johnny Scarano *had* gotten by the gate and shown up on her doorstep. Her confidence took a major hit and for a moment all she'd wanted to do was bury her face in Lane's broad, capable chest and cry.

Then he'd spoiled everything with his smart ass remark about parties.

Angry at her momentary lapse into wimpdom, *and* at the fact Lane was right, made her want to spit. She didn't know which she hated more— reacting like a wuss or being proven wrong.

Lane returned with his phone slapped against

his ear. She raised her head, listening to the one-sided conversation.

"No, I don't have him. I was in the bedroom when he busted in the door... Of course, he was armed. He lost the gun in the fight we had... She's all right, just a couple of bumps and bruises... No, he belted her pretty good. She dropped like a rock. Glass jaw."

Gabriella wanted to smack him for giving Roger that information. It made her sound like a has-been boxer.

"By the time I came to, he was already out the door."

Slowly rising to her feet, she fought a wave of dizziness and entered the kitchen to replenish the ice in the towel. When she returned, Lane was finishing his conversation.

"I agree. It's the only thing to do at this point. I'll call you in the morning... Right."

"So, what's the verdict?" she asked as he hung up.

"I suggest we get the hell out of here and go to a motel for the night. We'll make plans in the morning. Roger thinks we should pull out now and forget about the Casano deal. I agree."

"Of course you do."

"We could call the cops with the mugged-in-the-parking-lot story. The complex might beef up security, but we'd be prisoners."

"No cops. Ponzetti has several in his pocket, and the news would get back in no time. Then, Frankie would take on the role of protector. We'd never get rid of him."

"Suppose one of the neighbors heard the fight? *They* might call."

Gabriella glanced at the clock. "If that were the case they'd already be here. If the neighbors heard anything, it wasn't enough to alarm anyone."

"Scarano knows where you live *and* knows we won't call the cops either. Do it my way. We'll go to a motel. Pack up a few things." He ran a hand over his jaw and a look of sudden exhaustion crossed his face. "We'll talk more in the morning. And please, don't argue with me," he added when she drew a breath.

"I wasn't planning to. Maybe I *am* concussed, but I'll do it your way—at least until tomorrow."

She fingered her jaw and winced, then dropped her hands to her sides where she balled them into fists to hide the trembling. She hated giving in and being forced out of her surroundings.

She lifted her chin, saying, "Regardless of Roger's opinion, I think we can pull this off. It's only a few days away. We can hide out until then. Nobody will miss us."

"What about Frankie? He'll miss us. My bet is he'll show up tomorrow afternoon bearing gifts of remorse."

"Leave Frankie to me. I'll think of something."

"How do we explain the door? Johnny smashed it in."

"I'll call the manager tomorrow and say a former boyfriend got drunk and did it. He'll charge for fixing it, but who cares? They may even deny Frankie access if I tell them he did it."

A look of alarm crossed Lane's face. "Don't do that. We don't want Frankie pissed, just out of the way." He drew a deep breath. "Let's work on our story tomorrow. I'm bushed."

So was she. Weariness and pain left her wishing she could disappear with a snap of her fingers or a twitch of her nose, like that silly TV witch.

"All right, but keep this in mind—we stay for the wedding!"

On that note, Gabriella stalked back to her room, closed the door, and sagged against it. God, she hurt. Her head throbbed, and once again she cautiously moved her jaw.

Alone, she allowed herself the luxury of trembling. Her knees gave out and she sank to the floor, crying silently. Oh shit, how had all this happened? Three days ago, she had been blissfully unaware danger lurked anywhere on the horizon and now—she didn't want to think about it.

Drying her tears, she crawled over to the bed and pulled herself up.

Knock it off. Crying isn't going to help or make Johnny Scarano disappear.

She hated it when her weaker emotions took control.

She rose and scrounged a suitcase from the cluttered depths of her closet. Her fingers shook and the routine of packing helped calm her nerves, restoring her lost confidence. She *would* handle Frankie, they *would* kidnap Casano, and most importantly, they *would* stay alive.

It galled her to admit it, but deep down, Gabriella was glad to have Lane Hamilton around.

****

Before leaving, Lane took a few minutes to fix some of the damage to the front door. Luckily, the force of the blow had splintered the weaker wood of the door jamb. When Frankie left, Gabriella had been pissed and neglected to turn the deadbolt or use the chain. Johnny's footprint was clearly visible above the lock on the outside. Thank goodness the bastard hadn't destroyed the catch.

It took him two minutes to pack and gather his belongings.

"Do you have everything?" he asked before securing the door.

"Yeah, I think so. I don't keep files on my hits. I have the computer and the agency phone with me. There's nothing incriminating left behind. How about you?"

"Ditto. Let's get out of here."

They hustled down the steps and out to the car. He jammed the suitcases and laptops in wherever he could, then helped a subdued Gabriella into the passenger seat before slipping behind the wheel and taking off. He drove making frequent turns, monitoring the rearview mirror in case Scarano had found transportation and still lurked.

Lane braked at a stoplight. He didn't like driving the Porsche. The damned thing stuck out like a lighthouse beacon in the fog. Anyone searching for them would have no problem seeing the car in a motel parking lot, but they hadn't had much choice in the matter. Hers was the only car available.

The light changed and Lane accelerated down the empty street. At this hour of the night, the residential neighborhoods they cut through slept in peaceful darkness. Shooting down alleys and making quick turns, he merged onto the Dan Ryan Expressway, floored it, and then exited abruptly across four lanes of light traffic.

"Where are we going?" Gabriella asked.

"Don't know. I'd love to ditch this car and find something less ostentatious. I don't like the idea of a snazzy sports car sitting in front of our motel."

"Go to a hotel and have it valet parked in a garage."

It made so much sense he wanted to kick himself for not having thought of it. They could register under one of his identities and live off of room service. Gabriella had found Lane Hamilton, but she hadn't discovered the other two IDs hidden in his computer case.

On the corner, he spied an all night diner and remembered he hadn't eaten. He was starving. Gabriella had tied a scarf over her head to help hide the bruise on her jaw and from the way she kept fingering her temple, he assumed she must be hurting.

Should he chance stopping? He shot a glance into the rearview mirror. The street behind was devoid of traffic. He doubted anyone followed.

Pulling into the parking lot, he said, "I don't know about you, but I need to eat. How's the head?"

"Hurts, but I'll survive."

"There's a twenty-four hour drugstore across the street. You get us a table while I pick up some aspirin and an ice bag."

She nodded and he waited until she entered the diner before leaving the car. A few minutes later, he slid into the booth she'd selected, noting with approval Gabriella had chosen one along the back wall, away from the front windows.

He handed her a bag. "Here, take a couple of aspirins. We'll fill the ice bag at the hotel."

He stared, worried when she didn't answer, merely accepting the sack with another nod and a trembling hand.

"You sure you're all right?" he asked in a low voice.

Gabriella sighed. "Yeah. Just tired and sore."

A waitress appeared beside them. "What can I get for you folks?"

"I'll have a cheeseburger, fries and a coke."

"Just coffee for me—decaf if you have it," she said, her shoulders slumping.

"Sure you don't want anything to eat?" Lane asked.

He didn't like her reticence. It was out of character and he wondered again if he should take her to a doctor.

"No thanks, I had dinner."

Even under the scarf, the edge of the purplish bruise was visible. The waitress's eyes opened wide. She gripped her order pad and pencil tighter, shooting Lane a dirty look.

"Are you okay, honey?" she asked.

"I'm fine, really."

Lane didn't like this. If anyone came asking, they'd be remembered.

"This is my sister. Her ex-boyfriend got drunk tonight and roughed her up. The cops are looking for him, but I decided to get her somewhere safe until he's behind bars."

"Is that true, honey?"

Gabriella patted the woman's hand and smiled. "Yes, it's true. Could you recommend a good hotel? I need to rest. I'm so tired."

"Sure can. Try the Regency Arms over on Claymore Street. It's clean and not too expensive."

"Do they have a parking garage?" Lane asked.

"Yeah, and it's got security twenty-four seven."

Gabriella rubbed her temple. "Thanks. Could you bring me a glass of water? I've got one hell of a headache."

The water arrived and she downed two aspirins. Less than ten minutes later, the food and coffee appeared.

Lane wolfed his meal while Gabriella took occasional sips of coffee. Overcooked and dry, the burger tasted like crap, but would have to do.

As he paid, leaving a generous tip, he said to the waitress, "Please, if anyone comes asking about us, could you forget we were ever here?"

"Glad to, mister. And I hope the cops get the son of a bitch. Tell your sister she doesn't have to take that kind of shit from any man. I oughtta know, I have a violent ex myself."

He joined Gabby at the door and scoped out the parking lot. Other than the Porsche, it was empty. He helped her into the car and drove off.

"Are we going to this Regency Arms?" she asked.

"No, we're going to the Tower Plaza."

"Your idea of hiding out is on Michigan Avenue?"

"It has valet parking, room service, and would be the last place Johnny would think to look for us. I doubt Frankie would even think of it. Speaking of Frankie, how are we going to keep him off balance?"

Gabriella yawned. "I don't know. I'll think of something. If he comes by, do you think he'll notice the damaged door?"

"I don't see how he could miss it."

Lane kept a watch in the rearview mirror, driving down side streets until he was sure no one followed.

He pulled up in front of the Tower Plaza and handed the keys to the valet, then allowed a bellboy to carry their suitcases inside. The bar, situated near the entrance, had a few customers. Ignoring them, he walked past, guiding Gabriella, his hand on her elbow.

"Go have a seat in the lobby while I register. Keep your head down and that bruise under wraps."

He got her settled, selected an ID from his computer case, and approached the front desk.

"I need a room for a couple of days. Do you have any vacancies?"

"Yes, sir. Would you like a king or two queen beds?"

"The queens."

"Your name, sir?"

"Robert Ellis and my sister, Rosemary." He finished registering and returned to Gabby.

Walking through the lobby, he realized he couldn't have chosen more opulent surroundings. Marble and granite graced the floors and the tabletops while the lobby chairs bore damask upholstery. Dark paneling gave the walls a somber note and the lighting could only be described as subdued. It reminded him of a British gentleman's club. Johnny Scarano wouldn't get past the front door.

A few minutes later, he, Gabriella, and the bellboy were in the elevator heading to the tenth floor.

Lane tipped the man, then closed and locked the door behind him. He turned to find Gabriella staring at him, some of her exhausted stupor gone.

"One room?" she said, lifting an eyebrow.

"Do you really think I'm going to let you stay alone?"

"And who is the Mr. Ellis the bellboy thanked?"

"I'm Robert Ellis from Los Angeles and you're my sister, Rosemary."

"Rosemary? You've gotta be kidding. Nobody is named Rosemary."

"You are, so remember whenever you sign any room service tabs. And tip in cash."

"How many names do you have?"

"As many as Roger thinks I need. Now, I suggest you pick a bed and get into it. I'll get some ice for your head from the machine down the hall."

He slid out the door and returned in less than a minute grateful she hadn't fastened the chain lock. He wouldn't have put it past her. While he filled the ice bag, Gabriella exited the bathroom and slipped between the sheets. Lane handed it to her.

"Which hurts more?"

"It's a tossup." She placed it on the pillow next to her head and closed her eyes.

He ran a gentle finger down her cheek. "Sleep tight, Gabby. I'll keep you safe." He expected a pithy remark, but she remained silent.

Lane inspected his face in the bathroom mirror. Not too bad. The knock-out punch had landed just above his left ear. Hair would hide any bruising. His knuckles hurt like hell, but showed little signs of a fight. Thank God, mostly body blows had been thrown. Scarano had been wearing some kind of overcoat. It not only saved Lane's hands, but hampered the thug's movements. His cheek had reddened from where the book hit it. Luckily, the cut was on the inside of his lip.

He downed a couple of aspirins, then turning out the lights, stripped to his boxers, and crawled into bed.

Jesus, he was tired—tired and hurting. He should be making plans, but at the moment, he couldn't formulate a damned thing. Tomorrow. He'd worry about it all tomorrow. Then, from out of the darkness came a low voice.

"Thank you, Lane."

He hadn't expected it, and wanted to slide into her bed to hold and comfort her. Gabby was a gutsy, brave woman who sounded scared to death. He admitted to himself the woman had done more than worm her way under his skin and for a brief moment tonight, he'd thought he'd lost her. When he found she was alive, his heart started beating again. He had fallen for her and damned if he knew what to do about it.

Rolling onto his side, he faced her, the bed and her body a dim outline in the dark room. He'd never seen her vulnerable before. It made her human—far too human.

"You're welcome. Go to sleep, honey. I'm here."

****

Johnny stumbled through the front door of his third hotel since he'd arrived back in Chicago. The bored desk clerk didn't bother to look up from the magazine he read. A drunk staggering in at this hour probably wasn't an odd occurrence.

Clasping the banister, Johnny hauled his pain-racked, weary body up the stairs to his second floor room. He slammed the door shut behind him and plopped into the sagging chair next to a small table by the window. How long had he been walking and running? He had no idea. All he knew was that he'd come so close he could almost smell reinstatement into the family.

He poured a drink from the bottle of whiskey on the table, bolting it down his throat. The fiery liquid helped calm his still shaking nerves. For a drunk, the cousin had sure acted alert and packed quite a punch. After three years on the island, Johnny had gotten soft. He hurt all over.

Breathing heavily, Johnny stood and shuffled into the minuscule bathroom where he inspected his injury in the cracked mirror above the sink. The wound no longer bled, but the dried blood on his face gave him a garish look, like a Halloween mask from a horror shop.

Damn! Who would have thought a fucking shoe could have done so much damage? When the bitch had slugged him, he'd seen stars.

He turned on the water and washed up, then gazed at the indentation just above his left temple. A fraction of an inch lower and it could have been lights out—permanently. He glanced at his hands. The knuckles were scraped raw and bruised. By tomorrow, his face would show he'd been in a fight. Touching his ribs, Johnny breathed a sigh of relief. Nothing broken.

Returning to the other room, he slumped into the chair, poured another drink, gulped it, and then filled the glass again. He'd been a jerk to turn his back on the hallway. He'd never done something that dumb before.

One more thing to blame on the island and Vicelli.

The cousin had hit him like a freight train and the ensuing fight surprised him. Maybe Leo hadn't been as drunk as he'd thought. After landing the lucky punch, Johnny had decided to cut his losses and get the hell out. Shame he lost the gun. No matter. He'd pick up another one tomorrow. It's not like they were hard to find.

He pounded his fist on the arm of the chair. *Son of a bitch! I was so close! I almost had her!* This half-assed cousin had spoiled his revenge. Johnny swilled his drink and poured another.

Leo...Leo. For some reason, he had a problem placing the name with the face. They didn't fit and he didn't know why. A cousin Leo from Detroit who looked vaguely familiar. Uneasiness plucked at him. Something was wrong about it. But what? Bubbles. He needed to talk to her. Maybe he'd risk going back to The Topsy-Turvy tomorrow.

He guzzled half the whiskey. No. He'd gotten lucky tonight. Frankie and his cohorts had been drunk and distracted. Maybe he'd wait outside the club's back door like a fan, grabbing the stripper when she came out. Yeah. That might work.

Johnny bolted the rest of the booze down his throat and shoved the glass aside. The room spun lightly. Dammit! That fuckin' island had also destroyed his ability to drink. He'd become a ghost of his former self and it was all Vicelli's fault.

He clenched his jaw, ignoring the flash of pain radiating down his neck and then through his head. Tonight may have been a disaster, but he refused to give up. He'd come too far. He had to find another way.

Tomorrow, he'd hit the bars again to see what he could pick up. He hated to take the chance, but at the moment, it was the best he could do. Exhaustion and the booze made his head swim. He wasn't thinking clearly. He knew he missed something logical, but the thought slipped away like smoke on the breeze.

Johnny slouched in his chair. "You bitch! You beat me tonight, but I'll get you. You *and* your cousin, Leo."

Grabbing the bottle off the table, he tilted it to his lips and drank.

****

Gabriella came out of the nightmare to a blinding light and a pair of hands shaking her shoulders. Still in the grips of her dream, she struck out with her fists.

"Leave me alone, you bastards! Leave me alone!"

"Gabby! Wake up! You're dreaming."

Opening her eyes, Lane's staring face wavered into focus. The light beside the bed was on, and he gently shook her into full consciousness. Gabriella struggled to sit up, pushing his hands away.

"Leave me alone," she moaned.

Burying her face in her hands, she sobbed. He left momentarily, and then returned. She felt the smooth surface of a glass pressed against her lips and sipped the cool water. It slid through her dry mouth, down her parched throat, to settle in her churning stomach.

Lane smoothed her hair. "You were having a nightmare. Are you all right? Who's Jack?"

"I'm fine," she said through her tears.

Oh, God! What a time to have the death scene nightmare. It was the worst of them all. The nausea forced its way into her throat. She scrambled from the bed and raced into the bathroom where she threw up. Mercifully, Lane did not follow. She brushed her teeth, then returned and curled up in the bed.

"Do you often have nightmares?" he asked.

"I don't want to talk now."

She refused to look at him. Humiliation and anger at him having witnessed her crying and vulnerable stabbed deeply into her gut. Dammit! She didn't want to explain, and Lane would demand an explanation.

"What was it about? Scarano?"

"Not now, Lane." She took another sip of water and tried to compose herself.

"Gabby, you were screaming. It scared me to death. I thought someone had broken in."

"I'm sorry. Look, I'm fine. Just give me a few minutes and I'll go back to sleep."

"If anybody has a right to have a nightmare, it's you. Tonight was damned scary. Do you dream often?"

Gabriella couldn't bring herself to answer. All she wanted was go to sleep. The nightmare wouldn't return. They never did.

"Gabby, answer me."

"Just leave it be, Lane."

"No, Gabby. I won't. Nightmares aren't unusual in our line of work." His voice had taken on an understanding tone. "But if they cause you to wake up screaming, you need to talk about them."

"Oh, sure. Like I'm going to spill my guts to some shrink, so he can prescribe a bunch of sleeping pills and get rich. Forget it."

"Tell me about the dream, Gabby. If this is going to be a nightly occurrence, I have to know. The mission may depend on it. What was it about?"

Gabriella closed her eyes. Why not tell him? For the first time in her life, she felt the urge to share her fears. Maybe Lane would understand.

"This particular nightmare has haunted me since my father's death and has nothing to do with my job. I'm...I'm standing across the street from the La Scala Bravo restaurant. My father is inside dining with...with a friend. He's going to make a decision that will change my life, and I can't wait any longer to know."

"What decision?" Lane asked.

"That's not important. Daddy comes out. I wave and start to cross the street when this car roars up behind his limo. All hell breaks loose. Bullets fly everywhere. I try to run and help, but my legs won't cooperate."

"That's typical dream imaging. What happens next?"

"His dining companion walks out and is also shot. The killers take off, and I finally make it to the other side. Daddy is dead. So are his bodyguards. There's blood all over. I'm so numb I can barely take in what's happened."

"What about the other man?"

"He's still...," her breath caught, "...still alive. I step over Daddy and hold him. He dies in my arms."

"Do you have these nightmares often?"

"Often enough."

"Okay, that's a start," Lane replied in a quiet voice.

"What do you mean?"

"You kept screaming 'Daddy, Daddy' and another name." Lane paused, and then took a deep breath. "Who's Jack?"

Chapter Twelve

Lane's words, *Nightmares aren't unusual for people in our line of work,* slashed across Gabriella's mind. *Our line of work.* Did that mean Lane—Dante—considered her an equal? Could he really understand? Did he suffer from demons of the dark?

Maybe the time had come to unburden her soul and her psyche—to finally talk about everything.

Sitting up, she curled her legs under the covers and propped her back against the headboard, then clutched a pillow to her chest like a protective shield. She was about to expose her mind, no need to do the same for her body.

Gabriella glanced at Lane. He settled on the edge of her bed, his eyes warm and concerned, inviting confidences. He'd pulled a T-shirt over that muscular chest and his boxers resembled a simple pair of shorts. At the moment, he looked about as threatening as...well, a cousin.

She focused her eyes over his head on the far corner of the room. Taking a deep breath, the words overflowed. Six years of pain and anguish spilled out.

"Most of the nightmares started a little over a year ago. At first, it was just every once in a while—no big deal. I blew them off as stress related. After all, aren't dreams the mind's way of releasing mental stress?"

"I don't know. Maybe. Go on."

His quiet voice gave her confidence to continue. "Then, gradually, they became more frequent...more intense...more frightening. I'd wake up, my heart pounding or I'd be crying. Sometimes, I'd have difficulty distinguishing the dream from reality. I wouldn't be able to tell if I was in a maze of streets or my own bedroom. It would take a few moments for everything to be right.

"It affected my sleep. The dreams always come between four and six in the morning. I can't see a clock at the moment, but I'll bet it's close to that now."

"It's five-twenty," Lane said.

Gabriella bit her lips, shifting her gaze to her hands clenched on the pillow. She felt better and relaxed her grip. He hadn't interrupted, but the sympathy in his voice brought a lump to her throat.

"I got into the habit of staying up late, especially after a hit. I'd go work out or turn on the stereo and dance off the excess energy until I was ready to drop. Anything to exhaust myself and sleep through the night."

"Did it work?"

She nodded. "But sooner or later the nightmares returned. Sometimes, I can go back to sleep. At other times, I get up and try to plan my next hit. That's why I've had so many in the past year or so. It occupied my mind. I'd do anything to avoid thinking about the dreams. There were times I thought I was going crazy."

It was hard for her to admit that, even to herself.

"Let me guess, you went to a psychiatrist and he gave you a prescription for sleeping pills," Lane said with a knowing smile.

"Yeah. Stupid bastard. He charged me a fortune for the privilege of ogling my boobs and legs, and then had the nerve to ask if I resented my mother."

"And what did you say to that?"

"I told him to fuck off, of course."

Lane smiled. "Of course. Go on. What are the dreams about?"

Gabriella shifted slightly and fiddled with a ring on her finger. Even with the light on and Lane sitting on the edge of the bed, her heart thumped as she remembered.

"It's always like coming into a theater in the middle of the movie. I'm being chased and running for my life. I'm panicked, but manage to stay one step ahead of my pursuer. Sometimes I know who's chasing me and sometimes I don't. No matter which way I turn, I can never quite reach safety.

"Then, there's nowhere else to turn. I'm trapped. I'm carrying a gun, but it always changes into something silly like a banana or a tongue depressor. I see the shadow of a man. He lifts his gun and pulls the trigger. That's when I wake up."

"But tonight was different," he said.

She paused, not sure if she could continue. Jack had been her secret for a long time. To share him with a man she'd made love to just a few hours before almost smacked of disloyalty. Why, she didn't know. She sucked in another deep breath. She'd gone this far; she might as well go all the way.

"Yes, this one was different. It's the worst. I wake up screaming. I haven't had it in months." She dried her tears on the pillow. "I never came close to witnessing my father's murder, of course, but knowing what I do about the business, I could imagine."

His hand smoothed over her hair, then trailed down to cup and lift her chin. For the first time since she began her saga, Gabriella looked Lane in the eye. Understanding and compassion gazed back at her.

"Gabby, who's Jack?"

She decided to bring Jack back among the living.

"Jack was Jack Carpenter, my fiancé. He and Daddy had dined together in an effort to get to know one another. The hostess at the restaurant said Jack had paused to pick up one of those little candy-striped mints and compliment the meal. He was only a couple of seconds behind Daddy going out the door. If he'd stayed another five talking or unwrapping that goddamned mint, he'd still be alive."

Tears welled in her eyes. How many times had she played this out in her head? Jack lingering and living? Too many.

Lane handed her a tissue. "Tell me about him."

"Jack was wonderful, a computer genius. He formed his own software company at the age of twenty-five and three years later was rolling in dough. He was good-looking, but nothing spectacular. Blond hair, blue eyes, and so different from me. Nothing ever flustered him. He was always calm, cool, and in control. If a problem arose, he'd deal with it logically. My volatile personality amused him. He'd let me rant and rave, then kiss the hell out of me."

She wiped the tears from her cheeks and blew her nose. It suddenly hit her. Jack and Lane possessed many of the same personality traits.

"Deep down, I always expected Daddy to die by violence. But not Jack. He and I were supposed to live to a ripe old age, raising children and doing all the things any married couple would do."

"And the police came to your door in the middle of the night to give you the news."

"The minute I opened the door and saw the cops, I knew Daddy was dead. My first question was about Jack. When I learned he'd died, too, I fell apart. After the funerals, I took off for my aunt's in St. Louis. I spent the first two months crying until I picked up the paper one day and read about your exploits. The rest you know."

Lane took the sodden tissue from her fingers and handed her another one.

"I'm sorry, Gabby. It's tragic to lose two people you love in the same night. What did Jack think about your father's occupation? How did you ever meet?"

"It was Christmas and we argued over a cab. We decided to share and somewhere along the line exchanged phone numbers. He'd been in Chicago speaking at a seminar. By New Year's, I was in love. Jack's company was located in Dallas and for months I practiced a Texas twang. God, he was brilliant. He taught me everything he could about computers in the eight short months we were together."

"What did your father have to say about him?"

"Daddy was thrilled I'd fallen in love with a man not connected, and Jack didn't give a tinker's damn what Daddy did. I wasn't my father. They were at dinner so Jack could formally ask Daddy for my hand in marriage. It was old-fashioned, but Jack always did the right thing—until he opened that fucking restaurant door." Fresh tears flowed.

"Gabby, I can't tell you what to do about the nightmares. I'm not qualified, but when this is over, why not take a long vacation? Get out of the business for a while. You can always come back."

Shredding the tissue with nervous fingers, Gabriella had to ask, "Do you have nightmares, too?"

Lane compressed his lips, heaved a sigh, and nodded. "I did. Only mine came at the beginning of my undercover work. I dreamed I'd been caught and my captors were about to torture me. As my confidence rose, the nightmares faded. In a way, that scared me even worse. I took it as a sign of complacency. I forced myself to concentrate on the little things that could trip me up."

He smiled and separated the second mangled tissue from her hand, throwing it onto the nightstand.

"It's funny you should mention staying up to let off steam. I do the same thing. Until my mind winds down, I have to keep active. Only, I usually clean."

He grinned, and she had to chuckle. "That explains a lot. Did you see a shrink, too?"

"I made the mistake of telling Roger about the nightmares. He insisted on it. So, every couple of weeks I sat on a couch and talked to an agency approved doctor."

"And did he prescribe sleeping pills?"

"Of course. I don't like taking drugs of any kind. I never filled the prescription."

"Did he ask if you resented your mother?"

"Nope. My father," Lane replied with a laugh.

She laughed with him. "And what did you say to that?"

"I didn't tell him to fuck off, but after three months of nonsense, I quit going. I told Roger the dreams had stopped. Several months later, they did."

Lane rose and grabbed the pillows off of his bed.

"Scoot over. It's late, but we can still catch some sleep."

Gabriella didn't object and gave him room. Tonight she wanted to be held.

Pulling back the covers, he lay down next to her, and then turned off the light. Dawn peeked through a chink in the curtains. She snuggled against him as his arms encased her in a warm cocoon of safety.

He gently kissed the top of her tousled head. "Go to sleep, honey."

****

Awake, Lane listened to Gabriella's even breathing as she slept. A fiancé. The innocent bystander in the reports had been her fiancé. He hadn't suspected, and he was certain Roger hadn't either. Lane bet she'd never discussed him with anybody. Gabriella had kept Jack Carpenter close to the vest. And if he and Roger were in the dark, then so were Frankie and the rest of the families. Now her vendetta against the Ponzetti family made sense. He'd have to tell Roger, of course, but not until after they snatched Casano.

That last thought jerked him into a surprised awareness that he wanted Mr. Big as much as Gabriella.

She murmured indistinctly in her sleep and nestled her head deeper into his shoulder. Lane wondered if she was still in love with Jack. Then, he remembered her passion when they'd made love. Could she put the past behind her to make way for a new love? Jack was a wound that might never heal.

He tightened his arms around her. She was too young to say never again to love. She deserved another Jack Carpenter, not Dante Borelli or Lane Hamilton or Robert Ellis, all men looking over their shoulders for the rest of their lives in case someone put two and two together and recognized them. The only problem was he wanted Lane Hamilton to be the new Jack Carpenter.

The room grew brighter. He needed sleep. The next couple of days would be killers. He almost laughed at his terminology. Yeah, right.

Closing his eyes, he tried to clear his mind. When this was over they would have a serious talk about their future.

****

Gabriella picked up the phone and punched a number. "Room Service? Please send up one Island Chicken Salad with mango vinaigrette, one Steak Supreme sandwich, medium rare with fries, and a large pot of coffee."

"Yes, ma'am. And your room number?"

"Ten-twelve. How long will that be?"

The person on the other end paused for a second, and then said, "Forty-five minutes to an hour."

She sighed. Why did it always take so damned long? If they'd been in the restaurant, they wouldn't have to wait. "All right, but hurry it up if you can."

She hung up and walked to the window, gazing out at the pool and hot tub area. God, that whirlpool looked inviting. What she wouldn't give to sit in the warm waters letting the air jets pound the stress from her body, but Lane had been adamant about not leaving the hotel room until the wedding.

I'll be a basket case by then.

Her confession must have acted like a sleeping pill because as soon as Lane crawled into bed next to her, she'd known nothing until awaking thirty minutes ago.

Gabriella listened to the running water as Lane showered. She'd do the same when he finished. Turning from the window, she picked up a pillow from the bed, stuffed it into a chair, and then sat down.

Leaning her head back, she focused on the job at hand. The first order of business was to get a plan into place. It would have to be simple. They didn't have the luxury of time. And once Casano was out of the picture, they would have to make their escape. No lingering, but find the nearest door and leave.

Plus, the specter of Johnny Scarano hung over them like Jacob Marley hung over Scrooge. Johnny could put in another appearance at any time. If he found her once, he could do it again. Roger would infiltrate the All-Italian Club with back-up in some way, so what prevented Johnny from doing the same? It would take brass balls, but then Johnny was desperate enough, not to mention dumb enough, to try anything.

Lane came out of the bathroom, a towel wrapped around his hips. Gabriella licked her lips. He looked good enough to eat and her hormones kicked up a couple of notches along with her heartbeat.

"Did you order?" he asked.

She dragged her gaze away from his chest. "Yeah. It'll be about an hour. Why does room service always take so long?"

"It's noon. The restaurant is busy and they have to spare a waiter to bring it up. I also suspect the management has sensors in the rooms that gauge how hungry we are." He grinned.

"You're probably right on both counts."

Lane paused by the dresser and searched through the duffle bag sitting on top. The knot on the towel loosened allowing the strip of cloth to fall around his feet. Gabriella gazed at his heavily muscled thighs and firm derriere. Her mouth watered. Forty-five minutes to an hour, huh? Plenty of time. Then her eyes fell on the clock. Damn, fifteen minutes had already passed. With her luck, the waiter would arrive early. Oh, well. Later.

"If you're finished, I think I'll take a shower, too." She rose and headed towards the bathroom.

"Go ahead. When you get out, we'll start planning. We have to let Roger know something by tomorrow noon. He'll need to get our back-up in place."

Thirty minutes later, she was showered and dressed, ready to start work. Lane hung up his cell phone and frowned.

"What's up?"

"I called Roger with an update."

"Oh? What did he have to say? Are we on?"

"Yes, if we can come up with a sensible plan. He's already working on back-up and transportation."

"So, why the long look?" Gabriella asked.

"He had other news. They found the body of the missing security guard at the Maryland airport stuffed into a closet in the hangar. Roger's not pleased it took the Bethesda cops over twenty-four hours to notify him."

"Why did it take so long?"

"Local police don't like giving up anything to the Feds. He also told me the body of Ralph Puccio was discovered in a dumpster in the alley behind The Tavern. A bum rooting through the garbage found him. He'd been dead at least a day."

"This puts both murders at Scarano's doorstep," she said. A shiver raced down her spine.

"Without a doubt."

Gabriella clenched her jaw to keep her teeth from chattering. Lane had been right all the time. Johnny Scarano was a cold-blooded killer, and she had seriously underestimated him. He'd been right about them all. Never again would she think of them as easy targets.

Taking a couple of deep breaths, she forced her mind back onto the problem of snatching Casano. During her shower, Lane had taken out several files and spread them on the bed.

"Where'd you get those?"

"You never thought to search the computer case. The files and all sorts of goodies are in there. Come on, let's get cracking. We have a lot of work to do."

Her phone rang. Glancing at the ID, she said, "It's Frankie. What should I do?"

"Do you have a story in place yet?"

"No."

"Then ignore it. He'll call back or leave a message."

The ringing stopped and a few seconds later the message received feature beeped.

She picked up a file. "What do we do first?"

"While I read the file on Casano, I need you to make a detailed drawing of the All-Italian Club."

They worked in silence for ten minutes until her phone rang again.

"Damn, it's Frankie. Patience is not one of his virtues. I'd better answer or he'll be doing this all goddamned day," she swore.

"Make it convincing," Lane warned.

"Hello?"

"Baby, where are you? Are you all right?"

"I'm fine, Frankie," she said. "How are you feeling?"

"I'm okay, but where are you? I came to apologize for getting drunk last night, found you gone and your door damaged. It looked like someone tried to kick it in."

"Well, it was all right when I left this morning."

"I'll take care of it. Where's the management office? What kind of security they have around here anyway?"

"Oh, don't do that, Frankie. They might think you did it. You're not supposed to have the gate code. I could get in trouble."

"Where the hell are you?"

Frankie's tone was demanding. She had to think fast. Her gaze fell on a hotel brochure on the desk.

"I'm at a spa."

"A spa? What the hell are you doing at a spa?"

"Well, I just got out of the Jacuzzi and after lunch I'm getting wrapped."

"No, I mean *why* are you at a spa?" Frankie shouted.

She wanted to laugh at his frustration, but instead replied, "I've gained two whole pounds in the last week and I need to lose it before the wedding. I have a super dress and want to look scrumptious for you."

"Where's Leo? Is he with you?"

"No, silly. Leo got a phone call late last night. He had to go back to Detroit to take care of some business. I drove him to the airport and decided now would be a good time to pamper myself for a couple of days. I love to be pampered."

She mentally patted herself on the back. Her voice sounded silky, spoiled, and self-centered.

Lane snorted, a derisive look on his face. Gabriella waved a hand at him to shut up.

"Leo's gone?" Frankie's voice had perked up.

"He'll be back for the wedding. He said he really likes Chicago and may stay for a while."

"Swell." She ignored the dejection in his tone.

A knock sounded on the door and a faint call of "Room service" came through the panels.

"Oh, Frankie, honey, I've gotta go. My lunch is here. I'm having a salad with no dressing, yogurt, and Perrier."

"Sounds delicious, baby. I'll talk to you later."

She hung up, ejected a loud sigh, and tossed the phone onto the table.

Lane opened the door, and a waiter wheeled the cart in. He signed the tab, gave the guy a tip, and then locked the door behind him.

Starving, Gabriella grabbed her salad, setting it on the table in the tiny seating area in the corner. She shoveled lettuce and chicken into her mouth.

"Slow down, Gabby. We can always order more."

"I never had a real dinner last night. Besides, wait until tonight. The tab will look like the national debt."

He laughed and took a big bite of his sandwich. Curiosity got the better of her. She had to know more about him.

"Since I talked a blue streak last night, I think it's your turn. What's your story? Where were you born? Do you have parents or a family?"

"No. I have no one."

"That sounds lonely." She related to lonely. She put her fork down. "Please, tell me. I'd really like to know more about you."

He took another bite of sandwich and poured them each a cup of coffee. Taking her cue from him, she resumed eating.

"I was born in Los Angeles. I never knew my father and often wonder if my mother did. My earliest recollections are of seedy rooming houses or one bedroom apartments. My mother would roust me out of bed in the middle of the night to sleep on the couch so she could entertain men. I assume that's how she made money. That and the welfare she got for having me around. She saw to it I was decently clothed and cared for. Her need for the checks demanded it.

"She was also a drunk. I can remember coming home from school to find her passed out on the couch, the apartment a mess of smelly garbage, dirty clothes, and just plain filth. By the time I was ten, I knew that if I didn't clean the place, nobody would."

"So, that's where Mr. Clean comes from," she murmured. "What about school? Did you have any friends?"

"I liked school and loved the challenge of getting good grades. It was my only contact with normal people. I had plenty of time to study. Once I cleaned and made dinner, Mom would wake up and take off for the nearest bar."

Gabriella couldn't conceive of a parent who didn't care. Gus may have been a mobster, but he'd loved his daughter and always put her interests first.

"And friends?" she probed.

Why did she have the feeling their experiences in this line were the same?

"The few I had disappeared when Mom showed up at the school one day. I had no idea why she was there, but naturally, she was drunk. I kept to myself after that. No one wants the son of a drunk for a friend, and I was too embarrassed to explain my mother to anyone."

"How on earth did you end up in the FBI?" She'd finished her meal and refilled her coffee.

"The school periodically made us take aptitude tests and damned if I didn't score high in them."

"How high?"

"The ninety-nine point nine-nine percentile."

"Holy shit! What's your IQ?"

"A hundred and seventy-four."

She gasped. "But...but that's genius territory."

"So they say. I was placed in accelerated programs and graduated high school at sixteen, which was fortunate since that was the year my mother died. I knew that genius or not, the state would slap me into foster care. After the funeral, I sniffed out the nearest Army recruiter, lied about my age, and joined."

Her ringing cell phone interrupted him.

"Goddamn it! What does Frankie want now?" she fumed. "Hi, Frankie."

"Hey, baby? How was lunch?"

"Yummy."

"How about we go out for dinner tonight?"

"Oh, I can't. I need to lose those pounds."

"Well, how about I come over and keep you company?"

"I'm getting wrapped in a few minutes. Do you miss me, honey?" The stupid asshole must be in love after all.

"I'm just worried what with the door at your place."

She sighed. "Silly man. I'm fine. I'll call the super in a little while to look into it. Don't go there until I get home. Okay?"

"Yeah, all right. What are you getting wrapped

in?"

God, would he never shut up? She wanted to get back to Lane's story. Grabbing the brochure, she read off of it.

"They soak strips of cloth in herbs and other natural substances to give me an invigorating sense of well-being."

"They what?" He sounded confused.

"Oh, I've gotta go. They're ready for me."

She hung up and Lane exploded into laughter. "God, what a bunch of bull!"

"Thank God for this brochure. I can use it every time he calls." She tossed the phone onto the nightstand. "Where were we? Oh, yeah, you joined the Army."

Lane shook his head and gathered the dishes, then placed them on the cart and wheeled it into the hallway.

"Enough about me. We need to get started on this plan. How's the drawing coming?"

Okay, she'd go along with him for now, but sooner or later, she wanted to hear the rest of it.

"Almost done. Give me another ten minutes. Then you can study it while I read the dossier on Casano."

Nodding compliance, they settled down to plot the kidnapping of the century.

****

Johnny sat at the bar nursing a drink and dragging on a cigarette. He kept the bill of the baseball cap he wore pulled low over the cheap wig he'd bought this morning, its ugly strands hanging almost to his shoulders. He hated it, but it and the hat helped hide the bruises on his face. He looked like a bum, but then that had been his intention. So far, the disguise seemed to work. No one paid him any special attention.

"Johnny! Johnny, is that you?" a woman's high-pitched voice squealed from across the room.

He snapped his head around and saw a busty brunette in a skin tight sweater and mini skirt staring at him with a grin on her face. So much for a working disguise. Who the hell was she? The woman dashed across the bar to stand beside him, gushing on all eight cylinders.

"Johnny, I can't believe it. Gosh, I haven't seen you since I left the Topsy-Turvy. What have you been up to?"

Johnny winced. The bitch's voice carried into the next county.

"Fine," he answered as she slid onto the stool next to him. With the mention of the club, he placed her. Using the stage name, The Merry Widow, she stripped off widow's weeds to the music of some classical composer. He couldn't remember her real name.

"Buy me a drink?"

"Yeah, sure. What'll you have?"

"Bourbon, rocks," she told the bartender, then turned her gaze back to him. "You don't look like your usual self. You been in a fight?"

The bartender set the drink in front of her and said, "Can I get you anything else, Marlene?"

Of course, Marlene. She could talk a blue streak and always knew something about everybody. She'd left the club shortly before Vicelli had nailed him.

She shook her head at the bartender and took a noisy sip of her drink. "So, how's it been going, Johnny?"

"Look, couldja keep it down? I'm doing something special for Mr. Ponzetti."

"Oh, yeah. Sorry."

Maybe it was a good thing Marlene had shown up. Johnny needed information, and he needed it fast.

Ignoring the reference to a fight, he said, "The

boss is kind of concerned about Gabriella Vicelli and Frankie, know what I mean? This cousin looks a little odd and I'm tryin' to get the dope on him. You hear anything?"

"I know he's outta Detroit and that he and Frankie got wasted last night at The Topsy-Turvy. I talked to Raquel this morning, and she told me."

Johnny sipped his drink carefully. The stupid bitch was just as dense as Ralphie.

"Yeah, I heard that, too. Sal told me. Hear anything else? Mr. Ponzetti just wants to make sure Frankie ain't bein' two-timed or nothin'. Gabriella's been seen with a lot of different dates over the last few years."

"She wouldn't dare play Frankie for a chump. Besides, Frankie likes him. Hey, I know! Why don't you ask Bubbles? I hear she was all over the guy. Did you hear about Ginny? She's got the clap and you'll never guess who gave it to her. I heard it was..."

Johnny let Marlene ramble on. He had no interest in the private lives of strippers. He wanted to concentrate on Vicelli and her cousin.

After the fight and the booze last night, he'd awakened with one hell of a hangover, no plan, but still determined to bring the bitch to justice—mob justice.

He fingered his chin, and then winced when he touched some of the bruises. He'd like to settle the score with ole Cousin Leo, too.

Cousin Leo. It still didn't ring true. Something bothered him about the guy. He knew Gus Vicelli kept his younger brother and sisters out of the business, and this Leo looked too old to be Gus's nephew. As far as he knew, none of the Vicellis lived in Detroit.

He took another swig of bourbon and re-ran the scene at the club last night in his mind. On the surface, it had looked like a bunch of guys out having a good time. He remembered the laughter, and the clink of glasses being raised and slapped together. Still something about it bothered him.

Maybe it had to do with the fight and not the nightclub. It had been a cheap-ass fight and with the island years sapping his muscle tone, he'd been happy to get out when he had. Which reminded him—he needed another gun.

Johnny started to take another drink then stopped with the glass halfway to his lips. Shit! A gun! That was it! While he and Leo had rolled around on the floor, he remembered feeling the unmistakable shape of a gun stuck in the back of Leo's slacks.

If Leo had a gun, why didn't he use it? He could have shot him and the cops would call it self-defense. He'd be hailed as a hero by the Ponzetti family for taking out a man they thought to be an informer.

So, why didn't he use it?

Only one reason came to mind. He didn't want to call attention to either himself or Vicelli. If she worked for the Feds, then maybe he did, too.

Of course! That was it. That's what his mind had been fumbling for last night. As soon as the Feds knew about his escape, the first thing they'd do would be to send someone to protect the bitch. Oh, Christ! Why hadn't he thought of that before? He had to warn Gavino!

Once again, Johnny replayed the scenes from the club and this time, he pictured them with Leo as the law. Suddenly, the pieces of the puzzle fell into place with a loud click.

A lightning bolt shooting up his ass couldn't have stunned him more. A chill raced down his spine when he realized why the guy had looked familiar. He'd seen him once before from across another crowded bar in New York. The face was different, but the gestures the same—throwing back the head to laugh, the backslapping, even the way he saluted the toasts with his glass before slamming the contents down his throat.

The bar in New York came sharply into focus. He'd never forget it. Two months later, half the mobsters he'd been drinking with that day were in jail and all because of Cousin Leo. Only then his name had been Dante Borelli!

Chapter Thirteen

Johnny sat frozen with his glass halfway to his lips. His mind shifted into high gear. *Dante Borelli! Christ! This is it—my first class ticket back into the family.* Not only would he deliver Vicelli to Gavino, but the infamous Dante Borelli as well.

He, Johnny Scarano, would leap to the top of the mob hero list. Every Mafiosi in the world would know and, more importantly, fear his name. Hell, the New York bunch had a half a million dollar contract out on that son of a bitch Borelli.

His mind blazed away in fantasyland. He pictured Gavino slapping him on the back after selecting him to replace Frankie as the man to take over the Ponzetti empire. He visualized drinking the best champagne and booze offered in the finest restaurants in Chicago. Maître d's would know his name and bow when he walked in the door—without reservations, of course—to be seated at the best table.

And broads. He'd be seen with the most gorgeous and desirable bimbos in the city. And not just one. He'd have at least two or three on each arm. Every goon from every family in the whole fuckin' country would envy him. No more doing the bidding of others. No, sir! Now, he'd be the boss! He'd get respect!

Move over, John Gotti. I'm next.

"...and I hear an invite is next to impossible to

189

get. Boy, I'll bet it'll be the biggest wedding in years," Marlene said.

Johnny's attention swung back to the present. What the hell was she babbling about? Wedding? What wedding?

"Hey. Johnny, you listening?"

"Uh, sorry, Marlene. I was thinking about something Mr. Ponzetti asked me to do." He finally sipped from his glass and lowered it to the bar. "What were you saying about a wedding?"

"Casano's granddaughter is getting married on Saturday. Everybody is going to be there. I'd love to go, but no way can I swing an invitation. How about you?"

"Sorry. I don't rate that high."

Johnny paused to think. *But Gavino and Frankie do. And if Frankie goes, then his date would have to be...*

"I guess that means all the family heads will attend," he said.

"Probably. Casano would want a full house for the shindig even though rumor has it the bride is already preggers."

A wedding would be the one place all the dons could congregate without fear of reprisals. Female family members were not subjected to viewing mob justice. It would be a strictly social evening with eating, drinking, and dancing.

"Marlene, I gotta go," he said abruptly. "I have something important to do for the boss. Take care. I'll see you around."

"Yeah, sure, Johnny. I'll catch you later."

Johnny slid off the stool and hurried out of the bar to mingle with the crowd on the sidewalk. He should snuff the babbling bitch, but too many people in the bar had seen them and heard her call him by name. Shit. He hated loose ends. Saturday. That was only a few days away. Maybe it wouldn't matter if

Marlene lived or died.

Pausing to light another cigarette, Johnny stopped and peered up and down the street. Good. No one appeared to have followed him out of the bar. He took a deep drag of smoke, and then resumed his steps.

He had to figure out a way to crash the reception and to do that, he needed better information than Marlene could supply. He had to talk to someone in the know. He would be taking a terrible chance, but decided it was worth the risk to make contact with one of his family buddies.

****

Gabriella and Lane plotted for hours, living off of room service. The corridor resembled her kitchen with dirty crockery and silverware piled on trays stacked outside the door. They took a break to catch some sleep, and then began the process all over again.

"I still think we should snatch him between the church and the All-Italian Club." Gabriella liked that plan best, but Lane rejected it.

"No. I told you. That's when he and his bodyguards would be the most alert."

"Then I'll sweet talk him into a rendezvous just like I did the others."

Why did he insist on making this so difficult?

"Your old ways aren't going to work with him. He's too smart and has seen too much to be taken in by mascara and boobs." Lane ran his hand through his already mussed hair.

"All men are taken in by mascara and boobs. I have twenty-five of them on an island to prove it."

She slapped her notepad on the plate-strewn table. She wanted to throw one of the half-eaten croissants at him.

"Twenty-four," he corrected. "No. We have to be subtle with this one. He won't go anywhere without his bodyguards joined at the hip. And I still say you should stay in the background, keeping Frankie and Gavino off balance. Let me and the back-up take care of snatching him."

"And how do I explain my Cousin Leo disappearing with the Big Boss? How do I get out of the place?"

"I'll give you a sign before everything goes down."

"No fucking way. May I remind you that I've been at this for several years now? I know what I'm doing. He won't be nearly as suspicious of me approaching him. If you try it, those bodyguards will serve you up as hors d'oeuvres."

Lane inhaled deeply a couple of times while pouring another cup of tepid coffee for them both. Gabriella walked around the room, trying to relieve the tension. A little time in that hot tub and a few laps in the pool would help clear her mind, maybe give her a new perspective.

"Will you stop pacing?" he snapped. "You're distracting me. I need to think."

"Well, excuse me, but I'm wired. If I drink any more coffee, I'll crawl across the ceiling. I'm going down to the hot tub and pool."

He grabbed her arm as she turned. "No. We have to stay out of sight."

She jerked away. "Out of sight? As in inconspicuous? Have you seen the shit piled up outside the door? It practically screams, 'Hey, look. We're hiding out.' I don't see how an hour of exercise is going to hurt."

Lane rubbed his forehead. "Okay, you may be right, but let's do it after we have a plan."

Gabriella decided to humor him. At least he'd finally agreed to get the hell out of this room. She swore the walls inched in every hour. They'd get a plan—any plan—then perfect it later.

Her cell phone rang and she didn't need to see the caller ID to know who it was. Frankie called every few hours, but whether out of loneliness or suspicion, she couldn't be sure.

"God, not again," Lane groaned.

Shaking her head, she answered, "Hi, Frankie."

"Hey, babe. When you gonna be done?"

"Oh, honey, I'm getting the most scrumptious pedicure in the world." She had that damned brochure memorized. "First they scrub my legs and feet with raw sugar. Then they cover them with mud and hot towels. After that, they massage lotions all over from my knees down. It's wonderful," she concluded in a breathy voice.

"Yeah, but when are you gonna come home?" His voice had an edge of impatience.

"I don't know. When I'm done, I guess." To take the sting out of her words, she cajoled, "I'm getting a bikini wax just for you, sweetie, and I promise to wear my little black thong undies."

Lane shot her a look that clearly said he thought she was pushing it.

"I can't wait, baby, but why won't you tell me where you are? I wanna see you."

"Frankie, how can I pamper myself with a man around?"

"Are you sure you're not with some guy? It would make me real unhappy if you were."

"Now, Frankie, don't be that way. I don't like it when you're jealous—well, just a little jealous, maybe. Oops! I've got to go. It's almost time for my manicure. I can't talk on the phone until my nails are dry. Bye-bye, lovey. Can't wait for the wedding."

She hung up, exhausted from the conversation, then realized Lane was laughing.

"God Almighty! How stupid is Frankie anyway?"

"Pretty damned dumb, but smart enough to not buy everything I say. He suspects I'm with a man.

I'll have to do a lot of verbal dodging to keep him happy."

She tossed the phone onto the unmade bed.

"That's your job—keeping Frankie happy." Lane pulled a pad of paper towards him. "Now, let's try this plan again. Roger's going to need something good in the next few hours in order to set things up." He riffled through a file. "Casano is nobody's fool. He came up through the ranks and has more blood on his hands than Capone. He's also slippery as Gotti. The Feds thought they had him nailed on numerous occasions, but he wiggled free."

"I know. Even my father feared and admired him."

"God, this guy is something else," he said, reading the dossier yet again. "He once kidnapped the mayor of a suburb and refused to let him go until he agreed to a waste hauling contract with Casano's company. Talk about extortion!"

"The guy's lucky he didn't end up in little pieces," she replied, nibbling on a dried croissant.

"Casano also ordered the massacre at La Villa Mario. The son of a bitch killed two targets and five innocent bystanders."

Gabriella swallowed and sipped the coffee. She knew all about innocent bystanders.

"I remember when that happened. The remaining witnesses all said they hadn't seen a thing. The cops never nailed the triggermen," she said.

"What did your father have to say about Casano? Did he ever talk about him to you?" Lane closed the folder.

"God, no." She rose, pacing again. "Daddy never talked business in front of me. Anything I picked up, I heard accidentally. I didn't give the massacre any thought because I was only ten at the time, but in later years I heard him talking to some friends about

Casano and how ruthless he is. Daddy said something like, he'd kill his own mother if he thought it would improve his stature."

"And yet Gus Vicelli admired him."

She detected the censure in Lane's voice. It pissed her off. What did he know about her father? Only what he'd read in dossiers like the one on the table.

"Yeah, he admired him, but he also feared him. I guess we all have our fears."

"I guess we do. Come on, let's get back to work. How are we going to pull this off?"

Gabriella sat down and stared out the window. "Our job would be a whole lot easier if we could just eliminate the bodyguards for even a few minutes. Why can't we tranq 'em? He's got two and a driver. I can nail one, if our men can take care of the others."

"And how do we get close enough for that?"

"It'll be crowded in The All-Italian Club."

"And your plan is to whip out your dart gun, shoot, and then say, please follow me, Mr. Casano?"

"Don't be a sarcastic asshole. I was just thinking out loud. There must be some way to separate him from his entourage," she snapped back.

Lane sat back in his chair, a thoughtful expression on his face. His eyes focused on the wall opposite. She could almost see his mind chewing on an idea.

"What?" she asked.

"I think I know how we can separate them." He turned to look at her, a smile on his lips.

"How?"

"There's only one place the bodyguards won't follow him."

"Where?" She saw the gleam in his eyes and comprehension dawned. "Oh, my God. You mean..."

"Exactly. They won't follow him into the can. They'll go in first to make sure it's empty, but then they'll stand outside the door and see to it no one else enters. Where are the restrooms located?"

"Down a back hallway. If I remember right, there's a dumbwaiter for getting things up from the kitchen, the restrooms, and next to them, a lovely back staircase. The door leading to the alley is at the foot of the stairs." Excitement hummed, setting her heart beating faster. "We can eliminate the guards while he's inside and nab him when he comes out. Better yet, go in after him. I'll dart him and we can haul him downstairs into a waiting van."

Oh, this could work. Exhilaration eased some of the tension.

Lane tapped his pencil on the pad of paper. "Timing. How do we know when he'll have to go? And how do we cart him downstairs unseen. Suppose someone wants to use the restroom before we get him out? They'll see the guards and raise the alarm. We need to buy more time after we have him. He'll be a dead weight when the tranquilizer takes effect. And he has to remain quiet while we move him."

Gabriella listened to Lane's tapping pencil and thought before finally saying, "It would be a lot easier if those damned stairs weren't in the picture."

"I agree, but they are. Everyone will be up..." he stopped abruptly, stared into space then leaned back in his chair. "Gabby, where are the downstairs restrooms located?"

Of course! The answer sounded simple now. "Right below the upstairs bathrooms. The back door is less than thirty feet from the ladies' room, but how do we get him to go downstairs when upstairs is available?"

"We have to make upstairs *un*available."

"How?"

He shook his head and held up his hand. "Quiet. Let me think for a moment."

She sat back and watched as a smile, and then a

frown followed by another smile, flitted across his features.

"We have to arrange for the men's room upstairs to be out of order. Roger can have someone break in overnight and screw with the plumbing. When the owner calls a plumber, the agency intercepts the call and sends in our guys. It would be great if we could stake out the ladies room downstairs."

"We can," she said smugly. "The men's room upstairs is located next to the stairs, but downstairs, it's reversed. Any plumbing problems up can cause problems down."

"And before anyone can use the upstairs facilities, downstairs has to be fixed. That will give us the excuse to punch a hole in the wall between the two bathrooms downstairs."

"After all, the plumbers have to get to the pipes."

He grinned. "Absolutely."

"I hide in the downstairs ladies' room, get through the hole, nail him in the can, and you guys haul his ass out to the van."

She wanted to dance around the room. They had a plan!

The smile faded from Lane's face. "We still have to take care of the guards."

"We have one of our guys walk by and tranq 'em."

"Maybe, but we still have the problem of timing. We have to be in place before he decides he has to go. And we have no way of knowing that."

"Ipecac," Gabriella said.

"What?"

"Ipecac. A few drops in his drink and five minutes later he's puking his guts out. I'll tell Frankie I just have to say hello to Mr. Casano and, of course, I'll want to introduce him to my Cousin Leo. With you and Frankie as distractions, I'll slip it to him."

"Then we have a brief conversation of nice-to-meet-you, get into position, and wait?"

"It's so simple, it's scary."

"Too simple. I can think of a thousand things that could go wrong, most of which involve you," he said slowly, a frown on his face.

"What do you mean?"

"I don't like you administering the drops. If someone sees you, we're dead. I mean dead! And I don't like the idea of you being the one to lie in wait in the bathroom. I think you should slip away from Frankie and meet us in the van."

Gabriella tossed her pencil on the table and leapt to her feet, her hands fisted on her hips.

"No fuckin' way. If this is my last hurrah, then I'll be the one to shoot the goddamned dart!"

"Why do you swear like that? I wish I had a dollar for every time I've heard you cuss. I could retire tomorrow."

"Oh, go to hell! We'll both be retiring in a couple of days. What's it to you how much I swear?"

"I'm curious. I can guarantee you don't do it around mobsters. They don't like it when women use foul language. It makes them uneasy. If you swore like that around Frankie, he'd smack you." He folded his arms across his chest. "What's the purpose in swearing at me?"

"I learned a long time ago that swearing got me noticed. The dirtier, the better. All the girls in school thought I was scum anyway, so I decided to shock the ever-loving hell out of them. It worked. When I called Wendy Cooper-Smith a stupid cunt, they couldn't ignore me."

A furrow knitted his brow. "But it got you noticed for all the wrong reasons. They weren't going to think any better of you because you swore like a soldier."

"Those girls weren't going to think of me in any terms other than a mobster's daughter. I enjoyed shocking them. Maybe it's my perverse nature. I don't know. After a while, it became a habit—a way to let off steam."

"It's one I could do without. Suppose you try going cold turkey and stop swearing?"

"Why the hell would I do that?"

"To please me."

Gabriella snorted. "Drop dead."

"I'm going to charge you a dollar a word penalty every time you swear," Lane declared.

"Yeah? Well, kiss my ass and try to collect it." Lane burst into laughter, further angering her before she realized he'd deliberately tripped her temper. "Smart ass. Just for that, I suggest we go for that soak and swim. We can work out the details of the plan later."

"And where will we get bathing suits? I sure didn't pack one. How about you?"

"This is a fancy hotel. They have a gift shop complete with all the necessities, including swimsuits." She tugged on his arm. "Come on. You promised."

****

Gabriella lay on the bed, half listening, half dozing as Lane gave the details to Roger.

"I know, but it's the best we can do on such short notice... I'm not pleased with that either... Trying to slip someone in as a waiter will be a hard sell this time. They'll use staff they know. The best bet will be the plumbers... I agree with you wholeheartedly... We'll have a night to sleep on it and if you come up with any refinements, call me. The wedding is scheduled for two o'clock. The reception should start about five or so... Right, thanks."

"What did Roger have to say?" she asked.

"He thinks it's daring and dangerous, but possible. He also thinks you should stay out of the action."

Sighing, Gabriella flung her arm across her closed eyes. "Fuck him."

"You owe me a dollar."

"Fuck you."

"Two dollars, and that's not a bad idea."

The mattress sagged. She moved her arm and opened her eyes. Lane knelt over her, slipped her top off and unsnapped her bra. He was just as quick with her shorts and panties. Then, he pulled his T-shirt and boxers off and lowered his body between her legs. She knew she should smack him one, but the heat rose eliminating the thought.

She traced his lips only a couple of inches away with her fingernail.

"Oh, yeah? Then I demand a reduction in the penalty."

He opened his mouth and sucked her fingertip inside, his tongue gently licking. Her breath caught in her chest as the warmth increased. His erection nestled against the apex of her thighs and the pull of need throbbed deep within. Lassitude, heavy as her heartbeats, swept throughout her languid body.

Then the phone rang, destroying the mood.

"Aw, shit!" she snapped.

Lane laughed and rolled to the side. "Three bucks."

"Hello, Frankie."

"Hey, baby. What are you doing now?"

Lane propped himself up on his elbow and smiled. With a wicked grin and slow deliberation, his hand smoothed down her cheek to her throat, then on to her breast where he stroked the smooth flesh.

She sucked in a breath and glared at him.

"Hey, baby, you there?"

"Huh? Oh, yeah, I'm here, honey."

"So, what are you doin'?"

"I'm getting a massage."

Lane shook with silent laughter, then leaned over and took the erect nipple into his mouth where he laved and sucked.

Gabriella tried, but could not suppress a gasp.

"What was that? Are you all right?"

"Yeah, Frankie, the masseuse hit a knot. Oh, God, that feels good," she groaned.

Lane's hand slid down her belly to tangle in the curls below her navel. Slipping two fingers inside, he used his thumb to rub that pinpoint of sensitivity, all the while still using tongue and teeth on her breast.

"Oh! Oh, God!" She almost yelped.

"That must be one hell of a massage."

"You have no idea. I'm a mass of knots."

Lane increased the pressure from his thumb. Burning heat gushed through her body and along her nerves. She couldn't keep the whimpering moan in her throat from escaping. Unable to stop, her hips moved up and down as he stroked and pressed.

"Oh! Oh, damn! Look, Frankie, I've got to go. I'll talk to you later, okay?"

She hung up without bothering to say goodbye or hear if Frankie said anything else, then tossed the phone onto the floor.

"You son of a bitch," she panted.

Lane laughed and once again rolled over to wedge his body between her legs.

"Four dollars," he murmured sliding into her.

With a cry, Gabriella wrapped her arms around his neck and her legs around his waist, fastening her lips to his while they rocked and thrust.

****

"I still don't see why we can't have dinner in the restaurant," Gabriella grumbled. "I'm sick of room

201

service."

"Your bruise is still noticeable. How are you going to hide it at the wedding?"

"I'll get some make-up at the drugstore. That should hide most of it. If not, I'll think up something to tell people. I'll say someone accidentally hit me during aerobics. Don't worry."

"How's your head?"

She fingered her temple gingerly.

"The lump's still there, but my hair hides it. Doesn't hurt much at all."

"Good. Why don't you phone in our order while I take another look at this plan?"

She stared as he picked up the pad of paper. Ever since they'd made love this afternoon, he'd seemed preoccupied and distracted. The sex had been damned good and she'd lost another piece of her heart to him, but now his reticence had her wondering what he had up his sleeve. Did it have to do with the mission or with her personally?

Gabriella called in the order, and then joined him at the table. "You've been awfully quiet the past hour or so. What's on your mind?"

He shrugged. "This plan has too many holes. There are too many 'what-ifs' left uncovered."

"Yeah? Like what?"

"According to the dossier, he only drinks scotch and Italian wine. Will one of those cover the taste of ipecac?"

"It should. Maybe he'll be distracted by our conversation enough not to notice."

Lane put the pad down and shook his head. "I still don't like you putting the drops in."

"Well, someone has to do it, and I've done it before. I'm good at palming things. I'll slip it in while you're shaking hands. Everybody's eyes will be on you, not me," she replied impatiently. "I'll leave a few minutes later. Don't be such a worry wart."

"How are you going to get out of the room without Frankie noticing?"

"I'll lead him over to the corner furthest from the main stairway. I'll tell him I have to use the restroom, then circle around and take the front stairs. It'll be crowded. I shouldn't have any problem losing him."

"When you do, I want you to walk right out the front door, around the corner, and into the van. Things will get fast and furious real soon."

"I can handle it and have no intention of letting anyone else get the satisfaction of finishing off my career, is that clear?"

"It's clear, but it's not going to happen. The decision's been made. You'll be in the van. We'll take out the guards, nab Casano, and meet you in the alley."

"I won't do it, damn you! You won't have time to argue once I'm there," she snarled at him.

"Dammit! Why can't you for once in your life obey orders? Why does it always have to be your way?"

"I've been the one setting up and carrying out the hits since the beginning. I know what I'm doing and you assholes behind desks keep thinking you can second-guess me. I'm sick of it."

Her voice had risen and if this continued much longer she would explode like a bomb. How dare he and Roger decide to cut her out!

"You've been a pain in my ass for years!" he almost shouted. "For four years, I've been trying to keep you from sticking your head in a noose and you resist every order I ever gave. Dammit! I have three other operatives to control, but spend ninety percent of my time dealing and arguing with you!"

It took a second for her to digest his words. Then the implication of what he said hit home. The fuse burned fast, hit the primer, and detonated the bomb.

Chapter Fourteen

Lane wanted to bite his tongue. Dammit! He'd lost his temper and let information slip—again. Roger would hang him by his balls. He watched several expressions cross her face, then waited for the explosion.

Her eyes narrowed and she sucked in a deep breath.

"Control? *You're* my controller? You're the one who's been reading my reports for the last four years? You? And you say I'm a pain in the ass!"

She didn't quite shout, but he saw the fury in her eyes. He couldn't blame her. It must be embarrassing to meet the faceless person she'd sworn at and defiled with nasty names for years.

"Yes, I'm your controller and before you have a fit, remember the main goal is secrecy."

"Well, you sure as hell could have told me once you got here."

"You didn't need to know. It was supposed to be a quick trip into town, get you to safety, and then leave. I never expected to...to have the problems you've presented."

He'd almost let slip that he'd fallen for her. What the hell kind of an agent was he? Couldn't he keep any secrets anymore? Maybe fieldwork was no longer his milieu.

"*I've* presented problems? Would you like to know how much a pain in the ass you've been? I was all set to take out Gino Rosetti and you refused to give me back-up."

"That's because Rosetti wasn't the person we wanted you to eliminate. We didn't have anyone ready to infiltrate the Casano family at that level yet," Lane explained as patiently as possible.

"Then, all you did was criticize my report on the takedown of Duke Anseletti. It was a brilliant plan and worked perfectly."

She fisted her hands on her hips and glared at him. Two bright patches of red claimed her cheeks.

"Once again, you hit the wrong person."

"You gave me arguments on every thug I wanted to send away. I'm the one on the hot seat. I know the situations and should tell *you* who's next. Where do you and Roger get off telling me my business?"

"I told you, Roger and I have an overview of the entire project you don't. Face it. Your concern is revenge against the Ponzetti family. Your one-track mind gives you tunnel vision. You're no longer objective. I advised Roger to pull you from the project last year, but he refused."

Gabriella's lips curved in a smile that didn't reach her eyes. "Good for Roger. At least he knows my worth. You, on the other hand, are a first class asshole." Her smile broadened into a grin, and then she laughed.

"What's so funny?"

The laughter increased. "You! You're Tinkerbell!"

Lane closed his eyes. The heat of embarrassment flooded his face. Shit. "It wasn't my choice. Quit laughing. You're Medusa—remember?"

"Why Tinkerbell?" she asked, bringing the laughter down to a chuckle.

"Originally, everyone had code names from 'Peter Pan'. When I took over, I wanted to change it, but Roger said no, my other contacts were used to it."

"How does 'Medusa' figure in?"

"You were such a bitch on wheels, we felt it only logical. Captain Hook seemed too tame."

"Well, keep this in mind. I refuse to be pushed into the background on this job. I'm in and you'd better get used to it."

He knew when to quit. He'd tackle it later, maybe have one of the back-ups grab, gag, and then toss her into the van. At least, laughter had replaced the anger. God, this woman was like a Molotov Cocktail with a short-burning fuse. He never knew what to expect.

And is that necessarily a bad thing?

Her cell phone rang and she made a face. "Oh, God, not again."

"He's in love."

"He's a worse pain in the ass than you." She answered in a sugar sweet voice. "Hello-o-o, Frankie, how's my big, strong honey?... Of course I miss you... The massage? Oh, it was terrific... Well, naturally I made noise. It hurt."

Lane snorted, and then whispered, "Didn't sound like pain to me."

She glared and waved him into silence. "First the masseuse used this lumpy, wooden roller on all my tight spots. Then she pounded me with her hands, and after that she kneaded my muscles like bread dough. It felt wonderful. I was limp by the time she finished."

"I knew you'd admit it sooner or later," Lane murmured. "I felt pretty good myself."

This time, the look she shot him clearly said to shut up or else. After dinner, he'd like to explore "or else" further.

"You should try it sometime, Frankie. It really relieves the stress... What?... I'm about to have dinner. I'm allowed a big blowout tonight. I get to eat two ounces of steak, three carrots, three asparagus spears, and a salad. And for dessert, I'm having mixed berries with fake whipped cream... What do you mean 'is that all'? It's a feast! And guess what, I've lost those two pounds and three more besides."

Lane chuckled. God, she was good. She had to be if Frankie bought this crap. He wished he had a tape recorder. She frowned and shook her fist.

"Oh no, sweetie, I won't have time to go back to my place... Because tomorrow morning I have water aerobics followed by a mud bath and a facial. I've also scheduled an aromatherapy session... Aromatherapy. It's super. I get to bathe in scented water surrounded by aromatic candles to heighten my senses. It relaxes my inner physical self and soothes my soul—or something like that... But honey, then I have a hair appointment."

She rolled her eyes in impatient exasperation.

"Oh, don't be mad. You want me to look gorgeous, don't you... No, I can't. After I'm done, I have to go pick Leo up at the airport... Don't be that way, Frankie. I have my dress with me. We'll meet you at the church. Is that all right?"

Raising his finger into the air, Lane gave her a hurry up signal when a knock sounded on the door. She nodded. He opened it, signed the tab, and pushed the cart into the room.

"Oh, baby, I have to go. Dinner's here... I'm eating in my room tonight. I'm exhausted... I can't wait to see you either... I love you, too. I'll dream of you all night. I promise. Nighty-night, Frankie."

Gabriella hung up and dropped the phone on the bed.

"Damn, that's tiring. I'll be glad when this is over. I won't have to deal with Bozo the Hood any more."

Lane laughed and pulled two chairs up to the

table. He eyed the bottle of wine, reaching for the corkscrew.

"Trying to get me drunk so you can take advantage of me?" he asked. The cork left the bottle with a little pop.

"Naturally," she replied, sitting down and removing the lid from her steak. "And I'm still mad at you, Tink. You could have told me the truth."

"I suggest we put that particular argument aside. We have other things to think about." He poured them each a glass, then sat down and proposed a toast. "To the mission. May it go smoothly."

"To us. May we live long lives," she countered.

"Hear, hear. There are still a hundred things that can go wrong, but I learned a long time ago not to dwell on the negative."

He cut into his steak while she sipped her wine. They ate in silence for a few minutes, but the furrow on her brow suggested she had something on her mind.

"Can I ask you a question?" she said.

"Sure. What do you want to know?"

"I know about Dante Borelli and Lane Hamilton in the early years. What happened after you joined the Army?"

"I loved computers and math. The Army gave me an aptitude test. I did well and after basic was sent to computer training. Before I knew it, I was an analyst dealing with covert missions in Central America and the Caribbean. I should have joined the Navy. At least I would have seen the world. I never left Ft. Bliss."

Gabriella swallowed. "Where's Ft. Bliss?"

"Ft. Bliss is outside El Paso, Texas. You try being young and finding something to do in El Paso on Saturday nights. Doesn't happen. The only place I could get a beer was on base at the Enlisted Men's

Club. Ft. Bliss was four years of social suicide. Luckily, I loved my job and was good at it."

"So, you were only in for four years?"

"Army life wasn't my style. After discharge, I used my Army pay for college. I did a double major in Criminal Psychology and Computer Science at USC. I studied like crazy and graduated in three years."

"I'm impressed," she said, forking salad into her mouth.

It reminded him to eat. Lane cut into his steak again and wolfed down a third of it. He had to hand it to this hotel. The food was spectacular. His steak was tender and the seasonings perfect.

Gabriella nibbled on a French fry and cut more filet. "The newspaper accounts of Dante Borelli were thrilling. I kept thinking how I could do the same and avenge Daddy's and Jack's murders. The cops knew who'd done it, but couldn't make any charges stick."

"Those were strange, dark years. I've often wondered what would have happened if my bosses had let me stay. I think they were afraid I was getting too comfortable in my role."

She stopped eating and stared at him with wide eyes.

"You mean they were afraid you'd turn? That you'd become a family member?"

He shrugged and took the last bite of meat. Had they? "Maybe. I don't know."

Gabriella finished her salad and steak before working on the fries. Lane poured them another glass of wine.

"I take it the Witness Protection Program came next."

He finished his meal and sat back. "Yes. I stayed in it for a whole year before contacting Roger to get me the hell out of Dodge."

She laughed. "Bored, huh? Where were you and what did you do?"

"I was in Dodge—Dodge City, Kansas, and I sold used cars by day and did computer analysis for Roger by night." She shot him an amused expression. "It's the truth. My boss thought I was starting my life over from a personal family tragedy."

"Good pun. Was he a nice guy or an asshole?"

"Asshole is swearing. You owe me a dollar."

She made a face and refreshed their glasses with the last of the wine. "So, you joined the Alpha-Omega team and ended up as my controller?"

"Roger decided I was the one to handle you."

Lane jumped as Gabriella's foot slid up his leg to press lightly on his crotch, her toes wiggling. She gave him a lazy smile with full sexual promise in her dark, liquid eyes.

"Still think you can handle me, Mr. Controller?" she murmured, using her character voice.

He grabbed her ankle and forced her foot back an inch.

"I can handle Medusa with no problem. It's Gabriella Vicelli who gives me trouble."

She laughed and inched the chair closer until her foot made contact again.

"Oh, yeah? How?"

Lane dropped her ankle and stood. "I'll tell you later," he laughed.

Her gaze slid down his body, stopping just below his waistline. "Nice flagpole," she murmured with an arch in her right eyebrow.

"Let's run the flag up and see if you salute."

He pulled her out of the seat and into his arms where he planted a kiss on her lips. Moving quickly, he peeled her shorts and panties down her legs, then did the same with his clothing.

Hard as a brick, Lane sat down and hauled her

into his lap, his throbbing shaft impaling her in one swift thrust.

Gabriella fastened her lips on his. While their tongues clashed, she rode for a few strokes, and then abruptly stopped.

A moan formed in the back of his throat and he tore his mouth from hers.

"Don't stop!"

She laughed softly, resumed the motion, and then stopped again. She was killing him. Her warm, wet heat had sent his blood pounding through his veins, and he was ready to explode.

"Gabby," he growled in a barely audible voice.

"What's the matter, Tinkerbell? Can't take any more?"

No, he couldn't. "Damn you, Medusa!"

He slid his thumb up and down at their joining. With a cry, she moved and rode him like a rodeo queen as he thrust.

His passion burned with an ever-increasing intensity until the world went white-hot. Dimly, he heard her cries of "yes, yes" as he pumped his release a second after she climaxed.

Collapsing back in the chair, he waited for the world to spin again. She laid her forehead on his chest.

After a few seconds, Gabriella raised her head and gave him a deep kiss.

"Shall we stay seated? Do you want another dessert?" she murmured. Her eyes had that languid, satiated look.

He chuckled and kissed her back. "In a while. I'll be able to eat more later."

She laughed and rose. Dressed again, Gabriella wound her arms around his neck and pressed close, her hips rubbing against him, a look of pure devilment on her face.

He stroked her back and nibbled lightly on her

neck. It would be so easy to toss her on the bed, strip her naked again, and have that dessert. He was ready for round two.

God, she smelled good. He inhaled the scents of floral from her skin and citrus from her hair. Then, his eyes fell on the open files. The sight brought him back to earth. Damn. He sighed and pushed her away.

"Behave yourself. We have work to do," he replied steering her toward the work table. "I want to go over this again and plug as many holes as possible."

"What happened to not dwelling on things and all those negative vibes?"

"Never mind," he said rolling the dining cart into the hallway. "Let's just do it."

"We already have," she murmured.

He ignored her comment and pulled out a chair. "Have a seat."

She sat down and gave him a look indicating she would rather explore other avenues. Later, he told himself.

****

Johnny hunched his shoulders and lowered his head to stare at the tabletop in yet another dingy bar as a Muzio henchman walked past. He couldn't recall the guy's name, but remembered he helped take out Vittorio Gianelli a few years before.

Johnny held his breath until the man left. The last thing he needed was to run into a rival family member. This joint used to be a Ponzetti hangout. So far, he hadn't seen even a shadow of a Ponzetti.

Tossing a couple of bucks onto the table, he downed the last few drops of his drink and casually sauntered out. Dammit. That had been the third bar he'd checked out since leaving Marlene. No old friends had shown at any of them.

Johnny walked down the sidewalk, his step

slower and less buoyant than earlier. What if he couldn't make contact? How would he crash the reception? He had no idea when or where the wedding would take place. He assumed the party would be at the All-Italian Club. It had one front entrance, one in back by the alley, and several hidden doors in case of a sudden need for escape.

He sidestepped a bag lady with her shopping cart, then crossed the street and stopped to look in a store window. His eyes scanned the busy sidewalk in the reflection. All seemed normal—no one mimicking his actions or slinking in and out of doorways. Good. He wasn't being followed.

Johnny cut down a side street and took a series of alleys before once again coming out onto his street of choice. He quickened his pace and wondered which dive to hit next. The Paradise? No, it was too far away. He'd save it for last if he didn't find someone soon.

Maybe The Corner Bar would yield something, but when he arrived, he reversed his steps. The presence of guys holding hands told him the place had changed. No way would he find information here. He turned away, disgusted.

Shit. What's the world coming to?

Johnny stopped on the corner waiting for the light to change. Depression settled on his shoulders like a heavy winter coat. Jesus, there had to be a place where he could find some of the old gang.

Then he remembered Eddie's. It was a small out-of-the-way dump about six blocks away. Hookers liked it because of the fleabag hotel located across the street, and it was dark enough inside for him not to worry about being recognized.

He walked rapidly through the descending dusk. *This better work. I'm running out of bars and time.*

Turning the corner, he puffed a sigh of relief. Eddie's still stood, and he saw no hanging plants in the windows. In fact, the windows had so much dirt and nicotine residue coating them it was hard to see anything. That suited him just fine.

"Hey, baby. Want a little action?" a woman in a tight Spandex miniskirt asked.

Yeah, he'd love some, but had bigger fish to fry at the moment. "Get lost."

"Not your type? How about me?" another of the group of four said.

"Ten bucks and I'll give great head," a third proposed, reaching for him.

Damned whores. They're like cops. When you really need one, they're never around. When you have other business on your mind, they crawl out of the fucking woodwork.

Johnny jerked his arm away, snarling, "Beat it, bitch."

"I'm willing if that's what you want, honey," the last one replied, a smile on her crimson lips.

He grabbed her crotch and squeezed until she yelped in pain. "Keep it warm for me, baby, and I'll consider it when I'm done with business."

He released her, and pawing his way past the hookers, entered the tavern. He stood in the doorway a few seconds waiting for his eyes to adjust, then wandered up to the bar and ordered a whiskey. The bartender poured it never once looking up to see who had asked.

Good. Either the guy's too lazy to care or knows enough not to be curious.

He took his drink to a table in the back corner and sat down to wait. He sniffed the contents cautiously. The shit smelled sour and sharp. Taking a tiny sip, he gagged. The whiskey sucked. It was cheap and burned all the way down.

He'd give Eddie's a few minutes and if no one showed, he'd take a hike. Two men entered and sat at a table across from the bar. Johnny had never seen either before. A third guy followed.

Johnny's heart damned near stopped and he swallowed hard. It was Stefano "The Mangler" Vicente, a debt collector for the loan sharking end of the Ponzetti family. Vicious and unafraid, he was a complete psychopath. Even Johnny had kept his distance.

The Mangler poured two glasses of the rotgut down his throat and chatted with the bartender. Vicente certainly wasn't his first choice, but he needed information.

Johnny rose from his chair to approach Vicente when another customer strolled in. He sat down again quickly. This was better. The newcomer was Nick Accardi, one of the Ponzetti loan sharks. Accardi sidled up to Vicente. The bartender slapped a beer down in front of Nick, and then found something to do at the other end of the bar. The beer disappeared in three gulps. The two men spoke in whispers and a few minutes later The Mangler left.

Accardi must have someone not paying up. Even a blind man could see instructions had just been given to extract the debt owed.

The bartender returned and poured Accardi another beer. Making a decision, Johnny left his table and took the stool vacated by Vicente. Nick gave him a cold stare. Then recognition dawned.

"*Johnny?*"

"Hello, Nick. Long time, no see. How's it been goin'?"

"Jesus, Johnny, where the hell have you been? Rumor had it you rolled to the Feds."

"Naw. I'd never do that. Let's just say I've been doing a bit of undercover work for Mr. Ponzetti through Benny. It's very hush-hush."

Johnny felt safe saying this. Nick didn't have much contact with Gavino, Frankie or any of the inner circle.

"Yeah? What kind of undercover work?" Nick chugged his beer and slid a sidelong glance at Johnny. "What's with the long hair and beard? You look like a bum."

"Part of the disguise. I ain't been in Chicago."

The bartender came over and gave Nick a refill. Johnny also ordered a beer, taking a cautious sip. Better than the whiskey.

"Where you been?"

"Can't say, but I gotta make a report to the boss and Benny later. What you been up to?"

"Not much. Same old, same old. Things have been slow lately. I've still got my customers though."

Johnny listened and wondered how to pry information out of Nick as he talked about business. His story had to sound convincing. Nick was not Ralphie or Marlene.

"I hear Mr. Casano's granddaughter is getting married."

"Yeah. She's knocked up and the old man is pissed as hell, but he's footin' the bill for the whole shebang. I don't envy the groom, that's for sure." Nick drained his glass, and then lit a cigarette. The bartender set another beer in front of the loan shark. "You goin'?"

"I doubt it. When is it?"

"Tomorrow afternoon at St. Jerome's. Don't know the time."

"Shit. I'm tied up 'til late afternoon. I might make the reception as a gesture of respect though. It's at the All-Italian Club, I take it." Johnny gulped half his beer in excitement. The church was just around the corner from the Club.

"You'll have to ask someone else. I ain't invited."

Damn, he needed to know now. Either Nick was telling the truth or suspicious as hell. Change the subject. Take another tack.

"I hear Gabriella Vicelli is all but engaged to

Frankie."

"So they say. Her cousin Leo is in town from Detroit. I heard the cuz, Frankie, and some of the guys had a helluva time at The Topsy-Turvy a couple of nights ago," Nick said.

Johnny shifted on the barstool. He needed to talk to Bubbles. She'd have details on both the wedding and the reception. Knowing her, the bitch had probably finagled an invitation.

"The Topsy-Turvy, huh? I miss that place. Is Bubbles still there?"

Nick inhaled a long drag on his cigarette, blew out a stream of smoke, and crushed the butt into the ashtray.

"Hell, yeah. She's the headliner. I talked to Sal yesterday and she's all excited about the wedding. She's going with him. Can't you just see that old bastard with Bubbles on his arm? Shit, if he tries to fuck her she'll end up killing him."

"Yeah, that broad is enough to stop any man's heart." Looking around, Johnny dropped his voice and leaned closer.

"Nick, I need a favor."

"Yeah? What?" Nick's voice had a suspicious quality to it. He gazed at Johnny with narrowed eyes.

"I need to talk to Bubbles."

"So? Go to the club."

"I can't. The club is too public. I'm still undercover, but I need to talk to her tonight. Could you arrange a meeting, maybe between shows? Before I make my report, I have to ask her something."

Nick lit another cigarette and finished his beer before answering. Johnny waited, his heart racing. He wondered if his request sounded fishy.

"Don't need me for that. Just call the club and leave a message for her to meet you. Promise her money and she'll show." Nick slid off his stool. "Gotta go to the can. I'll be back in a minute."

Johnny watched Nick say something to the bartender, and then disappear toward the restrooms at the back of the room. The bartender set another glass in front of Johnny.

"Compliments of your friend. He said you might need to make a private call. The office is down the hallway. First door on your left."

Johnny eyed the man who turned away to rearrange the bottles on the shelf behind the bar.

"Yeah. Thanks."

He slid from his stool, made his way to the office where he closed the door, picked up the phone, and dialed. It rang six times before anyone answered.

"Topsy-Turvy Club."

"I need to speak with Bubbles. She there?"

"You gotta be kidding. Bubbles doesn't get here until right before show time," the man snorted.

"When she comes in, give her a message."

Johnny hung up a minute later, rejoining Nick who had returned, and resumed drinking.

"You get a hold of her?" Nick asked.

"Yeah. I left her a message to meet me out back between shows. Said I was a fan and would make it worth her while."

"That oughta do it," Accardi laughed. "That broad must make a bundle out of quickies. Tell her I said hi and hope to see her soon."

Johnny relaxed. Success. He'd get the info he needed and still have time to make a plan.

He checked his watch. "Hey, I've got to get goin'." He clapped Nick on the shoulder. "Good talkin' to you and you haven't seen me, right?"

"Johnny who?" Nick grinned and signaled the bartender for a refill.

Johnny walked out of Eddie's and past two of the four still hustling hookers, the bounce back in his step.

****

Gabriella pushed the hair off her face and massaged her scalp. She and Lane had continuously gone over the plan until she was ready to scream.

"Now, let's look at how you're going to get the drug into his drink again."

"Aw, shit! How many ways can I do it? Pack it up. I'm tired and had enough," she snapped. "It's as good as it's going to get."

Lane shrugged, but laid the pad aside.

"Okay, I guess we've covered as much as possible tonight. We'll go over the whole thing from top to bottom in the morning, and then go shopping. We both need dressy clothes."

Not even the thought of shopping perked her up. She stalked into the bathroom, slammed the door, then washed her face and brushed her teeth. Finished, she came out and he took his turn.

Gabriella didn't bother with a nightgown. Shedding her clothes, she slid beneath the covers. Lane turned out the lights and crawled in next to her.

She lay immobile for a few moments, then turned to him and encircled his neck with her arms. His hands moved slowly up and down her body. His fingers sent shivers dancing up her spine, and a shot of scorching heat kindled the embers of desire into flames.

"Lane," she whispered.

Together they skyrocketed into the night.

****

Johnny paced in the alley behind The Topsy-Turvy waiting for Bubbles to show.

He couldn't keep his sense of excitement from rising. In a few minutes, he'd have all the details he needed. He still had to buy a gun, but that wouldn't be too hard. Then tomorrow, he'd sneak into the reception, grab both Borelli and Vicelli, and present them to everyone as Feds.

He could see the surprise on Gavino's face, but the gratitude of Caesar Casano would be priceless. Then, the shit would really hit the fan.

He would expose the Feds as kidnappers and force the release of the men on the island. He'd let Casano have the pleasure of torturing and dispatching Borelli, but the bitch was his. He deserved the right to send her to hell. He'd start by ramming his dick in every available hole. Then he'd use cigarettes or a knife on her flawless face.

He laughed out loud and pounded his fists on his thighs. Yeah, he could hear her screams now. But he'd ignore her pleas and work his way to those tits she loved to flaunt in everyone's face. He didn't have a plan for her actual demise, but by the time he finished, Miss Gabriella Vicelli would beg for death.

He glanced at the back door of the club, and then at his watch for the hundredth time. Where the hell was Bubbles? The stupid bimbo was ten minutes late. Had she gotten the message? Maybe he should risk going inside to make contact.

Footsteps sounded behind him. Before he could react, someone stuck a gun in his back.

"Welcome home, Johnny," the voice growled in his ear.

"Let's go, nice and quiet like," the other man said.

His heart slammed into his chest and fear clawed at his insides.

"What the...Carmine...Joey, is that you?"

"The boss would like to have a little chat."

"How—how did you...?"

"Know where to find you?" Carmine finished with a laugh. "You figure it out, asshole."

Had Bubbles talked? No, impossible. He hadn't left his name, just the promise of a quick fifty bucks.

Nick! He turned him in to the family. Dammit! Where had he fucked up? He thought his story sounded convincing.

He swallowed what little spit he had left in his mouth and tried to bluster his way out.

"Hey, guys. You got it all wrong. I got valuable information for the boss. I know where all the guys who disappeared are being held. I know who's doing it."

Joey ground the gun into his ribs causing Johnny to grunt with pain. A car drove up next to them.

"Inside, Johnny. We're gonna take a little ride."

They shoved him into the backseat beside a third man he didn't recognize, then Carmine joined the driver and they sped away into the darkness.

Chapter Fifteen

Gabriella lay staring at the spinning ceiling fan barely discernable in the faint pre-dawn light. Exhausted from plotting and making love, she'd fallen asleep immediately only to awaken hours later.

Her mind teemed with disjointed images of Jack, her father, and Lane. The pictures jumbled together in the past, present, and future. She still felt vaguely disloyal to Jack's memory, and wondered what her father would think of her sleeping with the enemy.

Five years. Five years, and I've changed so much.

She had known and loved Jack for less than a fifth of that time. But the brevity of their relationship had not diminished the memory of its intensity.

She'd been mellower then, less cynical, less demanding, less angry and profane. Jack, God bless him, had made her laugh, using humor and gut-wrenching, toe curling kisses to soothe her temper.

By now, she and Jack should have been living the good life in a Dallas suburb with a four bedroom house and a couple of kids, doing mundane, boring things like mowing the lawn or grocery shopping.

Instead, she worked for the Feds.

Gabriella understood and accepted that she was a tool of the FBI. Roger used her just as she used the agency to promote her own ends. She'd become judge and jury, sentencing men to prison in the name of vengeance. And all of it was illegal as hell. It bothered her that Jack, with his deep sense of right and wrong, would disapprove.

Blinking away the sudden tears, Gabriella pushed her reminiscences into the back of her mind and concentrated on the business of abduction.

In her imagination, she saw how the kidnapping would go down. She and Lane had worked and refined the plot until it resembled a sure thing. If the backup could get into the club tonight and carry out phase one, then the rest would follow.

The usual attack of excitement and nerves before a hit had not yet arrived. It would—it always did. In the beginning, the clenching gut and pounding heart had frightened her, but she soon recognized it as the thrill of the chase and the satisfaction of putting away another scumbag like Scarano or Alberti.

Turning her head, she looked at the dim outline of Lane's body. He faced away from her and she resisted the urge to stroke the smooth muscles of his back. She returned to watching the fan and swallowed, unable to ignore her personal life.

She loved him or at least thought she did. Her fantasy love for Dante Borelli kept intruding on her feelings for Lane. And even though she knew the two men were one and the same, she viewed them separately.

And then there was her stubborn refusal to let go of Jack. She still clung to him like a security blanket, afraid if she released his soul, hers would die along with the thirst for revenge.

She rolled onto her side, staring at Lane's back, then slipped an arm around his waist and closed her eyes, willing her mind to cease this introspection. It confused her, and she didn't need confusion today. She needed rest.

Please, just a little more sleep and one last successful mission.

****

Lane watched the faint gray fingers of dawn slice through a crack in the draperies. His sleep had existed of catnaps. He reviewed the plan yet another time. Too many holes, too many flaws, and concocted much too fast. Then he wondered if their backup had succeeded in creating the plumbing problem.

Not your department. Concentrate on the take down.

They'd have precious little time to hustle a sick and vomiting Caesar Casano out the back door and into the van. Suppose they weren't able to eliminate the guards? What if Casano managed to cry out for help? What if someone else felt the call of nature and came down the stairs?

Stop it. Stop thinking about what can go wrong.

Roger would have only the best in position and, while getting Casano to the van was his problem, the escape and preliminaries would be his boss's.

Roger is meticulous and spends hours planning even the smallest detail.

Gabriella rolled over and he felt the warm touch of her protective arm slip around his waist. Whether she liked it or not, she would be in the van. He'd have a fight on his hands, but refused to do it any other way. He wanted her out of the line of fire if things went wrong.

And after the mission? What then?

If Scarano was still in the picture, how long would they have to remain in hiding? Suppose Johnny avoided both the Feds and the mob? What if he went straight to the media? A mobster with the court system on his side? The irony was too ridiculous to contemplate. Would he be able to return to D. C. and take up his old job or would he be forced back into the Witness Protection Program?

And what about Gabby? After this, her usefulness to Alpha-Omega would be over, at least in the field. He tried to imagine her in the role of controller and almost laughed out loud. It would serve her right if she got stuck in the position *he'd* had to endure for the past four years.

Going their separate ways in the program was out of the question. He had no intention of walking off into the sunset without her by his side. He loved her, and for once in his life, he wanted to be a selfish bastard.

Gabriella moved slightly and he felt the searing heat of her body close to his. Desire fanned into little tendrils of flame. He could tell from her breathing, she was not asleep.

Lane turned and looked into her eyes. Her hand stroked his cheek. He pulled her into his arms.

"Gabby," he murmured, feathering kisses along her forehead and face.

"I know," she whispered. "Make love to me, Lane."

His lips found hers and his hands caressed her back and shoulders, the skin slipping past his fingers like hot silk. She eased her leg over his hips and rose above him, her open mouth sliding down to his throat to his chest.

Gabriella's tongue found his nipples and her teeth nibbled while her hands stroked the hard muscles of his abdomen. Moving further down, she kissed every inch of his belly and explored his navel with thoroughness.

By the time she reached his inner thighs, nipping with teeth, and then soothing with tongue, he couldn't control the groan forming in his throat. It escaped while his heart pounded in his ears. His insides quaked.

Running her hands over his thighs, she looked up at him, grinning wickedly. Gabriella leaned over and took his throbbing shaft into her warm, velvet mouth.

Lane fisted his hands in her hair and pumped his hips. Her tongue licked and swirled, and her teeth scraped ever so carefully up and down.

Flames—hot, searing and almost uncontrollable—shot from his belly to every extremity. His groans turned to gasps as his lungs tried to keep pace with his heart, now hammering at lethal speed. Muscles clenched, then shook when Gabriella increased her actions. He neared self-destruction. A spring coiled tighter and tighter in his gut. In a few moments, he would reach overload.

"Gabby! I can't hold on any longer."

She released him, and with that wicked smile still in place, straddled his hips taking him deep in one powerful move. Lane shuddered and trembled. He tried to speak, to say something of love, but all he articulated were hoarse groans and incoherent words.

All at once, it didn't matter. She moved up and down, slowly at first, then faster and faster until he no longer thought, only reacted. He moved with her, reaching for that moment when the spring would snap.

They arrived together in an explosion of fire and sweet release. Crying out her name, he jammed her hips down hard on his and arched his back. Throbbing and pumping, he dimly heard her cries of ecstasy.

The freefall back to earth returned him to reality. Gabriella rolled over and lay next to him, panting.

"Gabby," he whispered.

"Shh," she hushed. "Don't talk. Not yet. Later."

She rested her head on his shoulder and kissed his neck. Lane turned his gaze upwards and watched the ceiling fan slowly twirl.

****

The sour taste of fear clogged Johnny's throat and coated the inside of his mouth. He remained silent. Talking to Joey and Carmine was useless. They were only doing their jobs. In a few minutes he'd see Gavino Ponzetti. That would be the time to tell everything.

He tried to control his shaking. The next hour would determine if he lived or died, and Johnny had every intention of living.

He assumed they would take him to the Ponzetti warehouse on Turner Street. That's where Gavino conducted all unofficial family business. Johnny had taken part in a lot of beatings and killings. He knew what to expect.

The city flashed past the dark-tinted car windows. He used the time to perfect his story from the time he first met Vicelli, to his abduction, and finally to Dante Borelli. He'd forget to mention the part about being drugged on the island and giving up family secrets. The boss didn't need to know that. He bet Gavino would let him live.

The silence grated on his nerves. That was the whole idea. He'd played the game in the past and been in Joey and Carmine's seats. Let the victim sweat and beg. He'd never realized how well it worked. Sweat poured from him like a race horse after the Kentucky Derby, and he hoped he didn't shit his pants. Being on the receiving end sucked hind tit.

He stared straight ahead as the car snaked through the streets and alleys, his heart pounding like a jackhammer. Johnny licked his dry lips, and then swallowed. He knew Joey felt him shaking. The gun in his ribs added to his fear. Joey loved to grind it into his victims and watch their faces contort in pain.

Finally, they pulled up to the back door of the

Ponzetti warehouse where Carmine, Joey, and the third man escorted him inside. The driver remained with the car.

They prodded him with the guns and wove their way between boxes of merchandise, some legal, some not, Johnny guessed. The dim lights allowed him to see the place was damned near full. A shipment had either just come in or was about to go out. Business must be good. A glance at the catwalk above showed a couple of guards with assault weapons pacing the narrow confines. He knew more men hid in the shadows, especially toward the back and the hidden hallway.

They emerged from the maze of containers into a large space in front of several doors. Johnny knew the one on the left was the warehouse manager's office. The one in the middle held files, the kind every legit business possessed.

That left the windowless third room on the right. They'd take him there. The family referred to it as the interrogation room. His heartbeat sped up and the sour taste in his mouth intensified.

Joey knocked on the door. It slowly swung open. He stared into Frankie's cold eyes. Carmine shoved Johnny in the back, and he stumbled through to stand behind a chair in the middle of the floor. Joey and Carmine entered and leaned back against the wall. The third man closed the door, remaining outside. In front of him, Gavino Ponzetti sat behind a desk.

"Johnny, nice to see you. Have a seat," he said. Frankie grabbed his arm and shoved him into the chair. "Wanna tell us where you been for the last three years?"

Johnny wet his lips and negotiated for his life.

"I was kidnapped and held prisoner on an island with a bunch of other guys from Chicago families."

He'd have to let the story unfold like a movie, or

he'd have no chance. Frankie, dumb as shit and engaged to Vicelli, might blow his brains out before he finished.

"You were kidnapped? By who?" Gavino asked, tapping a pencil on the desk.

His gaze bored into Johnny's and Johnny's heart accelerated. If it knocked against his chest and hammered in his ears any louder, he'd go deaf.

"The Feds."

He wanted to wipe the sweat trickling down the side of his face, but kept his hands clasped on his knees and stared back at his boss.

"The Feds? How'd they do that? Just walk up to you and say, 'Hey, Johnny, let's go'?" Gavino asked in a soft voice filled with menace.

Johnny licked his lips again. The soft voice usually preceded violence. He shot a quick glance at Frankie who glared back. He gripped his knees tighter to stop his hands from trembling.

"Sorta, boss."

"I need more than 'sorta.' If memory serves, you disappeared while at a restaurant."

"Yeah, that's right. I went outside for a breath of air and was shot by a tranquilizer dart. When I woke up, I was on this island."

"What island?"

"I don't know."

"Who shot you?" Frankie asked with a sneer in his voice and on his lips.

Johnny didn't look at Frankie when he said, "Gabriella Vicelli."

Frankie's fist nailed him in the jaw and sent him flying off the chair and onto the floor. His head went numb.

"You lyin' bastard!"

"It's the truth. I swear it." He fingered his jaw and spit blood from his mouth.

"You expect us to believe Gabriella has the

ability to do something like that?" Gavino's voice had hardened.

"That self-centered, little girl act is a fraud."

Frankie hit him again. This time Johnny saw stars before someone picked him up and tossed him back in the chair.

"You are talking about the woman I intend to marry!"

"You sap! She's using you, just like she used any number of guys to make contact with us."

Frankie's fist caught him full in the mouth, once again sending him to the floor. The numbness disappeared, replaced by pain. He swallowed the blood and spat out a tooth, then staggered to his feet.

"Enough, Frankie. Let Johnny talk."

"She's a Fed. She uses guys like Frankie to get into the All-Italian Club. It's neutral territory. She has a wide selection of targets. She lines up her next victim and when the time is right, she lures the guy into a secluded place and pow! nails 'em."

"She lures them? How?"

"Are you kidding? You've seen her. She's all tits and breathless. That's how the bitch got me. She had me so hot and horny I'd have followed her anywhere."

Frankie's foot connected with Johnny's balls. He screamed, fell to the floor, and grabbed his crotch. Pain ripped through him. Writhing, he sobbed and cursed Vicelli. This brought another kick to his back from Frankie. Joey and Carmine heaved him back into the chair where he sat, bent over, gasping, and grasping.

"So, Miss Vicelli *lured* you to a secluded place— where?" Gavino asked.

Breathing deep to stop the pain, Johnny croaked, "She got me in a limo at Carlucci's restaurant. There were several of us there. She came with Vito Morelli. During dinner, she slipped me a note to meet her out back for a few minutes. Vito was talking business and never noticed when she left for the can. I opened the limo door all set for a quickie, but got a dart in the neck instead."

"Liar!" Frankie screamed.

He slammed his fist into Johnny's stomach. Pain tore through him and he puked bitter tasting bile.

"What happened after the dart?"

Gavino smiled as though carrying on a normal conversation with a friend. It scared the crap out of him and a gush of fear made Johnny shake uncontrollably.

"I don't know. I woke up in some kind of house on an island, feeling like shit."

"What island?"

"I don't know. Nobody does!"

"That's right, you said there were others of us on this island. Who?" Gavino twirled the pencil between his fingers and stared at Johnny with snake's eyes, deadly and hypnotic.

"Duke's there along with Carlo Marianni, Lou Rizzo, Lefty Lefkowitz, Bobo Rabinsky, and others."

Gavino stopped fidgeting with the pencil and leaned back in his chair. He shot a look around the room at the other three men.

"How did you escape?"

Johnny breathed easier now. He told his boss about the unguarded plane and hiding onboard, then making his way to Chicago.

"So, why not come directly to me? If you had, we wouldn't be having this discussion now."

"I wanted to bring Vicelli in to you."

"And all this time on the island, what did you do?"

"Not fuckin' much." He told them about life on the island, trying to make it sound as boring as possible. He didn't want Gavino thinking he'd been at a country club.

"You just sit around and play cards? I assume there are guards," Gavino questioned.

"Of course. They're all over the fuckin' place. You can barely move without a guard."

"And how did you manage to board the plane with all these guards around?"

Johnny hesitated, reluctant to admit he had been playing golf. And in a tournament, no less.

Frankie slapped him across the face, hard. "Answer my father, you bastard!"

"I usually went for a walk at that time of day. For some reason the guard never showed. When I saw the plane, I took a chance."

"Johnny, I have the feeling you're not telling me everything. We have a bunch of guys on an island with guards, but I haven't heard you say anything about interrogations. I never met a Fed yet who wouldn't take advantage of asking questions. Did they ask you questions, Johnny? What did you tell them?"

Johnny's heart pounded faster as if ready to burst. His vision swam with dizziness. His stomach muscles clenched, and he wanted to puke again.

"Of course they did, but I never told them nothin', boss. I swear it. They tried, but I held out. I'm loyal. That's why I wanted to bring Vicelli to you. To show my loyalty. That's why I escaped."

"I see. The others try to escape?"

Johnny swallowed. Gavino's questions boxed him into a corner. The trembling increased. Fear scented sweat flowed from his pores. Panic bubbled under the surface like a covered pot about to explode from the pressure.

I still have an ace in the hole. Borelli.

He sucked in a deep breath. "I don't know. They're all fat, dumb, and happy. Not a drop of loyalty among any of 'em."

"Are you telling us that out of all the men on this island, only you held out? That the others squealed to the Feds?"

Shit. Gavino wasn't buying it.

"I don't know about them, but I never said nothin' to nobody."

"Johnny, why is it I just don't believe you?" Gavino sat back and nodded to Joey and Carmine.

Johnny steeled his body for the punishment to come. Joey held him upright while Carmine worked him over. Fists slammed into all parts of his body. His nose broke along with several ribs. He puked again after taking several shots to the gut. A kick on the back of the knee buckled his leg. Joey let him slide to the floor where the two of them aimed kicks at his head, back, ass, and thighs. Pain enveloped him from head to foot. He pissed his pants.

Through swelling eyes, Johnny saw Gavino and Frankie stare. His boss's face remained impassive, but Frankie's bore an avid look of satisfaction. He obviously enjoyed the show.

Then, Carmine grabbed Johnny's arm and pinned it to the floor with his foot. In one swift motion, he grasped the wrist and pulled up sharply, breaking the bone.

Johnny screamed in agony and did what every other sucker did. He begged for mercy.

"Please," he pleaded through battered lips. He tasted blood mingling with the flavor of fear. "Stop."

Gavino motioned the guys away. Johnny lay on the floor, sobbing and clutching his arm.

"Johnny, I'm gonna ask you again. What did you tell the Feds?"

"I...I didn't. I swear," he replied, gasping.

At a nod from his boss, the two thugs moved in. They once again kicked him, including his broken arm. Johnny passed out. He came to, his head and shoulders wet. Joey stood over him holding a pitcher.

He sobbed and puked blood.

"Johnny, why prolong this? Just tell me what I want to know and it'll stop. Trust me."

When he remained silent, the men stepped forward. Johnny broke.

"Okay, okay. I'll tell you."

Joey and Carmine lifted him from the floor and deposited him in the chair. The pain from his broken nose and arm almost had him passing out again, but he hung on squinting at Gavino and Frankie.

"That's better. Now, tell me everything." Gavino's voice sounded smooth, as though talking to a frightened child.

Johnny swallowed more blood and shivered. He had no choice, but there was still Borelli.

"Yeah, I talked. So did everyone. They drugged us. I don't know what they used, but I can remember this guy asking questions about the family and our operations. I tried not to say anything, but it was like truth serum or something. I had no choice."

"I'm real sorry to hear that," Gavino said, his voice back to soft.

A gush of fear oozed through Johnny. Now! Now was the time to spring his surprise.

"Wait a minute. I got other information for you."

"Like what?"

"Cousin Leo ain't her cousin."

"Who's Cousin Leo?"

"He's a Fed pretending to be Vicelli's cousin from Detroit. Frankie knows him. They were at The Topsy-Turvy the other night."

He shot a glance at Frankie, happy to see him look uncomfortable. The smile had slipped from his lips.

Gavino looked up at his son. "Frankie? Who's this Cousin Leo?"

Frankie glared at Johnny. "He's Gabriella's cousin from Detroit. He's one of us. He knows the right people and events."

His father frowned. "Gabriella's cousins are all in legitimate occupations. Gus saw to it no other member of his family would be in the business. I checked it out before I had him hit. I didn't want some hot-headed relative seeking revenge."

"He's not that close a cousin. Something about a grandmother and a sister."

"What about The Topsy-Turvy? Why am I just now hearing about this? I go out of town for a couple of days and you end up at a strip joint with a Fed?"

"For cryin' out loud, he's Gabriella's cousin. She introduced us. I took Leo out on the town one night. A bunch of us were there. We got drunk and had a great time." He kicked Johnny in the ankle. "This lyin' piece of shit doesn't know what he's talking about."

"He's a Fed, you moron," Johnny spat out.

He hated Frankie. The stupid asshole didn't have the brains to head the family. It stuck in his throat that an act of birth would allow it.

"How do you know?" Frankie challenged.

"If she put me and all those guys on the island, who else could he be except a Fed? And I know something else."

"What's that?" Gavino said.

"Remember when you sent me to New York a few years ago? On my last night there, the guys took me to a nightclub. At another table a bunch of Tiziano family members whooped it up. One of the guys turned out to be Dante Borelli."

Johnny saw the gleam of interest in Gavino's eyes. He stopped lounging back in the chair and sat forward, his hands pressed onto the desktop.

"Borelli? Are you sure?"

"Damned right I'm sure. Two weeks later, the shit hit the New York fan when his undercover days ended and all those hoods were arrested. I got a flash for you. Cousin Leo and Dante Borelli are the same guy."

He watched as astonishment raked across his boss's face. Frankie just stared, his mouth hanging open.

"That's not possible. After the trials, he went into the Witness Protection Program. The New York guys have been trying to find him for years," his boss said, leaning back again.

"Trust me. It's him."

Gavino glared at him, and then turned to his son. Fumbling in his pocket, he tossed a set of keys across the desk.

"Frankie, in the locked cabinet behind the hidden door in the office you'll find the file on Dante Borelli. Bring it to me"

Frankie left. No one said anything until he returned with a yellow folder. He slapped it on the desk where Gavino opened it and extracted several photos. He held them up for Johnny to see.

"Is this Cousin Leo?"

"Hell no," Frankie snapped. "The guy doesn't look a thing like that."

"For someone that important the Feds would get him fixed up." Johnny tried to keep the sneer from his voice. No sense in pissing off Gavino, even if his son was a moron.

"And how would you recognize him all fixed up?" Frankie asked, curling his lip.

The stupid fuck. Frankie better start sweating a little, too.

"The face might not be the same, but I was at the club that night. I watched him. The way he slapped you on the back, threw back his head when he laughed, and even how he slammed down his drinks were the same. It took me a while, but I finally remembered. That's why I made contact with Nick. Bubbles was with you guys. She was all over

Borelli. I thought maybe she'd have information for me. I wanted to bring him in, too."

"Bubbles? You expect to get anything sensible out of that stupid cunt? Shit, she crawled all over him so she could suck his dick," Frankie snarled.

"Yeah, but she didn't. You guys left and I followed. I wanted to nail Vicelli. I broke down her door. The next thing I knew this cousin and I were rolling around in a clinch. I fought him off and scrammed."

"I don't believe a word of this. You'd say anything to save your ass," Frankie yelled.

"Frankie, we can't just ignore it either," Gavino said. "If Johnny is telling the truth, then Gabriella and her cousin or whoever he is, are a big problem. We'll have to do something. You should have told me about this cousin when he showed up so I could've had him checked out. A simple phone call to Detroit will tell us one way or the other."

Gavino pulled out a cell phone and scrolled down the list of names before hitting a button, and then waited a few seconds.

"Yeah, Bruno, Gavino Ponzetti here. I need a favor and it's urgent. Hold on. What's this Leo's last name and which Detroit family?"

"Carpetti and the Narello bunch," Frankie answered.

"Hello, Bruno. I need some information on a guy named Leo Carpetti with the Narello family up there. You ever heard of him?"

Johnny wanted to smile through his pain. Bruno had been a Detroit Ponzetti informant for years. He knew everything about everybody. Gavino kept in touch—just in case something came up.

"He's supposed to be a cousin of some sort to Gabriella Vicelli, Gus's daughter... Yeah, I know, but this would be a distant kind of thing, a second or third cousin... No, no other information. Hold on.

Frankie, did he tell you anything other than that?"

"Not really. He mentioned a few incidents he said happened a couple of years ago, but that's all."

"No, Bruno, that's all. You ever hear of him... Leo Carpetti... Yeah, I'll wait." Gavino covered the phone with his hand and told Frankie, "He's on the other line. He says the name sounds familiar and he wants to check it out."

Johnny's heart lurched. Jesus, had he made a mistake? No, no way. He knew Vicelli was a Fed. He didn't often use logic, but this time logic demanded Leo was, too. And Johnny was certain about the Borelli connection. He waited almost ten minutes with his heart thumping in his ears and pain radiating through every nerve in his body before Bruno came back on the line.

"Yeah, Bruno, I'm still here. What have you got?... You're absolutely sure?... How long ago?... I'll be damned. Okay, Bruno, thanks a lot. You've done a good job. I'll talk to you later... Yeah, no problem. Bye." Gavino hung up and looked at Johnny. "Leo Carpetti was a very lower echelon enforcer in bookie operations for the Narello family. He died five years ago in a shoot out with police."

If he could, Johnny would leap to his feet and shout. He'd been right! He'd done it! He'd unmasked the FBI agent most wanted by the mob from coast to coast. He glanced up at Frankie.

The man stared at the photo on the desk in horror, his breaths coming in strange, gasping pants.

"I...I don't believe it. Gabriella...all this time..."

"...has been playing you for a sucker," Johnny finished.

"I've been talking to her on the phone for the last couple of days. She...she said she was at a spa wanting to get beautiful for the wedding."

"Why would she want to go to the wedding?" his father asked, a frown knitting his forehead. "With

Johnny on the loose, she should be a hundred miles away from Chicago."

"After the fight with Johnny, you'd *think* they'd be long gone by now," Frankie muttered.

Gavino's scowl deepened. "Unless she and this guy are planning another take down."

"Shit!" Frankie exclaimed. "Everybody's going to be there. Who could she want?"

"What's it matter? Me, you, Casano...it could be anybody. We can't let either her or this cousin close to anyone until we find out if he really is Dante Borelli. I think Johnny's right about Gabriella, too." Gavino set his jaw angrily. "I'd say she drugged your drink at the party last week so she could kidnap Marco."

"Yeah, they were talking together over in the corner."

Johnny took great satisfaction when Frankie's face turned a deep shade of red.

"That fuckin' bitch!" Frankie screamed. "She made an ass out of me."

"I'd have to say so, son. The contract is yours. Bring her and this Leo to me, but don't see her until you have to. Call and make up some excuse for not meeting her at the church. We'll take 'em down at the reception."

"No, no!" Johnny pleaded. "I've waited three long years for this. I've laid awake nights on that fuckin' island planning how I'd do it. I've earned this. Do what you want with Borelli, but I want her."

Gavino gazed at him with a small smile. "We'll talk about that later, Johnny."

"And I want to come back into the family. I'm giving you Vicelli and Borelli. Doesn't that show my loyalty?"

"Indeed, it does, Johnny, but you broke the code of silence. It wasn't your fault, but you broke it just the same. Sorry."

Johnny watched in growing horror as Gavino Ponzetti nodded to Carmine and Joey.

"No! No!" Johnny screamed.

He'd lost his fight to stay alive. The barrel of a gun pressed against the skin behind his ear.

Chapter Sixteen

Shivering, Gabriella walked through the front door of The All-Italian Club on Lane's arm and climbed the staircase to the second floor. The weather had taken a turn for the worse. A cold wind blew and clouds had moved in. She didn't consider it a good omen. She shivered again, dismissing it as superstitious nonsense.

The All-Italian Club was packed. Lane had insisted on arriving late to ensure lots of distractions. She hoped it worked, but a sense of foreboding had her scanning the crowd.

They'd checked out of the hotel a little before noon, then stopped at Marshall Field's to buy the proper clothing and make-up. A loose hairstyle hid the lump on her head, but the bruise on her jaw was still noticeable. Lots of foundation and powder helped. With any luck at all, the dim lighting in the club would help conceal the contusion.

A Casano family bodyguard stopped them at the top of the stairs. He leered at Gabriella while patting down Lane. He was clean, but the idiot didn't check her. The dart gun lived in its usual place on her thigh. Roger's backup team should have smuggled a couple of real guns in with their toolboxes.

Fluffing her hair further around her jaws, Gabriella now experienced the familiar rush of nervousness preceding a hit. With it came a heightened sense of her surroundings. The babbling voices and the smells of garlic, beer, and wine intensified. Her gaze swept from side to side automatically, seeking possible problems.

She still puzzled over a phone call from Frankie earlier. He'd apologized for not being able to meet her at the church. Something had come up and he would see her at the reception. That enabled her and Lane to ditch the ceremony, too. Yet, she couldn't shrug off a nagging worry something was wrong. Frankie hadn't sounded like his usual self. His voice had a distant and distracted edge to it.

"Time to check in with our backup," Lane said, his lips close to her ear. "Will you be all right on your own for a few minutes?"

"Yeah, sure. I don't see Frankie or Gavino. I wonder where they are."

"Probably dealing with the problem. The less we see of them, the better. Be back in a few minutes."

Lane disappeared down the stairs, and she grabbed a drink from a passing waiter. Circulating among the crowd, Gabriella nodded and greeted the people she knew all the while keeping her eyes open for Frankie and Casano.

It didn't take long to find the latter. Caesar and two bodyguards stood off to the side accepting congratulations from the guests. He looked relaxed, and she noticed he drank red wine. Good. It would mask the taste of the ipecac they'd bought at a drugstore, and which now lay secure in the bottom of her purse.

"Everything's in place," Lane whispered, rejoining her. "Two of the guys are in the ladies room and two in the men's. They have one stall out of order and a three-foot hole in the wall behind it. The bodyguards will run 'em out, but with Casano sick they might not be thorough and check out the closed stall."

"Good. Casano's over there and drinking red

wine. How soon do you want to do this?"

"Wait until the dancing starts. The wedding party will be introduced and the lights dimmed for a few minutes. That'll be our best chance. Quit looking around like you expect J. Edgar Hoover to leap out at any moment. It's not in character," Lane admonished.

Gabriella sucked in a deep breath.

"Sorry. Nerves. Once we get started, I'll be fine."

"Okay, introduce me to some of the people you know. Make it look natural."

For the next twenty minutes, she steered Lane from one group of people to the other saying all the right things. Nevertheless, she had an uneasy feeling. Had they forgotten something? Her mind raked back over the plan. No. They had covered all the bases, yet she sensed an unexplained tenseness in the air. It distracted her, and they didn't need distractions at this late hour.

Lane mingled with the other mobsters, his manner breezy and cool. He looked like he didn't have a care in the world. She envied him and tried to get her mind back on track. The wedding party would arrive soon. She'd be better then.

"I've been looking all over for you," Frankie said in her ear.

She jumped. She'd almost forgotten about him.

"Oh, hi. Isn't this a lovely reception?" she said.

"Yeah, it's great. How was the ceremony?"

"It was so beautiful. I cried. They make such a lovely couple. I wish you could have seen it, sweetie."

"Me, too."

Gazing around the room, she asked, "Where's that handsome daddy of yours?"

"He can't make it. He's got business downtown."

Gabriella didn't like this. Frankie spoke in terse tones and hadn't once called her baby. She wondered what could have pulled both Gavino and Frankie away from the big boss's party.

Holy shit! Maybe they'd heard about Johnny. If so, it could make her and Lane's job easier. The Ponzettis would have other fish to fry. But what if they'd nabbed him already? Scarano could be singing like a canary. The thought made her stomach clench, and she swallowed to quell the nausea. No, if they had Johnny, she wouldn't be standing here. The Ponzetti henchmen were probably scouring the city for their former comrade.

"Well, I think it's a shame you had to miss it. I hope nothing's wrong," she probed.

"Nothing that can't be taken care of," Frankie replied. "Where's your cousin?"

"Over there."

Frankie grasped her elbow and pushed her in Lane's direction.

"Hey, Leo. Lookin' good. Glad you could make it. How were things in Detroit?"

"Frankie! Glad to be here. Detroit is Detroit. Know what I mean? I had a little business to conduct—the kind I couldn't ignore. Late payment penalties. Get my drift?"

"Yeah, I get your drift." He refocused his attention on Gabriella, gazing at her through narrowed eyes. "That spa must have been something else. You look great."

"Thanks, Frankie. You should try it sometime."

He stared hard at her jaw, and by reflex, she pulled a lock of hair forward.

"What happened to your face?" he asked.

Her fingers strayed to the bruise. "Oh, that. I...ah...had a little accident during water aerobics. Some woman nailed me with her elbow."

"Where is this spa?"

"Uh, out in the western suburbs, near Glen Ellen, I think." She handed him her glass. "Honey, could you get me another drink?"

His lips curved into a tight smile. "Sure. Another red wine," he said glancing at the bruise again.

"Yes. Thank you."

She waited until Frankie disappeared into the crowd, and then turned to Lane.

"Something's wrong. Frankie's all uptight and hasn't used one endearment."

"I noticed. Is Gavino here?" Lane asked, sweeping the room with worried eyes.

"No. Do you think they may have heard about Johnny?"

"Let's hope so. That'll keep both Scarano *and* the Ponzetti family off our tails. Unless..."

"Unless what?" Gabriella asked when he paused.

"Unless...they've actually captured Scarano. That could explain why Gavino isn't here. They may be grilling him as we speak."

Lane's worried look deepened. Since those had been her thoughts just moments ago, her worry increased, too. Things had been off key ever since they'd arrived.

"I don't like this. It has a funny feel to it," he said. "I'm thinking we should grab the guys and get the hell out. I'll go down the front. You use the back stairs and get to the van parked in the alley."

"Now who's showing nerves?" The thought of bailing out this close to the target and with a plan in place didn't sit well. "If Scarano isn't dead already, they're looking for him. And if he talked I'd be dead, too. The son of a bitch is out of our hair. I'm sure Roger has people scrounging for him in every sewer in Chicago. And they've got several days' head start. The Feds will get him first, and we can continue with Alpha-Omega as before," Gabriella remarked, a tad impatient.

"If they torture him, he'll spill his guts about who dispatched twenty-five men to an island."

"We have a good plan, and Roger has the best backup. We should be all right. Even if the Ponzettis have captured Johnny, it would take them a while to extract information. And they can't just snatch me from the All-Italian Club without a ruckus. Here comes Frankie."

Frankie handed Gabriella her drink and slid his arm around her waist.

"Come on. Let's say hi to everyone," he said, steering her toward a group of people.

For the next several minutes he led her and Lane through the crowd, never leaving them alone. Frankie drank heavily and his gaze constantly searched the room.

Some of Lane's worry rubbed off. Gabriella shivered in the warm room. Frankie had become a goddamned leech.

The glad-handing continued as he introduced Lane to damn near everybody. Suddenly, she wondered if this was a stalling tactic of some kind.

Then, they found themselves in front of the Big Boss, Caesar Casano.

"Mr. Casano, I'd like you to meet my fiancée, Gabriella Vicelli."

Casano nodded and smiled. "My pleasure, Miss Vicelli. I knew your father quite well, God rest his soul."

"I'm so pleased to meet you, Mr. Casano. I remember Daddy talking about you."

Damn, this fucked up the entire plan. It was too early. How would they drug Casano now?

"And this is her cousin Leo Carpetti from Detroit."

Caesar Casano gave Lane a hard stare and didn't offer to shake hands.

"A pleasure, Mr. Carpetti. I'm glad you could join us." The smile he bestowed on Lane did not reach his eyes.

"Thank you for having me. It was a lovely ceremony."

Gabriella wanted to scream. The timing was all wrong. They might not get this close again. Unfortunately, even if she'd wanted, she couldn't get the ipecac out of her purse. Frankie had glued himself to that side of her body. The purse lay trapped under her arm.

"Yes, it was. I hope you're enjoying the reception, too. What brings you to our fair city?"

"I worry about Gabby being alone and decided to visit. I've heard a lot about Frankie. As her oldest male relative, I should keep an eye on her."

"Very commendable, Mr. Carpetti."

One of his bodyguards pivoted to block the path to his boss as another man walked up.

"Nice to have met you both," Casano said, turning to meet the newcomer. They had no choice except to move on.

The lights dimmed, and the DJ announced, "Ladies and gentlemen, may I present the parents of the groom, Mr. and Mrs. Anthony Rosetti!"

Gabriella fumed. Now, the goddamned wedding party arrived? They couldn't have managed to get the fucking pictures finished ten minutes earlier? She wanted to cry with frustration. Casano now stood on the opposite side of the room, out of reach.

With the introductions over, the dancing began; first the bride and groom, then the rest of the wedding party, and finally everyone else.

"Come on, let's dance," Frankie said, not giving her a chance to refuse.

Gabriella sensed big trouble. The whole plan had gone awry. They'd never get close to Casano again, and it didn't look as if Frankie would leave her side. Lane's idea to call the whole thing off sounded better and better.

Frankie insisted on the next three dances also.

When the last one ended, she put on her little girl act one final time.

"Frankie, will you excuse me for a minute? I have to go to the ladies room." To make it look good, she kissed his cheek. "See you in a couple. Now, don't you move. I don't want to lose you in this mob."

"Sure. No problem."

She scooted through the crowd looking for Lane. *We have to get out. Now!*

****

Lane's worry increased. They had planned for just about every conceivable scenario except Frankie clinging to Gabby like ivy. And now, with the introduction to Casano taking place early, the whole plan had gone down the toilet. It was something they'd neglected to consider. *Too much to cover and too little time. What else did we miss?*

Lane's antennae now picked up on every little vibe, none of them good. He sensed disaster coming fast. They needed to leave. Now! Dancing—that was the way out. He'd dance her over to the front stairs, collect the backup, and go.

He turned to claim Gabby for a dance, but Frankie beat him to it. He stood by himself feeling alone and naked. Then an unexpected voice murmured in his ear.

"L-e-e-o, have you been avoiding me?"

Shit! Bubbles! How the hell had she gotten in and what did it matter? He had to get rid of her.

She slid around in front of him, plastered her body against his, and gave him massive lip suction.

"Bubbles, baby, I didn't expect to see you here."

"Of course I'm here. Sal brought me. I didn't want to miss the social event of the season. Come on, honey. Dance with me."

Dancing with Bubbles was the last thing he wanted, but afraid she'd create a scene if he refused, he steered her onto the dance floor where she once again rubbed her body all over his. He tried to keep moving, but the crowd restricted them to but a few feet.

"Shouldn't you be dancing with Sal?" he asked.

"Oh, phooey! The silly man is sitting at a table with his buddies getting drunk. I want a little action." Her hand found the front of his pants, and she winked. "Know what I mean?"

He pulled her hand away. "Yeah, baby, I know what you mean, but this is a dance floor and a wedding reception. The timing's not right."

Lane scanned the couples around them for Frankie and Gabby. He spotted them on the opposite side of the floor. Damn!

The dance ended and Lane steered her toward the bar. "Can I buy you a drink?"

"Sure, sweetie. A Cosmo."

"Why don't you go find us a table and I'll deliver."

"Okay," she replied in a cheerful voice. "Just don't take too long."

He watched her totter away on her ridiculous high heels, her rear end swaying in a tight spandex dress. Strapless, it stopped at mid-thigh. If she bent over, anyone looking would have an uninterrupted view from all angles.

As soon as she left his line of sight, Lane wound his way through the noisy crowd toward the front staircase. He needed to clue the guys in so they'd be ready when he and Gabby came down.

Downstairs, he turned for the men's room and got a nasty shock. Two men stood at the back door looking like they meant business. One had parked himself along the wall at the foot of the back stairs and the other leaned against the door itself. The back escape route was blocked.

Lane ignored the goons and entered the men's room. It was empty and he went straight to the first stall—the one with the "Out Of Order" sign on it.

"Hey, guys, it's me."

A man stuck his head through the hole in the wall. "What's up?"

"We got trouble. Things are all screwed up and the back entrance is blocked. I think the Ponzettis may have found Johnny, and he's now singing an Alpha-Omega tune. I'm calling this off. Get out and bring the van down the alley to the corner. We'll meet you."

"When?"

"As soon as I can get us out. Call Roger. I want the company plane ready to go."

"Wait a minute. Here's a gun," the man said handing it to Lane who slipped it in his pocket.

"Thanks. Hope I don't need it."

The man nodded and Lane heard the sound of tools hurriedly being replaced in toolboxes. He exited the men's room and headed upstairs to find Gabby.

He paused at the ballroom entrance when an arm encircled his waist from the back and a hand squeezed his ass. Bubbles. Did this woman never give up?

"Where's my drink, honey?"

"I was just getting it. Did you find us a table?"

"Yeah, it's over here."

She pointed. Lane's heart sank. It was just a few feet away from the upper foyer and staircase. He steered her over where she gave him another suction kiss before planting her butt in a chair. Lane removed his suit coat and tie, dropping them on the seat next to her.

"Let me get you that drink. I'll be right back, baby."

He turned and made his way towards the bar. Gabriella sidled up.

"Everything's fucked," she said.

"I know. We've got to get out of here. The back

door is being guarded, so once you're down, head straight out the front."

"How do you know that?"

"I've just come from downstairs. Go. The van will be waiting on the corner. It's parked in the alley. I'll be right behind you."

She nodded. "For once, I agree with you."

"Hurry! Go while the dance floor's crowded."

Gabriella nodded again and took off for the staircase. She soon disappeared in the throng.

He breathed a sigh of relief and glanced at his watch.

"L-e-e-o, where's my drink?"

Bubbles twined her arm through his and stuck like an octopus as her other hand played with the buttons on his shirt.

Maybe it only seems like she's got eight arms. He had to dump her and fast.

"Coming up. One Cosmo for the lady," he told the bartender.

"O-o-o, thank you. I'm so thirsty." She downed it in one long swallow, and then tugged on his arm again. "Come on, baby, I wanna dance."

Had Gabby made it out yet? Surely, it wouldn't take her but a minute to make her escape and race for the van. He bet she ran like the wind, even in those spike heels she wore. Hell, given her talents, she could probably run a four minute mile in the damned things, especially if the thugs downstairs tried to follow. Now, he had to ditch Bubbles.

"How about another drink and we go sit down?"

"No," she pouted in a slurred voice. "Wanna dance."

"We can do both."

"Okey-dokey," she replied, grinning.

He ordered another Cosmo, handed it to a woozy Bubbles, and then danced her across the mobbed floor to the table where he deposited her in a chair again.

"I gotta go to the can, baby. I'll be right back. Don't go anywhere, okay?"

"We'll dance some more?"

"We'll dance forever."

Lane left Bubbles drinking her Cosmo with a happy expression and made a beeline for the front stairs. The two men from below had moved up the steps and now stood at opposite ends of the hallway. Their cold, hard stares told him he had trouble. His heart pounded and fear simmered just below the surface. He decided to stare them down.

Then, a gun barrel ground into his right kidney. They moved in and each man took him by an arm.

"Mr. Borelli, I presume," Frankie's voice said in his ear. "Search him, boys."

Lane's heart did more than pound. It hammered at full ramming speed. They knew! How the hell had they figured it out? He cursed silently and tried to bluff his way out.

"Frankie, what the hell's goin' on?"

The thugs searched him roughly, finding the gun within seconds.

"Now, where did you get this? I know Casano's boys gave you the once over when you arrived. You must have friends on the inside, right Borelli? So do we."

"Borelli? What the hell are you talkin' about? Who's Borelli?"

"Aw, you disappoint me. I expected something a lot better from Dante Borelli," Frankie replied in a smooth voice. "Get goin'. We gotta see my father. He'd like to meet you." He pushed Lane down the stairs.

"Dante Borelli? The guy who brought down all those New York guys? Why would you think I'm him? For cryin' out loud, Frankie, I'm Gabby's cousin."

"Yeah, and I'm the Easter bunny. We found Mr. Scarano. He told us all about Gabriella Vicelli and her dart gun. My boys will bring her along later. He also told us how he once saw you in New York. Plastic surgery can do wonders, but it can't change how you laugh or move. Now, let's get goin'. I'm about to gain a lot of respect."

They hustled him out the back door and shoved him into a waiting limo.

Lane broke out in a cold sweat. Fear churned his insides and made him want to puke. He'd never faced capture before, but had watched a few terminations. They had not been pleasant.

God forgive me, Gabby. My past has just signed our death warrants.

Chapter Seventeen

Lane always promised himself that if he were caught—really caught with no hope of escape—he would not make up stupid stories to gain freedom. He would go down like a man, defiant and insulting with his last breath.

Now, faced with that very situation, he was surprised to find his mind working on an escape plan. Shoved into the back seat of a limo, Lane spied the agency van at the opposite corner of the alley out of the corner of his eye. He hoped Gabby and the guys noticed his unorthodox departure. Even though facing the wrong way, he hoped they'd make an attempt to follow.

The car pulled out of the alley, turned left, and sped away. He breathed a brief sigh of relief. At least they hadn't hauled Gabby out of the reception and dumped her in with him. She must have made it to the van.

Praying his backup had seen everything, Lane tried to calm his galloping heart and buy some time, or at the least, some credibility.

"Frankie, what the hell is goin' on? Why would you think I'm Dante Borelli?"

Frankie turned in the front seat to glare at him. The look on his face reminded Lane of a madman. Sweat dampened his forehead. Crazed eyes glowed with rage and hate. Lips curled back, baring his teeth, and his nostrils flared.

"Johnny talked a blue streak right before Carmine here put two behind his ear. We know all about the island, the kidnappings, and you. He saw you in action once."

"Who is this asshole, and why would you fuckin' believe him?"

Frankie snorted and curled his lip further. The glow in his eyes intensified.

"He's one of our guys Gabriella sent away. And I believe him because he had nothin' to lose. He told us about your fight the other night and surprise, surprise—I see you're sporting a few bruises. I also noticed Gabriella's. Did Johnny slug her, too?"

"I told you. I had to take care of some business in Detroit. It got a little rough."

"Yeah. That must have been interesting business since the real Leo Carpetti's dead. Has been for the past five years," Frankie spat out. He raised his gun and shoved it to within a few inches of Lane's face. "You son of a bitch! Not only are you a fuckin' Fed, but you've probably been bangin' *my* fuckin' fiancée in the bargain! I oughtta blow your fuckin' head off right now!"

Frankie's voice rose to a scream and the gun wavered indicating his adversary was close to losing control. Lane swallowed hard, and for an instant thought Frankie would pull the trigger.

"Hey, Frankie, calm down," Carmine said. "Your father wants him delivered alive."

Obeying, the Ponzetti family heir apparent lowered the gun with a shaking hand, wiped a line of spittle from his lips, and turned around to stare out the windshield.

Lane wet his lips and tried to think coherently. His insides quivered and shook, and his mouth was desert dry. He knew what to expect from Gavino, but Gabby would be on the receiving end of a horrific interrogation. She'd used Frankie, and then exposed him for the idiot he was in front of his father and family members.

The car raced down side streets and alleys until Lane had no idea which direction they headed. The silence stretched as did his nerves. He forced his breathing to slow. No use in hyperventilating. He would need all internal resources if he wanted to get out of this alive, although that possibility shrunk with every passing second.

Leo Carpetti. Roger must have used the name of a former Narello family member. It didn't matter. The Ponzettis knew Carpetti was bogus, but were they convinced they had Dante Borelli?

Maybe he could buy Gabby a little time if the goons brought her in. His mind stayed busy plotting a sensible story until the car pulled up at the rear of a warehouse.

The thugs jerked him out of the car and rolled up a garage type door, then nudged him inside.

"Prop it open a little. It's hot in here," one of the guards in the warehouse said.

Pushed and shoved, he wound through a sea of boxes and cartons with two other thugs grasping his arms and Joey grinding the gun into his back. Frankie led the way to a cleared space in front of three doors. He stepped forward, knocked, and then opened the one on the right.

The hoods heaved Lane into the room. He fell on the floor, his hand making contact with a dark, damp spot. From the metallic smell, he knew it was blood. The room stank of sour sweat and vomit.

"Hello, Mr. Borelli. Have a seat," Gavino said from behind a desk.

Rising from his hands and knees, Lane did as ordered, his eyes taking in the surroundings at a glance.

The room was square, measuring about twenty by twenty feet and other than the desk, unfurnished.

A straight-backed chair sat under a naked light bulb suspended from a cord in the ceiling, the harsh light bright and glaring. Squinting, he saw a door in the right hand corner. He reasoned it led to a hidden hallway for a quick exit.

"So, Mr. Borelli, what have you got to say for yourself?"

"First of all, I don't know what you're talking about. Frankie here says some asshole is saying I'm a Fed. It's a fuckin' lie. My name is Leo Carpetti. I'm part of the Narello family in Detroit."

"Good try, but my sources in Detroit say that's not possible. Leo Carpetti is dead."

"Your informant is wrong." Lane injected a sneering tone into his voice.

Gavino smiled. "I don't think so. Now, where are my people? What have you and Miss Vicelli done with them?"

"Gabby? She doesn't have anything to do other than shop. She's an airhead."

"I thought she was your cousin."

Lane swallowed. "She is. My grandmother and Gus's mother were sisters. That doesn't make her any less an airhead."

"Forgive me if I don't believe you."

Gavino nodded and one of the thugs stepped in front of Lane, his fist lashing out to catch him on the jaw. His entire head exploded as if hit with a battering ram. He flew out of the chair and landed on his side. Other hands roughly jerked him upright and back into the chair.

"Now, Mr. Borelli, I want to know exactly where my people are located and how this organization you represent works."

"I can't tell you because I don't know what you're talking about," Lane replied, fingering his jaw. It hurt like hell and he hoped it wasn't broken. He steeled himself. This was just the beginning. He thought of Gabby and prepared to take whatever they threw at him. He had to give her time.

Gavino nodded again and the two goons closed in.

****

Finally free of the crowded dance floor, Gabriella headed for the stairs, and then stopped when one of the Ponzetti thugs came up, barring her way. Left with no choice, she whirled and strode toward the back. Another man emerged from that stairwell. She recognized both from the Ponzetti party where she'd dispatched Alberti. She assumed that if she tried, they'd prevent her from leaving. The Ponzetti's had the escape routes blocked.

Now what the hell am I going to do?

Without breaking stride, she entered the ladies room, frantically trying to get her nerves under control. Instinct told her whatever had stuffed the broomstick up the Ponzetti family ass must have been huge.

Shit. Lane's right. Maybe they do have Johnny and are just waiting for the time and the place to grab me. And if they suspect me, they'll suspect Lane, too. God, maybe they're ready to grab me now.

Her stomach churned with nausea, and she recognized fear. Her heart pounded with staccato beats. Her head swam, and her fingertips tingled with the first signs of hyperventilation. She had to regain control. She also had to get out of this john, and tell Lane they were trapped.

Gabriella sucked in a deep breath, opened the door, and ignoring the man on her left, turned right, and walked calmly down the hall. She skirted the edge of the crowded dance floor looking for Lane when a hand grabbed her elbow. She whirled around ready to strike and faced a drunken Sal.

"Hey, Miss Vicelli. Bubbles deserted me. Did Frankie desert you, too? How about a dance?" His words slurred and he swayed on his feet.

"Actually, I'm looking for Frankie," she said trying to sidle away.

"He won't mind if I dance just one dance with his fiancée."

Before she could protest, he swung her into the swirling jam of dancers. She decided to endure it. To refuse might draw unwanted attention. She craned her neck looking for Lane. In the dimly lit room, Gabriella couldn't see beyond a few feet. Too many jostling couples blocked her view.

Sal's sweaty body reeked of bourbon and he tromped on her feet. His idea of leading was barging into other couples. They bounced around the floor like hapless balls in a pinball machine. The dance went on forever.

Gabriella gritted her teeth and tried to maneuver Sal's booze soaked, stumbling body towards the edge of the dance floor.

Mercifully, the music ended. Her strategy had worked. The bar stood on the opposite side of the room from where they'd stopped.

"Oh, Sal, thank you. That was nice. Would you be a dear and get me drink? Red wine is fine," she said, batting her eyes. The silly voice had disappeared, but he was apparently too drunk to notice.

She gave him two seconds to disappear in the crowd before whirling and pushing her way past laughing, inebriated guests. She searched for Lane, while also scanning the crowd for Frankie. It would be just her dumb luck to run into him now. She didn't see him. She shivered and paused in the archway to the upper foyer. Intuition told her something was wrong.

Where was Frankie? She turned and took another look around the crowded room. Not a sign of him. And he'd been stuck like glue only a short while ago.

That's strange. He should be panting after me. What the hell is going on? Where is he?

Gabriella experienced a heavy sense of dread. Gavino was a no show. Frankie had disappeared. And she didn't see Lane anywhere. Even the goons had departed. Maybe Lane had gotten out and waited for her in the van. With the Ponzetti men gone, her brain screamed, "Get out now!"

No, if he didn't find me already in the van, he'd have come back. I know it. So, where's Lane?

Her scalp prickled and her heart pounded. The stomach churning fear returned.

A loud hiccup from her right brought her head whipping around. Bubbles sat slumped in a chair by herself at a table for six.

"Hi there!" the blonde said, cheerfully raising a glass.

"Uh, hi Bubbles. What's new?"

It had been a rhetorical question. Gabriella shifted away from the blonde and toward the staircase.

"I heard a lot of neat gossip just sitting here all alone. Do you know Johnny's back in town? You know Johnny, don't you? He's a friend of Frankie's. I used to see him at the Club all the time." Bubbles hiccupped again.

Gabriella froze in place. Johnny? What the hell did Bubbles know about Johnny? She recognized Lane's coat and tie on the seat next to the stripper.

"Yeah, I know Johnny. You say he's back in town?"

"That's what I heard one of Frankie's boys telling a guy. I wonder where he went. He was always real nice to me." Bubbles drained her drink. "Could you get me another Cosmo? Leo said he'd get me one, but he never did."

"Leo?"

"Yeah. We danced, and he said he'd get me a drink, but he's gone. Where is everybody?"

"My question, too. I'm looking for Frankie."

"Oh, they left together," Bubbles said, licking the inside of her empty glass.

Gabriella's heart missed a beat. "What?"

"Yeah. Leo started to go downstairs to the can and Frankie followed him. They met Carmine and Joey and all left together."

"When? How long ago?" she asked, her voice rising in panic.

"Oh, I don't know. A few minutes, I guess. No, maybe ten or fifteen. I can't remember. I went over to the railing to remind Leo about my drink and saw them. Then, they were gone and someone else brought me a Cosmo. Will you get me another?"

"Yeah, sure."

A new sense of urgency had her taking action. If Frankie had captured Lane, then they were really fucked. Johnny had spilled his guts, and she would be next on the hit parade—literally. She couldn't figure out why Frankie hadn't grabbed her first.

Gabriella sped away from the babbling Bubbles and made a beeline for the stairs, racing down them for all she was worth. The time for subtlety had passed. Lane was in danger, and she had to do something about it. She needed to contact the backup.

She reached the foot of the steps when two figures detached themselves from the wall where they'd slouched, as if waiting for her.

"Miss Vicelli, come with us," the first man said.

"Yeah. Nice and quiet like. Mr. Ponzetti wants to have a word with you," the second guy added.

She knew these guys were nothing more than glorified flunkies—deadly flunkies to be sure, but flunkies just the same, their sole purpose in life to take orders. It also meant their intelligence levels weren't high. Gabriella lifted her chin. She could take them.

They closed in on either side of her, grasping her arms in firm grips, and then half-walked, half-dragged her toward the hall and the back door.

Trapped! Fear surged. Her bravado shrank, while shaking legs and a pounding heart threatened to incapacitate her. She wasn't her father's daughter for nothing. She knew exactly what kind of fate awaited both her and Lane.

No, by God. If this is the end, I refuse to go down without a fight.

She sucked up her courage, then clenched her jaw and stiffened her spine, prepared for battle.

Chapter Eighteen

Gabriella bit back the fear. When in doubt, make a scene, she remembered Jack telling her. It would buy her a few moments of time from an attacker. She could almost hear his voice.

And anything can happen in a moment.

The narrow hallway did not allow the three of them to walk together. One thug moved ahead toward the back entrance leaving her with the second. Now!

She raised her foot bringing the stiletto down with all the force she could muster, aiming for the upper part of his foot near where it joined the ankle.

Bullseye!

At the same time, Gabriella balled her right fist and pivoted, grinding the heel deeper into the man's foot. She put all her weight behind the punch delivered to his solar plexus. He yelled at the pain her stiletto caused, and then the air rushed out of his lungs when her fist connected.

The first man, hearing the commotion, raced back, slinging his arm around her throat.

"You bitch," he snarled, tightening his hold and dragging her backwards.

Collapsed onto his hands and knees, thug number two tried to suck air while at the same time attempting to grab his injured foot. The dark stain spreading up the leg of his pants told her she'd drawn blood.

With her breath choked off, Gabriella tensed her muscles and drove her elbow solidly into her attacker's stomach just like Jack had taught her. When his grip loosened, she repeated the action. He let go. In a flash, she whirled and swinging viciously, planted her foot squarely in his crotch. He howled and dropped like a rock.

The goons lay writhing between her and the back door. She ran for the front, but underestimated the man whose foot she'd gouged. He tripped her. She fell to the floor with a thud. Gabriella scrambled to her feet, but a hand now clasped her ankle. She pulled and looked over her shoulder.

The man attempted to drag her toward him. The other guy still crouched, grasping his balls, and gasping in pain. He clawed under his jacket for his weapon. She had no time to reach for her dart gun, so using her purse she nailed the thug grasping her ankle in the head. The heavy metal fastener caught him right between the eyes. With a grunt, he dropped her ankle just as she yanked back. The momentum sent her tumbling onto her backside.

She scrambled to regain her footing, but panic made her foot slip. The man had finally pulled his gun, pointing it in her general direction. In the small confines of the hallway, she'd be hard to miss. The men's room door was next to her. She had no idea what she'd do once inside, but any port in a storm, and the waves had built to monstrous proportions.

The back door flew open. Two plumbers burst in. Scooting backward, Gabriella heard two soft plops, then silence. It took her a second to realize both of her potential kidnappers were dead.

"Miss Vicelli, are you all right?" one of the plumbers asked. The other man stepped over the bodies and helped her to her feet.

"Yeah, but Lane's missing. Frankie's got him."

She'd never seen fresh kill and had to swallow

hard at the sight. She wanted to throw up, and then sit down and bawl like a baby.

"We think so, too. Let's get out of here. There's no telling if anyone heard the noise. Come on. The van's on the corner."

She clutched her purse in a death grip. The two men helped her as she ran on shaking legs out the front door and down the street. She rounded the corner, spotting the van in the alley. The second guy shoved her into the backseat, and then followed while the first man jumped in on the other side. The driver took off. A fourth man rode shotgun.

"My name's Mark. This is Pete. The guy up front is Will. Larry's driving. What the hell happened in there?"

She gave them the *Reader's Digest* version. "Lane was right. We should never have attempted this. Now he's caught. What made you guys come through the back door?"

"When Lane scrapped the plan, we left by the back entrance. Two men looked us over, but we spun them a tale about needing more equipment, and they let us go. They knew what was going down and didn't want witnesses," the man named Larry said.

Mark continued. "We got in the truck and waited on the corner like instructed. As we left a car backed up and parked. A few minutes later, Pete sees four guys come out, get into the car, and drive away." The driver glanced into the rearview mirror. "Are we being followed?"

"No. We're clear." He pulled over to the curb. "We knew something was wrong when neither you nor Lane showed. Then, a second car pulled up and two guys got out. It didn't look right. Pete and Mark went back to check."

Gabriella grabbed the agency phone from her purse. "I've gotta call Roger. We have to find Lane."

She punched in Roger's number. He answered

on the first ring. "Warwick here."

"It's Gabriella. We got big trouble. The Ponzettis got a hold of Johnny. He spilled his guts. Frankie kidnapped Lane, and they damn near got me."

"Hold on."

"Don't put me on hold, goddamn it!" she yelled, kicking the seat in front of her when he did.

"How long ago did this happen?" he asked a few seconds later.

"How long ago did they leave?" she asked Pete.

"Ten, fifteen minutes, tops."

"Ten or fifteen minutes."

"Any idea where they went?"

"How the hell should I know? Call an informant, you asshole. I need more men. And cops. Call the cops."

"Relax, Gabriella. Put Mark on the line."

She handed the phone to him with irritation. "Here, he wants to talk to you."

Mark took it from her. "Yes, boss... No, I don't think so. We weren't sure it was Lane to begin with. If it wasn't, butting in would blow our cover... Sorry, Mr. Warwick, but we had to pop 'em. They had Miss Vicelli... All right... Yeah I remember hearing that... Where's it located?... Gotcha. We can be there in ten minutes."

Mark hung up and looked at Gabriella.

"Mr. Warwick says he'll take care of everything. He thinks they've taken Lane to the Ponzetti warehouse. They use it for interrogations."

"Interrogations, my ass. They use it to kill and torture people. Where's it located?"

"Over on Turner," Will told her.

"Then what the fuck are you waiting for? Get your asses in gear. Every second counts." She snapped her fingers at Mark as the van shot away from the curb. "I'll need a gun."

"I don't think Mr. Warwick would approve of you

going in with us," Larry said.

"Look, Helio Castroneves, just drive the fuckin' van. Warwick has no choice. Neither do you. Quit wasting time."

"She's right. Let's go," Mark said. He reached into a bag at his feet and handed her an earpiece with a slender threadlike wire attached to it. "This is for communications."

Gabriella screwed the earpiece into her ear and anchored the microphone under the strap of her dress.

Larry drove hard and fast through the streets of Chicago. The weather had deteriorated. Dark clouds pregnant with rain hung low overhead. In the distance, thunder rumbled. Dusk had long since passed, even though the hour was not late.

"Good. The weather will help us," Pete muttered as he shrugged his way into a Kevlar vest. Mark and Will had already done the same and now checked their guns.

"How do you figure that?" she asked.

"The thunder and rainfall will mask any noise we make. You'd better stay in the van. We only have four vests."

"Go to hell. I'm in. What's Roger's plan? Or is he making it up as he goes along?"

"He's calling in the local feds and the cops, and also letting the mayor and the media in on it. In Chicago, it's sometimes hard to tell friend from foe," Mark replied.

Larry parked the van down the street from the warehouse. Gabriella's nerves hummed with an odd combination of excitement, fear, and dread. Her hands shook. Was Lane still alive? She said a little prayer and concentrated on the next order of business.

"So, how do we get inside?" she asked.

"We can't waltz in the front door, that's for

sure," Larry said.

"Will, Pete, go around to the far end of the alley. Take cover if you can. Larry, Gabriella, and I will do the same over here," Mark instructed.

"They'll have guards on the door," she warned.

"Of course they will. I've done this a few times before, honey. They'll also have several goons inside, just in case. Are you ready?"

Honey? Gabriella wanted to give a pithy reply, but decided to let his snarky comment go. Lane came first.

"Yeah, I'm ready."

The five of them exited the van. Keeping low, she ran across the darkened street as the first raindrops fell. Will and Pete broke off, scuttling down the side street. She, Mark, and Larry crouched behind a dumpster full of several days' worth of trash and garbage. The rotting food stank and as she knelt, her knee made contact with a squishy mass of decaying fruit. A rat scurried for cover.

Mark peeked around the edge of the bin, and then whipped his head back. "They've got two guys on the back door and three or four cars parked along the alley."

"Can we use the cars as cover?" she said.

Mark didn't answer, but tapped the center of his earpiece. Gabriella did the same to her device, realizing they could all hear each other. He spoke into the microphone.

"Pete, Will, you in place?" he whispered.

"Yeah," came Pete's hushed reply. "We're inside a recessed doorway about a quarter of the way down the alley. The goons covering the door are too busy smoking and trying to stay dry to pay much attention."

The rain, light at first, had steadily increased. Its patter on the concrete sizzled as though boiling. Gabriella wiped the moisture from her face and tied her hair into a sloppy knot. A few straggling strands clung to her face and neck.

"Hold on. I've got an idea." Mark turned to her with a challenging stare. "Think you can distract those two morons on the door?"

"I've been distracting men for years. What do you want?"

"I don't know. Stumble down the alley. Tell them your car won't start or something. Just get them to come toward you, so Pete and Will can get behind them."

"Are you nuts? Even with the rain, they'll hear them coming."

"Just do as I tell you."

"Remind me to plant my foot up your ass when this is all over." One of the guys bit back a chuckle as she raised her skirt and extracted the dart gun. "At least I can get one of them. If we're lucky, the rain and darkness will hide what I've done until our guys can get close enough to take the other one out."

Without waiting for a reply, Gabriella crawled away from the dumpster to the end of the alley where she stood. She sucked in a few deep breaths to steady her nerves, concentrated on Miss Cameron's acting class, kicked off her shoes, let loose a scream, and ran down the alley. Someone swore as she passed the dumpster.

"Help! Help me!" she hollered, keeping the gun close to her side.

Only Superman could have ignored her, and the two guards were not Superman. They turned and ran toward her.

"Help! Help! He tried to rape me!"

"Who, lady? Where'd you come from?" the first man in line asked.

She raised her gun and shot the dart into his neck. He staggered toward her, falling into her arms. She struggled to stay on her feet and hold him. Her gun clattered to the pavement. The second man ran up.

"What the hell's goin' on here?"

"Rape! Rape!" she cried again.

The man looked over her shoulder. "Who? Where? What's wrong with Eddie?"

Eddie weighed a good two hundred twenty pounds, and Gabriella slowly sank to her knees. The second man was so engrossed with the scene in front of him it gave Pete the chance to catch him right behind the ear with a gun butt. Two more sharp blows did the job. He fell on top of Eddie sealing her fate on the wet, ripe pavement.

"Get 'em off me," she demanded.

The others ran up, quickly trussed and gagged the two guards with duct tape, then dragged them over behind the dumpster.

"Rape?" Mark said to her. "Jesus, you could have screwed us all."

"Shut up, asshole. It worked, didn't it? That car business was lame. He'd have given me a quarter for the nearest pay phone and told me to hit the road. Yell something ridiculous. It works every time."

"Stop arguing. Let's get inside," Will said.

Gabriella agreed.

"Here, you're going to need this," Mark said, handing her a nine-millimeter Glock.

The door to the warehouse resembled a garage door and was doubtless used to load and unload merchandise from trucks. At present, it was wedged open two or three feet by a crate. They rolled under it and took up positions behind the containers on either side.

Mark pointed, and she saw a catwalk above her head. Off in the distance, two figures with guns lounged against the railing, puffing on cigarettes.

A sense of déjà vu rippled through her. The scene looked hauntingly familiar. Her pounding heart increased its speed. Gabriella looked up at the catwalk again and remembered her nightmare—the one where Johnny had caught her. God, was she now clairvoyant? She shivered and forced her mind back onto rescuing Lane.

The dimly lit warehouse and the boxes in it cast shadows onto the dark floor. From somewhere up ahead, the glow intensified. Instinct told her that was where they'd find Lane.

A flash of lightning followed by a peal of thunder made her jump in surprise. The heavens opened and rain cascaded down, drumming on the metal roof.

"Okay, everybody, spread out and stay low," Mark said into the mike. "The rain is perfect cover. Will, get up on the catwalk, and let us know how many guys are guarding it." He turned to face her. "Stick close. I don't want you getting lost."

She resisted the temptation to call him a filthy name, but when she had Lane safe and sound, the arrogant prick would hear more than his fair share.

Will's voice came over her earpiece. "I count four guys up here, and I see two more on the ground in back, but I don't know what they're guarding."

"Might be a hidden door for a quick getaway. Where are you now?" Mark asked.

"There's a landing where the ladder meets the walkway. I'm behind a big spool of cable."

"Good. Stay put until we locate Lane, then take out as many as you can before getting the hell down."

"Roger."

Mark moved to his right indicating for Gabriella to follow. She bent low and moved after him. The Glock weighed a ton, and she gripped it with a sweaty palm. A trickle of perspiration slowly made its way between her breasts. She felt dirty and wondered if the smell rising from her body was due to the garbage or her fear.

The two of them dodged from box to box. She assumed the others did the same. Finally stopping, Mark tapped her on the arm and jerked his head to the far right. She shook hers and pointed in the direction of the light. He frowned and grasped her arm, pulling her behind him as they wove their way closer to the wall. She wrenched her arm free and glared at him.

"Stop that! Do what I say," he hissed.

"Damn you. They're probably holding Lane close to the light source. Even now, someone may be about to pull the trigger and blow his head off."

"In which case, we can't do a damned thing about it. Our job is to also catch these guys."

"You cold-hearted bastard!"

"Look, Lane knew the odds of this hare-brained scheme. I don't know how you talked him into it, but he's a professional. Do as I say."

That'll be the day.

"Pete, where are you?" Mark asked.

"On the left just below the catwalk."

"Larry?"

"Also on the left, but closer to the center of the room. I can see a clearing in this sea of cartons. I think Gabriella's right. They must be holding him near there."

While Mark spoke with the men, Gabriella took the opportunity to turn back the way they had come. Within seconds, he disappeared from view. Fuck him. She headed for the clear space and Lane.

Mark's voice sounded in her ear. "Gabriella! Gabriella, where the hell are you?"

She jerked the earpiece out and stuffed it down the bodice of her dress not wanting his yammering to distract her. She dodged around a crate, and stumbled over something soft. Unprepared, she fell.

It took a second to realize she'd fallen on a body. The pale light illuminated the corpse's face and she smothered a cry. It wasn't a pretty sight. Battered almost beyond recognition, she assumed he'd met the usual mob justice and been shot. Then it dawned on her who it was—Johnny Scarano. Had to be. Who else?

Bile, strong and bitter, rose in her throat. It was the second time in an hour she'd seen a dead man. The incident in the hallway happened so fast it had barely registered. She forced herself to swallow the vile taste.

Gabriella rolled off Johnny and lay on her back breathing through her clenched teeth for a few seconds until the nausea subsided. Mark was right. Her scheme was hare-brained, and she had talked Lane into doing something he knew wasn't logical or likely to succeed. If Lane died, it would be her fault. Taking one last look at Johnny, she shuddered.

God, please don't let Lane come to this.

She forced her mind back onto rescue and crawled away from the late Mr. Scarano. The light. She had to get to the light. With renewed determination, she inched her way around another box.

****

Frankie's fist slammed into Lane's stomach again. His gut wrenched, but had nothing left to throw up. Carmine and Joey held him upright by the arms. If they hadn't, he'd be lying in a heap on the floor. Frankie's foot connected with his balls. Lane howled. This time the goons allowed him the luxury of falling. He writhed as the pain radiated throughout his body. Tears flowed from his eyes and snot dripped from his nose.

He gasped and shuddered, barely hearing Gavino say, "Are you ready to tell me where this island is now, Mr. Borelli?"

"I...I don't...know...nothin' 'bout...no island," Lane said in a tortured whisper. "And my...name...isn't Borelli."

Lane didn't think the pain could get any worse until Carmine's foot made heavy contact with his ribs. A loud cracking told him at least one, perhaps more, had broken. His breaths came in hard, rasping pants, and it hurt like hell. He couldn't draw enough air and wondered if one of them had punctured a lung.

Joey's foot hammered into his buttocks and spine and for a brief instant his entire lower body experienced a sharp tingling, then numbness. Christ! Had the bastard broken his back? He'd prefer a bullet to life in a wheelchair.

The thugs tossed him back into the chair like a rag doll. The numbness subsided allowing the pain to return. He didn't know how much more of this he could take. How long had he been here? An hour? Ten? Longer? Was help on the way? He had no idea. His world had shrunk to enduring pain and the determination to stay alive.

"Mr. Borelli, I must ask you again. Where is this island?"

Gavino's smooth voice came at him through the sea of throbbing pain, his image wavering in a strange red haze.

Groaning, he croaked, "Don't...know...nothin'."

Gavino nodded, and Frankie's fist adorned with brass knuckles come toward his face.

****

Gabriella peeked around the corner of the container giving her shelter. Ahead, she saw more boxes and paths. While she advanced, the light had grown brighter. She had no clue where the rest of the men had gone, nor did she care. She focused on finding Lane.

She chose a path and crawled silently to the next carton. Through the wooden slats, she smelled the strong aroma of coffee and wondered if drugs had been stashed inside. Probably.

She peered around the box. Another choice of pathways. Damn! Didn't anything lead directly to the light? Then she realized there was a method in the seemingly random, chaotic placement of containers. The maze would delay any intruders like the Feds or the cops, giving the Ponzettis a chance for escape.

She bet the warehouse offices were located along the back wall with at least one having a door leading to a hallway and easy outside access.

Gabriella stopped to orient herself. Yeah, the back wall should be toward her left. Another quick glance confirmed it. The light emanated from that direction. Without hesitation, she chose the left hand path and reached her objective.

A final look-see around the box showed a small cleared space and three doors. Two had frosted glass, but the third was solid. She also spied two guards in front of the third door. Directing her gaze upwards, she noticed two of the guards on the catwalk overhead. The far ends of the walkway receded into the gloom. The men smoked and talked, not paying much attention to what happened below. Will had confirmed four guards, and she assumed the other two were somewhere in the darkness.

Gabriella didn't want a one-on-one confrontation. If Gavino and Frankie heard a commotion they'd snuff Lane before making a getaway. She'd left the tranquilizer gun in the alley—it'd only had one dart anyway—and wrestled with how to take the guards in front of her out of commission.

The men talked and gestured. Keeping to the shadows, she inched closer in an effort to overhear the conversation. The rain still pattered on the roof, lessening with every passing second, and the occasional peel of thunder represented a double-edged sword. It masked her approach, but also prevented her from hearing what the thugs had to say.

She crouched behind the last box, straining to make out their conversation.

"...can you believe it? ...think he's...Borelli?"

"Why would he come out of...don't make no sense."

"Yeah. I think...on this one. Can't be Borelli."

Gabriella's heart lurched in her chest. Shit! Now she understood why Lane had been snatched first. Borelli had been blown.

"...are the other guys with Vicelli? Should have...by now. Think something happened?"

A cry of pain had them all turning their heads towards the solid door. Gabriella winced, and then rejoiced. The sound could only have come from Lane. He was alive!

"Asshole sure is taking it."

"...he's got endurance."

With the rain now reduced to a light shower, she clearly heard the sounds of a thorough beating taking place. The sounds of flesh meeting flesh, grunts, cries, and laughter rang through her head. A scream made her shiver. How much more could he stand? She needed to take action—now!

Backing up a ways, she fished the mike from her bodice and screwed in the earpiece.

"Mark, where are you?" she whispered, hardly breathing.

"Where the hell are *you*?"

"I'm in front of the office doors. Lane is in the one on the far right, the one with the solid panels. He's taking a terrible beating. Are you in position?"

"Get out of there. Let us handle it. We'll be set in a few minutes."

"You son of a bitch! You've had a lifetime to get set. Move your ass."

Then she heard in the distance the sound of sirens. No! It couldn't be! Sirens? She also heard Mark curse.

Yeah, right. Friend from foe. Obviously, at least one cop was not a friend. She spared a glance above to the catwalk. Even though the rain had slowed, the guards up there didn't act as if they'd heard anything. The guards below looked towards the side of the warehouse.

"You hear that?"

"Sounds like a siren. Think it's heading our way?"

"Can't tell. Maybe it's just a regular cop siren goin' to a wreck or somethin'."

"Should we tell the boss?"

Gabriella couldn't wait much longer. If they told Gavino, he'd kill Lane and escape.

"Now!" she hissed into the mike.

"Not yet. I'm not in place."

"Fuck you!"

Crawling to the edge of the last container, Gabriella knelt, raised her gun, and supporting her right hand with her left, tightened her finger on the trigger.

Chapter Nineteen

Lane made an important discovery. The human body could take only so much pain, and then the sensory systems shut down. He existed in a fog, not quite unconscious, but neither did he experience the sharp, gut-wrenching pain.

Frankie's fist came at him again in slow motion. His head snapped back, and he tasted fresh blood. Exploring the source with his tongue, Lane noted the sensation of cool, dry air on its tip. His cheek had been sliced clean through. Joey and Carmine held him upright while Frankie pounded away. Now, the heir apparent pummeled at his stomach. Breathing was impossible.

The thugs released his arms and let him fall to the floor, and then dumped him back in the chair. Pain still racked his body. Broken bones ground together. His nose, a cheekbone, and several ribs had gone. Looking down, he noticed his left arm had twisted at a grotesque angle. When had that happened?

"Where's the island?" Gavino asked.

Lane turned a blurry gaze toward his tormentors. Gavino still maintained the air of an aristocrat, but Frankie had the lean, hungry look of a predator. He'd shed his jacket long ago and his white shirt, open to mid-chest, was splattered with blood. Frankie stepped back, a feral expression in his eyes, and panted with exertion. The room reeked of blood, sweat, vomit, and fear.

"Don't...know...told...you," Lane mumbled.

Frankie moved in again when Gavino stopped him.

"Hold on. He's almost out. We can't get information from him if he's unconscious. Take a breather."

The thugs and Frankie gathered around the desk conversing in low tones. Lane didn't care. As long as they left him alone. His head fell forward until his chin rested on his chest.

Though his body barely felt the pain, his mind still functioned with reasonable clarity. He worried about Gabriella. Had she been captured, too? Was she getting the same treatment in another room? He strained to hear the conversation, but the buzzing in his ears prevented it. Gabby was smart and resourceful. If she could escape, she would.

Go, honey. Run like hell. Get out of town and into the program. A new name. A new place. A new background. You'll be safe.

His mind drifted. Where and when could Johnny have seen him? And how could he have recognized Borelli after the plastic surgery. Frankie—or was it Gavino—said something about gestures. Yes, it could have gone like that. Gestures and mannerisms were almost impossible to change.

Funny. He spent all those years on the inside of the Tiziano family only to get nailed by a lowlife, small time piece of shit like Johnny Scarano. In spite of the pain, he almost laughed at the irony.

Lane raised his head. The thugs still conversed. He accidentally moved his broken arm. The rest had given his body a chance to throw off the numbing effects. Pain ripped through him. He clenched his teeth.

The beating hadn't produced the desired information. Maybe that's what they discussed now.

The *real* torture. It would begin soon. He wondered which method they'd use. In New York, he'd heard the guys bragging about several forms—none pleasant.

Would they hang him from a meat hook and use various parts of his body for target practice? Maybe they'd press cigarettes or flatirons on him until his flesh sizzled. A baseball bat was a painful way to break bones. Electrodes on the genitals was an oldie, but a goodie.

He'd once been in on a discussion about the worst revenge ever extracted. One guy swore he'd seen a candidate take a bullet up the ass, while another thug insisted he'd taken part in a killing that involved skinning a man alive. Lane hoped they'd been bullshitting. He had passed fear a long time ago and was now into existing.

Carmine left the desk and strode over to the far corner of the room where he picked up a baseball bat. Looked like he'd get the broken bones routine. Frankie grabbed him by the hair, and landed two vicious jabs to his mouth. Blood spurted.

"Mr. Borelli, I am weary of this charade. I'm going to ask you one more time—where is this island?" Gavino said.

"I…don't know…and go to…hell."

Gavino sighed and nodded to Carmine and Joey. Joey grabbed his left leg while Carmine swung, bringing the bat down on his kneecap. Bone splintered and crunched.

Lane screamed.

****

Gabriella's hand wavered for an instant, and then she heard the sirens again, closer this time. Wetting her lips, she inhaled a deep breath, and squeezed the trigger.

The gun bucked with the recoil. The resulting boom almost deafened her. A look of amazement came over the face of the man closest to her. A bright red stain mushroomed in the middle of his chest. He slowly crumpled onto the floor. She re-aimed and squeezed again, nailing the second guy in the throat. It took less than two seconds.

Then, all hell broke loose.

Mark and the other team members yelled in her earpiece. Gunfire erupted from every conceivable location. She threw herself behind a container. This was no dart gun. These were real bullets and she'd just killed two men.

Oh, my God. I am my father's daughter.

For the first time in her life, she acknowledged Gus Vicelli had been a killer.

Gabriella pressed against the side of the box and the floor, trembling and shaking as if in the grip of a fever. For the past five years, she'd only played FBI agent. This was real danger and death. She didn't like it.

She sobbed wondering if one of the gunshots booming throughout the warehouse had killed Lane. Wood splinters rained down as bullets slammed into the boxes. The stench of cordite and gunpowder burned her nostrils and throat. A scream and a body crashing into containers told her Will must have nailed one of the guards on the catwalk. A second later the sound repeated itself. Two down.

Then in her earpiece, she heard, "I'm hit! I'm hit! Fuck! It went right through my vest. The sons of bitches have cop-killer bullets! Oh, shit!"

It was Will. His voice ended with an odd gurgling noise followed by silence. She realized a man had just died. Too sickened to swear, Gabriella ripped the earpiece and mike from her body, and flung it aside. Never again did she want to hear something like that.

The gunfire didn't abate, and she crawled back until she had another box between herself and the offices. She had to get a grip on her emotions. Her heart raced to the point where she thought it would explode or leap from her chest. She breathed as though having run a marathon. Little black dots swam in front of her eyes. No, no! Now was not the time to faint!

The sound of cursing, angry men and the crash of bullets came from all directions. She smelled death and tasted fear in her mouth.

Suddenly, the door to the interrogation room was flung wide. Carmine, Joey, and Frankie ran out, crouched low with guns blazing, and dove for cover. Through the open door, she saw Gavino holding a gun on a man in a chair. Lane! They hadn't killed him! Gavino wouldn't hold a gun on a dead man.

Gabriella tried to get a clean shot, but too many boxes blocked her line of fire. She crawled from one container to the other. Two slugs missed her head by inches. She swung her gun to the left and fired. Joey spun around, dropped to the floor, and lay still.

Carmine ran for the protection of a carton further away. Bullets from unknown sources slammed into him. He hit the ground and ceased moving. Frankie followed Carmine's route, his gun spitting bullets before he dove behind a container.

Outside, sirens blared. The cops had finally arrived.

Gabriella focused her attention back into the office. Gavino still stood in front of Lane. Biting her lips and trying to steady her hands, she raised the gun and fired.

Shit! She missed Gavino, but apparently hit the light. The room went dark. At the same instant, a shot rang out from the office.

"No!" She scrambled to her feet, and ignoring the danger, raced for the room.

****

The pain from his broken kneecap washed over

Lane. He sat gasping and shuddering, praying the numbness would return or that he would die. He had no more endurance.

"Mr. Borelli, why put yourself through this? Tell me what I want to know and I swear the boys will drop you off at the nearest hospital."

"I...can't tell you a damned thing...because I don't...know a damned thing," Lane replied.

"We have Miss Vicelli. She's waiting in another office for her turn with Frankie and the boys. Tell me what I want to know, and I'll let her go. She's so beautiful I'd hate to see her face carved up like a Halloween pumpkin, wouldn't you? Spare her. Talk to me."

It was tempting. God, it was so tempting, but he knew Ponzetti lied. They could never afford to let Gabby go free. He wondered if they really had her. If they did, she'd be the perfect catalyst to force information from him. A few moments of watching them beat her and he'd sing. He knew it, and so did Ponzetti. For the first time since his capture, hope rose. She'd eluded them. If his tortured lips could smile, they would.

His thoughts were confirmed a second later when a shot echoed from just outside the door. Another followed. Then the warehouse erupted in gunfire. Gabby!

"What the hell!" Frankie yelled.

Gavino dropped behind the desk. The other three men dove for the floor.

"Stay down!" Gavino ordered.

Bullets blew through the door, raking the walls. Screams and shouts filtered in to them.

Lane had no energy to throw himself out of the way of a possible stray round. He sat and prayed. Time stood still, and he had no idea how long the gun battle lasted.

"Carmine, take a look," Frankie said.

Carmine opened the door a couple of inches. Bullets found the crack and smashed into the wall a mere foot from Gavino's head.

"Close the fuckin' door!" Gavino screamed, his pseudo-suave, cultured tone gone. "You nuts or something?"

"They got Tony and Little Nero," Carmine reported. "I saw 'em about ten feet away from the door."

"Kill Borelli! Kill him now!" Frankie shouted.

A bullet from close range ripped through the wall and plowed into the desk.

"When I say so," his father yelled. "Carmine, Joey make a break for it. Frankie, go with 'em."

"What! Why me?"

"Because I said so, you asshole! If you hadn't had the hots for that bitch, we wouldn't be in this mess. Go redeem your sorry ass!"

Frankie rose to his feet, pale and shaking. He nodded at Carmine and Joey.

"Let's go."

Carmine jerked the door open, and the three made a dash for cover, guns firing. The sound of battle ricocheted off the walls of the enclosed space. Gavino crawled from behind the desk, a gun in his hand, and stood in front of Lane.

"He...won't...survive," Lane said.

"I know. He's my son, but he broke the code. He talked to you about family business, didn't he?"

"Yeah. Not...too bright."

"I always knew that, but the business was destined to be his. By the time he took over, I'd be dead and beyond caring." Gavino shrugged. "Are you Borelli?"

Lane shook his head, ignoring the pain. "Just...sent to keep...lady safe."

"I'll give you this. You got balls. So does Vicelli. In a way, I admire Gabriella. She's avenging her old man's death. I understand that. Shame she's a woman. She'd have made a great don. The lady has vision."

Two more bullets sliced into the wall behind Gavino forcing him to duck.

"Time for me to leave." He raised his gun and took aim at Lane's head.

Lane tensed. The light bulb over his head shattered. He threw himself to the left as Gavino fired, landing on his broken arm. He screamed. Gavino didn't bother checking to see if he'd killed Lane, but headed for the door in the back wall. Within seconds, he was through it and gone.

Pain radiated from every nerve in his body. He shook with it. But he was alive. He wanted to cry. He passed out instead.

****

The gunfire wound down to an occasional shot. The cops and FBI agents shouted for the thugs to surrender. Gabriella dove to the floor again when a couple of stray rounds whizzed passed her head. Regaining her feet, she finally made it to the office door.

With the bulb destroyed, the only light in the room filtered in from the warehouse. It was dim at best, but strong enough for her to see a desk, an overturned chair, and a body on the floor.

She choked back a sob, knelt, and rolled Lane onto his back. Even in the semi-darkness she saw he'd been badly beaten. But was he alive? She placed a trembling hand on his chest, and then sobbed. His heart beat strong and steady.

"Lane? Darling, are you all right? Talk to me, honey."

She caressed his cheek, nauseated when her hand came away slick with blood. His left arm bent at an unnatural angle. She wondered how many broken bones he had.

Stroking the hair from his forehead, she leaned down to kiss it, tasting blood. The bastards had worked him over good.

"Come on, honey. Wake up. Please," she begged.

Lane slowly opened his swollen eyes into narrow slits.

"Gabby. What...what the...hell took so long?" he whispered.

Biting back a strangled laugh, Gabriella buried her face in his chest and tried not to cry. She lifted her head immediately when he groaned.

"Broken...ribs," he muttered.

"The stinkin' bastards. What else is broken?"

"Arm...kneecap...nose. Not sure. Hurts...to breathe. Quiet out there."

"The cops came. I guess they're rounding up the last few holdouts." Another shot sounded from outside the room. "Well, most of them anyway."

Lane attempted to sit up, and then fell back with a gasp.

"Don't move. I'll get you to a doctor." She leaned over and kissed his battered lips.

"Easy, sweetheart. Need to...heal. Appreciate...the thought."

She laughed softly. This was the Lane she knew and loved. Battered, beaten, and in pain, yet still giving her orders and joking about it in the bargain.

If he could joke, so could she. "Okay, no kissing, but there's no reason why I can't screw your brains out is there? They didn't hurt *that*, did they?"

"Nope. *That's* fine."

"Good. Danger makes me horny."

"Sounds...like love."

A tide of tenderness washed over her. "Yeah, I guess it is," she replied.

"How...'bout that? Took *how* long to realize I...was missing?"

"They damn near got me, too. We came as fast

as we could."

"Took the long way."

"Asshole. We got here, didn't we?"

"Another day...another dollar. Kids will have one hell...of a college fund."

His words sank in. Joy she never expected to feel again filled her from head to toe. Without using words, she said a gentle goodbye to Jack.

"Do you mean it, Lane?"

He raised his hand to stroke her cheek, but failed. It fell back to his side. "I mean it, Gabby."

His voice had weakened and she wondered how much blood he'd lost and was still losing. She had to get him to a hospital fast.

Before she could reply, the light in the room diminished. Twisting around on her knees, Gabriella saw the silhouette of a man in the doorway.

"Hey, baby," Frankie said.

Gabriella's heart lurched, and then slammed in her chest. Oh, God. She'd forgotten about Frankie. He stood before them, his face in deep shadow, but she noticed his left arm hung limp by his side with blood dripping from his hand onto the floor. The outline of a gun showed clearly in his right.

Lane's hand fumbled for her gun lying between them. He had an impossible angle and would never hit Frankie. Using the darkness as cover, she brushed his hand away and closed hers over the grip. She had no idea how many rounds remained.

"Hello, Frankie."

"You're a Fed."

"That's right. I'm a Fed."

"Why?"

"Because your father murdered mine. Unfortunately, an innocent man died with him—my fiancé. My sole purpose in life was to bring you animals down, eliminate you like I would any vermin I found crawling around my apartment."

"You filthy bitch! You made me look stupid in front of my father and the whole family!"

"Not hard, Frankie. All your brains are in your dick, and from what I've heard, you're not too impressive in that department either."

Gabriella tightened her grip on the gun and eased it off the floor a couple of inches. When the time came, she'd need to move fast.

Frankie's breath hissed in and out. "You've been doin' him, haven't you? Screwin' Dante Borelli, super cop. Did it give you a thrill? Do you get off on it, baby? Huh? You wouldn't give me the time of day, but you're fuckin' him like a rabbit, aren't you?"

She laughed with derision. "Morning, noon, and all night long. He's got the dick of death, Frankie."

"You fuckin' bitch! I'm gonna kill you both!"

Frankie's hand trembled as he raised his gun. Gabriella raised hers faster and to her surprise, raised it with a steady, calm hand. She squeezed the trigger again and again until the clip emptied.

The impact of the bullets crashing into his body threw Frankie backwards. When the firing ended, he lay staring at the ceiling with sightless eyes, half his chest torn away.

Gabriella dropped the gun and sat down hard. She trembled. Fear and delayed reaction raked her from head to foot. Tears overflowed, and sobs tore from her throat. She laid her head on Lane's chest.

His hand patted her hair. "Good job, Agent Vicelli."

The beam of a flashlight sliced into the room as a man stood in the doorway. "FBI. Are you two all right?"

Chapter Twenty

Gabriella gazed at the turquoise and emerald waters slipping by below from the window of the company jet. Roger and Lane sat up front relaxing, having a drink, and talking in low tones. For the moment, she preferred to stare at nothing.

The past month had been a blur of hospitals and safe houses. In spite of her insistence on staying with Lane, the FBI had hustled her out of the warehouse and into a car, taking her to a house where she'd undergone debriefing. Hours later, they allowed her to see him.

She still shuddered at the image. In the cold light of day, he looked a mess. His face resembled a crazy quilt with stitches running in every direction. A plastic surgeon repaired his broken nose and cheekbone and would work on eliminating the scars at a later date. An orthopedic surgeon had repaired his broken jaw and replaced Lane's shattered kneecap with a hunk of plastic. He'd walk again, but with a limp. The doctors strapped up his broken ribs, and he sported a cast on his left arm as well as the one on his leg. By luck and by God, the beating hadn't damaged internal organs.

Roger insisted on moving both her and Lane from house to house and hospital to hospital with Lane changing names along the way. Gabriella still looked over her shoulder. Even with agency men on guard twenty-four-seven, she wondered if one day she'd round a corner and find herself staring down the barrel of a gun with a mobster on the other end.

Gabriella refused to leave Lane's side, and didn't care enough to ask about the outcome of the warehouse battle. Someone told her Larry and Pete had been wounded, but unlike Will, would survive.

She also heard Gavino Ponzetti had escaped and was in seclusion, supposedly mourning the death of his son. Lane told her about the conversation he and Gavino shared just before she shot the light out. She still didn't understand how a man could sacrifice his son—a scumbag idiot or not.

They'd dealt the Ponzetti family a hard hit. Most of the seasoned henchmen were either dead or in custody. A search of the warehouse revealed drugs, guns, and stolen auto parts from chop shops crated and ready to go overseas, along with legitimate merchandise.

A concealed closet contained several locked file cabinets and the files in them yielded a gold mine of information. Names, dates, shipments, and numerous bank account numbers in the Caribbean and Central America came to light. No detail was too small. The entire Ponzetti organization lay before Federal and state prosecutors. Why Gavino kept them was anybody's guess. Arrogance? Overconfidence? Just plain stupidity? Who knew? It was only a matter of time until the Feds indicted Gavino Ponzetti on charges under the RICO Statute. Rumor had it Caesar Casano was ready to move in and take over what remained of the Ponzetti empire.

Let him. His time will come eventually.

Gabriella had no more interest in the mob or bringing it down. The Ponzettis were finished. That's all she cared about. That and Lane.

Lane's remarkable constitution enabled him to heal rapidly. The stitches came out a few days ago, and most of the bruises had faded into a dingy yellow giving his face a slightly jaundiced look. While still appearing like he'd been in a fight—or an automobile accident as the agency told some of the doctors—he rebounded with amazing vigor. Already his evil sense of humor returned. Even now, he and Roger laughed.

They were on their way to the island. Roger and Lane had business to discuss with the security staff and the prisoners. Gabriella was mildly curious about it. Other than somewhere in the Caribbean, she still had no idea where it was located. Only Roger and the pilots knew, and they weren't talking.

Her gaze slid back to the front. She unsnapped her seat belt and joined the men.

"What are you laughing about?" she asked sliding into a seat next to Lane.

"Just the mission," Lane said, smiling at her.

"You find something amusing about it?"

"Some aspects are," Roger replied. "For instance, Mark still can't get over you telling him to fuck off and doing your own thing."

"Mark has a stick up his ass. He was going to let Lane die in the hopes of capturing a bunch of thugs."

"I'm glad you decided to be a loose cannon and save mine." Lane grinned. "What did he say when you told him what he could do with himself?"

She shrugged. "I have no clue. I ripped the earpiece out and threw it away."

In her mind, she still heard Will's god-awful death gurgle and suppressed a shudder. She'd never forget it.

"You did a great job, Gabriella," Roger said. "By taking control, you saved Lane's life. Mark needs to learn how to adapt to changing situations. He's a good man, just inexperienced."

"Yeah, the asshole damn near got us killed."

"He's not all that different from you. In fact, the last five years are a testament to your determination. Sometimes you bordered on the psychotically stubborn, but you always got your man."

Roger's words embarrassed her. She wasn't used to praise from anyone and hadn't dispatched those goons for it. Still, it felt good to have someone approve of her actions—psychotic or not.

"Casano was my only failure," she said.

Roger frowned and sipped his drink. "We all got greedy. Won't happen again."

Lane's understanding smile had her changing the subject. "What happened in the warehouse?"

"I'm a little curious about that myself," Lane said. "Once the fighting started, I don't remember much other than talking with Gavino before Gabby found me and blew Frankie away."

"Our team took out quite a few of them before the cops and local FBI arrived. Gabby nailed four. Will got two before he died. Larry, Pete, and Mark accounted for a few more."

Roger rose to refresh his drink, raising his eyebrows at the two of them. They both declined.

"Why did they come in with sirens screaming?" she asked. "I heard them a mile away. So did the goons."

"No one seems to know, but they're checking into it. My guess is one of the mob moles was in on the chase. Don't worry. Sooner or later we'll find out who it is and deal with him—or her."

"Provided mob justice doesn't deal with the person first for not getting the message out faster," Lane murmured, sipping from his glass.

"So, I suppose the cops got all the credit for the bust," Gabriella said.

"Of course. We leaked that something was going down to the media. When they showed up, we made sure they talked only to the Chicago PD. As far as they're concerned, the FBI merely assisted on the bust. The Chief of Police and the mayor have already declared the raid to have been the result of an ongoing investigation."

"What was the total body count?" Lane wanted to know.

"One of ours and eleven of theirs, including Frankie, Johnny, and the two at the reception. A couple slipped out the back door with the boss," Roger replied.

"Damn, it shouldn't have been that sloppy," Lane countered.

"I know, but things happened so fast we didn't have time to plan ahead."

"What happened at the All-Italian Club?" Gabriella asked. "We left two dead guys in the hallway downstairs."

"One of our informants had wangled an invitation and said it didn't take long for the shit to hit the fan. A couple of Casano's men heard the commotion, went downstairs, and found them. I gather the room cleared rapidly. Our informant claims Gabby hadn't disappeared down the steps any more than three minutes earlier."

"Holy shit! We must have been getting into the van. A few seconds later and we might not have made it to the corner," Gabriella exclaimed.

"Casano left immediately for the safety of his compound. The wedding party left shortly after as well. Two bodies in the joint put a damper on the festivities."

"What about us, Roger? Will the mob be looking for Gabby and me?"

"Probably. We planted a news story that the bodies of two unidentified people—a man and a woman—were found in the warehouse. Whether or not they buy it, is anybody's guess."

Lane pursed his lips and stared into his glass. "Once the shock wears off, they'll start checking out the area hospitals. Eventually, they'll find what they need."

Roger took a deep breath and exhaled in a rush.

"That's possible, but we inserted a death certificate in both your names in the coroner's files."

Gabriella closed her eyes. "My poor aunt. She'll wonder why there's no funeral."

"We've already talked to her and told her the truth. She told friends you died in an automobile accident and held a closed casket mock funeral a few days after the fight. Then, she had you cremated and the ashes scattered."

She stared at Roger in both disgust and admiration.

"What the hell did she cremate?"

Roger grinned. "Nothing. We filled the casket with rocks. She poured the ashes from her fireplace out of a helicopter flying over St. Louis. By the way, you had a marvelous send-off."

"Fuck you, Warwick."

"So, what happens now? Is Alpha-Omega still in business?" Lane wondered.

"We exist, but under a different agenda. We'll still drug and eliminate, but it won't be by the same method. And of course, we'll still slip our guys in whenever possible. The Chicago mob will be wary for a while, so we'll switch venues—maybe Kansas City or Miami. Our main focus is keeping our men inside safe from any upcoming purges."

Gabriella rose and poured herself a generous shot of vodka, and then resumed her seat. Roger didn't have to tell her she would no longer play a role in the organization she helped found.

"What about Gavino? He knows what we did. Johnny told him. Do you think he might use it as a bargaining tool to slither off the hook on the RICO thing?" She couldn't stomach the thought of Jack's killer getting a walk. "Jesus, you don't think he'd sell out and end up on the island, do you?"

Lane snorted. "The ultimate irony? No, I don't think Gavino Ponzetti will say much of anything. He's a don and dons don't turn. He'd rather go to prison and try to rebuild his empire from there."

Gabriella turned on Roger. "He can do that?"

"It's possible, but unlikely. Once he's gone, Casano will take over. Ponzetti will be lucky to stay alive—in or out of prison. Besides, we're already spreading the rumor that Johnny Scarano had been in the Witness Protection Program and came out because he had delusions of killing Ponzetti and Casano, then taking over."

"So, anything he may have said will be dismissed as the ranting of a mental case," Lane replied.

"More or less," Roger concluded. He shook his head, tipped his glass, and swallowed. "I'm sure Ponzetti will try to cut a deal with the information Scarano gave him, but he has few specifics to barter, and the witnesses are dead. I suppose some hotshot Congressman or Senator looking for good press will form an investigative committee, but we've covered our tracks."

Gabriella polished off her drink and rose for another. So far, Roger had everything under control, and while it was not perfect, it came close. She felt badly about her aunt and would miss seeing her from time to time. Her father's family had not been close.

She resumed her seat and shot a glance at Lane. He looked tired, but smiled, then winked. He had spent the last few days resisting the pain pills in a show of macho posturing. At the first flicker of discomfort, she vowed to shove one down his throat.

Lane tapped the bottom of his glass on the heel of his hand. "You know, with Scarano and Frankie dead and Ponzetti's organization on the verge of disappearing, now would be a good time to plant a snitch in The Topsy-Turvy Club. It's still a hangout and someone will take over. Information flows in and out like a mountain stream in winter melt off."

"We've had an informant in place for over five years, before Alpha-Omega officially opened for business," Roger replied with a half-smile.

"What! Why the hell didn't you tell me?" Gabriella demanded. "I could have used the information he gathered in planning my hits."

Roger shot her a sardonic look. "This may come as a shock to you, but not everything at Alpha-Omega concerned you. The division has grown a bit since its inception. We knew The Topsy-Turvy would be a gold mine and made it a priority."

Lane finished his drink and set it on the table.

"Good for you. I imagine a bouncer or a bartender could pick up a lot of loose information. I hope he can survive the coming purge."

"Nice fishing expedition, Lane," Roger said, grinning.

"I had to try."

"Quit being a tight ass, Warwick. Just tell us who it is," Gabriella snapped, pissed off at being out of the loop.

"The club manager is a Ponzetti family man and he gets his bouncers in-house. He also vets the bartenders. They're the obvious choice for undercover work. Slipping one in under the radar would be hard."

"Are you gonna fuckin' tell us or not?" She hated these cutesy-pooh games the director played. He loved making them wait. She bet he'd been a pain in the ass in an interrogation room.

"Dollar," Lane said quietly.

Oh, shit. Were they back onto that? "Go to hell."

"Two dollars."

Roger laughed. "Our information comes from the

least likely source. One they'd never suspect."

Gabriella glared wanting to explode, but said nothing. A gurgling snort from Lane brought her gaze to his face.

"No. It can't be!" He chuckled.

"Who?" Her patience wore tissue-thin. If they didn't stop this bullshit, she'd open the door and toss both of them off the plane. Maybe thirty thousand feet of nothing would make the smart asses think twice about screwing with her.

"Bubbles?" Lane's laughter built, and he clutched at his broken ribs.

Gabriella's jaw dropped. "That bimbo is a fuckin' Fed? You can't be serious!"

"Three bucks."

She flipped Lane the bird. "You gotta be kidding me!"

"Miss LaRue is not a federal employee, which makes her a paid informant, an independent contractor if that sounds better. Nor is she as dumb as she appears. We approached her when she was still a waitress. Every two weeks a deposit is made to an offshore account in the Caymans."

Bubbles? *Bubbles*? It boggled her mind.

"She was the informant at the wedding?"

"Yes, and she wasn't as drunk as she let on. We got some good information from her after the fireworks," Roger confirmed.

"I'll just bet I know how she gets her information," Gabriella said with a sneering tone.

"Since she is not one of us, her methods are her own. She can retire in another couple of years."

Lane still chuckled. "I'd love to read what she had to report on Leo Carpetti."

"You were from Detroit and the cousin of Frankie's empty-headed fiancée."

"Empty-headed? That bitch! I'll snatch her bald and pull her implants out through her ass!"

"I thought that was what you wanted people to believe," Lane said, still laughing. "Good job!"

"Fuck you!"

"Four dollars—and fifty cents for the finger."

Before she could respond, the fasten seat belt sign flashed as they prepared to land on the island—somewhere in the Caribbean.

****

Lane maneuvered on his crutches down the plane steps with the help of Roger and the pilots. The cast on his arm hampered mobility. His ribs still hurt, but this leg cast was a pain in the ass. Plus it itched.

He finally reached the bottom. He and Roger headed in one direction, while the pilots entered the flight ops Quonset hut. Security guarded the plane. There would be no repeat of the Johnny Scarano escape. Gabriella stayed onboard, saying she'd dispatched these guys once and had no desire to see them again.

Tapping his way across the tarmac, Lane wondered at the wisdom of making contact with the prisoners. If an escape happened once, it could happen again. And if it did, he'd just as soon not have his face remembered.

Roger held open the dining hall door for him. Inside, they met the director of the island, Al Navarro, and then turned to face the twenty-four men seated at the tables. They stared back with mixtures of curiosity, suspicion, and speculation on their faces. Since Johnny's escape they'd been in lockdown with the cable TV disconnected. Navarro lifted the isolation this morning.

The director led them to a table in front of the others, and then said, "Gentlemen, this is William Smith and his assistant, Edward Jones. They have something they want to show you."

"Don't give us no bullshit," a man replied. "I

don't know who his assistant is, but Mr. Smith is Roger Warwick, former head of the FBI."

Al looked taken aback, but Roger smiled. "Mr. Marcianni, you were the best consigliere in Chicago. You knew everybody and everything."

"Who's the guy with you? Looks like he's been worked over by pros," another man asked.

"He really is my assistant and his name *is* Ed Jones. Unfortunately, he was involved in an automobile accident a few weeks ago."

"So, what's he doin' here?" yet a third man wondered.

"He doesn't like inactivity, Bobo."

"So, what you want to see us about?" Carlo asked.

Roger handed a folder to Navarro who distributed photos from it around the tables. Roger sat while Lane took over, standing in front of the prisoners.

"As you see, those are the bodies of Johnny Scarano, Frankie Ponzetti, and other Ponzetti family members."

"Jesus, what the hell happened?"

Lane recognized the speaker as Lou Rizzo from the Muzio family. He looked younger than his photo. The tropics apparently agreed with him.

"Johnny got careless and talked to the wrong person. This is the result. The Ponzettis killed him. A short time later police raided the Ponzetti warehouse on a tip. This is the price of escape. Even if you make it back, you'll end up just like Johnny. You all broke the code," Lane warned.

Carlo shook his head and gazed at Johnny's graphic demise. Roger insisted on bringing the goriest photos in the hopes of hammering home their fate if they tried to escape.

"Poor dumb bastard. I told him this would happen, but he was so set on exposing Gabriella

Vicelli, he refused to listen. I told the guys he was dead meat the minute we heard he'd gotten free. How'd he do it?"

Lane glanced at Roger who nodded.

"He stowed away in the plane. We had an unfortunate security lapse, which will never happen again."

"So, Frankie's dead. What about Gavino?" Marco Alberti said.

Lane eyed the newest member of the island. He had a mean, angry look on his face.

"Gavino Ponzetti is alive and still leads the family, but we expect to indict him soon on the RICO Statute. The mob's days are numbered."

Bobo smiled. "The mob will always be there."

Lane shrugged, but said nothing. What could he say? Bobo was right.

Navarro stepped forward. "If you have no other questions, I suggest you return to your cottages. Starting tomorrow morning, all privileges will be restored."

Most of the men rose and filed out of the room, talking among themselves. Only Bobo and Carlo remained.

"Uh, Mr. Warwick, we need to talk to you," Bobo said.

Lane eased his body into a chair. His ribs and knee hurt like hell. If Gabriella noticed she'd force him to take one of those damned pills.

"I have a few things I need to do in my office. Have a good trip back to Washington," Navarro said and left.

Carlo gazed again at the late Johnny Scarano.

"Don't look so sad, Carlo," Bobo said. "You tried to warn him, but Johnny was dumber than week old shit. It ain't your fault."

"You wanted to talk to me?" Roger asked.

Bobo pushed the picture across the table and

said, "Yeah. It's about the golf balls."

Lane wasn't sure he'd heard right.

"Golf balls?" Roger questioned.

"Yeah. The last shipment we got was light. You think some of your guys are stealing them?"

"I doubt it," Roger said with a smile.

Lane marveled at the irony of a mobster accusing the FBI of theft.

Bobo continued. "Anyway, some of the guys are just learning. They slice and hook the shit out of them. With the vegetation around here, finding 'em is almost impossible."

"I'm sure we can send a few more," Roger told him. "Anything else?"

Carlo slipped on a pair of reading glasses, then took a piece of paper out of his pocket and unfolded it.

"Yeah. I was going to present this to Navarro, but since you're here, I might as well give it to you. We also need more tennis balls. The salt air and humidity does weird things to them. They go flat fast. Lefty Lefkowitz wants to have a tennis tournament in a few weeks."

"Didn't he organize the golf tournament where Johnny escaped?" Roger asked.

Bobo grinned. "Yeah, that's our Lefty. Always was a great organizer. He started the Thursday night poker games and he's teaching some of us how to play bridge. Nine or ten take lessons. That's enough for two tables."

Lane wondered if he'd tripped into a *Twilight Zone* episode. With the photo of Johnny's horrendous death not six inches away, his friends negotiated for more amenities. It was a good thing Gabby wasn't here. Club Med for hoods would not go over well.

"Anything else to make your stay more comfortable?" Lane asked. Neither Carlo nor Bobo appeared to notice the sarcasm.

"Art supplies," Bobo reminded Carlo.

"Right. A couple of the guys want to try their hand at painting. And Lou Rizzo wants to know if you can send down some books. He'd like to start a library. A few of the boys also regret not finishing high school—in Joey's case, grade school. Maybe we can set up our own GED program."

God Almighty. Alpha-Omega is turning into Mobster U. They'll be asking for coeds next.

Roger had the look of a man under siege. "Art supplies and books...yes. I'll take the continuing education thing under advisement and let you know." He glanced at his watch. "Is there anything else?"

Bobo cleared his throat in an apologetic manner.

"Uh, we were wondering if maybe...well, our social life is a little limited."

Good God, bring on the coeds.

"We wondered if we could have a little get-together out by the pool before dinner."

At first Lane didn't understand. Then he did. "You want happy hour?"

Bobo beamed. "Yeah. A little beer, some wine and whiskey would be nice. The beer especially. Pepsi and poker just don't cut it. The same with Monday Night Football."

"I'm not sure that's a good idea, but I'll think about it."

Lane couldn't believe his boss even contemplated agreeing to any of this.

"Are we finished now?" Roger asked.

Carlo looked at Bobo who nodded his head.

"Yeah, I guess that's it."

"It should be," Lane replied. "You guys are sitting in the lap of luxury."

"It ain't half bad," Bobo conceded.

"I kind of enjoy it," Carlo confessed. "I never played golf or tennis before, and I like bridge. It's a game of strategy." He shrugged. "You know, I could never get too mad at Gabriella. She did what she thought she had to do. That took guts."

Lane remembered Gavino saying almost the same thing in the warehouse.

"I'm sixty-two, a widower with no kids. Who's gonna miss me? This way I get to live out my life in peace and quiet. Most of us here feel that way. All except Alberti, but he'll come around."

"Some of the guys worry about their wives and kids, though," Bobo said.

"We've made sure your families are financially secure. We set up college funds and bogus investments to see them through with the explanation you did it in case of a sudden disappearance," Roger said. "You can tell the guys."

The two former mobsters nodded and left the building. Lane stared at his boss.

"They're like a bunch of sheep. Are we drugging the food or something?"

Roger raised his eyebrows and smiled.

"I don't freaking believe it," Lane said. "When I retire, can I come here?"

Roger laughed. "Come on. You and Gabriella go on to your final destination, while I have a little talk with Mr. Navarro and his security staff."

****

Lane re-entered the plane. Gabby sat in a seat watching him with an eagle eye.

"What are you grinning about?" she demanded.

He eased himself into the chair next to her and said, "Nothing. That's not a grin. It's a grimace."

"Are you in pain?" She reached for her purse where the dreaded pain medication lived.

"I'm more tired than anything."

The pilots entered, nodded to them, then closed the door and headed for the cockpit.

"Where's Roger?"

"He has a few things to discuss with Navarro. We're going on to another island. The plane'll come back for him."

"Ah, yes. The Witness Protection Program. What kind of future is that? We won't be allowed to be ourselves or go where we want," she said in a grumpy tone.

"Sure we will, provided we don't visit Chicago or New York."

The engines started. She leaned her head back and sighed.

"I never actually thought about the future. I was goal oriented, even if the long-term goal was illogical. I pretended to be an FBI agent. I realized it while cowering behind boxes scared to death I'd be shot." She gave him a half-smile. "You once called me a spoiled little girl. You were right. I didn't care about anything except *my* agenda. It damn near got us killed, and could have brought down Alpha-Omega. I was a selfish bitch. I'm sorry."

Gabriella bit her lip and looked away. "I thought revenge would be sweet. There's nothing sweet about pumping a bullet into a man's neck or blowing away half his chest. It's disgusting. I don't ever want to do it again."

Her admission and apology surprised him. To cover his confusion, he tossed a manila envelope into her lap. "Funny. I never thought I'd end up with Medusa."

"I like Medusa better than Tinkerbell. What's this?" she asked, picking it up, and undoing the clasp. A sheaf of papers fell into her lap. She flipped through the pages.

"Our new identities," he told her.

"Mr. and Mrs. James Langley? We're married?"

"I'm willing to make it legal if you are."

Lane wondered if the sudden rush of warmth was due to a quirk in the air conditioning or coming from within. Several expressions flashed across her face. As a proposal, he supposed it was kind of shitty. Maybe he should try to sell her on the idea.

"We'll live on the island of St. Albans. It used to be a British protectorate, but they gained independence about fifteen years ago."

"I see." She smiled. "Langley. Someone has a warped sense of humor."

"Sheer coincidence. We were FBI, not CIA."

"I see my new name is Maria, and we're from Australia. Won't our lack of an accent seem a little strange?" she countered.

"Read the bio. It says we lived in Hawaii for the past ten years. We lost our accents."

The plane taxied to the end of the runway.

"I hate to break this to you, but I'm only twenty-six. I've been hanging out with you since I was sixteen? Does that make you a dirty old man?"

Lane chuckled. "Read on. You lived with your parents who have since passed on. We've known each other for only three of those ten years."

"Knowing Roger, he probably has a headstone in the local cemetery with my parents' names on it. So, what do we do on this island to keep from going stir crazy?"

She looked him dead in the eye, the ends of her lips curling upwards. It was challenging and drop dead sexy at the same time. For the first time since he'd been beaten, he felt desire stir to life. Casts and broken ribs or not, he wanted her.

"I'll work as an analyst for Alpha-Omega. Roger will keep me on to do profiles. I suppose you'll stay at home cooking, cleaning, and looking after the kids."

Gabriella snorted, but had a hopeful look in her eyes. Maybe she liked the idea of kids. He did.

"I think we should change places, Mr. Clean. Maybe, I'll open my own business. I could always sell expensive clothing and accessories online. Me transforming into a Stepford wife would bore the crap out of you. I might even turn over a new leaf and stop swearing."

"Damn! There goes the college fund."

"Dollar!" She smiled with a wicked expression in her eyes. Then, the smile faded. "Are you sure, Lane? About marrying me, I mean. I'm a pain in the ass and opinionated as hell. But there's one thing you can always count on. I'll never stop loving you."

Lane pulled her onto his lap and kissed her, ignoring the stabbing pain from his midsection. The discontent of the last five years had vanished. When he wasn't analyzing bad guys, he'd find something else to do. And Gabriella would be with him.

"I meant every word. I love you, Gabby. While they were beating the hell out of me, I realized that for the first time in my life I had a reason to live. I fought Roger tooth and nail not to come to Chicago, but if I hadn't, I'd still be bored stupid telling other operatives what to do.

"You kept me on my toes before we met. Maybe I was half in love with you even then. You were bold and daring. I admired those qualities as much as I hated dealing with your stubbornness and inability to follow orders."

She kissed him lightly, and then asked, "Think you can stand retirement? If I recall, you kind of liked getting back into wise guy mode."

"Retirement? Who's retiring? Lady, life with you may end up a challenge, but it'll never bore me. We'll have our share of arguments, and our arguments turn me on. Afterward, we'll make love." He paused. "You know, you haven't said yes yet."

"I'm thinking about it." She yelped when he pinched her bottom. "Ouch, that hurt. I'd better say yes."

Lane laughed, and then sobered. "There'll be no

more Frankies or Johnnys to give you nightmares. I promise I'll keep you safe and love you forever. Trust me."

He kissed her again and felt the tears sliding down her face, before realizing they mingled with his.

The jet roared down the runway and lifted into a perfect bright blue sky—a sky as bright as their future.

A word about the author...

I was born in Indianapolis, Indiana, but lived for many years in Memphis, Tennessee, which I now consider home. I have two adult children and four grandchildren. At present, I reside in Fort Lauderdale, Florida, with my husband, Bruce, and two dogs, Lucky and Liza.

I've been a serious writer for six years and belong to RWA, Florida Romance Writers, River City Romance Writers, the special interest chapter of RWA, Kiss of Death, and Mystery Writers of America, including the Florida chapter. I achieved PRO status in 2004. I also co-chaired FRW's 2007 Fun In The Sun Conference.